DM Quillman was born in London in 1942 and read modern languages at Cambridge. After a brief and not particularly successful teaching career he worked as a legal executive with a leading firm of City solicitors until 1992, when he turned to freelance legal translation, a profession he continues to practise. His interests include classic detective fiction, jazz and Tottenham Hotspur. He divides his time between homes in Hertfordshire and Devon.

A Saint Emerging

D. M. Quillman

A Saint Emerging

Vanguard Press

VANGUARD PAPERBACK

© Copyright 2024
D. M. Quillman

The right of D. M. Quillman to be identified as author of
this work has been asserted by them in accordance with the
Copyright, Designs and Patents Act 1988.

All Rights Reserved

No reproduction, copy or transmission of this publication
may be made without written permission.
No paragraph of this publication may be reproduced,
copied or transmitted save with the written permission of the publisher, or
in accordance with the provisions
of the Copyright Act 1956 (as amended).

Any person who commits any unauthorised act in relation to
this publication may be liable to criminal
prosecution and civil claims for damages.

A CIP catalogue record for this title is
available from the British Library.

ISBN 978 1 80016 960 9

This is a work of fiction. Names, characters, businesses, places, events and incidents are either the product of the author's imagination or used in a fictitious manner. Any resemblance to actual persons, living or dead, or actual events is purely coincidental.

Vanguard Press is an imprint of
Pegasus Elliot Mackenzie Publishers Ltd.
www.pegasuspublishers.com

First Published in 2024

Vanguard Press
Sheraton House Castle Park
Cambridge England

Printed and Bound in Great Britain

It was supposed to have been the start of a new phase of life for David and Helena Halstow, when they moved from a Home Counties dormitory town to East Anglia.

But only a few months later David dies suddenly, leaving Helena alone in a town she hardly knows.

This story, simple enough but with profound issues beneath the surface, chronicles the first year of Helena's widowhood. It tells how, through a combination of Helena's courage and the grace of God, her life is ultimately transformed.

"Pure soap, maybe, but not without a certain fragrance." — *The Book Cellarer*

1

WINTER, 1980

Past midnight. Unbelievably, it was already the second Friday.

Helena sat silent and alone, with unwanted but undismissable images pursuing one another through her mind.

Paradoxically, there was some consolation in being left to herself for the first time. First Claire, then Chris, and finally Karen had come, and she had been grateful for their support; but now she had been able to assure her children that they could leave her and go to bed, and the quietness of the night was an unspeakable relief. It was something she had always appreciated after an evening crowded with family or other guests. She consciously took several deep breaths and began to order her thoughts. Emotionally she was still numb, but her mind was clearing. Slowly and painfully she forced herself to review the events of the last few days.

David had been working hard — "We couldn't stop him," Keith Ormondroyd, his boss, had said to her — and his brief-case, when he came home (later than he had usually got home at Colmleigh), was always full of files and papers, which had kept him occupied for two or three hours in the evenings, with few exceptions, since the move. On the Monday evening he had looked tired, certainly, and although he had meant to start painting the ceiling of the spare bedroom, Helena had taken pity on him and agreed that the job could wait for a few weeks longer. He had reviewed a draft agreement that needed urgent approval, and had then decided to watch a late film on television. Helena had got herself ready for bed; then, coming downstairs to see how long she would have to wait for David, she had heard a peculiar noise, something between a grunt and a gasp, from the lounge where he was sitting. The film was a violent and noisy one — she had never quite understood the passion he had for westerns — and initially assumed that she was hearing the death-throes of one of the characters in it; but suddenly she had raced to the lounge door, to discover David half-way between the armchair and the floor, struggling for breath, perspiring and white-faced. He had been inarticulate, but clearly in pain, so she had rushed to the telephone to call a doctor, only to realise that, although they had registered with a practice on their arrival in Danesburgh, they had had no occasion to visit the surgery, and consequently she had no idea of the number. Precious seconds passed while she fumbled her way through the directory. She could only get the answering service, which gave her the duty doctor's number. Fortunately, he had been at home, and, to do him due credit, arrived within ten minutes. He was a correct and courteous Indian with great brown eyes behind pale-rimmed glasses, and infinitely careful in his speech. He had taken a single look at David and telephoned immediately for an ambulance, politely seeking Helena's leave to do so even as he picked up the receiver, not that she would have thought of refusing; had suggested that she get dressed again, for she would be going straight to the hospital with David. Inwardly panic-stricken, she had nonetheless been ready to follow the ambulance driver and his assistant as they carried David on a stretcher to the vehicle. He was conscious then, and as the ambulance raced away, looked up and whispered, "My God! These fellows must be late for their cocoa." Then seeing her face, he had added, "It's all right, love, this is nothing to worry about."

But as the ambulance drew up to the doors of the hospital, wide open and brightly lit, another spasm had twisted his mouth and caught his breath in a sob; and she watched the driver's assistant leaning over her husband, at once uncomprehending and knowing perfectly well what had happened. The crew had taken him into the hospital at something approaching a gallop, doctors and nurses had seemed to appear from all directions, lights had flashed, and one of the nurses had taken her swiftly by the hand and led her to a waiting-room. But by then she had known what she must expect, and when the house doctor appeared, she had not needed him to tell her that David was gone; she was already enveloped in a despairing rage that vainly sought an object. The whole of the medical service had functioned with perfect efficiency. Not a single detail could be faulted.

"I'm very sorry, Mrs Halstow," she heard him say. "We really did do everything we could, but it was a massive attack, and he was already too far gone when they brought him in. Just sit here for a minute. I'll get someone to be with you, and we'll organise a cup of tea." The nurse who had shown her to the waiting-room appeared again. Helena scarcely noticed.

The night passed. Helena had drunk one cup of tea and refused a second. The church clock nearby, clearly audible at that time of night, struck quarters, halves, full hours. Two further emergency cases were brought in, with a sudden quickening of activity in the corridors. Helena had strained her eyes towards the high windows, searching for a first hint of daylight; but it was still far too early, and she had rested her head in her hands, as she was doing now, and closed her eyes, abandoning, for the moment, her struggle to make sense of the night's events. When she looked up the sky had begun to lighten, and the staff were preparing to attend patients with the first round of hot drinks. Soon the morning papers were deposited on the waiting-room table. Outside, motorcycles and cars could be heard, and then the buses. Danesburgh was waking; but David would not wake again.

Then the melancholy round of formalities had begun. First, Helena had received and stared unbelievingly at David's clothes and shoes, his watch, his ring, all neatly packed in a polythene bag. Then she had been invited to the office to collect the certificate. It had been in an envelope.

The friendly nurse had appeared once more as she made her way towards the double doors. She must have been close to the end of her shift. "Are you all right, Mrs Halstow? Can I get you a taxi?"

"Oh, please."

The taxi had come promptly, and the driver, observing Helena's drawn expression and heavy eyes, had remained tactfully silent. Helena handed him the fare with a generous tip and let herself back into the empty house.

***

In the course of that night, disturbing visions of Karen and Chris had passed through here mind, but she had shrunk away from them. She needed her sister; Claire must be the first to know. She reached for the telephone.

Claire's steady voice at the other end, "Helena? What is it?"

"Oh, Claire, it's terrible. It's David, last night, he had a heart attack… he's gone."

After the slightest pause, Claire's response was firm.

"Oh, my poor dear. I'm coming straight over. I'll be with you in a couple of hours. Have you been up all night?"

"Yes."

"Then have a cup of hot milk or something and put yourself to bed till I get there. Do Karen and Chris know?"

"No, not yet."

"Don't tell them, then, not till I'm there with you. Listen. Unless you want to talk about it now, I'll grab a cup of coffee and get on the road straightaway. See you soon."

Aware that Claire's arrival in two hours' time was more than she had dared hope for, Helena had allowed Claire to replace the receiver. She took her sister's advice and warmed some milk, which she sipped slowly, and then climbed the stairs and undressed. When it came to going to bed, however, she found herself unable to do it; she had always detested sleeping alone in the double bed, and on the odd occasions when David had to be away for a night she had preferred to occupy the single bed in the spare room. That option now seemed too painful, and she put on her dressing gown, and, picking up a pillow, had gone back down to the lounge and stretched out on the new settee, where she had dozed fitfully until at last she had heard Claire's small Renault pulling up outside, and her sister's brisk footsteps approaching.

At the door, they had looked at each other for an instant.

Helena, in her dressing gown, slight and pale-faced, her dark hair flecked here and there with a little grey, looked as if she were fifteen years older than her sister, instead of a mere four. Claire, who was fairer, taller and more strongly built, and whose face, still scarcely lined, still bore traces of the freckles that had been her despair as a girl, exuded a healthy vigour which, she was sensitive enough to realise, might at times seem overpowering.

The sisters embraced each other.

"Oh, Claire, you are good to come so quickly. All this way! Are you sure Bernard and the boys will be all right?" she enquired anxiously. Claire's boys were, to put it mildly, a handful. Aged twelve and ten, respectively, they had all their mother's energy but had yet to acquire any of her discreetness, if they ever would. They had adored David, who had entered whole-heartedly into their games and activities — football, cricket, space wars, wrestling — while Bernard himself, though used to entertaining them, found himself all but ignored.

"Of course, they'll be all right. It's half-term. Bernard had planned a couple of trips with us — they'll just have to do without me. It won't do them any harm to live on beans and sausages for a few days, they'll think it's like being away at camp." Andrew was a Scout, Martin was a Cub, and Bernard himself had been a Scoutmaster for some years. If anyone was well equipped to look after a couple of healthy boys, it was undoubtedly Bernard.

Claire had taken in the situation as she spoke. Although she was clearly exhausted, shocked and distressed, Helena was totally in control of herself.

"Have you been able to sleep for a while?"

Helena nodded, although she was not certain it was true. Waking or sleeping, she felt as though she were in some atrocious, endless dream. Claire noticed the pillow on the settee, and understood.

"Oh, Helena, you should have gone to bed, as I told you. Never mind, I've got something with me that'll help you to sleep. Now I'll just take my things upstairs, if that's all right with you, and then we'll have a talk about everything."

"Of course. The spare bed isn't made up, but perhaps you could have Karen's room for the time being. I don't know whether she'll be able to come just yet."

Claire disappeared upstairs, and descended a few minutes later, fresh and calm.

"Can you bear to tell me what happened?"

Helena had tried to relate the events of the night, faltering but dry-eyed. Once or twice she flinched, as though Claire had probed a wound. When she reached the moment of her arrival home, she was trembling. Claire put an arm round her shoulder, but Helena had already calmed herself. Claire had always admired her sister's self-possession, but reflected now that it might not always be an asset. The effort had left Helena drained. Claire came to a decision.

"Now you rest again for a while. I'll be nearby. Later on, we'll have something to eat, and then this afternoon we'll sort out what has to be done. Rest now."

Helena had sunk back on to the settee, and after one or two false starts, had fallen asleep.

***

When she awoke again, it was after half past one. She could hear her sister moving plates and cutlery about in the kitchen, and cooking smells reached her nostrils. Claire came in with a tray bearing scrambled eggs on toast, a small salad and a cup of coffee.

"Oh, you dear," said Helena, suddenly feeling very hungry. Claire returned to the kitchen and fetched a similar tray for herself, and the sisters settled themselves comfortably to the meal.

"By the way," Claire said over her second cup of coffee, "your next-door neighbour — Mrs Broughmer, isn't it? — called around midday. She heard the ambulance in the night and guessed something was wrong, but she didn't know you were back from the hospital. I told her what had happened, I hope you don't mind. She seems very nice. Have you got to know her yet?"

"No, not really. Just the odd word or two. We've been — we had been — so busy since the move, what with trying to get the house straight and sorting Karen's flat out. Thank you for telling her, Claire, anyway. It's… it's one off the list."

It was the first mention of breaking the news. Claire had asked Helena whether she would rather leave it to her to tell Karen and Chris. Helena had felt that it was her own duty to do so, but she knew how difficult it would be.

"Karen will be devastated. She adored David, she's so much like him."

"Well, then," said Claire sensibly, "don't ring her direct. Speak to her line manager first and ask her to explain that something serious has happened and tell her to phone you back. That'll give her a bit of an advance warning, and it'll make sure there's someone there with her. I think I'd do it at about four o'clock, then there won't be too much of the afternoon left, and with a bit of luck they won't expect her to carry on with her work once she knows."

At four o'clock, Helena phoned Karen's office. The response came about ten minutes later.

"Mum?" Karen's voice was agitated. She seemed to have difficulty in speaking, as if something were interfering with her breathing. "What is it? What's happened?"

"Karen, darling... It's your father. He was taken ill very suddenly last night, it was a heart attack, a massive one. The doctor came and got an ambulance for him, but..." Helena nearly broke off, but forced herself to continue, "...It was no good, I'm afraid. He died just as we got to the hospital."

A silence, then Karen's voice came again, faintly. "Oh... no, no, no. Not Dad." A clunk. Helena could envisage her, her hand over her eyes, the receiver laid down on the desk. Then Karen spoke again. "Mum, what about you? Are you all right?" That foolish, banal question that springs to everyone's lips.

"Yes, dear," Helena said gently. "Claire is here with me. Don't worry about me for the moment. Listen..."

But Karen's initial shock had metamorphosed into fury, involuntarily directed against her mother. "Why didn't you tell me this morning? Didn't I have a right to know straightaway? I suppose you thought I couldn't take it. Mum, I'm twenty-one, I'm not a child any longer."

The anger in her voice caught Helena off guard. She looked hurt and bewildered. Claire gestured to her to pass over the receiver.

"Karen, dear, please listen. Your mother's been up all night. She's been badly shocked, much more than you can tell over the phone. Try to understand. I came over this morning as soon as she told me, and made her rest all morning and most of this afternoon. It was me that suggested we shouldn't tell you until later in the day. I'm sorry if that was the wrong decision, my love."

Karen's next words were accompanied by a distinctly audible sob. *That's better*, Claire thought.

"No, Aunt Claire, it's all right. I'm sorry. Please tell Mum, I'm sorry. It wasn't fair of me. Oh, God..."

She broke off. Claire hoped that whoever was with her was sensible and sympathetic. She passed the received back to Helena.

"Karen," said Helena. "It's all right, my darling, I do understand. Can you manage now? Will they let you go back to the flat, or somewhere quiet for an hour or so?"

"Yes, I think so. Oh, Dad. He was so full of life. Why this? Why?"

It was a question Helena had not formulated coherently in her own mind. She had no answer, and tried to set it aside.

"What about this evening? Will you be alone in the flat?"

"No, I don't think so. Gill didn't say she was going out. I think she's got to study or something."

Gill was Karen's flatmate. They had met by chance at a disco six months earlier, when the family had still been living in Colmleigh. It had turned out that, when Karen had decided not to leave Colmleigh, Gill, whose parents had just gone through a somewhat unpleasant divorce, had come to the conclusion that she would rather move away from home; and the girls had believed they had sufficient in common to make flat-sharing a reasonable proposition. Helena hardly knew Gill, who had tended to be away at weekends with various friends, and had had some reservations about the arrangement, but since Karen enjoyed her job and the financial independence it brought, and there were few comparable opportunities in Danesburgh, she had given in. Now she wondered again whether it had been a mistake.

"Karen, dear, the funeral is on Thursday. I won't expect you to come before that unless you really want to, but come as early as you can on the day, will you, please?"

For the funeral had already been arranged. After lunch, Claire had gently urged Helena to see to immediate business, pointing out that it was best to get it out of the way as quickly as possible. In Danesburgh it was easy enough, with Claire driving, to attend at the register office, a prefabricated building behind the Town Hall, and visit Mr Forbes's funeral parlour, and still have time to start composing letters to the insurance company, the bank, the building society, the solicitors. Later, they would prepare an obituary. On reflection, they had decided that this had better be placed in the Colmleigh local paper, rather than the Danesburgh Gazette, since many more people there had known David. But after that, Helena needed half an hour to collect herself before she felt ready to speak to Karen.

Chris could not be reached immediately. He should have been back at his lodgings, a terraced Victorian artisan dwelling in Leytonstone, by five; but he had apparently gone to see a fellow student after the afternoon's classes, to take a look at a motorcycle, and was not expected back until later. Helena asked his landlady, a Mrs Byles, to tell him to call as soon as he came in.

Mrs Byles sounded inquisitive.

"Oh yes, of course I'll tell him. I'll tell him right away. Oh Gawd, I hope it isn't anything serious, like."

Helena had the uncomfortable feeling that Mrs Byles meant the opposite.

"Yes, Mrs Byles, I'm afraid it is something serious. You may as well know, my husband died suddenly last night. I doubt whether Chris will be able to get away immediately, but I'd like him to come as soon as he can. He won't need to be away for more than a few days. You will keep the room for him, won't you?"

"Oh, of course I will. Of course." Mrs Byles was gratified at being entrusted with the sad news. "Oh, the poor, poor boy. Oh, I am sorry. What a terrible thing, when he's only just started at the Poly. Oh dear, oh dear… Well, well. Do you know, I was only saying to my friend Daphne the other day, 'Do you know', I was saying, 'I don't know when I've had a nicer lad staying here than young Chris', I said to her, 'he must come from ever such a nice family', I said…"

Helena interrupted a politely as she could. "Thank you, Mrs Byles. You're very kind. I'm glad you're getting on with Chris. You'll tell him to phone me, then? Oh, and would you ask him to reverse the charge if he likes, if he's short of change. Goodbye, Mrs Byles, and thank you again."

Mrs Byles had hung up, clucking sympathetically, and probably relishing what she had heard.

Having got that far, Helena was all for continuing with the dismal duties until everything possible had been dealt with, but Claire had thought it was enough.

"You'll have to tell David's parents, I'm afraid, but I'll tell Mum and Dad. Karen can pass the word round in Colmleigh — she won't mind doing that for you. Didn't David have a brother in Australia? Do you have his address? We'll write to him."

The round of calls had gone on. David's father took so long to speak that Helena was afraid for a few moments that he had been taken ill in his turn. Elspeth McCallogh, Helena's mother, immediately began to make plans to travel south with Frank, her husband. This meant arranging for a nurse to look after her invalid sister, Marie, and therefore had to be done promptly.

Then Chris came on the line.

"Mum, Mrs Byles has just told me. I'm shattered, I can't believe it. He seemed quite all right yesterday. Oh lord, poor Mum. Was it awful?"

"It was, rather. And it still is. But your Aunt Claire is being a marvellous comfort. She came straightaway this morning, and she'll be staying till Thursday evening. How soon do you think you can come?"

Chris had worked hard for his place at the college, and was not finding the course particularly easy. Helena would have loved him to come then; but he really should not miss any more classes than was absolutely necessary, and in any case, how could he help in Danesburgh?

"No, Chris, you stay where you are till the afternoon before, and try not to let this put you off your work, if you can. I know you'd come if you could."

Chris had a moped, which he used to travel from his lodgings to the college, and for short trips about the local area. He was quite prepared to ride it all the way to Danesburgh, but Helena managed to dissuade him.

"Come on the train. Claire will pick you up at the station. I'll only worry if I think you're on the road on that thing."

***

By the evening, Helena was once again exhausted. So, indeed, was Claire, who had taken it upon herself to keep house for Helena for the week, and by the end of the day had used up even her abundant energy. With kisses on the cheek, they retired to their respective bedrooms. Claire, concerned though she was about Helena, could not face the prospect of the next three days without sufficient sleep, and did not stay awake long. Helena, on the other hand, found that her thoughts were racing again. She turned over, dozed momentarily, but then, wide awake again, took a book and tried to read to calm her mind. No good. She gave up and finally moved over to the window, where she placed her bedside chair and sat, looking at the stars in the clear night sky and the few street lamps that were all she could see of Danesburgh. For a moment she felt alone in a strange country, even though she could hear Claire's steady breathing in the next room. Only twenty-four hours had passed since she had been in the hospital waiting-room, with a nurse holding her hand and offering her tea. Now she sat in her room, sleepless and longing for the dawn to come once again.

Nine more days had passed. The events of those days were already beginning to merge and become confused. Then had come the funeral; and now it was over. And Helena had still not shed a single tear.

***

David is dead... dead... dead. I am a widow. A widow.

Helena was deliberately torturing herself now, scourging herself with the most pitiless words she could find. She repeated them in her mind again and again, until the sounds finally lost their meaning, and with it, the power to inflict pain. Still there remained the dull ache, the nightmare sensation, the unreality.

An idea came to her. Quietly, she reached up to the top shelf of the wardrobe and took out the family album. She carried it downstairs to the kitchen and opened it on the table.

She began to turn the pages.

Images of past holidays and parties, almost forgotten. Their old home Karen in Brownie uniform. Chris dressed up for some school play or other.

And David, David everywhere, laughing, playing, gently teasing, carrying one or other of the children on his shoulders, or on his own with a boat or a plane or a castle in the background. Real. Solid. As though he would be there forever.

Oh, David.

The key had turned. Helena's shoulders shook and the tears came at last, releasing her from that intolerable burden of self-control she had borne all week. She wept, wept and was comforted. Karen, whose own sleep had not been easy, came down early in the morning with the idea of making her mother a cup of tea and was astonished to find her slumped over the kitchen table, fast asleep, eyes red and hair falling haphazardly over her forehead. This was a mother she had never seen before.

"Mum," Karen whispered. Helena stirred, and waking, held out her arms.

"Oh, my darling girl," she whispered.

And mother and daughter embraced each other in a moment of tenderness.

***

The weekend passed in the intimacy of family mourning, the harshness of grief tempered by the warmth of their love for one another. They hardly needed to pass the front door, for Claire, ever practical, had taken the opportunity, during the days before the funeral, to lay in sufficient provisions for several days more, no doubt concerned lest Helena should overlook essential matters in her bemusement. But in fact she would have perceived a startling change in the sister whom, only a couple of days earlier, she had been guiding through the formalities of bereavement, as though a labyrinth.

The dullness had left Helena; she now seemed anxious to grasp at every memory of her husband, as if the chance would be lost for ever if it were not taken then and there. The weather, overcast but dry during the week, had broken, and rain spotted the outer glazing of the patio doors. Inside, the family wrapped itself in a grief which, paradoxically, brought its own pleasures, recollections, moments of deep contemplation, and for Helena, echoes of David's voice, reflections of his ways in the two children, adult in stature now but in her eyes combining all their past ages, from infancy to teen-age years, as she reviewed the days of her marriage.

They piled all their photograph albums on the lounge carpet and spent hours studying the pages, from the stilted wedding photographs taken by Maurice Cumber ('still life with bridesmaids', David had called one of them), to the summer holiday snapshots, mostly Chris's, taken in Snowdonia, where they had camped for a week, and Malaga, where they had slept until noon and danced until four in the morning. In the earlier part of the year both Karen and Chris had talked about arranging their own holidays, but David and Helena had persuaded them to postpone their independence for another season; and thought Helena, *what a blessing they had*, for, perhaps against the odds, the holiday had proved an outstanding success. Their friends in Colmleigh had been surprised to learn that they still intended to go away as a family; most of those friends knew only too well that their rapidly maturing children would have hated the idea. But David had had a knack of binding them all together — a talent he had exercised to good effect during his National Service, at the end of which he had been offered the opportunity to train for a commission (and, after some thought, declined it, seeing his future elsewhere), and in his job, where he had been noted for his ability to get the best out of his colleagues, and later his subordinates, by virtue of a combination of infectious enthusiasm, shrewd psychology and natural authority.

Helena's eyes began to water. Karen noticed, and steered her away from the subject of their holidays.

"Mum, you know I always like hearing about how you first met Dad. Tell us the story again, will you? Please."

This, she knew, would lighten Helena's mood, for it had been one of their best anecdotes, related to many a dinner guest over the coffee and liqueurs. Fresh from National Service, David had been a sales representative for a smallish company that specialised in an early type of espresso coffee machine, similar to those used on the Continent. Espresso bars were then becoming fashionable, and David's brief was to interest owners of ordinary cafés and restaurants in this new means of preparing coffee. This was not so difficult in the London area, but David's ingenuity and stamina were severely taxed when it came to selling in the provinces, particularly in the north.

Helena, in the meantime, had settled with her parents and Claire in a suburb of Newcastle-upon-Tyne, where her father had been promoted to a position of moderate authority in H.M. Inspectorate of Taxes. She had done well in her final school year and been awarded a place at Durham University, where she was to read English; she had vague ideas of becoming a librarian. With the intention of getting together a little money to supplement her grant, she had taken a temporary summer job as a waitress in a restaurant situated on the top floor of a local department store.

David had had an unrewarding morning, the local people being generally more partial to instant coffee than the espresso variety. He had found his way into the store with the intention of buying some razor blades, and since it was then about half past twelve, decided that the restaurant would be as good a place as any to have lunch. Helena, of course, had come to serve the meal. She had been rather intrigued by this young man from the

West Country, who seemed so out of place among the Newcastle matrons who formed the majority of the store's customers.

At the end of the meal, David had just ordered coffee for himself when a tremendous crash in the kitchen shook the restaurant and probably the whole floor of the building, causing one or two of the more nervous customers to jump, drop paper serviettes on the carpet and slop tea and coffee into their saucers. The restaurant itself was known as the *Coffee Pot*, and was popular for mid-morning refreshments as well as lunches, the name being derived from an enormous earthenware jug, from which coffee was dispensed into copper pots to be served at the tables. It was this jug that had, for some reason, crashed on the tiles of the kitchen and now lay in several jagged fragments amid a morass of liquid and grounds. Helena was not in any way to blame, but her gasp, as she passed his table, caused him to look up.

"What was that, then? I hope there wasn't anybody underneath it, whatever it was!"

Helena had to smile. "It was our coffee pot, I'm afraid. Nothing else would make a noise like that. I'll go and see."

She had walked quickly over to them kitchen door and taken in the scene, the manageress trying with a mop to clear enough of the floor to make a path for herself to the service hatch.

"Oh, dear! Can I do anything to help?"

The manageress had looked up, cross and perspiring. "Yes, my lass. You can come and clean up here while I send out for a new pot. I'll have to apologise to the customers, the ones that are waiting to be served."

"Don't send out, madam."

David was standing behind Helena.

"I beg your pardon, sir?" The manageress was perplexed at being addressed as 'madam' by a customer.

"Just wait a minute while I nip out to my van. I've got something in there that'll solve your problem in no time."

He was off to the lift. Helena watched him go, conscious that she had not yet presented him with the bill. What if he simply didn't come back? Would she have to make up the loss from her own pay? It would make a significant gap. But David was back within minutes, carrying a cardboard carton in his arms, and a packet of coffee protruding from his jacket pocket.

"This machine will make cup after cup of fresh coffee..." and he launched himself into his familiar sales routine. "You dispose of the grounds as you go along, together with the filter. Or you can put them on your potted plants. It's always hot, it's always fresh and none gets wasted. You've got a power point in the kitchen? Good. Fill up the machine, plug it in and serve your customers. No charge. I'm always glad of an opportunity to demonstrate the product."

Thus was espresso coffee introduced to the store's customers, some of whom manifested cautious approval. David was invited to meet the management, and stayed for most of the afternoon. He returned to the now misnamed 'Coffee Pot' for tea in high spirits, having made a sale and agreed to loan his demonstration machine to the company until the new one was delivered. He engaged Helena in conversation and finally made a date with her for the local cinema that evening. Helena had been doubtful at first, but sensing that the young man's evident resourcefulness did not necessarily imply any improper intentions, agreed, on condition that he should drive her home immediately at the end of the film.

The programme had consisted of an Ealing comedy, not exactly new, but they had both enjoyed it, and each other's company. David had duly driven Helena home in his van, and very briefly met her parents, before departing to his commercial hotel, a squalid building close to the main railway station.

"Good night, Helena. Thanks very much for coming out with me. You've really made my day. First the sale, and then the date! I hope I'll see you again one day." They had exchanged addresses and telephone numbers, only half seriously. And the next day David had left for Middlesbrough, there to pursue further the uphill task of selling his coffee machines, while Helena had returned to the 'Coffee Pot', where she endured the teasing of the other staff for several days thereafter.

That recital naturally led to further reminiscences, the correspondence, for example, between Helena and David while she had been at Durham, punctuated by occasional meetings in the vacations. David's changes of job — every time they met he seemed to be representing a different company; at one moment he would have a new type of cleaning fluid, at another it would be electric typewriters, and on yet another occasion camping gear; but it always proved to be something for which the demand suddenly increased; he had an unerring instinct for merchandise on the point of discovery by the general public, and a knack of getting in first with retailers. Thus he had progressed over the years to computers, leisure centre equipment, integrated business systems; more recently, before the move, he had been with a London firm of marketing consultants. The Danesburgh office, an off-shoot of that firm, had shown every sign of prospering, despite its relatively remote location.

Then there were the remarkable coincidences that had brought the whole McCallogh family south just as David had begun to work in the capital, as a reward for his consistent success in the provinces, for a large plastics manufacturing company. Frank McCallogh had received his final promotion to one of the big City districts; Helena, having completed her degree course, had managed to secure a probationary post at a library in one of the London boroughs, a pleasant south-western suburb. Claire had passed her G.C.E. examinations and was beginning her nursing training at a specialist college, also on the south-west side of London. They had looked for a convenient centre from which to travel to their various places of work, and had settled on Colmleigh, about thirty-five miles out, a market town which had metamorphosed into a dormitory suburb with the advent of the Southern Railway, yet had retained a little of its original character.

Returning from her first day at the library, Helena had found David waiting for her at the station. At that time he had been renting a flat in Wimbledon, and had been on a sales trip to Colmleigh during the day. Quite by chance, or so he had maintained, he had met Elspeth McCallogh in the shopping centre. He had known, of course, that the family were moving to that area, but when Helena had last written to him, she had been unsure of the date of their removal. He had admitted afterwards that he had rather hoped to bump into Helena herself at the time, although he knew that hope to be unrealistic. To meet her mother had been better luck than he had had any right to expect. He had naturally insisted on taking Elspeth to lunch, and it had not been difficult, from what he learnt in the course of their conversation, to calculate the likely time of Helena's arrival at the station. Hence the reception, which Helena found welcome and only a little contrived, once she had got over her initial surprise.

In truth, neither of them had had any serious doubt that they would one day be married. Helena had discovered in David a remarkable combination of qualities which she admired, his fundamental reliability and level-headedness, which appealed to her Presbyterian upbringing, were allied to a spontaneity and drive that had stamped him as totally different from her father, the quiet Scot and persistent, hardworking but inconspicuous civil servant, yet rendered him acceptable in her parents' eyes. He would have made a good American, Helena sometimes thought. He had those characteristics of commitment, guilelessness and enthusiasm; and perhaps that was more than coincidence, for in the two preceding centuries several generations of Halstows had emigrated from Gloucestershire to the New World, where they had established themselves by exercising similar virtues.

What David, for his part, had been attracted to in Helena was something which, modest as she was, she rarely contemplated, although she would have been astute enough to realise that her intelligence complemented his enthusiasm, her quietness tempered his occasional outbursts and that her faithfulness had been amply demonstrated during her student days, when she had been the subject of much attention from various able and courteous young men; perhaps most of all he had prized that self-possession which had served her so well during the recent dark hours, and had enabled her to bring to every decision they had made together a considered wisdom which had, more often than not, accorded with his instincts, if not with his emotions.

Helena had gone silent, as the memories succeeded one another, while Karen and Chris sat equally quiet, not wishing to break into her thoughts. She realised, and apologised.

"I'm sorry, my dears, do forgive me. I was remembering some very happy times before we were married. Oh, I don't mean that getting married spoiled anything, quite the opposite. It was just that that was where I'd got to, if you see what I mean."

"Mum, you were happy with Dad, weren't you?" Karen asked quietly. "I mean, I always thought you were, but when I talk to some of my friends and they're always on about the rows their parents have, when they haven't already split up, well, I wonder sometimes if..."

"If we were putting on an act for you?" Helena finished for her. "No, we never needed to do that. I know some people do, but yes, we were happy. I don't mean we never argued, but I can't remember ever having a really serious quarrel with your father. I suppose we must have been exceptionally fortunate, then."

She considered this. Certainly, their marriage had been free from most of the usual causes of tension — incompatibility, unfaithfulness, financial strain. David had been no deceiver; even as a salesman he had always relied on enthusiasm rather than duplicity to persuade his customers to buy, and she had never had any reason to doubt his honour. On the financial side she had rarely had any cause to worry, and her own natural thrift had helped to see them through the few periods they had experienced when money had been scarce. No, hers had been a stable and joyous marriage. One of those 'made in heaven', as Susan Cumber had once enviously described it when she and Maurice had been going through a bad patch. Which made it all the worse now... *no,* Helena thought, *I won't cry again, it wouldn't be fair to the children, I'll have enough time for that later,* and she deliberately turned her mind to recalling the moments that would bring them amusement, or highlight their father's character. Like the time, six months before their wedding, when David had announced, to her horror, that he was thinking of hiring a pipe band for the reception. That had been a joke, as it happened; but he had been absolutely serious when he had asked her to leave the honeymoon arrangements entirely to him, so that all she had known, even as they left for the airport, was that their destination was a city in southern Europe. It had turned out to be Naples, which David had somehow or other found time to explore during a brief spell in Cyprus towards the end of his National Service. It had been one of his rare misjudgements, for Helena had found the climate too hot and the city too noisy and dirty; but she had been fascinated by the history of the region, and spent enjoyable days visiting museums, art galleries and archaeological sites, with David accompanying her uncomplainingly, although she suspected he would rather have been on a beach. Characteristically, however, he had had an alternative plan prepared, just in case Helena should not be quite as happy as a bride should be on her honeymoon, and despite her fervent protests that their being together was quite sufficient, they had left Naples early in a hired car for Rome, whence they had travelled on to Paris by train and then back to London by air when the time came. Helena brought out the familiar, now fading, photographs, Vesuvius (which she had flatly refused to allow David to visit again); the Vatican; Montmartre and Notre-Dame. David posing as an ice-cream seller, an American tourist, a cartoon Frenchman in striped shirt and beret, with a baguette under his arm and a bottle of *vin ordinaire* in his hand. She had to admit that David's sense of humour had never been subtle; to him, however, the whole of life had been fun, and he had never needed to use laughter as a defence against its sourer side. His kind of humour had been broad, but rarely gave offence; and on the few occasions when it did he knew how to relieve the sting with a quick and gracious apology.

Helena revived the episode of the Cumbers' gnome. Both Maurice and Susan, who had no children, spent a great deal of time and ingenuity adorning their home with antiques of dubious authenticity and their garden with rustic furniture, stone rabbits and other ornaments of the type easily obtainable from garden centres, intended to set off the mathematical precision of their lawns and borders. On one of their trips to the local nursery, they had brought back a plaster well, about seventy-five centimetres high, beside which a placid gnome, a red cap on its head at a rakish angle and a clay pipe between its teeth, sat with rod and line, apparently fishing.

This was on a Saturday in the summer, and it so happened that the school fete had been taking place on the same day. Among other trophies, Chris had won a goldfish in a polythene bag full of water. The fish had looked distinctly unwell even then, and although Helena, taking pity on it, had turned it out into the largest glass jar she could find, pending the acquisition of a proper fish tank, which would have to wait until Monday, it failed to survive to the end of the day.

Chris had wanted to bury it; but David spotted the chance of what he considered a harmless bit of fun, having noticed the gnome on his way home. After dark, he had crept into the Cumbers' garden via a side gate, and with the aid of a torch and a bent pin, had contrived to attach the fish to the gnome's line.

The Cumbers had invited the family to tea on the Sunday afternoon, to be enjoyed in their garden, using one or more of their rustic tables. The forecast was for a warm day, and David had calculated that by four in the afternoon the fish would be making its presence known.

Unfortunately he had reckoned without the two young and boisterous Siamese cats owned by the Cumbers' neighbours on the further side. When let out in the morning, the animals immediately became aware of the addition that had been made to the ornamental well, and were quite naturally moved to investigate it further. Being unable to reach the fish with their paws, they were obliged to knock the whole ornament over, and since it had been perched on a corner of a rockery above the level of the patio, the fishing gnome fell heavily on to the paving and was summarily decapitated. All this occurred before the Cumbers were up; but as Susan drew back the bedroom curtains she was just in time to see the two startled cats disappearing over the fence, while the gnome's head, now pipeless, rolled half way across the patio. Susan detested the cats in any case, since they were constantly digging in the flower beds, and the incident provoked a furious row between the Cumbers and their neighbours.

On hearing of the disaster and its consequences, however, David had immediately confessed to his part in the affair, and had not only driven straight to the garden centre to buy an identical replacement for the ornament, but had also gone to see the neighbours, who were relatively new to the district and whom he knew only by sight, and seen to it that peaceful relations were restored.

It says much for David's character (and Helena's diplomacy), that by the end of the afternoon he had been completely forgiven by Maurice and Susan Cumber, for whom he eventually became something of a legend.

In retrospect the whole episode seemed rather childish and tiresome, of course; but what stood out in Helena's mind was David's simple glee at the prank, his immediate concern at the unforeseen outcome, and his instant and practical reparations. In any event, he had not made a habit of perpetrating practical jokes, and had only permitted himself that one on the strength of having known the Cumbers for years. He and Maurice had met when both had joined the Colmleigh squash club at about the same time and had played in competitions together. Despite their very different personalities, they had become and remained good friends, and David had been best man at Maurice and Susan's wedding. This recollection set further memories in train; and so the talk, and the photographs, and the moments of silence, re-created David among his family, so that for a short while they almost believed that he was only away for a few days on business, and would be home in person as soon as that business was concluded.

***

Then Karen, quite unintentionally, dispelled the illusion.

"Mum," she said, "what will you do now?"

"Now" changed everything. It was a question Helena had put to the back of her mind, although she knew it must soon find its way to the fore

"I don't know, dear, It's much too early. I need time to think."

"Wouldn't it be best if you came back to Colmleigh?" Karen continued hopefully.

Helena was silent. She knew that Colmleigh had been Karen's only home, and that she had passed her infancy, her schooldays, her first few months at work, her earliest tentative romances, against that constant background; her friends, her landmarks, her memories were all there. It was natural for her to urge her mother to be restored to the picture.

Chris said nothing, but his face did not mirror Karen's eagerness. He, in contrast, had never enjoyed living in Colmleigh; he had made few friends, spent much of his time in solitary walks or cycle rides, or searching, without much success, for rare ornithological species. Danesburgh was within easy reach of two or three nature reserves, in addition to being a centre for local agriculture. He had looked forward to getting to know the area when he came home for weekends and vacations.

Karen was still talking.

"I mean, it's not that I don't like it here, but it seems such a long way away…"

Chris interrupted her. "At least you've got the car."

"Yes, but it's not the same as when we were all together." Karen swallowed hard, realising the import of what she had just said. Her face crumpled, and she put her hands over her eyes. It was Helena's turn to put an arm round her daughter.

"I promise you," she said gently, "that I really will think about it, and if I can't settle here I may very well consider coming back to Colmleigh. But please do give me time. I've only just got here, after all, and I want to be fair to Chris, as well. It won't help him at college if we're moving home every other week. I hope you'll come over when you can, too, of course.

You may sometimes feel like getting right away for a day or two, and I love having you here."

"But you'll be so alone all week." Karen clutched at a remaining chance of persuading her mother. "What will you find to do, Mum? This place is so dull."

Dullness, to Karen, was the unforgivable sin; but Helena remembered something David had once told her when he had been trying to explain the satisfaction he derived from his job.

"People will tell you that this place or that place is dull," he had said. "But I've been in most of the towns in this country at some time or other, and I've never yet found a place where there wasn't something of interest. It's no good just looking at the museums and monuments, though. They're the past, they're dead. Get talking to people; they're what keeps a place alive. I've sat in pubs that seemed like the end of the world, and heard stories that were better than anything you'd find in a book. True stories, I mean, or stories that passed for true, anyway. I wish I'd had time to write a few of them down, they were so good. And the old boys that used to tell them, they were better than music-hall comics. They'd got the expressions, the timing... Marvellous."

Helena hardly saw herself as a collector of folk tales, sitting in pubs with pencil and paper at the ready; but David's words were still clear in her mind as she replied.

"Well, I suppose it may seem dull to you. At the moment, I can't tell. Ask me again in another six months or so. Maybe then I'll have formed an opinion."

"Six months!" Karen echoed, as though she found it incredible that her mother could already be looking so far ahead.

"Dear Karen! Try to understand. Moving house once was bad enough; I can't go through all that again for a while. And then I've got to sort myself out, see whether I can cope on my own or not. I can't just go on as if your father were simply away for a week or two, and I don't want to be wallowing in memories and sympathy from friends all the time, it would only make things worse. You saw what Mrs Cumber was like at the funeral. She wouldn't know what to say to me for months. Then there's money, too. It's such an expensive business moving, and the house prices are much higher in Colmleigh than they are here, because it's so much nearer to

London. It's not that I'm afraid of being short of money, but I'll still have to be careful. It may not work for me to be here, but I think I ought to stay long enough to find out. Don't you think Dad would have agreed?"

She was on firm ground now. David had managed to wrest success out of many an unpromising business situation by sheer patience and determination. "I managed to wear their resistance down in the end," he would sometimes comment after a particularly tough battle for a sale, during his days on the road.

Karen, Helena thought, *will try to wear down my resistance in the same way. She's as tenacious as David was, when something matters to her.*

For the moment, however, Karen was acquiescent.

"All right, then, Mum. See how you get on. But," she couldn't help adding, "I still wish you were coming back."

And for the rest of the weekend nothing more was said about the subject.

***

At Epping Underground station, the next morning, Karen and Chris parted in very different moods.

Never very talkative at home, Chris had engaged in the barest minimum of conversation since he had arrived on the day before the funeral. His natural reserve, combined with an awkward sense of not knowing quite the right things to say on such an occasion, had caused him to hope that taciturnity on his part might be interpreted as discreetness. Helena could only guess at his feelings. He had always detested shows of emotion, and she could remember various occasions when he had turned away with evident distaste when Karen had dissolved in tears at some minor upset or other; and then, although he had loved his father no less than a son should, he was cast in such a different mould from David. For him, sports and games had been something to be endured, at home as at school, try as David would to interest and coach him; and he would grasp any opportunity to avoid a social event. The one thing he had acquired from David was an interest in machinery; apart from his ornithology, he enjoyed nothing better than tinkering with internal combustion engines, and his dexterity had brought him a number of casual friends who, although they had little else in common with him, were glad enough to call on him for assistance when their old motorcycles, or even older cars, required attention. He hoped to use that talent as a means of supplementing his income while studying, and was keen to build up a circle of college acquaintances who might put a little work in his way.

Chris had left Danesburgh with a new resolve tempering his grief. Unlike his sister, he had not excelled during his early school years, doing the minimum work that was necessary to keep out of trouble; but having scraped a handful of 'O' levels, he had suddenly realised that a number of his companions whom he had not regarded as particularly able had done rather better than he; and slowly, with much encouragement from both parents, he had improved to the point of gaining two reasonable 'A' levels and a place at the polytechnic; whereas Karen, having dazzled her teachers up to the end of her third year, had suddenly begun to find school somewhat childish in the two years leading up to her 'O' levels, and consequently achieved relatively disappointing results. Inevitably, she had preferred to leave school and try to make her way in the adult world; with the result that, after five years at her office, she was still in a relatively junior position, and seemed quite content to stay there.

Chris was still adjusting to the different demands of college work, not to mention the minute front bedroom, more of a box room, at Mrs Byles's house, in which he had to prepare his work; but he felt that he had suddenly matured in some way, accepting a new range of responsibilities. He would earn his father's posthumous approval, he decided, not that David had ever been more than mildly critical when one of his school reports had been on the acerbic side; but he suddenly felt that he had a family tradition to uphold, and should Helena, or indeed Karen, need his support, he would make sure that he was capable of providing it. His grief was surmounted by a kind of excitement. He meant to emerge from his father's shadow. He would be equal to his father one day. Different, but equal.

Karan, by contrast, was perplexed as she resumed the long drive back to Colmleigh. It had never occurred to her that her mother could bear to stay on in Danesburgh for an hour longer than was absolutely necessary; and now, even though she understood Helena's reasoning perfectly well, at an intellectual level, she still felt hurt and rejected. Her father had been her anchor during her adolescence; he had invariably collected her from parties, put her boy friends at their ease even as he assessed them, swum and played tennis with her, practised new dance steps with her, listened to her records with every appearance of enjoyment; she had loved him fiercely and defended him vigorously when friends complained about the incomprehensible adult race. Now she felt totally bereft, and angry at the unfairness of it all.

When she finally reached the flat she found Gill still sprawled on her bed, listening to a radio through earphones, with a half-empty cup of coffee on the table beside her. It was then about midday, and Karen had to be in the office by two.

"Oh, hello," Gill drawled. "Have you had a rotten time?"

Karen looked at her. Suddenly the independence which had seemed so attractive a week earlier had lost its appeal. She would have given anything to be able to go back to their old semi-detached house just off the main road into Colmleigh, for the lunch her mother would have had ready for her.

She replied with an effort, "Yes, 'fraid I have, rather. I suppose I'll get over it in time. Look, Gill, I've got to go to work this afternoon. How about a quick something in town? I've got a few spare luncheon vouchers."

"Can't be bothered now," said Gill lazily. "But I'll do dinner tonight, if you like. Donna and Max showed me how to do stuffed pimento on Saturday night. It's an experience."

So Karen had to have lunch alone in a burger bar in Colmleigh High Street, where the thermoplastic floor was piled high with shopping bags, the neon lighting flickered incessantly and the smell of fresh and stale cigarette smoke mingled nauseously with those of frying oil and the perspiration of the cooks.

Karen's workmates were sympathetic, but busy. When she returned to the flat in the evening, Gill was in the kitchen, surrounded by eggs, herbs, bowls of rice and other, more outlandish, comestibles, while a thin, long-haired young man, wearing rimless glasses, who was seated on the divan in the living-room, contrived to smoke and strum a guitar at the same time.

"Oh, there you are, Karen," Gill called from the door. "You know Steve, don't you? No? Oh, well, this is Steve. My flatmate, Karen. Be nice to her, won't you, she's just lost her father."

Steve mumbled some expression of sympathy and resumed his musical exercise.

"I've invited Steve to share the meal. I hope you don't mind," Gill explained. "His landlady kicked him out. He's got somewhere to go, but nobody to cook for him."

Karen assented, feeling that perhaps it would be good for her to listen to someone else's troubles. Steve, it appeared, was a second-year anthropology student at London University. He talked undergraduate politics, while the girls made coffee, washed up and then played records for a couple of hours. Finally, he left.

"Oof! What a bore," Gill complained. "I think I'll pass him on to Hilary. She's political. She'll *argue* with him."

Karen yawned, lifting he hand to her mouth.

"Oh, God, I'm sorry," Gill became apologetic. "You must be all in after that drive, and work on top of it. Come on, you get to bed and I'll bring you some hot chocolate."

How can Gill take things so much in her stride, Karen wondered. It must be her background, you'd have to learn that sort of indifference, you couldn't be born like it.

As Gill came in with the chocolate, she gave Karen a slightly twisted smile. "If you feel like a good howl, don't mind me. Your father was super, wasn't he? I only met him once, but I thought then, if only I'd had a father like that. What a life. You have someone marvellous and you lose him, while I've got four parents telling me what to do, and I sometimes wish I could be rid of the lot of them. They made a mess of their lives, and I'm not letting them mess up mine. If I get in a mess at least it'll be of my own making. It's so unfair, isn't it? There's no sense in it. You just have to go on trying to make something out of it."

For a moment, tears stung the inside of Karen's eyelids. *Yes*, she thought, *I suppose I shall try to make something out of it. Mum and Dad never needed to, though, or at least they didn't seem to. Everything seemed to fit together for them. But with Dad gone, the whole world seems to have fallen apart. Oh, God. What will Mum do?*

And not greatly consoled, she fell into a troubled sleep.

***

Helena, meanwhile, had reached a similar conclusion, although she would no doubt have expressed it rather differently. Having waved to Karen and Chris until the car had turned the corner of the cul-de-sac and disappeared, she had gone back indoors with a curious sense of peace.

The house was a modern one, detached with four bedrooms and a central staircase, about five years old, and built on a small development where the designs varied to a reasonable degree. The garage, an integral part of the building, still accommodated the company car, which, Helena knew, must be collected during the following week; she had learned to drive, but had only done so in emergencies, such as when David had been in bed with influenza and a vital document had needed to be delivered to the office. Transport was a problem she would have to tackle soon, but in the meantime she wandered from room to room, taking stock.

The home still spoke more of its previous owners than it did of David, and that was all to the good. Had he had time to work on it, she would have been reluctant to alter anything; as it was, she made up her mind that one of the first things she had to do was redecorate the lounge and the master bedroom. The low ceilings, white woodwork and veneered doors meant that this would not be too arduous a task, and furthermore the bedroom walls still wore their original emulsion; evidently the previous owners had not thought it worth the effort to paper them.

Helena looked out through the window at the small, rectangular back garden, mostly laid to lawn, with a concrete base where a greenhouse had stood and a small shed; beyond the rear fence, a spinney, and then open fields. It was quiet compared with Colmleigh, where the traffic had flowed ceaselessly along the arterial road half a mile away, and where from the early hours of the morning neighbours were leaving to travel up to London. Here it was only the birds that had woken Helena early, until she had had to shut the window, even when it was really too warm to be comfortable, in order to achieve a full night's sleep. David had normally slept through it all, but recently she had noticed that he had been half-awake at intervals throughout the night; perhaps a warning sign? But he had so rarely been ill; the usual occasional influenza or stomach upsets apart, he had never suffered with his health, and even when she knew he was enjoying his job in London rather less, he had shown few signs of strain at home. How ironic that his death should have occurred just after they had moved to this far more peaceful environment.

Helena sat down on the bed, her eyes misty, and permitted herself a few more tears. She had known that she would want to weep again, and had made up her mind to indulge her emotions a little once the children had left. This particular spasm, however, did not last long. She washed her face, combed her hair and began to think about colour schemes.

After a while, the doorbell rang. It was Rhoda Broughmer, Helena's next-door neighbour, who, mindful of the promise she had made to Claire after the funeral to keep an eye on Helena, had decided to invite her to lunch. She was agreeably surprised by the change she observed in Helena; what she had originally regarded mainly as a neighbourly duty now promised to be a potential pleasure. Helena accepted willingly, appreciating her neighbour's thoughtfulness and hoping for a measure of support.

Over lunch, Helena found herself recounting further stories she had half-forgotten, while Rhoda listened, occasionally mentioning a similar experience, or inviting Helena to elaborate a little further. Then it was Rhoda's turn for disclosure; her husband Eric was a consulting engineer with a local company, and they had spent some time working in East Africa, until a worsening political situation had forced them to return home. They had their own personal tragedy, a daughter killed in a road accident, twenty years earlier. There was also a married son in the Midlands, with two small children, of whom Rhoda was proud to the point of embarrassing herself.

Rhoda clearly led a busy life. The letter rack in her kitchen was full, and the calendar on the wall marked with numerous future engagements. Helena had already noticed that she had numerous and frequent visitors. *I'd better not take up too much of Rhoda's time*, she thought, and found an excuse not to stay; but she was much encouraged by the couple of hours they spent together.

By the end of the afternoon Helena had formed a redecoration plan, to be put into practice during the coming week. In the evening she had planned to deal with the correspondence that had been building up for some days, letters of condolence to acknowledge, forms to complete, one or two bills, and a pile of circulars and advertisements which she had put to once side, not being sufficiently interested to read them. Now, having taken out her pen and paper and laid them on the table, she felt totally disinclined to start.

Darkness had fallen, and she felt alone again; a grey haze of melancholy somehow inserted itself between her eyes and the writing paper. At last she gave up and instead went and found a favourite Beethoven concerto, and played it over to herself on the record-player, trying to give her mood some kind of musical expression. She loved classical music, and had often wished David had shared her taste; although they had been to a few concerts together, he had tolerated rather than enjoyed them, preferring popular big bands — Ellington, Dorsey, Glenn Miller; for him, music had been for dancing, not for listening to, and Helena recalled his enthusiasm for every new dance craze, and his unflagging energy on the dance floor; even that summer in Malaga, he had hardly missed a dance, urging Karen to take her place when she had had enough.

The concerto came to an end. Back in her memories, Helena had scarcely listened; but the music had its effect, for she felt settled again, and her melancholy had lifted. She knew now, however, that the tasks she found repugnant would have to be undertaken in daylight; she could not confront them once it was dark. She decided to adopt a routine whereby the correspondence would be dealt with in the mornings, leaving her other chores, together with any painting and decorating, until the afternoons and evenings. This, she hoped, would leave her sufficiently tired to sleep at night, without recourse to tablets. She had a bath, made herself a hot drink, and for the first time in days, slept naturally, free from the tormenting image of the coffin disappearing through the curtains.

***

The next few days passed as Helena had planned. She dutifully wrote her letters in the morning, doing her best to distance herself from them emotionally, as though they were some kind of homework from her schooldays. Having found a local branch of a national do-it-yourself chain store that would deliver decorating materials, she was able to busy herself in the afternoons with sandpaper, filler and paint, wearing the oldest clothes she could find. The appearance of the lounge began to change; it was lighter, and somehow seemed bigger. The carpet was in far too good a condition to need changing immediately, she concluded, but perhaps it could be cut down and used elsewhere at a later date. She bought a couple of indoor plants, and a print of a Highland scene she had rather liked when she had seen it in the Danesburgh art shop. Without realising it, she was beginning to remodel her surroundings as part of her process of adjustment.

She introduced herself to her neighbours on the other side, whom she had hardly seen. Their names were Colin and Judith, and they had a cabin cruiser somewhere on the Broads, where they spent most of their weekends. They were horrified to discover that they had been entirely oblivious of the drama of the previous weeks. Colin worked for an estate agent and promised to look out details of one or two suitable bungalows, should the house prove too much for Helena to manage on her own. But they were of a different generation, and Helena realised that she had little in common with them. She saw Rhoda Broughmer when she could, and at Rhoda's request Eric reconnected the wall lights and ornamental central chandelier in the lounge, which David had promised to do for her. Eric, however, was as reserved as Helena herself, and would not stay long.

Chris came home at the weekend with a rucksack full of books. He evidently intended to take his studies seriously. He assisted Helena with some of the painting, and the hanging of some new curtains; but for much of the time he withdrew to the study, where Helena found him immersed in technology. She was a little disappointed, but not really surprised, for communication between them had not been fluent since he had grown up. That was not symptomatic of any strain in their relationship; he simply did not find it easy to talk. It was not until he opened the garage door to look for a pair of wellingtons, with a view to a rare stroll across the fields, that he ventured to speak up.

"Mum. The car's gone?"

"Yes, dear. It had to go, of course. It belonged to the company."

"But how on earth are you getting about, then?"

"Well, I haven't had to do much travelling this week. I've only been into town once. I went on the bus. It's quite a regular service."

"Mum, that won't do. You can't rely on public transport all the time. I bet there aren't any buses at all on Sunday, and you can't possibly use taxis, they charge the earth. You'll have to buy a car of your own. I'll look after it for you."

Helena protested a little, but promised to consider it. When, later in the week, she came to give the matter some serious thought, Chris's logic seemed irrefutable. A sudden one-day strike by the local bus company's employees, called as a result of some alteration to the schedules, decided her. She told herself that, outside what passed for a rush hour there, Danesburgh, was a quiet little place that represented few hazards for the inexperienced driver, unlike Colmleigh, where, all day long, everyone seemed in a rush to get somewhere. She bought a copy of the local paper, consulted Eric Broughmer about dealers, and worked out some figures. David had had an unencumbered endowment policy, taken out through a broker friend before they had moved to Colmleigh, and she had submitted a claim under Claire's guidance during the days before the funeral. Thus prepared, she was ready, when Chris reappeared after another week away at college, to approach a garage recommended by Eric Broughmer. At that time the garage had nothing suitable, but the owner promised to look around, with Helena in mind, for a reliable vehicle; and a month or so later, she and Chris between them settled on a modest second-hand Ford with only one previous owner, who had kept it serviced and looked after it reasonably well. This, Helena thought, was likely to suffice her, bearing in mind the limited amount of driving she proposed to do, for a few years at least.

Chris was satisfied. "Now you'll be able to see us a lot more often," he said. Helena was less certain, for the long drive to Colmleigh, never mind having to cross London, filled her with apprehension. Winter, moreover, was approaching, with its attendant fogs, frosts and snow.

"Let me get used to driving again," she warned him.

And when she collected the car, freshly tested, serviced and valeted, she had to summon all her courage to put it in gear and drive the mile and a half home. Although she achieved this without mishap, and successfully stowed the car in the garage, she nevertheless felt shaky enough to pour herself a gin and tonic, which, she persuaded herself, was as much by way of a celebration as a stiffener.

It was close to the end of November. Some of the mornings were still bright, but by mid-afternoon it was usually damp and misty, if not actually raining, and the autumn reds and golds had given way to the duller browns and yellows in which the countryside prepares itself for the dead season. Helena had spent several weeks unhurriedly restyling the interior of the house; it now reflected a subdued good taste, in keeping with her situation.

There were few ornaments, for Helena did not care to continue exhibiting the souvenirs she and David had brought back from their holidays abroad; a single family portrait, taken by a professional photographer a couple of years earlier, stood on the bookcase; she had a more sentimental photograph of David, which she felt belonged in her room. The Highland scene hung above the York stone fireplace, and on the other wall she had fixed a rectangular mirror with a view to augmenting the daylight from the window.

All this had kept Helena quietly occupied through the early days of her widowhood. More and more, however, she found herself counting the hours to Chris's return on Friday evening. The evenings, predictably enough, were the hardest times to bear, spent in hope that the telephone would ring and Claire's voice, or less frequently Karen's, would enquire how she was and bring her up to date with their own goings-on. Loneliness had never before seemed a serious threat, but now she was undeniably becoming acquainted with it. Busy herself as she would, she was intermittently aware, all week long, of a dull, profound emotional ache, which invaded her whenever she paused, and reached its most acute level at bedtime on nights when no one had telephoned. She argued with herself that it was something she had to expect, and determined not to burden anyone else with it, and to be busier still the next day. All the same, that ache remained with her through the weeks, to the point where she feared the weekends would become the focus of her whole existence.

Without intending to do so, she intimated as much to Claire in the course of one of their evening telephone conversations.

"It seems to me," Claire commented, "that you ought to look for a nice little job of some kind. You know you always meant to work again, once the children grew up. Something to get you out of the house all day and give you the chance to meet people. No library work, mind. You don't want to bury yourself in books any more. Have a look at the local paper, see what's going."

"Not very much, by all accounts," Helena replied, "but you're right, of course, I ought to have thought of that a week or two ago, but it seemed too early then, somehow. Perhaps if I practise my touch-typing I might find a secretarial job. There must be something, office staff are always coming and going, aren't they?"

The conversation passed on to other matters — the progress of Claire's boys at school; a proposed theatre trip, to which Claire invited Helena, as an excuse for an outing. But it was for the following Friday night, and Chris had already made arrangements to come home early, so, with a little regret, Helena had to decline the invitation. She, in turn, invited Claire to come over for a weekend, with Bernard and the boys, before Christmas; but this, conversely, did not fit into Claire's diary. In the end they agreed to meet during the Christmas holidays.

For some years the two families had been accustomed to seeing a great deal of each other over Christmas, getting together at one home or the other, before David and Helena had moved to Danesburgh. Usually Mr and Mrs McCallogh had also been there, until they had returned to Scotland on Frank's retirement. David's parents had been less frequent visitors, usually just before or after the festival; it had always taken a great deal to entice them away from the West Country ("quite rightly", David would have said), and had been particularly difficult in recent years. They had their friends, whose company they tended to prefer, and the children were too much for them, especially when they were all there at the same time. Bernard's mother would also visit them; she was a cheerful, rotund old lady who took great joy in her two grandsons, but also had a soft spot for Karen and Chris, and invariably bought them more thoughtful and elaborate gifts than their degree of kinship really justified.

"What will you be doing at Christmas? I've been meaning to ask."

Helena was silent for a moment. Family gatherings, she reflected, were becoming a thing of the past. The move would have seen to that in any event, not to mention the age the children had reached, even if... even if David had still been alive, she forced herself to complete the thought. And then, her parents would not relish another trip south in mid-winter, even if Aunt Marie consented to be left in the care of a neighbour for a few days; and who wanted to be left with the responsibility of looking after someone else's ailing elderly relative over Christmas? No, this year it would be a quiet Christmas, just herself and the children.

"Oh, I expect it'll just be the three of us this year. It's a long way for Mum and Dad to come at this time of year, and they've got Aunt Marie getting more and more dependent on them, haven't they? And David's parents never used to make the effort to come to us at Colmleigh, so I'm sure they won't want to come all the way up here. Never mind, we'll come and see you just before Christmas. Karen can come straight from work if she can't get a day off."

These plans left Helena feeling a good deal better, and her first thought was to practise driving as much as possible in the next few weeks, to prepare herself for a trip to Croydon, where Claire and her family lived. She would drive Chris back to Leytonstone, perhaps, after the weekend, to get accustomed to the metropolitan traffic without actually having to cross the capital.

Then she remembered Claire's advice, and on the Friday, spent some time perusing the "situations vacant" in the Danesburgh local weekly, in search of possible employment. At first sight the prospects were not encouraging, most of the vacancies being for supermarket shelf stackers, chicken jointers, dressmaking outworkers and the like; but one advertisement then caught her eye. This was for a secretarial position at Danesburgh Cartons, a smallish factory on the industrial estate, just off the ring road. She hesitated. *I'm a librarian*, she thought, *I've no office experience*; but her determination won. *I can type, I can make appointments as well as anyone else, and I'm not saddled with the local accent* (which, although not unpleasant in itself, was decidedly rural). *I can spell, I'm not likely to go off somewhere without notice, and I certainly shan't be applying for maternity leave. I must have a reasonable chance of being taken on.*

She hesitated once more, and then, with sudden resolve, went over to the telephone and dialled the number of Danesburgh Cartons.

***

Living away from home was chafing Karen, as a new shoe, however smart, may chafe the heel; she still did not regret her decision to remain in Colmleigh, but Gill's personality was proving very different from her own. Although she might have preferred not to admit it, Karen took her job very seriously, and if anything went wrong at the office she could be irritable, or tearful, or both, in the evening. On such occasions she missed her parents' calm common sense, their ability to cheer her. By contrast, Gill, although ostensibly engaged in a correspondence course for some certificate or other, rarely seemed to open her books, much less settle to writing anything; she lounged about the flat, scruffy and unkempt, making coffee, smoking and listening to records, a good deal of the time. Or she would go off to the university campus and stay there until late in the evening. The flat always seemed to be full of strangers, thin, bearded young men in sandals, or earnest girls in shawls and beads; some were genuine students, others merely adopted a student-like appearance for reasons of their own. Karen found their company tedious. They seemed to presume to understand the world and its problems on such a mean foundation of experience. They, in turn, tended to discount her; once or twice she wondered whether one or other of the boys might show an interest in her, at least for her looks, but they mostly seemed to have girl friends, of a similar cast of mind to their own, elsewhere. Even if she had admitted to herself that she would have liked a weekend with her mother in Danesburgh, she would have been uncomfortable about leaving the flat, fearing that someone quite unacceptable might use her room while she was away; *one whiff of pot, and I'm out of here,* she thought more than once, but even then wasn't sure whether she really meant it.

Gill was quite unable to understand Karen's reservations.

"They're quite all right," she would say. "They might look a bit odd to you, but they're absolutely harmless, and some of them are brilliant. I mean, look at Pete. He's got Hegel and Kant absolutely taped, hasn't he? No problem. He's working on his own version of existentialism now, he'll probably write a doctoral thesis on it later on. Maybe they'll name it after him, and then you'll be able to say you knew him in his early days. I wish we'd lived a hundred years ago. I'd have been his mistress, and he'd have written me hundreds of letters, and I'd have kept them all and published them years later, when he was famous. He will be, you know. Famous, I mean."

Karen had her doubts about this. For a long time she had sensed that Gill was trying to acquire a reputation for intellectual brilliance by association, a kind of reflected glory, no doubt with a view to establishing her superiority over her parents and their respective second spouses; but she lacked the ability to express those thoughts coherently, and in any case, she would not have wished to hurt her flatmate. Gill was capable of genuine thoughtfulness, but for a good deal of the time she seemed to be wrapped in dreams, and not at all certain of where she was going or why; for all her affectation of worldly wisdom, she was too concerned with escaping from her recent past to think much, or clearly, about the future. There was a certain naivety about Gill which, while admittedly irritating, had a certain appeal for Karen, who was beginning to feel responsible in some measure for her flatmate's moral welfare. *God knows*, she thought once or twice, looking at Gill's slight, untidy figure sprawled on the sofa or the divan, a lock of lank dark hair falling over her face, *God knows what she might get mixed up in, with all these weird people, if I weren't around to keep an eye on her*. Then she would reprove herself for sounding too much like her Aunt Claire.

All the same, it was that sense of responsibility, as much as her determination to manage on her own, that kept her there for several weekends in succession.

***

The response to Helena's job application took her by surprise. She had rather expected a form in the post, to be filled in and returned; instead, a cheerful male voice with an accent from the eastern suburbs of London invited her to come along for an interview the same afternoon. *Well*, she thought, *I seem to be on the shortlist already. I wonder if there's something wrong with the company that puts people off working there.* She asked Rhoda Broughmer whether she knew anything about it.

"I don't know anything much ," Rhoda replied. "All I do know is that most of the local industry's been having a hard time just lately. Some of those factories must be operating on a shoestring to keep going. Anyway, why not go along to the interview? You can always say no if you don't like the look of it."

So, just before half past two, Helena carefully parked her car in one of the spaces marked out in white on the tarmac outside the Danesburgh Cartons building. It was one of a row of modern, brick-built factories and warehouses, all much alike on the outside, with a high row of reinforced windows, a loading bay at one end, and a small suite of offices, with a first-floor section added, at the other. As she walked through the lobby the sound of machinery, overlaid with piped music, assailed her ears. She reached the reception window, behind which a plump girl of about twenty was filing her nails. She looked up as Helena approached. *Bored stiff, by the look of it,* Helena thought.

"Can I help you?" the girl enquired in a routine tone.

"Good afternoon. I'm Mrs Halstow. I have an appointment here at a quarter to three."

"Just a minute." The receptionist took out a dog-eared appointment book and turned the pages with a nicotine-stained forefinger.

"Oh, yes, here it is. I'll tell Mr Farrelson you're here. Would you like to sit down?" The girl's manner was polite but indifferent. She moved to a small switchboard, pressed a switch.

"Mr Farrelson, I have Mrs Halstow here to see you."

The reply was inaudible. The girl turned to Helena again.

"Would you like to go up to the first floor, please? Mr Farrelson's room is on the right."

Helena climbed the stairs, which were carpeted in the middle with a strip of cheap brown material of some sort. At the top she found the door already open. Mr Farrelson was seated behind a teak desk adorned by a large blotter and a couple of worn-looking files. He was a thin, sallow-faced man in his thirties, with a receding hairline and gold-rimmed glasses. He gave Helena a cheerful smile.

"How do you do, Mrs Halstow? Thanks for coming so promptly. Sit down, won't you?" He indicated a straight-backed chair with teak arms and black vinyl upholstery.

"Now, you've come about the secretarial job, haven't you? What sort of experience have you had?"

Helena decided to be truthful.

"Not a lot, actually — not in an office, that is. I trained as a librarian. But I have done some work you could call secretarial. For my husband. You know, typing letters, telephone, filing, book-keeping and so on. When he was working at home a lot."

"I see. Did you have to work under pressure?"

"Sometimes there was a lot to do, yes. Not all the time, of course, but there were peaks now and again."

"Was this recently?"

"No, not very. A year or two ago. Before we moved to Danesburgh."

"M, h'm. What line of work is your husband in?"

"He was a marketing consultant."

"*Was,* you say. Does that mean — please don't be offended if I ask — that he's been made redundant?"

Anything but, Helena thought, with a touch of bitterness.

"No. He died a few weeks ago."

Mr Farrelson looked confused and embarrassed.

"Oh, dear. I am sorry. What a rotten question to ask you. You know, I hear of so many redundancies, half the girls' husbands here are out of work at the moment. I do apologise."

The gaffe, however, was not without benefit for Helena, for it gave her a kind of moral advantage. From then on, without exploiting the fact, she was treated with something approaching deference.

"Well, Mrs Halstow," Mr Farrelson said at the end of the interview, "it seems to me that you could do the job with no trouble at all — at least, the secretarial side; but I don't know whether it would appeal to you, with your level of education. I'll tell you what I'll do, I'll give you a bit of a run-down on what we do and how we work here, and then you can think about it over the weekend and let me know on Monday. How's that?"

Helena agreed, inwardly rather surprised at the continuing lack of formality. It was not the way they had done things in Colmleigh, when Karen had been applying for jobs, much less in London.

"Well, as you can see, this is a small business. We collect waste paper from all over the place, and press it into various grades of cardboard. Then we make it up into boxes and send it out to stores, warehouses, packing depots, factories and so on. We have contracts with a few supermarkets and department stores, and a number of casual customers who order consignments from time to time, maybe three or four times a year. We employ about thirty-five people altogether on the shop floor, plus half a dozen of us out here in the office. We've had a hard few months lately, but business seems to be picking up again now, and Christmas is usually good for a few extra orders. You know, for the January sales and so on. But we've had to prune our workforce a bit, and that's why we didn't replace our previous secretary straightaway when she left."

Helena wondered whether that explained the dilapidated appearance of the files.

"Because we're so small, our jobs have to overlap to some extent. I'm the general manager, or at least that's my job description, but I also have to know about the transport arrangements, and a bit about servicing the machinery. If someone's off sick we all share their work until they get back."

I suppose that's why it was you that answered the telephone when I rang, Helena thought.

"So, if you take the job on — and I have to say we can't offer a fantastic salary, not by London standards, anyway — you'll have to accept that it isn't all typing and filing and making telephone appointments. You'll come into contact with the shop floor workers a bit, and they're a mixed bunch, like you'd find anywhere else. Our previous secretary doubled as a personnel officer and a good deal more besides. We were sorry to lose her, but she was moving away. It was hard work, but I think she enjoyed it, most of the time at any rate. Do you think you could cope? As I said, give it some thought and let me know on Monday. We certainly haven't had a better applicant, so I think I can say the job's yours if you want it."

Helena stood up. The speed at which all this had been delivered had left her a little bemused.

"Thank you, Mr Farrelson. Yes, I'll let you know on Monday."

***

Well, Helena reflected as she drove home, this is just the sort of thing Claire recommended. Something that'll keep me so busy all day that I shan't have time to mope.

She would think about it over the weekend; but in reality, she had made up her mind already.

And as it turned out, that was just as well, for the weekend was to prove singularly inconducive to further reflection. When he arrived in the morning, Chris was clearly suffering from the early symptoms of what promised to be a particularly vicious cold, and had to be put straight to bed with a dose of aspirin and hot lemon. He had taken advantage of a rare free day, occasioned by the absence of a couple of lecturers, to make a trip to the Essex marshes with a fellow ornithologist on the back of a motorcycle, and had got soaked to the skin by the late autumn drizzle in the process.

Helena felt a smidgen of guilt, her natural concern being compounded by fear that she would catch Chris's cold herself and thus be obliged to start work while feeling under the weather, and as a result was uncharacteristically irritable. Chris was unrepentant, and uncomplaining so far as the cold was concerned; but he had received some encouraging comments from his tutors, and was rather disappointed at his mother's apparent lack of enthusiasm.

Helena did her best to explain.

"I'm sorry if I did sound cross with you, dear, but I do think it was silly of you, going off bird-watching at this time of year. And then, well, I've got a job. I'm starting on Monday, and I was afraid of catching your cold just when I need to be well."

Chris was startled.

"A job. Mum? Do you need a job?"

"Well, yes and no, dear. It's not so much the money, although a little more always helps. It's really so that I've got something to do during the week. It's a bit lonely here on my own."

"What sort of job is it?"

"Well, I'm supposed to be a secretary, but I've an idea there may be more to it than that. It's at Danesburgh Cartons, over on the industrial estate. Actually I haven't formally accepted it, but I'm almost sure I will. It might be quite interesting."

"But Mum, you've got a degree, and you're a trained librarian. Why on earth do you want to go to some third-rate factory to work? There must be better things you could do."

Helena smiled. "The degree and the library training are a long time ago now. Anyway, maybe it was time I tried my hand at something different. Your father was never afraid of a new challenge, was he? That was why we moved here."

"I don't think Dad would have liked you to waste your training," Chris objected. "He'd have said 'make the most of the ability you've got'. That's what I'm trying to do. Isn't it?"

Helena seized the opportunity of turning the topic of conversation back to Chris's own work.

"Yes, dear, and I really am pleased that your tutors think you're making progress. I know you can achieve things if you put your mind to it. Have you got much more to do this term?"

"Well, I've got a couple more test papers coming up. I've brought the books so that I can revise a bit for them. A couple of hours tomorrow and another couple on Sunday should be enough."

"Have an early night, then, and don't try to read now. You'll feel better in the morning. Good night, dear."

Helena left Chris to sleep off the cold (she hoped), and settled herself to watch an episode of a classic serial on television.

Not for long, however. Almost immediately the telephone rang, and Helena got up with a touch of impatience, which was dispelled as soon as she lifted the receiver.

"Karen! Hello, dear. How nice to hear your voice. How are you?"

"I'm fine, thanks, Mum. Listen. I'm in a call box, so I'll have to be quick. Can I come over tomorrow? I'm sorry I didn't ring before, but I've been so busy this week, and I'd love to see you. Gill's going up to London for the weekend, so I'd have been here on my own."

"Of course you can, dear. You know you're always welcome. Will you stay over?"

The pips sounded. Karen barely had time to say, "See you about midday, then." And the line was cut off before there was time to say goodbye to her. Helena was pleased, however; she had detected echoes of the old Karen, blithely flitting in and out of the house, cheerfully egocentric, but always disarming her parents with a smile and a hug. It would be nice to have both her children at home with her for a normal weekend. She willingly resigned herself to missing the rest of the episode and baking a batch of scones instead.

***

Karen's telephone call had not been made on a sudden impulse, nor as a result of a change of heart about Danesburgh. It was after lunch next day that this became clear to Helena. Karen and Chris had dutifully assisted with clearing up (a tradition Helena had successfully nurtured). Chris was even less articulate than usual, having all but lost his voice, but otherwise did not appear to be suffering too severely, and they were sipping coffee in the lounge. All the usual family questions had been asked and answered — health, work, relatives and friends — and Karen now felt ready to approach her mother on a slightly more delicate matter.

"Mum... can I ask you something?"

She leaned forward, her eyes on Helena's face.

"Yes, of course, dear. What is it?"

"It's about Christmas. You're expecting both of us, aren't you?"

Oh, Lord, thought Helena, she wants to go off somewhere else.

"Well, I was, yes. Have you got some other plans, then?"

Karen gave her that disarming smile. "Oh, no, Mum, it's not that. What I wanted to ask was, what would you say if I said I'd like to bring someone else as well, for Christmas, I mean?"

A boy friend? Helena thought. A number of young men in Colmleigh had asked Karen out on dates from time to time; but Karen had given no indication of any serious attachment so far.

"Well, that depends," she said cautiously. "Who exactly were you thinking of?"

"It's Gill, Mum. You know, my flatmate. She hasn't really got anywhere to go at Christmas, not where she'll enjoy it. Both her parents have married again now, and she doesn't feel as if she fits in anywhere. Her Mum and Dad finished up hating the sight of each other, and she says whenever she goes to see them it's a sort of reminder. So she'd more or less decided to stay on her own in the flat. And I said 'oh, no, you can't do that, what a miserable way to spend Christmas', and before I thought about it I said I'd ask you if she could come to us."

Helena was touched at the impulsive offer, in spite of some mild apprehension. She hardly knew Gill; the sharing arrangement had been set up on the strength of the girls' having known each other at school, although they had not been close friends at that time. Gill, a year younger than Karen, had stayed on into the sixth form, but the disintegration of her family life, which had accelerated over her last two years at school, had taken its toll of her powers of concentration, and she had not been able to secure a place at a university or college, although, with a commendable late effort, she had achieved two marginal 'A' level passes. As a sop to their consciences, her parents, who would have been much better pleased if she had gone away to college, had agreed to pay her share of the flat rent, while, as a last resort, she struggled with a correspondence course. The Cumbers knew her parents slightly and did not speak particularly well of them. Still, Helena reasoned, she herself had nothing against the girl, and if Karen had taken pity on her and wanted to bring her home for Christmas, then good for Karen; it was encouraging that she should be concerned for her friend, and perhaps the effort of entertaining a stranger would distract Helena herself a little from missing David.

"Well, my love," she said at length, "if Gill would really like to spend Christmas with us, I don't see any reason why she shouldn't come. But what do you think, Chris?"

Chris had no objection. He was mildly intrigued by Karen's description of Gill, and thought it would be interesting to see whether she matched it.

"Yes, bring her, Karen," he croaked. "We'll make her welcome. Won't we, Mum?"

In the evening, he took himself off to pursue his studies and nurse his cold, while Helena and Karen, on an impulse, drove into town and managed to obtain two of the last stalls tickets for the local repertory company's final performance of *Brief Encounter*. It would not have been David's choice, but Helena thoroughly enjoyed the stylised charm of the play. Karen, to whom such period pieces were unfamiliar, was perplexed by the characters' self-restraint, and surprised by their final decision not to meet again; she thought of Gill's parents, and of a couple of office acquaintances of hers, whose indiscretions were notorious. To her they seemed to be constantly at pains to prove that they were doing nothing to be ashamed of; but she could hardly be openly disloyal to the generation, so her only comment was, "It wasn't exactly what you'd call exciting, but I enjoyed it in a way."

When they arrived home Chris was already asleep, having made himself a hot drink and taken a couple of aspirins. His books lay open on the dining-room table. Karen took a look at one.

"Wow," she remarked. "Our Chris is turning into a real boffin, isn't he? I can't understand a word of this."

Helena smiled. "Yes, he's really working hard now. He's taken it very well, losing Dad. I was afraid it would break him up, but instead he seems to have settled down to studying all the better. I'm sure he misses Dad, of course, although he doesn't say very much. But it's made him suddenly a lot more serious, and that's something I want to encourage. It means he's growing up. What about you, though, dear? You've been away so much of the time since then, and I've missed you. How have you been coping with it all?"

Karen was silent for a few moments.

"I miss Dad too," she confirmed at last. "I sometimes ache inside with it. It seems such a waste. I think I'm still more angry than sad; like Gill says, it's not fair. She's got a real father and mother, and a stepfather and a stepmother as well, and she doesn't want to know any of them, but I really did love Dad, he used to brighten up the day for me so often, especially when I first started work and had a hard job getting used to it. Why do you think things like that happen, Mum?"

"I don't know, my love. I suppose everything has to have a reason. If I ever find out in this life," Helena concluded, "I'll tell you, never fear."

***

They slept in late on Sunday, and after a sketchy breakfast, drove out a little way into the country, in Helena's car this time, to a nearby reservoir, where Chris, whose cold was beginning to ease, scanned the waters through his binoculars for unusual wildfowl. The tally was unimpressive, but he was not discouraged; he would come again in the spring and summer. They stopped on the way back for an aperitif at on old thatched inn where, in an adjacent paddock, ponies and goats vied for the attention of visitors on an unusually mild December morning.

Lunch was a leisurely meal, followed by a quiet couple of hours, during which they passed the sections of the Sunday newspapers about. Chris read the science supplement; Karen devoured the fashion pages, and Helena lost herself in the literary reviews, after which they managed between them to solve a few of the clues to the prize crossword before finally admitting defeat.

After that there was tea, and television, and the rest of Sunday slipped quietly away. Karen and Chris left at about eight, and Helena was left to prepare herself for her new job. She got her typewriter out and typed a few lines. Not too bad, and the company would surely have a better machine than her old portable. She went to the wardrobe and looked out a white blouse and a pleated skirt, dark but not too sombre, which she hung carefully on the door handle. She had a leisurely bath and contemplated the morrow.

The factory floor, she knew, started work at eight o'clock. She would need to get there in good time, ready to start work immediately if needed; so she went to bed a little earlier than had been her custom recently. The bedroom, and the bed, had been cold, lonely places since October, and she had deliberately made a practice of staying downstairs until sheer fatigue drove her there. Tonight, almost for the first time, she was thinking ahead again, rather than back to the past. It might not last, once she got used to the job, but for the time being it marked a significant improvement in her morale. Once the children had telephoned briefly to confirm their safe arrival home, she was able to sleep soundly all night.

***

Monday morning was mild, damp and still. When Helena rose it was still dark, the street lamps in the close gleaming wanly among the almost leafless branches of the trees. She dressed quickly, boiled an egg and made some toast, which she ate in the kitchen, listening to an early-morning radio programme. It has been David's habit to tune in to Radio Luxembourg, and she tried to locate it; but when she succeeded the result was a cacophony of heavy-metal rock music, which she felt obliged to turn down to near zero, as though someone might be disturbed by it. She quickly switched to a news magazine programme, and then, as the announcer gave the eight twenty-five time check, turned off the radio and went out to the garage to start the car.

Having nervously, but successfully, negotiated the route to Danesburgh Cartons, through traffic rather heavier than it had been on Friday afternoon, Helena triumphantly parked in a vacant space on the factory forecourt. Work was already in progress; a large van was unloading bales of paper on one side of the bay, while on the other side a fork-lift truck, controlled by an overalled lad with greasy dark hair, was setting out pallets stacked with bundles of cardboard, presumably to be loaded into the same van when it was empty. Machinery could be heard thumping and clattering inside the building, and piped music fluted overhead. Helena made her way upstairs to the office and knocked on the door.

"Come in!"

Mr Farrelson was there with another man, stocky, balding and bespectacled; they were examining some printed dockets. "Oh, hello, Mrs Halstow. I didn't expect you to be here at this hour! I guess you must have made up your mind to accept the job, or you wouldn't have come, would you?"

"Yes," said Helena, "I thought I'd come early, so that I could start learning what I had to do straightaway if you wanted me to. But please don't let me interrupt what you're doing. I'll sit and wait outside if you prefer."

"Not at all, not at all. Well, welcome to Danesburgh Cartons. We're all on Christian name terms here, so I'll introduce you as we go along. This is George Bushmell, our transport manager."

The bespectacled man shook Helena's hand in a firm, dry grip. He grinned. "I hope you know what you're letting yourself in for, Mrs…?"

"Halstow. But it's Helena, if we're going to use Christian names."

"And I'm Brian," Mr Farrelson added. "Well, George, these look all right, don't they?"

"They'll do. Well, mustn't hang about. I want a word with young Kevin about the Transit. It looks as if something's dented the side. I'll let you know if I think we need to make a claim." George Bushmell disappeared through the doorway, nearly colliding with a tall, serious-looking man who was about to enter at the same time.

"Morning, Jim. You all right now?"

"Yes, I think so, thanks," said the newcomer. "I had a bit of pain in the shoulder over the weekend, but it's a lot better this morning. It won't stop me writing, anyway."

"Jim Sergent, our accounts man," Brian Farrelson explained. "Jim's the one who keeps us in the black — most of the time, anyway. Jim, this is Mrs Helena Halstow, our new secretary. Jim had a bit of a bump in his car on Friday morning," he went on. "So he wasn't here when you came for the interview. We sent him down to the hospital for a check. That reminds me. How's your first aid?"

"I used to know a bit," Helena admitted. She had taken a course at school, and had occasionally asked Claire to bring her up to date. Generally she had had no difficulty in dealing with the usual kind of minor injuries the children had suffered in the course of growing up. "I've a sister who's a practice nurse at a doctors' surgery. I can always ask her to give me a refresher course."

"Fine. We won't ask you to deal with anything serious if we can help it, but occasionally someone gets a knock or a cut, you know, with the machinery and so on. Anything drastic, you can call a doctor, or we do also have an arrangement with Plasmos, down the road if it's a real emergency. They're much bigger than us and have a private company nurse of their own. She'll usually come at short notice for us. The important thing is, if anything happens you make a note in the accident log as soon as you've done whatever's necessary, and if anyone says there's a fault in the machinery, let me know at once. The inspectors are hot on the health and safety regulations round here, and so they should be, of course. If it's not an accident, I mean if anyone's taken ill, there's small section screened off as a sick bay behind the reception areas, you can take them there. Think you can manage?"

"If it doesn't all happen at once," said Helena with a smile that belied her apprehension. "I'm sorry to hear about your accident, Mr Sergent. It must have spoilt the weekend for you."

Jim Sergent returned her smile, but without managing to look any less serious.

"It wasn't really so bad," he said. "I twisted my shoulder a bit, but the worst thing was having to hire another car, because my own was undriveable for the moment. I live out in one of the villages, you see, and the bus only runs twice a day. Never mind, it's at the repair shop now and I'll have it back by the end of the week."

He went off to hang up his coat.

Brian Farrelson grinned. "We call him 'Lucky Jim', when he's not there, of course. Poor bloke, you wouldn't believe the things that have happened to him. Worst thing, of course, he lost his wife a couple of years back. Cancer. It happened in the space of six months or so. Saw her go from a lovely woman to a bit of skin and bone. Tragic. Oh, I'm sorry, I shouldn't be going on like this when you've just been through something similar yourself."

"No need to apologise," Helena said quickly. "In a way it helps to realise that you're not the only person to have lost someone you loved. It was a terrible shock, of course, but I don't know what I'd have done if I'd had to watch my husband slowly fading away. It doesn't bear thinking about."

"Well, anyway," Brian Farrelson continued, "poor old Jim...". But poor old Jim was coming back, and Brian had to curtail the recital of his misfortunes.

Helena met a few more of the staff in the course of the morning, between spells of work. There were two maintenance men, Bob and Ernie, who came to check a fault in the loudspeaker system. One was tall and bearded, the other short and grey-haired, and both had pronounced local accents, which Helen suspected they deliberately exaggerated for her benefit. There was Diane, the receptionist, whom Helena had seen the previous Friday, plump and bored; she lit her first cigarette as soon as she had taken her coat off, and thereafter was rarely to be seen without one either between her lips or smoking itself away in an ashtray. And half-way through the morning Helena had a surprise. She was studying a diagram Brian Farrelson had given her, representing the various stages whereby waste paper was converted into cardboard, when a feminine voice with an accent at least as strong as Bob and Ernie's spoke into her ear,

"Would you like tea or coffee?"

Helena looked up into the mischievous eyes of a slim black woman, some six feet tall, with tight curls and gold earrings standing out against the dark skin of her face. She wore a factory overall that scarcely reached her hips, and under it a yellow jumper and sky blue slacks. She gave Helena a broad smile.

"Face doesn't exactly match the voice, does it? I'm Josie Barritt. I'm glad you've come. These gentlemen are very nice, but they need a lady around to keep them in order. I do my best, but I only come in twice a day."

Helena returned Josie's smile and introduced herself, once again.

"Well," she added, "I haven't really had time yet to find out what my official duties are, never mind keeping anyone in order. Oh, yes, coffee will be lovely, thank you very much. I'm sorry if I didn't respond very quickly at first, I was concentrating on trying to see how the processing works."

Josie briskly distributed tea and coffee around the office, moving with an easy grace. Another beaming smile and she disappeared again, her curls almost brushing the top of the door frame. Helena caught sight of her a little later, wheeling a metal tea trolley between the rows of machines, and exchanging banter with the workers, the smile flashing out at every turn. She wondered how Josie kept it up. Then she turned back to her study of the machine floor layout.

At lunchtime George Bushmell reappeared, and he and Brian Farrelson went off into town, where they evidently intended to spend the lunch hour in one of the pubs, with friends or business acquaintances. Jim Sergent reached into his desk and produced an unimaginative-looking pack of sandwiches, an apple and a Thermos flask. Gravely, he offered Helena one of the sandwiches.

"That's very kind of you," she replied, "but I think I'll pop into town. I've a little shopping I ought to do." She got up and fetched her coat.

Once outside, Helena thought of driving into town, but then remembered that on the opposite side of the ring road there was a public open space with a footpath that led directly to the market square. She could walk it in the time it would take her to find somewhere to park her car. She set off on foot.

Monday was not a market day. On another day, the square would be full of wooden stalls topped with coloured canvas, and would be echoing with the traders' shouts; but today there was only the noise of the traffic, and people walking to and from the shops. Danesburgh town centre offered few options so far as restaurants were concerned, and Helena was reluctant to commit herself to a full meal anywhere for fear of being late back to the office on her first day. She had almost decided to skip lunch altogether, when she noticed a poster attached to a notice board propped against the doorway of the town's Norman church, inviting all and sundry to a 'poverty lunch'.

This evoked a memory. As an undergraduate she had occasionally been to something similar, organised by some religious or humanitarian organisation, she couldn't remember which. Soup and a roll, perhaps some fruit, that kind of thing, no standing on ceremony and no waiting about; it was really the latter consideration that appealed to her most. She made her way through to the hall at the back, from which there emanated a smell of vegetable broth, and a murmur of conversation. Entering, she found about a dozen people standing about in groups or sitting at Formica-topped aluminium trestle tables. Among them was a young clergyman, fresh-faced and fair-haired, talking to a couple of leather-jacketed teenagers. He caught sight of Helena, excused himself and came over to her.

"Welcome," he said pleasantly. "It's nice to see a new face. Can I offer you some food?"

"Thank you," Helena replied. "I hope I didn't interrupt your conversation."

"Not at all. We were just discussing something we're planning for our family get-together after Evensong in a couple of weeks' time. Please sit down, won't you?" He motioned Helena to a chair and quickly brought her a tray with food on it from the hatch. The fare was much as Helena remembered it, a bowl of soup, a roll and an apple. The soup was hot and the roll fresh.

"Thank you," she said again. I really wasn't expecting to be waited on."

"You're very welcome. It's part of my job, after all. We're called to serve one another, literally as well as metaphorically. I happen to think that includes the very simplest things. I'm the curate here, by the way, my name's John Farthing. Are you new to Danesburgh, perhaps?"

"Yes, I haven't been here very long," said Helena. "Only since August. I've just started a job at one of the factories on the industrial estate, and this is my lunch hour." She wondered momentarily why she felt disinclined to enlarge on the subject, much as she had been reluctant to stay in the office at lunchtime, where Jim Sergent might have drawn her into conversation.

"Oh, well, I mustn't keep you talking, then. The lunch hour is a precious break, you won't want to waste a minute. Please feel welcome to come in any Monday, though, we hold our poverty lunch every week. And of course we'd love to see you at our Sunday services. Will you excuse me now?"

He got up and went to greet a couple who had just come in, and whom he evidently knew.

Helena in turn got up and left, placing some coins in the bowl she found by the door. She called very quickly at a couple of shops and walked briskly back to Danesburgh Cartons, arriving just as the church clock struck two.

Jim Sergent looked up from his ledgers, which were already open on the desk in front of him again.

"Ah, there you are. Did you find somewhere to eat?"

"Yes, thank you. I found they were having a 'poverty lunch' at the church, so I went in there for a few minutes."

"Oh, yes. Well, I imagine they're glad of all the support they can get for that." Helena fancied she detected a slightly sour note in his voice. She applied herself to her work without saying any more.

The other men came in two or three minutes later, still discussing some management topic, but George Bushmell almost immediately picked up an attaché case and departed for an appointment with the insurance company. Brian Farrelson dug out a pile of carbon copy invoices from a filing cabinet.

"Well," he said, "back to work, I suppose. These are some of our bills from last month. Can you have a look at them please, Helena, so that you'll be familiar with the way we set them out? These are our copies, and they're not paid yet, so for God's sake don't lose any of them. When they're paid we stamp them and put them in the 'paid' file, and Jim keeps them. When you're ready I've got some more to send out, so I'll ask you to type them."

The afternoon passed uneventfully, and by five o'clock Helena felt reasonably confident about the secretarial aspect of her job. It was not, in reality, particularly demanding, and she wondered whether it would still be providing her with sufficient interest after a few weeks.

She spent most of the evening renewing her knowledge of first aid with the assistance of a manual Claire had passed on to her, planning to recommend the purchase of a suitable book on behalf of the company, to be kept in the office for reference, not having observed the presence of any such book there during the day. Claire telephoned to ask how she had got on, and after a fairly brief conversation Helena went to bed content with the first day's work and optimistic about her prospects. It was still lonely, but she was tired enough not to dwell on that, and soon fell asleep.

***

The next few days proved busier than the first. Helena's secretarial routine remained calm, but one or two mishaps occurred on the shop floor, and she found herself putting her recently renewed first-aid skills into practice rather earlier than she would have wished. There was a badly cut finger, and a bruised and swollen foot on which some heavy item of equipment had accidentally fallen; one girl was brought to the office almost screaming with toothache, and had to be driven to the nearest dental surgery as an emergency case, and another had a petit-mal episode, fortunately not close to any of the machinery. This required Helena to remain in the sick bay with the girl until a brother arrived to take her home, by which time it was nearly five o'clock, and she stayed on for half an hour to log the various incidents.

One incident left her ruffled and rather upset. It was Thursday afternoon, and she was sorting some of the week's correspondence, with the object of bringing it up to date where possible. Both Brian Farrelson and Jim Sergent had left the office for the moment. There appeared in the doorway a tall, amply-built woman of indeterminate age, whose hair was dyed the colour of ripe blackberries, and whose face was so heavily laden with make-up that the colour and condition of the skin beneath could scarcely be guessed at. Her eyes were thickly ringed with mascara, and her lips, as red as a freshly painted pillar box, parted to reveal a shining full set of dentures. This apparition startled Helena, and she wondered for a moment whether she might be looking at a transvestite; but the voice soon dispelled that idea, for it was patently that of a woman of about fifty.

"'Ello, dear. Can I 'ave a word wiv yer — private, like?"

"Well, there's no one else here," Helena agreed, wondering what might be coming.

"Well, wha' I wan'ed to ask was, could I have an advance on me wages, to tide me over till tomorrer, see? That uvver secretary what was 'ere, she used ter let me 'ave a fiver, you know, on account, and take it orf me pay on the Friday."

Helena was taken aback. She thought for a moment.

"Look, I don't want to be unhelpful," she replied, "but I really don't have any authority to advance you money. The wages don't come from the bank until tomorrow, so I'd have to take it out of the office petty cash. I'll speak to Mr Farrelson or Mr Sergent about it as soon as I see one of them. Would you like to come up again just before five o'clock?"

But the woman was already on her way to the door. She marched out in evident disgust, muttering something Helena was almost certain was "toffee-nosed cow", and almost colliding with Josie Barritt, who was bringing in the tea. Near-collisions in the doorway seemed be a feature of office life at Danesburgh Cartons. "Oh, sorry, Topsy, didn't see you there."

Josie's smile was undimmed. "Marlene been up asking for money, has she? I thought she'd probably try it on with you. Don't take any notice of her, she's not a bad girl really, but she gets kind of frustrated when she hasn't got enough left for her bingo on a Thursday night. You should see her when she's won something, though. Friday morning she'll be all round the shop floor telling everybody about it. Maybe she'll win a hair-dryer, and another time it might be a pearl necklace. One time it was a portable colour television, can you imagine? Like a dog with two tails, she was. You can't blame her, she has a hard time, her husband hasn't had a regular job for years. And if she wins something like some chocolates or some biscuits, as often as not she'll bring them in and share them round."

"What did you say her name was?" Helena asked.. "And what was it she called you?"

"Marlene. Marlene Smetters. She's been here for years. And she calls me Topsy. They all do, down on the shop floor. You can see why, can't you?" Josie chuckled. "Topsy 'just growed' — and so did I!"

Helena had to smile too. "I see what you mean. Do you get teased a lot?"

"I did to begin with. Once or twice I was a bit hurt. But they all know me now. And anyway, it doesn't do to be over-sensitive, and I've got a lot to be thankful for. I might have ended up in one of the big cities, with no job at all." Another dazzling smile. "I'd better go, or they'll be wondering downstairs where their tea is. But don't worry about old Marlene, she'll soon get over it. She might be able to borrow a fiver off someone else. It wouldn't be the first time." She paused in the doorway. "Are the gentlemen coming back? If they are, I'll save them a cup."

Notwithstanding Josie's cheerful advice to forget the matter, Helena was still smarting inwardly, in a way that was unfamiliar to her. When Brian Farrelson returned he was quick to endorse the line she had taken, which mollified her a little.

"Yes, Peggy, that was our last secretary, did lend her a pound or two once, out of the petty cash, but we gave her a rare ticking-off over it. Apart from anything else, it messes up our accounting system. No, you were absolutely right, and Marlene should have known better. Don't worry about it one bit."

Even then, the insult had not totally lost its sting. *Toffee-nosed cow, is it?* she thought. *Well, let her cross my path again, and we'll see whether the toffee-nosed cow has horns.* She went home still disgruntled, and it took an hour and a half of Mendelssohn to restore her to a peaceable frame of mind.

***

Right up to Christmas, the weather remained mild, although the sky was often overcast and the air laden with moisture. At the factory, however, the mood was bright. The prospect of a holiday encouraged everyone, especially with the promise of a modest bonus, which Jim Sergent had satisfied himself the company could afford, and had been approved by the management generally. Work would not be resumed until the New Year, and with those incentives the cardboard was tumbling from the machines and cartons were being stacked in every available space. Brian Farrelson even took on a couple of university students to help to make them up. *White Christmas*, *Sleigh Ride* and *Winter Wonderland* blared incessantly from the loudspeakers. The office was festooned with tinfoil, holly and balloons, and in one corner a small Christmas tree presided over a few of the company's smaller products, suitably enveloped in gift wrap.

Serious business conversations were interspersed with polite enquiries about everyone's plans for the festival. Jim Sergent, who lived alone, was treating himself to a week in Funchal. He had a married son, but did not like to impose on the couple. Brian Farrelson and his wife, who had no children, were spending the holiday with Mrs Farrelson's parents. George Bushmell, who enjoyed riding in his spare time, had been invited to a large country house to lend a hand in the stables, according to a long-standing annual arrangement. Only Helena herself seemed to be staying at home. This was accepted as natural, and no further questions were asked.

One afternoon, when Josie brought the tea in, Helena asked her about her plans for Christmas.

"Oh, we'll all be at home, having a nice rest. We don't often get the chance of a long break together, you see, 'cause we all work. Except my little boy, he's at school of course. He's all excited, you know how they get just before Christmas. I've promised to take him to see Santa Claus in the town one afternoon, when school's broken up."

Further conversation revealed that Josie lived with her son and her parents in a council house just the other side of the ring road. Helena suddenly noticed that Josie wore no ring, and wondered whether it would be better to move off the subject of her family; but the tea girl was not in the slightest embarrassed.

"No, I'm not married, never have been. I was very, very silly a few years ago. I met an American airman, from one of the bases. He said he'd marry me, and I believed him. Instead of that, it turned out he had a wife on the base and another in Philadelphia. I never did find out which of them was the real one, if either was. Anyway, he flew back to the States and I was left with Wesley." She smiled, but her eyes remained serious, in a way Helena had not seen them before. "But my parents were marvellous. Dad said to me, "Now, Josie, you've done wrong, but that's between you and the Lord, and we won't let it come between us. And it's surely no fault of that baby that's coming. So you just pray for forgiveness, and we'll say no more. We'll do everything we can to help you bring him up, and nobody is going to say he hasn't got a proper family." The smile was broadening again. "You know, it was my parents that chose his name. Mum loves singing hymns, and Dad used to be mad on cricket, so it was really the only choice." Now she was laughing. "It's a bit of a squash at home, but we don't mind."

There was no more time to talk that day, but Helena was interested, and over the next few days, took whatever opportunities came her way to learn more. Josie had been born in Danesburgh and lived there all her life. Her father, who had studied mechanical engineering in his native Barbados, had come to Britain with the intention of improving his skills and making a better career for himself than he could at home. He had been accepted for the Air Force, as a member of the ground staff, and had rapidly learned to service aircraft. During one period of leave he had returned home and married, bringing his wife back with him. They had originally intended to move back to Barbados after a few years, but finding themselves accepted as part of the local community, they had stayed on. Josie's father had retired from the Air Force and now specialised in agricultural machinery, although he also occasionally worked on a crop-spraying plane. Her mother was a school meals supervisor at a primary school near their home; just now she was threatened with redundancy. Josie herself had been serving tea and coffee at Danesburgh Cartons for a little over a year, since Wesley had started school.

They were evidently a contented, close-knit family, which no doubt accounted for Josie's unfailing good humour, but Helena could guess the pain Josie's affair with the American airman must have caused her parents, and found herself feeling angry at the way it had ended. She wondered whether she herself could have come through such an experience without bitterness, as Josie seemed to have done, and concluded that, equable though her own temperament was, she would have raged inwardly for a long time afterwards.

At home, Helena's time was entirely taken up with preparations for Christmas. Each evening she lifted carrier bags full of food or gifts from the car; some for posting, others for delivery by hand. One large bag was marked for Karen to collect a week in advance and take to Claire, whom Helena would not be seeing before the holiday. There were cards to be written, and Helena missed Karen's assistance with addressing the envelopes. But when she picked up the first envelope that came in the post addressed to David and herself her heart almost stopped, as the whole wretchedness of grief swept over her again. She knew, of course, that such moments were to be expected, but this one took her by surprise, and she was unable to carry on writing cards for a while, as tears blurred her vision. *Maybe I've been too busy with my new job*, she thought, and felt guilty that David's memory, his absence, had been thus pushed to the back of her mind, when it was not yet three months since his death; and she went and fetched the photograph album, and spent half an hour turning the pages, without tears this time, but quietly mourning. *I sometimes used to wonder what I'd ever do without you*, she thought. *Now I'm finding out, and yes, I'm coping, but my God, I wish you were still here.*

But the moment passed, and she felt better in the morning, with the prospect of the office routine ahead of her. It was good to have grieved for a while before the children arrived, for no one wanted to be miserable at Christmas. The cards that made her uncomfortable were put away in a drawer. There would be plenty more to display without them.

***

At the flat, Karen and Gill were making their own preparations. Karen had promised to fashion some decorations, and was busy with various kinds of coloured paper, foil, cardboard and paste. Gill was in the kitchen, melting down a few old candle-ends in the hope that they could be moulded together and tinted. Eventually she gave up.

"Oh, damn, this isn't going to work. I'm going to make some coffee instead... Karen?"

"Just a minute." Karen was concentrating on cutting out an awkward shape. "Sorry, I'm listening."

"Is your mother religious, at all?"

The question took Karen by surprise. "Well, I don't really know. I think she believes in God. Probably. I don't think Dad did, though. We never went to church..."

"Do you? Believe in God, I mean."

"I don't really know, either. I've never thought about it much... What about you?"

"I suppose it might make some sort of sense out of life. But when you see the kind of things that happen, how can you? No, I don't know. But I sometimes think I'd like to believe."

***

The factory was working on Christmas Eve, but it was to close soon after two, with the dispatch of the last consignment of boxes. Everywhere in the building, the workers coordinated their efforts with the machinery in a way they only achieved when an early end to the day depended on it. Vans arrived, and were unloaded and reloaded as though the men themselves were driven by the same energy as their equipment. Wage packets were handed out, complete with bonuses, and even Marlene Smetters seemed satisfied. No one stopped for lunch. At a quarter to two the doors clanged shut on the final lorry load, and a cheer echoed from the steel girders of the hangar. The shutter came down on the loading bay, and the workers streamed out of the factory.

The office staff gathered for drinks before leaving. Helena would rather have got away quietly, for she still had things to do at home, and Karen and Gill would be arriving in time for tea; but she felt obliged to stay for half an hour, long enough to shown that she felt herself to be a member of the team. Brian and George were in an exuberant mood, and even Jim Sergent seemed pleased with the pre-Christmas figures.

"Although," he pointed out, striking a slightly jarring note, "there's no guarantee that it'll continue into the New Year."

At that point Helena insisted that she really must get away, and assuring everyone of her very best wishes for Christmas, she descended to the car park with the sound of the men's voices still ringing in her ears, and turned her mind to the tasks that remained to be done at home.

***

Chris was already there, of course, his college term having finished several days earlier. He had divided his time between the inevitable books, with which he had seemed to be more burdened every weekend, and wandering about the town, browsing in shops and stores, inspecting their supplies of electronic equipment, and weighing up the possibility of buying a personal computer, still a rare and expensive instrument, to assist him in his studies. Today, however, he had professed his intention of helping his mother as much as possible, and sure enough, when Helena arrived home, she found pans full of peeled vegetables in the kitchen, and the gigantic turkey they had bought together the previous weekend was thawing out on top of the domestic boiler. He had also made up a snack of sorts, consisting of various tinned and packeted foods, accompanied by fruit, toast and coffee; the sort of thing Mrs Byles occasionally permitted him to prepare for himself on the odd occasions when she was out for the evening.

The lounge was hung about with streamers, crêpe paper bells and balloons, and in one corner a five-foot Christmas tree stood in a patch of prematurely shed needles. Karen and Chris had insisted on this when they had come across a small plantation about five miles out of town, where the trees were being sold at prices significantly lower than they would have had to pay in Colmleigh. Cards were strung from one corner of the chimney breast to the other, and stood on every available surface from waist to eye level. Whether consciously or not, they had all tried to re-create the kind of Christmas setting they had been accustomed to in Colmleigh; but of course it lacked the extravagant touches that David had loved to add, especially when the children had been small. One year there had been a full-size Santa Claus figure, which a Colmleigh store had ordered and then for some reason rejected, and which David had bought from the display-material suppliers at a huge discount, hidden in the loft and placed just inside the front door, last thing on Christmas Eve, to be discovered by the children in the morning. On another occasion he had found a musical box with the figures of four carol singers outside a cottage, one of them holding a lantern; when you wound it up, it played *Good King Wenceslas*, the lantern moved up and down, and at the same time the door of the cottage opened and an old man appeared and stretched a hand out towards the collecting jar.

That musical box, Helena supposed, must still be packed away in some case or box, although she was unable to remember whether it still worked. It would have pleased her to see it again, even though it had nearly driven her mad when they first had it, because the children wouldn't leave it alone. Carol-singing, the real thing, seemed to have died out; she recalled the groups that used to stroll from one lamp post to the next, singing traditional carols and collecting for some charity or other; now, those you did hear were relayed over the loudspeaker of a van, which sped through the residential quarters and was gone before you could identify what it was playing. A few small boys did still wander around in twos and threes, but all they seemed to know was *We wish you a merry Christmas*, or at best the first verse of *Away in a manger*, and you felt they would just as soon have been in front of the television at home. So Helena rather missed her *Good King Wenceslas* musical box, and would have liked to unearth it for the festival, but it would have taken far too long to root through all the boxes and cases that still remained unopened since they had been packed in Colmleigh.

There was just time to clear up Chris's improvised meal and check the guest room one last time before Helena heard Karen's Volkswagen pull up outside. She opened the front door a little early in order to welcome Karen and Gill as they climbed out.

"Here we are, Mum. You remember Gill, don't you? God, the traffic today. I feel worn out."

Helena surveyed her daughter and the friend she had brought with her. The contrast between them was striking — Karen, tall and elegant in a smart suede jacket and dark green dress, might have stepped from the pages of one of the glossy magazines she studied so intently, whereas most of Gill was concealed within the wrinkles of what appeared to be an enormous fisherman's jersey, extending both above and below her outer cover of a labourer's donkey jacket, and left little visible of her black cord jeans. Her pale face, grey eyes and untidy shoulder length hair heightened the healthiness of Karen's complexion, the lustre of her copper-coloured hair and the light in her brown eyes. David had once claimed that she derived her looks from an ancestor of his, the famous Red Rose of Stow, who was reputed to have been a beautiful witch with the power to turn men into trees and bushes, and who, on seeing the Witchfinder General's agents approaching her cottage, was said to have walked calmly out into the back garden and transformed herself into a standard rose to escape the flames. Unfortunately, the spell had proved irreversible.

Karen gave her mother a hug and Gill shook her hand.

"It's awfully good of you to invite me, Mrs Halstow." She glanced through the door to the lounge. "What absolutely super decorations. We were trying to make some at the flat, but I'm afraid they didn't come to much in the end."

Chris appeared behind Helena. Karen called to him.

"Come on, Chris. Come and be introduced. Gill, this is my brilliant brother, Chris. He's into electronics and all that sort of thing. Chris, this is Gill Aubray — spelt with an 'a'. She reckons it's French originally. Gill's doing a correspondence course with the Cosmopolitan College."

Both Chris and Gill went a little pink. "Not very successfully," Gill mumbled. Chris, predictably, was unable to find anything to say and simply grinned in what he hoped was a friendly way. Helena broke in.

"Well, come on in and sort yourselves out. I'll have a cup of tea ready for you when you come down."

"I'll just get the bags first," said Karen. She opened the boot lid and extracted two cases, one of medium size and another smaller case which Helena recognised as one of her own, lent to Karen when she had first moved in to the flat, and finally a battered-looking hold-all, presumably belonging to Gill.

"Chris, you might give the girls a hand."

"What? Oh, yes, of course." Chris took all the luggage at one go and struggled up the stairs.

Ten minutes later they were sitting round the fire in the lounge, drinking tea, Karen had renewed her make-up and perfume, a superfluous gesture, Helena thought, but typical. Gill had evidently combed her hair, but despite having shed the donkey jacket, she looked as lost as ever in the depths of the fisherman's jersey. The conversation was a little laboured to begin with, notwithstanding Karen's bright chatter. Helena's eyebrows rose at her daughter's account of the office party and the quantities of Bacardi and Coke that could be consumed in an afternoon.

"...and it was really funny, Mum, there were Mick and Terry looking at each other and saying 'Can you remember where we left the car? No, nor can I!'"

"I hope," Helena said severely, "that you were not in a similar state."

"Oh, no, Mum, of course not. You know what I do, I take one drink and pretend to sip it now and then, and like that I can make it last for hours. I don't even like it much, anyway. It's just that some of the people make a thing of seeing how much they can take. It's silly, isn't it? But you do get to see what some of them are really like at these parties. It's quite a revelation."

Chris grinned again. "I bet it is."

"I got drunk at a party once," Gill said suddenly and earnestly. "Really drunk, I mean. I got so dizzy I couldn't stay standing up, and in the end I just curled up and went to sleep. When I woke up everyone else had gone and I felt really awful. I had to phone home and my father came and fetch me, it must have been thirty miles. He was furious with me; it was two o'clock in the morning. That was when my parents were still together. It didn't help them in their relationship, either. They started on at each other as soon as I was in bed. I could hear them. I felt really guilty."

Helena was startled at this disclosure. Is there something about me, she wondered, that makes these youngsters so ready to tell me their secrets? First Josie's confessions, and now this. Certainly they seemed far more open than her own generation, let alone that of her parents. Of Gill's family background she knew only the outline that Karen had provided for her, by way of introduction, apart from one or two comments from Susan Cumber, of doubtful reliability. From the way Gill had spoken, Helena had no difficulty in deducing that the break-up of her parents' marriage weighed heavily on her mind. *Well, if she wants to talk about it... but not while Karen and Chris are here.* In any event, intoxication was hardly a suitable topic for a family gathering on Christmas Eve. Helena deftly changed the subject.

***

After supper they all piled into the Volkswagen and drove into town. Danesburgh could hardly compete with the lights of the West End and Trafalgar Square, which they had been in the habit of visiting from Colmleigh on Christmas Eve, but it had its own charm, with the floodlit Norman tower of the church standing out against the dark sky, the lights strung between the lamp standards in the town square and a solitary hot-chestnut seller trying to catch the attention of the late-evening shoppers, for one or two stores were open until the very last minute. Helena strained to catch a glimmer of the magic she had known; then, with a sudden pang, she missed David's arm round her shoulder, and blinked back the tears for an instant. Karen and Chris laughed and talked as they walked across the square; Gill was silent, as though in a dream. It was in varied moods that they returned home for hot chocolate and bed.

Much later, with Karen and Chris already asleep, Helena, as she in turn got ready for bed, detected a strange aroma and the landing. *Oh no, please, God, not marijuana*, was her first thought; but then she was suddenly transported in her mind to Naples, with a vision of one of the churches she had visited there, on her honeymoon, all those long years ago. The source seemed to be in the spare bedroom. She tapped quietly on the door, and peering in, discovered Gill, still fully dressed, intently studying what appeared to be a wooden crib scene. From a brass ash tray, which Helena had placed on top of the chest of drawers on Karen's recommendation, and which now lay directly in front of the tableau, there rose a thin plume of smoke, while in the tray itself there lay a tiny incandescent fragment of some sweet-smelling substance.

Gill became aware of Helena's presence.

"Oh, God, I hope you didn't think there was a fire. I'm so sorry," she said.

"It's quite all right," Helena replied. "This is rather lovely. Did you bring it with you specially?"

"The crib, yes. It was a present from a favourite aunt and uncle of mine when I was small. They died years ago. My uncle made all the figures, he was very good at making things like that. I always take it if I go away at Christmas. And then the incense, well, a friend of mine brought some round to the flat a few weeks ago, and left a little bit. I thought it was a nice idea. After all, the Wise Men brought incense, didn't they? Or at least one of them did. It can't do any harm, can it?"

"I'm sure it can't." Helena smiled again. "Good night, my dear. I hope you sleep well." And she quietly withdrew, pulling the door to behind her. *Poor child*, she thought. *She is all mixed up. But rather sweet, in a way. I must try to make her feel at home. It doesn't seem as if she does anywhere else at the moment.*

She just made out the sound of the church clock striking midnight as she pulled the quilt around her shoulders.

***

The echoes of a full peal of bells from the church were hovering on the air as Helena drew her curtains back in the morning. She had been awake for a while already, but hearing no sound from the other bedrooms, she had preferred to delay going downstairs for as long as possible, to avoid disturbing the children. Now, however, the cooking had to be tackled. She heaved the turkey from its roost atop the boiler and set about garnishing it.

Once the fowl had been slid into a hot oven, which it only just fitted, Helena set about rousing the family with the incentive of cups of tea. Christmas morning, once a time of high excitement, was now a sedate affair, a chance to make up for the late nights of the previous week, by lying in until what at one time would have seemed a disgraceful hour. Helena was inclined to be indulgent; *of, all age groups,* she thought, *adolescents find the least pleasure in Christmas Day — neither engrossed in unwrapping presents, nor yet ready to savour the leisurely gossip of a prolonged family get-together.* There was no reason why they should not relax and enjoy a late morning.

Karen, however, was already seated at her dressing-table and examining her appearance in the mirror when Helena gently tapped at her door. "Happy Christmas, Mum. Oh, tea, super." She dabbed at her face with a cotton wool pad. "I think I've got a spot coming, what a pain."

Chris was still fast asleep, one of his computer books lying on the carpet beside his bed. The small desk by the window was all but invisible beneath an untidy heap composed of more books, charts and diagrams. Helena found herself wishing he had a hobby he could pursue in winter without risking his health; at present, he seemed to be making no real distinction between study and leisure. She admired his application and recognised it as an expression of the quiet determination that characterised the McCallogh side of the family, but at Christmas she would have liked him to be perhaps a little less focussed.

Gill too was still asleep, her face turned to one side and half-hidden by an outflung arm. The fading aroma of the incense still lingered in the room, the exotic images it conjured up contrasting oddly with the grey and cold of an East Anglian December morning. As Helena turned to leave, Gill stirred, opened her eyes and blinked two or three times, as if uncertain of where she was. Helena said "Good morning Gill. A very happy Christmas to you,. my dear," and was rewarded with a truly seraphic smile.

"Oh, Happy Christmas. This is marvellous. I was having a dream... but I think this is miles better than the dream I was having," Gill said a trifle hoarsely. "This is a lovely place. Isn't it peaceful."

Helena was touched, and also struck by the fact that Gill could enthuse over something Karen found difficult to appreciate. Certainly it was quiet. The bells had ceased; by now the faithful would have assembled, to adore Christ the Lord according to their various traditions. It had occurred to Helena that she might offer to take the family to church; once or twice she and the children had gone with Claire and Bernard and the boys, back in Colmleigh, but her strongest memories were of the noise made by the innumerable excited children, almost drowning the voice of the unfortunate Minister. Karen and Chris had been bored and fidgety, and David had politely declined to accompany them at all. *Better leave the question of church*, she reflected, *and just make the day as relaxed and enjoyable as possible.*

Helena's neighbours on both sides having gone away the previous day, there was no movement in the close. There was little incentive for anyone to venture outside into a mist which the sun was unable to pierce. None of the family hurried downstairs. At last the buzz of Chris's electric shaver became audible in his room, and a few minutes later, dutifully carrying his cup and saucer, he emerged into the kitchen, where Helena was engaged in peeling brussels sprouts.

"Happy Christmas, Mum. Good grief, are the girls not up yet?"

"I dare say they'll be down before long. Could you make some toast for me, do you think? I've just got to finish these."

Chris complied. It was Gill who appeared next; although Helena had offered her the option of a leisurely bath, it seemed that her toilet had been as perfunctory as Chris's. Barefoot, she wore the cords and jersey in which she had arrived the previous day. In her arms she carried a cardboard carton, which Helena found rather too reminiscent of the factory.

"Mrs Halstow, I hope you don't mind," Gill began. "You see, I didn't really know you or Chris, so I didn't think I could very well bring you anything personal, you know, as a present. So I wondered what to do, and in the end I thought maybe the best thing would be to help towards the food, so I brought these bits. For all of you. I hope you'll like them."

She put the box on the kitchen table, and Helena opened it. It contained an assortment of delicacies in tins, jars and packets, the names on most of which were foreign and totally unfamiliar. Gill had clearly exercised a great deal of ingenuity in her search for a suitable gift, and great care in her choice. At the very bottom, carefully wedged into a foil tray, there was a chocolate Yule log surmounted by a tiny gold coronet.

Chris inspected the array with an expression that said much more than his verbal response of "Hey! Terrific! Thanks, Gill." Helena added; "It's lovely, my dear. I'd never have thought to buy anything like that," but Gill had already disappeared again and returned half-hidden behind an enormous bouquet of white roses.

"Oh, my dear," said Helena again, "where on earth did you find those? They must have cost a fortune, especially at this time of year." She gave Gill an unexpected hug. "Thank you so much. I must put them in water straightaway. Chris, what's happening to that toast?"

Karen, as usual, took longest to wash and dress. Finally she made her entrance in a carefully selected combination of beige jumper and slacks, her hair shining.

"Happy Christmas, everybody. Happy Christmas again, Mum. Is it really as late as that? Sorry, I didn't realise I'd been so long."

"Look here," said Helena, "we'd better have breakfast. The turkey won't be ready until about four o'clock."

She was trying to make it the kind of Christmas Day to which Karen and Chris were accustomed, and they instinctively fell into step. Over breakfast they exchanged small gifts; the larger presents, and those received from friends and relatives, were stacked round the tree, to be opened after dinner. Breakfast would start late and end where lunch normally began, and in the usual way a stroll would follow; but the mist and damp rendered that idea unattractive. Once breakfast was over, therefore, they all sat in the lounge and sought ways of entertaining themselves for a while.

Although the custom had declined somewhat since the children had grown up, they had always played games at Christmas. David, an inveterate competitor, had been fond of the kind of board game where you make enormous quantities of money as quickly as possible, preferably bankrupting your opponents in the process, and had encouraged a willing Karen, and a rather less enthusiastic Chris, to play as though their lives depended on winning, with Helena keeping the bank and everyone's tempers in check. They had also invented some silly games of their own (*Useless Inventions, What They Found Out After the Calamity, Unseasonal Greetings*), which had heavily depended on David's imagination and energy and were limp without him there to give them life. Nothing was said, but all three of them found it impossible to contemplate anything competitive, and Gill, away from the chaos of the flat, could discern the effect of the absence of a leading spirit at a festival. In the end they settled for Scrabble, at which Karen excelled. Gill was seeing her flatmate in a different light here; Karen, self-effacing and almost wordless when the great student debates raged, was talkative and positive in her attitudes here, and occasionally impatient with Chris, whose talents were decidedly non-verbal. Having rapidly run up an unapproachable score, she proposed drinks and mince pies and had them ready on the dining-room table by the end of the game.

The Christmas Day rituals succeeded one another. Telephone calls were made to greet distant members of the family. Gill was invited to call her parents, which she did, but very briefly. The family dutifully watched and listened to the Queen's speech, making little comment.

The meal to which they sat down soon after four left them in such a state of torpor that they scarcely had the energy to open their parcels. The gifts were mainly of a practical nature, and Helena had particularly instructed the children to keep within a sensible budget. Karen, not without an element of mischief, had bought Gill a book entitled *The Art of Plain Cooking*, which Gill accepted graciously and made a mental note to return the compliment by giving Karen a Thai cook-book she had noticed when browsing in London. Once again, Helena found herself longing for a touch of David's ingenuity, and although she would not allow herself to grieve in the family's presence on Christmas Day, she could not entirely dispel the sense of desolation that had threatened to engulf her during the days she had spent at home. She looked at her children, who seemed contented enough, and then at Gill. Was the day proving unbearably dull for her? Helena leaned forward.

"This must seem very unexciting for you," she said quietly. "I'm afraid we haven't really got used to my husband not being here any more. He used to organise everything, you see, the parties and games and so on. He was so good at it; we couldn't possibly do anything to compare with it."

Gill looked a little surprised. "No, really, not at all. I'm having a super time, a real change." She could not possibly have conveyed to Helena, who had never experienced anything of the sort, the spiral of tension that had bedevilled every occasion when her parents had been forced to be together, with no means of escape, over the last three or four years; and then the division of her affections and loyalties, the intrusion of strangers into her intimate family circle, and finally the realisation that her presence in either of the newly formed households constituted a threat to the re-creation of a stable relationship, which both her parents were seeking in their new marriages. The spectre at the feast... She shook her head to dismiss a momentary stab of anguish.

Helena divined none of this, but perceived that something had caused Gill's face to cloud, and had the uncomfortable feeling that she had done more to allay her own passing sadness than to put the girl at her ease. She wondered how that could best be achieved. Apart from the brief revelation of the previous evening, Gill had maintained a polite diffidence from which Karen had not sought to draw her out, and Chris did not possess the interpersonal skills to attempt to do so. Helena had hoped that their common student status might provide an opening, but they were worlds apart in their different disciplines, and their conversations had not progressed beyond the initial courtesies,

"What are you studying?"

"Electronics and computer technology. What about you?"

"Well, it's called social science and applied psychology, but everything I've read so far seems to be full of politics. Do you get involved in politics?"

"Not really. One of our lecturers keeps going on demos and that kind of thing, but we get fed up with it. It means he doesn't have time to go through our work properly."

So with Chris shy, and Gill withdrawn, it was left to Helena and Karen to keep the conversation going as best they could. The poor daylight had long since disappeared, and there was no point in going outside; by common consent the television was switched on again, and *The Man with the Golden Gun* became the centre of their attention until tea, which on Christmas Day came at around eight o'clock and even then was scarcely needed. All was calm, time seemed forgotten, everyone seemed contented, but Helena could not convince herself that the day had been a success. She felt a distinct disappointment, a kind of dissatisfaction that refused to leave her. She was not grieving for the past now, but rather for the present. The day had turned out to be neither a religious festival, nor an out-and-out bacchanalian feast, but rather a missed opportunity, although she could not have said for what.

"I don't know," she pondered aloud. "Christmas Day seems to have become a day when you just sit about and eat and drink. I'm sure there ought to be something more to it."

Chris grinned. "Suits me, Mum."

Karen looked curiously at her mother. "I think I know what you mean, Mum. I've been trying to put my finger on it all day. Something's been missing. It's not just Dad. It was there before, but he used to disguise it with lots of fun and games. Christmas never quite seems to measure up to what it's supposed to be, does it? All that preparation and advertising and everything, and then it's over almost before it's started."

"Come on," said Chris, "there's two more days' holiday yet."

"Yes," said Karen, "but they're not really Christmas. I mean, Boxing Day's really just a winter Bank Holiday, and the day after that you go into town to spend your Christmas present money and try to see what's coming up in the January sales. All the best has gone out of it by then. I think it's a bit like Cinderella, the magic wears off at midnight on Christmas Eve. Gill, you're dreaming again. Do you think Christmas Day is an anti-climax?"

Gill reflected. "Not this Christmas. It's been peaceful. I think it's the first peaceful Christmas I've had for years. There was always a lot of squabbling at home, and then they'd make a horrendous effort to be nice on Christmas Day, season of goodwill and all that, but even if they managed that they were back to normal by half-way through Boxing Day. So I used to dread it, but I suppose it was never quite as bad as I expected, either."

Karen smiled. "Well, that's honest. I often wonder whether those stories you tell about your parents are a bit of an exaggeration."

"No more than the ones you tell about your dad," Gill replied, rising a little to Karen's slightly sardonic tone. The she reddened. "Oh, dear, I'm sorry, Mrs Halstow. I didn't mean…"

"That's all right, my dear," Helena said hastily, quelling Karen's angry look. The last thing she wanted was for Gill to retreat into her personal cloud again. "But, personal problems apart, I still think Christmas is losing its character, and I'd like to know why."

"We all grow up," Karen said huffily.

"I don't know what you're on about," Chris declared.

"Well," said Gill, "I think Christmas is such a peculiar mixture of myths and legends that it sort of evaporates unless you can concentrate it into a sort of atmosphere that keeps everything else out. It's best when it's dark. Last night, in town, there was still something of the atmosphere about, and even first thing this morning, with the bells…"

"First thing?"

"Well, when I woke up. I know it was late. But as soon as I pulled the curtains and saw the fog, that altered everything. Fog has nothing to do with Christmas. It belongs in November, or January maybe. And then you always know what's going on in the world these days. War, plane crashes, mountain rescues, strikes, all that sort of thing. They interfere with Christmas. Before we all knew so much, people felt that once they'd done something good, like, say, handed out some food to the poor or something, then they thought they could shut themselves in and celebrate with a clear conscience. Have you ever read *The Great Adventure*?"

Blank looks.

"You know, *Le grand Meaulnes*.[1] I had to read it at school, in French. We had a teacher who thought it was wonderful. It's not bad, actually... a bit slow... Anyway, there's a part of it that's about Christmas, and one phrase stuck in my mind. The grandparents used to arrive, and then it says 'they used to shut themselves in for a long week of pleasure'... something like that. They were insulated. Whatever went on outside didn't touch them."

"It sounds a bit selfish to me," Helena commented doubtfully.

"Yes, don't you see? It had to be. All the other days, you could be as charitable as you liked. Afterwards, the tradesmen came round for their Christmas boxes. And the servants could have a party. But it was still restricted to the people you knew. Everyone looked after the people around them, no further. Otherwise you couldn't enjoy it properly."

"So do you think," Helena asked, "that we're all nostalgic for the days when no one knew anything that happened outside their own village? If that's the case, we might as well get used to the fact that Christmas will never be like that again."

"Nothing," said Gill portentously, "is ever the same again. You sift out your best memories, and mix them together into one lovely dream, and of course it never comes true. The best you can hope for is to be able to add an extra memory now and again."

"My God, Gill," Karen interjected, "when are you going to start writing for *Woman's Own*? I could do with a drink. What about you, Mum?"

---

[1] Novel by Alain-Fournier, published 1913.

"We'll all have one," Helena replied, "and then it's bedtime, I think. Let's see whether we can find a reason to go out tomorrow. I think we need it."

She caught up with Karen in the kitchen.

"Karen, you were rather rude to Gill just now. I dare say you spar with her a bit in the flat, but you ought to remember she's our guest here."

Karen was already repentant. *As David would have been*, Helena thought.

"I know, Mum. I'll apologise to her in a minute. Actually, she's used to me, says it does her good sometimes to be brought down to earth when she gets into one of her dreamy moods. Still, you're right, I shouldn't have talked to her like that."

She put her head round the door. "Sorry, Gill. Don't take any notice of me, will you?"

"My fault," said Gill. "I was rambling on a bit, wasn't I? Now, if that had been my dear parents, they'd still be cross with each other at midnight."

"It is midnight," said Chris with another of his grins.

"Good heavens," exclaimed Helena, appearing with a tray. "So it is. We'll call it a day when we've had these, shall we?"

***

Boxing Day dawned as misty as the previous evening, but by half past eight the mist began to clear, and by ten a pale sun was beginning to glimmer over the opposite row of houses in the close. Helena suggested a walk out as far as the Feathers, and around mid-morning they set out, suitably coated, scarved and booted, although Gill's donkey jacket, jersey and trainers were beginning to give the impression of growing on her like some additional skin. The old main road out of Danesburgh had become a great deal quieter since the construction of the ring road, which it joined further out. The sparse traffic moved briskly, as though anxious to shake off the sluggishness of the previous day. In the open country, the brown fields were speckled with grey and white gulls, a few of which circled overhead with plaintive shrieks, and from somewhere further over came the deep bark of a large dog, evidently intent on chasing them. The sun became stronger. It was a morning to lift the spirits, to create the illusion that the winter might be on the turn already, whatever foul weather might await them in the next few weeks. The flat landscape had a kind of bare, thin-stretched splendour, which nevertheless gave a hint of the richness that would come with the spring. As they rounded the curve from which the Feathers could first be glimpsed, they all stopped together, without a word to one another.

The Feathers was an inn of genuine antiquity, at least in part, as the roughness of some of the oak beams attested, but was more generally a tribute to architectural mimicry; set well back from the road, it presented a conventional visual combination of timber, rendering and red brick, but with a greater degree of harmony than is usual in such buildings. The bay windows and heavy oak doors were visible from outside, the original chimneypiece had been carefully restored, and it was even possible to sit in the ingle nook if you arrived right on opening time. At the side and back there was an L-shaped garden area with rustic tables and chairs, looking damp and forlorn. All this was, of course, familiar to all of them except Gill; but what halted them was the courtyard which, although normally crowded with parked cars, was now alive with riders on horseback, in a scene splashed with red coats and resounding with cheerful talk. It was the Boxing Day Meet. In one corner perhaps twenty or thirty hounds were being kept in order by the Master; from a closer distance the riders could be observed lifting stirrup cups, and the clatter of hoofs could be heard as the horses shifted impatiently.

"Well," said Helena. "There's a bit of Old England for you."

Karen groaned. "We'll never get near the place while that lot are there."

But as they approached, the hunt moved off, the leading riders taking a small private road that flanked the inn, with the hounds quietly following. One straggler was being petted by a small child, which it evidently enjoyed, for it had to be called sharply to join the rest of the pack. By the time Karen, first as usual, led the others into the courtyard the crowd had mostly dispersed, and only one or two patches of horse dung remained as evidence of the meet.

Inside, the inn was crowded with townspeople out to take the air, local farmers with their families and one or two regulars who complained, not too seriously, about being turned out of their usual corners. Karen had nevertheless managed to secure a table, and beckoned to the others urgently to join her before the chairs were taken. Chris went to the bar to order, and it was some time before he returned, threading his way between tweed jackets and camel-hair coats.

"There you are," he said. "What a crush. I don't think I'd have come if I'd known it was going to be like this, though. Too much of a fight to get served."

"Oh, but I wouldn't have wanted to miss the hunt, would you?" Helena protested. "It's years since I saw a meet like that."

"I'm surprised you agree with hunting, Mum." Karen, as usual, was ready to take an opposing view. "It's all very pretty when they get together in the morning, but they'll probably end up covered in mud. And what about the poor old fox, if they find one? All those hounds, it wouldn't stand a chance if they caught it."

"Maybe they won't find one, " said Helena, ever anxious to prevent discord. "And I suppose if they do it's always got a chance of getting away."

"Well, I hope it doesn't." Chris was unusually forthright on the issue. "Foxes are just a pest. I remember one year when we went out to the reservoir from Colmleigh. Springtime, it was, and there were twenty or thirty ducklings at one end, just hatched. The warden tried to protect them, but by the next week they were down to about fifteen, and in the end less then ten of them survived. It was foxes, weasels, stoats — not to mention local cats. Every time they came out of the water, there were less ducklings on the reservoir afterwards. The warden said it was mostly foxes. They couldn't keep them away."

"It's just the balance of nature," Gill suggested. "Everything preys on everything else."

"Except foxes," said Chris. "That's why they ought to be kept down. I don't mind how it's done."

"But why do all these people want to *hunt* a fox?" Karen complained. "It's not as if you could eat foxes. There must be better ways of controlling them. And those hounds, they look so harmless. Why do they suddenly go wild when they catch a fox?"

"People often look harmless too, when they're not," said Gill. "Or, rather, they're harmless until they're confronted with a certain situation, and then their animal instincts take over. It's the hunters who want a kill, as much as the hounds."

"I don't see what for," Karen objected.

"Well, primitive men didn't only hunt for food." Gill was warming to her subject. "They hunted their enemies, as well, or anything they thought was a threat to the security of the tribe. That's why they started hunting tigers in India, or wolves in Europe. Foxes aren't much of a personal threat, but they do cause a lot of harm to domestic fowls. And then, I suppose, the fox represents everybody's idea of a criminal — cunning, ruthless, no moral sense, coming at night to kill and steal, and then escaping quickly. In people's minds, out here in the country at any rate, foxes are evil. They shouldn't just be destroyed, they need to be taught a lesson first. The hunt is about vengeance, really. You can see how angry they get when the hunt saboteurs spoil it for them. It seems out of all proportion until you realise that hunting is a moral issue for them."

"Good God," said Karen. "And I thought this was a civilised country. You make us all sound like savages."

"We are civilised," said Gill, and her voice was tinged with bitterness. "If we weren't, we'd leave the foxes alone and kill one another instead. We'd have tribal feuds, like the Campbells and the MacDonalds, all over the place, any time there wasn't a war on with some other country."

"Get on," said Chris. "Who's talking about wars and tribal feuds? We're just sitting in a country pub having a drink before lunch on Boxing Day. I mean, what could be more civilised than that?"

Karen agreed. "I don't think all this psychology is doing you any good, Gill," she pronounced. "It's making you go sour on life. You're better off not trying to fathom out people's deepest motives, if it makes you feel miserable."

Gill produced her best smile. "Sorry, everyone. I promise not to cast a blight on Boxing Day. What about another drink?" and she insisted on buying a second round, in spite of their protests.

They strolled back chatting easily, with none of the tension that had emerged the day before. Helena found herself musing about the disparity between Karen and her flatmate. Altogether her father's daughter, Karen possessed a temperament that demanded constant activity, and made her impatient with what she perceived as vagueness or a lack of purpose or common sense. Helena found this, which she had readily accepted in David, a little difficult to reconcile with her own idea of the feminine graces; she would have rather it had been Chris who had inherited it. Although not exactly a dreamer, he had so far showed little evidence of his father's drive. Gill, on the other hand, reminded Helena quite strongly of one or two of her university acquaintances; a gentle, urban romantic, who would probably have been a contented humanist if it had not been for her disturbed family background. *What an assortment we are*, Helena thought, *no wonder it's taken a couple of days to settle down with one another*; but she was pleased with the morning, and felt that it had made up a good deal for the shortcomings of Christmas Day.

The afternoon passed comfortably. They watched more television, played more records and talked a lot. At one point the ancient battle lines between science and art were drawn up. Chris maintained that the time would come when all music would be programmed by computer, entirely by reference to frequency, tonality, metre and volume; it would then be possible, by drawing up corresponding scales for light and sound, to create a synthesis of visual art and music, to be experienced by eye and ear simultaneously, and while he thought of it, why not include aroma as well? This, in condensed form, was the burden of his argument. To which Gill replied that, however sophisticated the technology might become, it was still no more than a tool whereby the artist's imagination and skill were expressed, and in any event, the whole idea had been foreseen and suggested in principle, if not in technical details, by the likes of Baudelaire and Rimbaud. She then had to explain who these latter persons were, and elaborated a little on what she knew of them. Upon which Karen commented that they sounded like a typical couple of French eccentrics (to refine her actual words a little), moving Gill to spring to the defence of her supposedly Gallic forebears. Helena realised with some relief that both girls were now following a well-trodden path, free from malice or animosity. Chris retired from the fray, feeling himself outpointed by Gill's wider general knowledge and debating ability; but he made up his mind to prove his point, one day when he had sufficient time and a computer of his own.

For the rest of the holiday they were all at ease. Gill demonstrated her culinary skills, conjuring some quite extraordinary dishes from the remains of the turkey and ham. Helena got out her sewing machine and completed a dress she had started to make with Karen months earlier, before the move. Chris immersed himself in various technical magazines. Then it was nearly the weekend, and Claire rang to invite them all over to her on the Saturday.

Helena summoned up her courage and drove them to Croydon, where they submitted to the more energetic entertainment devised by Bernard and the boys. Here Chris was in his element, coaching his cousins to peerless levels of expertise in the "Space Invaders" game that had been the most eagerly awaited of their Christmas presents, while Helena and Claire exchanged quantities of news, confining themselves almost entirely to the kitchen and dining room. Gill and Karen chatted with Bernard's mother, who had a happy knack of putting her grandchildren's generation at their ease. The day sped past, and they were back in Danesburgh just before midnight, feeling as if they had only just set out in the morning.

Karen and Gill were due to return to Colmleigh the following day. They had been invited to a New Year's Eve party, and expected that they would need most of New Year's Day to recuperate. Sunday, therefore, was a day for tidying up, packing gifts, loading Karen's car and checking petrol; even though Chris had a further week before he would have to go back to the Byles household in Leytonstone, the day bore all the marks of the end of a holiday. No one was in a hurry to get up in the morning, and they went out for lunch by way of a final celebration, toasting the New Year a little prematurely, after which they returned home to complete the dismantling of Christmas. The tree and the decorations might remain for a few more days, but Helena felt that they represented nothing more than an empty shell now, and rather wished that they might be removed there and then.

"Not until Twelfth Night, Mum," Karen insisted. "You might want to have some friends in or something. And Chris will still be here, of course."

Chris, in truth, was not particularly concerned about the decorations, but Helena gave in and agreed to maintain the appearance of the festival until the proper day.

The time of Karen and Gill's departure arrived. Karen gave her mother a perfunctory hug.

"Bye, Mum. Thanks for a lovely Christmas. See you again soon."

She was evidently ready to plunge into the Colmleigh whirlpool again. Gill, on the other hand, was rather more wistful, less sure about the advantages of the flat.

"Goodbye, Mrs Halstow. It's been really super, it was so good of you to have me. You'll come and see us before long, won't you? Goodbye, Chris, I hope your studies go well this term."

"And yours too," Chris returned. "Safe journey, both of you."

And a couple of minutes later the car had turned the corner and was gone.

"Tea," said Chris. "I'll make it, Mum, if you like."

Left to herself, Helena suffered a moment of sadness. She told herself sternly that it was nothing more than any mother would feel when one of her grown-up children left again after a spell at home; but the slight melancholy was combined with a certain uneasiness, which she thought was probably associated with Gill. It seemed strange and wrong that she had somehow been able to relate more easily to Gill than she had to her own daughter. Not that she and Karen had at any moment been at odds with each other; perhaps it was simply that Gill's temperament was closer to her own. In addition, there had been an undercurrent of profound distress in the way Gill had talked, and she felt a longing to be able to do something to help, without knowing either what or how; and then, was Karen not equally in need of comfort and support? She seemed to have come through the loss of her father without an emotional crisis; but such a crisis might simply have been delayed. If so, she would need help. Perhaps so would Helena herself. It had been a peaceful Christmas, but not exactly a merry one.

"Here you are, Mum," Chris was saying, handing her a steaming cup of tea. "You were miles away, weren't you?"

"I was," Helena admitted. "Do you think those girls are all right, Chris?"

"They should be. There won't be a lot of traffic on the roads tonight."

"No, I didn't mean on the journey, I meant generally. They seem an odd pair to be sharing a flat. So unalike."

"Oh, I wouldn't worry, Mum. I reckon they can manage all right. They're not exactly stupid, either of them."

Helena gave up. Chris possessed little sensitivity where personal relations were concerned. Or maybe it was just lack of experience. He could do with a sensible girl friend of his own… She looked at him affectionately, trying to imagine him married, with a wife and family demanding his time and distracting him from his computers and his ornithology. *No. Not just yet.*

"What's the matter, Mum? Have I got a mark on my shirt or something?"

"No, dear. Thank you for the tea. You're right, I was lost in thought. Crystal-gazing, I suppose, in a way."

"Crystal-gazing?"

"Trying to see into the future. It all seems so dim and cloudy at the moment."

Chris was surprised. "Does it? I thought you were getting yourself nicely settled now, what with the job and everything."

"Oh, yes. It's not that side of things so much. It's about us — all of us. I feel as if we were caught in a kind of no-man's-land at present. As if one kind of life ended when your father died, and we're all waiting for another one to start, but without any idea of what it might be like. Never mind. I expect I'm just indulging in a little day-dreaming; you'll do the same one day when you have a family, and after all, it's the time of year for that sort of thing."

Chris laughed. "Dream on, Mum," he said. "Only don't map out the future for me, will you? I want to keep my options open."

2

SPRING, 1981

The New Year brought a change in the weather. The wind swung to the north, and by mid-afternoon flurries of light snowflakes were beating against the windows. Chris looked uneasily at the heavy clouds and the garden, which was already disappearing under a layer of white.

"It looks as if we're in for a lot of this," he said.

"Never mind," Helena replied. "At least we don't need to go out today."

The snow continued into the evening and for much of the night. In the morning, even before the curtains were drawn back, it was discernible by the white light filtering through and the silence outside. After a while, however, a few scraping and sweeping noises began to be heard, together with attempts to start unwilling engines. Chris donned a pair of wellington boots that had belonged to David and cleared the drive, and Helena drove out very gingerly, allowing herself a few extra minutes to reach the factory. Fortunately the ring road had already been gritted, and heavy vehicles had reduced the snow to a low bank of brownish slush on each side and in the centre of the carriageway.

At the factory, a mood of resignation prevailed. The loaders wore woollen hats and scarves and thick gloves. Inside the building the heating was already operating at full volume, and the tube lighting stood out brightly against the dim portion of sky that was visible through the high windows. No one wanted to work near the outside doors. Upstairs in the office, there was little time for the usual polite enquiries about Christmas before urgent work took over. Helena quickly slipped back into her routine, thinking now and again of Karen and Gill and wondering whether the snow had been as heavy in Colmleigh.

Chris stayed at the house for the rest of the week and packed his bags on Sunday, ready to leave for college again. Karen had elected to stay at the flat that weekend, and so, rather than undertake the drive to London, for the snow had not yet cleared, Helena put her son on an afternoon train with a packed lunch, instructing him not to use the moped until the roads were negotiable.

For the next month or so the job took up Helena's days, leaving the evenings for domestic chores or, when those were negligible, such leisure activities as could be pursued at home. Family contacts were strictly limited to telephone calls while travelling remained difficult, except for Chris, who came home each weekend, invariably with a bag bulging with college work, through which he proceeded to toil for hours at a time, saying little, right up to his departure early on Sunday afternoon. Helena drew on her reserves of patience, finding this a tedious period; she longed for the spring, for the end of Chris's term, for the kind of weather in which driving would not be an ordeal; and she longed for companionship. The pangs of loneliness were less acute now, but they were still persistent.

One Tuesday morning in February, the telephone rang unusually early, just as Helena was about to leave for the factory.

"Mum? It's me, Karen."

"Hello, darling. Is something the matter?"

"I don't really know, but it may be. It's Gill. She's gone."

"Gone?"

"Well, she wasn't here when I got back on Sunday." Karen had been at Claire's that weekend, on a combined shopping and social visit to Croydon. "The place was in a terrible mess. There were bottles everywhere, and someone had been sick in the bathroom, and the whole place smelt of bonfires or something... I thought Gill must be away until late, and I went to bed, but she didn't come back yesterday, and she still isn't here this morning."

"Has she taken her clothes, dear?"

"I don't think so, not all of them. Her books are here... I wouldn't worry if she'd told me, but she said she was going to friends in London, and she'd be back last night."

"Well, I suppose they might have invited her to stay on a bit."

"Maybe." Karen sounded unconvinced. "But it was the state of the place that worried me most. I don't know who was here, or who let them in. But I didn't like the look of it at all. Or the smell. And most of all I didn't like the idea that someone had been in here while we were away."

"Do you really think Gill would have let someone have the key, then?"

"I don't know. Some of the people that have been here recently have been pretty weird, and they could have talked her into anything. She might just have said they could have a party here while we were away."

"Without asking you?"

"Well, she's a bit more easy-going about that kind of thing than I am. I'd have said no. Or I'd have stayed to see what went on. But Gill's so worried about keeping in with her friends, that's why they're always coming here, one or two at a time."

"Have you looked for a note?"

"Yes, Mum, of course I have. I've had to go right through the flat cleaning it up. I didn't have time to do more than the bathroom when I first got back. But I couldn't stand it like that for long. And I thought they must have been smoking pot, so I went round making sure they hadn't left any of the stuff anywhere. I knew one of Gill's friends had been in trouble with the law when they found some in his room. It wasn't really fair, he hadn't even been using it."

"Did you find any?"

"No, thank God. Either they'd smoked all they had or they'd taken it away with them. But I had to leave all the windows open all evening. Can you imagine, at this time of year? It was freezing. I've sprayed all round with air freshener today, and it's a lot better now."

Helena looked at the clock that stood on the chimneypiece in the lounge and which was visible from the hall.

"Karen, dear, I shall have to go or I shall be late for work. Are you really worried about Gill, or has she done this kind of thing before?"

"Yes, but not for this long. I'm a bit worried, but maybe she'll phone today. My guess is she's with someone who's made an impression on her. You know Gill now. She likes these weird intellectual types. Maybe she's in a squat, or a commune, somewhere in London. Anyway, I've got to go, too. I'll phone you again tonight. 'Bye, Mum."

Karen hung up, leaving Helena short of time. *Never mind*, Helena thought, *I've been getting in early every morning. One odd day when I'm a few minutes late won't matter.* She put on her coat and went to back the car out of the garage.

The snow had given way to an intensely cold spell, and a hard frost had turned the ground to rock and the roofs to silver. Even though Chris had recharged the battery, the Ford took several attempts to start. By the time Helena turned off the ring road it was already a quarter to nine. She drove cautiously down the spine road of the industrial estate, between the industrial buildings, and as she approached the forecourt entrance of Danesburgh Cartons she became aware of another vehicle about to overtake her. At the same time a van emerged from a gateway almost opposite, turning left to face her.

What happened next haunted Helena for months afterwards. The overtaking driver, in a five hundredweight van, tried to pull up, but even on a good road surface he would have found it difficult to avoid a collision. The ice concealed between the ridges of the ribbed concrete made it impossible. Instead of meeting the other car head on, the van spun on its own axis, caught the other vehicle a glancing blow, and mounted the pavement. A small boy, who had apparently been reading a comic as he walked past, was sent crashing against the boundary wall and fell in a heap on the footpath, his satchel sliding under the van, which came to rest against one of the pillars of the warehouse gateway. The whole sequence of events took place in a few seconds and almost seemed like part of a cinema film; except that in films no one really got hurt, and the little boy was lying very still indeed.

Suddenly grasping that what she had witnessed was real and serious, Helena drew her car up by the kerb and ran across to him. At the same time the van driver emerged very shakily from the damaged van and the driver of the other car also got out, evidently ready to set about him, verbally if not physically.

As she came close Helena realised with a slight surprise that the child was black. She checked his pulse; he was alive, at least. She was vaguely aware of the car driver starting to reproach the other man, a youngster not much older than Chris, who seemed dazed and incapable of any speech other than a stream of foul language, repeated in a monotone. Helena cut in.

"Look, I need you to phone for an ambulance, this boy's hurt. Go into Danesburgh Cartons, they'll let you use their phone. My name's Helena Halstow, I work there."

She went mechanically through the first aid routine putting her coat over the boy's curled-up body and her scarf gently under his head. Concussion, she guessed, but they would have to check at the hospital for fractures or other injuries. In the meantime she could not risk moving him. She waited impatiently for the man to return from the factory vestibule.

The younger man clearly needed attention as well. Helena beckoned to him.

"Would you go and sit in the reception room at Danesburgh Cartons? They'll look after you for a few minutes. You'll have to stay till the police come, I'm afraid."

"*Police*? Oh..." the youth launched into a further dismal string of obscenities, which exasperated Helena.

"Now, stop that," she said sharply. "Pull yourself together. It's not you that's hurt, you've had a very lucky escape. This poor little chap got the worst of it, through no fault of his own. We'll get him to hospital, and then we'll have to report the accident. Can you get the van off the footpath?"

The young man nodded. "I think so, yer," he said, and made his way back to the van, limping, as if he had twisted an ankle or a knee. The van started, and with a loud rasping sound from one of the front wheels, climbed off the footpath and crawled a few yards along the warehouse drive, where it came to a halt.

By that time the other driver had returned from the office and moved his own car to the side of the road. He came over to Helena, picking up the split and dirty satchel on the way.

"Poor little devil. Fancy him getting hit like that when he wasn't even in the road. I'd like to wring that young lad's neck. Where is he?"

"Not now," said Helena. "He's had a nasty shock too. The little boy's concussed, I think. The sooner he gets to hospital the better."

She looked at the satchel, then opened it with the ideas of identifying the child. There could not be so many black children of primary school age in Danesburgh. Suddenly, without looking any further, she knew who he was. Wesley Barritt — Josie's little boy.

A blaring two-note klaxon sounded; the ambulance was arriving. Helena had a sharp reminder of the night the ambulance had come for David, and flinched involuntarily. The vehicle pulled up, and Wesley was gently moved on to a stretcher and lifted inside. The ambulance was gone again in seconds.

Suddenly aware of the cold, Helena retrieved her coat and put it on. A police car drew up, and a young constable got out. He enquired of Helena and the other driver as to what had happened, and then suggested that he should record their replies in the factory vestibule, where the young van driver was waiting, still shaken and very nervous; formal statements would be needed later.

Helena had started out from home ten minutes late, and those ten minutes had expanded into an hour and a half; yet she could not start work. She felt obliged to catch Josie before she left home to come to the factory, explained her intention to the constable, and looked out the list of staff addresses. Having found the address, she started out towards the car, but as luck would have it, Josie herself was already approaching the building. There was no time for Helena to weigh her words. She would have to trust to instinct.

"Josie."

"Hello, Mrs Halstow. My word, isn't it cold. You'll be glad of your coffee this morning…"

"Don't go in for a minute, Josie, something's happened this morning that you ought to know about."

Helena explained what had happened as briefly and gently as possible, emphasising her hope and belief that Wesley was not seriously injured. Josie's hand went to her mouth, and she took several deep breaths.

"Dear Lord," she said at last, "and only last night I was telling him to take care crossing the road in this icy weather. I should never have let him go on his own."

"He wasn't in the road, Josie. The van went up on the footpath. Look, let me take you over to the hospital. Don't worry about the tea this morning. I'll get Diane or someone else to make it. Come along."

Pausing only for a word with Diane, who with unaccustomed graciousness agreed to make and distribute the tea, Helena led Josie to the car and drove her to the hospital.

"You go in if the Sister says you can, I'll wait here for you." Helena indicated the waiting-room. Josie disappeared in the direction of the children's ward, leaving Helena in the company of a couple of young mothers who had presumably been asked to wait until the doctor had made his rounds. Nothing had changed, Helena found herself thinking, since the previous time she had been there; the cracks in the ceiling plaster, the patch of bare wood on the skirting board, the Formica-topped table with the same pile of ancient magazines. At least the flowers in the vases were fresh, perhaps supplied by the Friends of the Hospital or a local church.

After a matter of ten minutes Josie returned, much more like her usual effervescent self.

"Have you seen him? Is he all right?"

"Yes, they think he will be, but they're going to keep him in for a night or two to make sure. It seems he came round in the ambulance and found it all very exciting. He's still got a bit of a headache, and he was a bit worried about what had happened to his satchel. But he's made friends with the little boy in the next bed, and I heard one of the nurses say "Now, Wesley, you mustn't make Jason giggle like that, he's still got his stitches in." Josie laughed, as much from relief as amusement.

"Does he need anything?"

"No, they say it's only for a couple of nights at most, it's not worth fetching anything."

"What about visiting later on? He'll want to see you this evening, won't he?"

"Well, I thought I'd come up on the bus."

"Oh, Josie, they're so unreliable. Look, supposing I run you up here again at the end of the afternoon, and come back to pick you up at the end of visiting time?"

"That's really kind, Mrs Halstow. But you've done more than enough for me already. It's a mercy you were there when it happened. I can't begin to thank you. It's a wonderful thing how the Lord puts the right person in the right place at the right time."

Helena had hardly regarded herself as an instrument of Divine providence; she thought, with a certain irony, that if the Lord had put her a few yards further forward or back the accident might not have occurred at all. A little embarrassed, she escorted Josie back to the car and took her home to tell her parents what had happened. Josie invited her in to meet them, but Helena politely declined, on the grounds that she must now endeavour to make up the working time she had lost.

"I'll see you this afternoon, then," she concluded. "And don't go waiting for the bus. It's no trouble at all for me to give you a lift up to the hospital."

Diane met her at the factory door.

"Is the little boy all right, Mrs Halstow?"

"They think so, at the hospital. He's staying in overnight so that they can make sure. But he's conscious, and doesn't seem to have anything worse than a bump and a headache."

"Oh, thank God. We were ever so worried, you know, when the policeman was in here, and that boy, he looked so frightened."

Helena wondered what had become of the boy, and also the other driver, who, she realised belatedly, might have to bear a share of the blame... *Well, no doubt that will come out if the police decide to prosecute.* Helena mounted the stairs to the office and plunged straight into a minor crisis over an order that had unaccountably been duplicated. This took what was left of the morning to resolve, and, exhausted and hungry, she decided to go over to the snack bar in town to have a quiet lunch and collect her wits.

The town centre was usually quiet in mid-week, and the snack bar half-empty. Today, however, it was unexpectedly crowded with schoolchildren, and there was hardly a seat to be found. Helena collected soup, quiche and vegetables, together with a cup of coffee, and enquired of the cashier why the place was so full on a Tuesday.

"Something's gone wrong with the kitchens up at the school, and they can't use them this week, so they've told the parents the kids can come over here if they like. Always has to happen at the coldest time of the year, doesn't it? It's good business for us, but don't they make a racket? I'll be glad when they're all back in their classrooms."

The hubbub was certainly phenomenal. Boys shouted to one another across the tables; girls shrieked with laughter. A small group of teachers occupied a table by the door, but were themselves deep in conversation. Helena consumed her lunch, which she had intended to spin out for the best part of an hour, in less than twenty minutes, and escaped into the cold again. She was about to take the footpath back across the gardens, but suddenly turned the other way, crossed the square and pushed open the heavy oak door of the church, with its great iron bolts and bands. She passed through the vestibule, not pausing to look at the notice board or the bookstall, and seated herself in one of the rear pews.

Here, at least, it was peaceful. The thick stone walls and stout doors excluded all but the loudest noises from outside. Helena gazed up at the arches surmounting the high pillars, the altar with its cloth of embroidered red velvet, the stained-glass window at the east end. The sun was on the southern side, but the sky was clear and the figures of Christ and the apostles stood out clearly; below them Helena could just discern the words of the Ten Commandments and the Lord's Prayer in Gothic script. The decorations were neither rich nor imaginative, but they were in harmony with the unpretentious air of the building; they imparted to her a sense of being one of many generations of worshippers kneeling in prayer on the carefully-sewn hassocks, or filing silently to the altar rail to take Communion. Helena knew little of the Anglican tradition, and it was many years since she had attended a church service; but the calm of the building refreshed her mind, and she relaxed for a moment, eyes half-closed, pondering the morning that had gone before.

First, Karen's telephone call, which, having at first obliterated by the accident and all that had followed, now returned with sudden clarity. What most concerned Helena was Karen's evident alarm. Having lived with Gill for several months, Karen must have become reasonably familiar with Gill's character and habits. Helena thought back to Christmas, to the frail, unkempt girl who had stirred her compassion with her sad eyes, her sweet smile and her incense. A storm in a teacup, quite possibly; yet Karen, whose common sense Helena readily acknowledged, had been anxious enough to call at eight o'clock in the morning. That had set in train the rest of the morning's troubles. If she had left home at her usual time she would in all probability have been at her desk by the time Wesley set out for school.

That was not to say that the accident might not still have happened to someone else; but why should it have happened at all? Though not responsible, she had become involved, just as she felt herself involved where Gill was concerned, even though Gill was no responsibility of hers. Helena closed her eyes completely, wondering whether she could have any influence on either situation. She had done what she could for Wesley, and there seemed to be a good chance that he would be none the worse for the accident; what about Gill?

It was at that instant that she felt it. Afterwards, she found it difficult to describe, a feeling of consolation, somewhere deep within her, such as she had not experienced at any time since David's death; a moment of relief, of partial perception without full understanding, a sudden calming of the spirit, as when a child racked by a nightmare awakes and recognises the familiar surroundings of his room, knows that his mother is near, and that one moment of truth is sufficient to dispel his anxiety and allow him to sink back into peaceful slumber – all of that would approximate to what Helena felt at that moment. It was not an answer to prayer, for Helena had not been consciously praying; but perhaps she had, without being aware of it, and if her prayer, if any, had been for others, the answer had unquestionably been for her. She had entered the church simply in search of a place of quietness, and had suddenly caught a glimpse of a different sort of peace altogether. What it meant she could scarcely begin to guess; it defied analysis, and in any event she was not disposed to examine the reality of her experience. She looked around her. The church was exactly the same as it had been five minutes earlier, but it was no longer a foreign, unfamiliar environment. As she got up, she felt confident about Gill, about Wesley and about her own future in Danesburgh. She left the church with a sense of gratitude she did not know how to express; on an impulse she placed some money in the offertory box by the door, and emerged with a slight sense of shock into the market square.

She walked back through the gardens, wondering exactly what had happened to her. Her vague recollections of Sunday school gave her no clue. She did not regard herself as a religious person, and indeed the very adjective had become somewhat distasteful to her, partly no doubt as a result of David's attitude. Yet this was something unexpected and unsought, and she was convinced, if only for that reason, that it was not simply a trick of her imagination. As she crossed the road to Danesburgh Cartons she decided to seek out the young curate she had met at the Poverty Lunch and speak to him about it. After all, he belonged to the church. If anyone knew anything about it, he should.

After the various crises of the morning, the afternoon passed without any unusual incidents. At five o'clock Helena found Josie waiting for her, and they climbed into Helena's car together, to the surprise of one or two workers who happened to be leaving early that day.

As Helena left Josie at the hospital door and watched her go in, carrying a bag containing one or two of Wesley's favourite books and toys, she realised that her feelings about the hospital itself were already changing, it was no longer merely the grim scene of David's last moments, but once again a place of care and healing and hope.

She had offered to collect Josie again just after seven.

"It really is kind of you, Mrs Halstow," Josie had said. "I won't forget what a friend you've been to me today. You know, when I got home in the middle of the day I thanked the Lord because Wesley wasn't badly hurt, and then I said 'and please bless Mrs Halstow, 'cause she's been so good to me."

"It was the least I could do," Helena had replied rather awkwardly, giving Josie a curious look. She had a distinct suspicion that if she enquired further she would discover that Josie's prayer had coincided with her experience in the church, and her natural reserve prevented her from disclosing such a private matter to someone whom she liked, but hardly knew; she would have hesitated to entrust it even tom her own family, except perhaps for Claire. Josie wore her simple faith as easily as if it were one of her brightly coloured jumpers, with no self-consciousness, while she herself, in common with most of the people she knew, regarded religion as a sort of thermal undergarment, warm and comforting, possibly, but in no circumstances to be displayed in public. It was with that bizarre image in her mind that she waved Josie goodbye and drove home.

The telephone call she expected did not come before she left for the hospital again. She wandered into the waiting-room, still mulling over the day in her mind. The passing of a few hours had not dispelled her new-found sense of security; if it had, she might have dismissed the feeling as an emotional response to a peculiarly stressful morning. The anguish the waiting-room had once caused was now totally absent; the sight of nurses and orderlies no longer made her look away as her eyes misted. Josie arrived, beaming.

"How is he, Josie?"

"Oh, he's fine, thank you. They've taken X-rays to make sure, but Sister says they're ninety-nine per cent certain there's no fracture. He's had fish fingers and ice cream, and now he's in there watching the end of *Doctor Who* with the rest of them."

"That's lovely," said Helena. "He'll be home tomorrow then, will he?"

""Yes. As soon as they confirm the X-rays are clear. They'll let me know if I ring."

"Well, just let me know, and I'll bring you up her to collect him." Josie tried to protest, but Helena would have none of it. "Now, have you had some tea?"

"I had a cup of tea before I left, and my mother will have something ready when I get back," said Josie. "Would you like to come in and have tea with us? You'd be very welcome."

"Thank you, Josie," Helena said, "but I'm expecting a call from my daughter. She's got something on her mind at the moment. I wouldn't like to miss her. But I would like to meet your parents, all the same. Perhaps I could just come in for a moment to say hello when Wesley comes home."

Josie smiled that dazzling smile. "They'll be delighted to meet you," she said.

Helena drove Josie home and then proceeded back to her own house with considerable caution, for the temperature was already below freezing. Her fingers were numb, for she had not bothered to put on any gloves, and it was difficult to put the key into the lock. She succeeded on the third attempt, and sat down for a moment to enjoy the warmth of being indoors again.

Karen's call did not come until it was gone ten, and her mood was entirely different from that of the morning.

"Sorry I didn't phone earlier, Mum. It's Greg's birthday, and we've been out celebrating. I like Greg," she went on happily. "He's asked me to a party this weekend. I think he might be getting a bit serious. He's already taken me out to lunch twice in a fortnight."

"Has he, indeed?" said Helena. "What sort of lunch?"

"A proper lunch. At that Greek place, you know. He's got a friend who knows the owner. He can always get a corner table."

"He sounds a useful person to know, then," Helena commented in a neutral tone. "Now, what about Gill? Have you heard from her?"

"Oh, Gill," Karen replied as if she had forgotten the original purpose of her call. "No, I haven't heard anything. But don't worry, Mum, I'm sure she's all right. She may be a bit dreamy, but she's not stupid."

"Even so," Helena reasoned, "do you really think you can leave it at that? People don't usually go away like that without telling you, or at least leaving a note."

"Well, what can I do?" Karen's voice sounded a little impatient. "I'm not her nanny. She's free to do as she likes as far as I'm concerned, so long as she pays her share of the rent and electricity and so on. I don't feel inclined to go down to the police station and report her missing, she'd probably turn up the next morning, and then I'd look silly."

"No," said Helena. "But I think at least one of her parents ought to know. They may have heard from her, anyway, or have some idea where she might be. Have you got a telephone number for either of them?"

"No, I haven't, but I should be able to find he father's number in the directory. There can't be many Aubrays in Colmleigh."

"Do you know him to speak to?"

"Yes, I suppose so. He came to the flat once or twice when we first moved there, to bring things of Gill's that she'd forgotten. I'll phone him tomorrow, it's a bit late to bother him tonight. Thanks for the advice, Mum. Love to Chris when you see him."

Helena could not help smiling as she put the receiver down. Greg had evidently replaced Gill in the course of the day as Karen's main preoccupation. Helena recalled him vaguely from before the move, at a party they had held, a well-spoken, well-mannered young man with an air of knowing where he was going. That would appeal to Karen, and she, although not exactly a flirt, knew how to turn on the charm when she had a reason to do so. Fortunately she could also judge a situation and recognise danger signs. She and Greg would undoubtedly make an attractive couple; and it was not surprising that, at twenty-one, Karen might speculate as to whether a boyfriend was getting serious. More evidence of change in her own life. When Karen married, as she no doubt would, it would presumably fall to Chris to give her away. Helena doubted very much whether the idea would have occurred to Chris.

She shook her head gently; no use peering that far into the future. And again there came to her that comforting feeling that had never completely left her since her visit to the church; and again she wondered what it meant. She went to bed very tired indeed, but utterly tranquil, despite the day's anxieties.

Next day brought further reassurance. Wesley was discharged from hospital early in the afternoon, and Helena was able to take a late lunch hour to drive him home with Josie. She met Josie's parents briefly, Mr Barritt, greying, quiet and dignified, and Mrs Barritt, diminutive by her daughter's side, but with the same liveliness and grace of movement. Both of them clearly adored Wesley, who dashed from one to the other, receiving hugs. Like Josie's, their gratitude for Helena's assistance seemed altogether out of proportion to what she had actually done, and she felt a little embarrassed. She diverted their attention to the child, commending him for his immaculate behaviour at the hospital, and was half-relieved when the time came to drive Josie back to the factory for the afternoon tea break.

The cold weather continued until well into March. Even Chris, who was usually indifferent to the cold, had begun to complain when, for the third week running, he returned to a freezing room at the Byles' house after the weekend. "I didn't expect her to keep my room heated all weekend, but it wouldn't have done her any harm to turn the radiator on for half an hour on Sunday night. She knows well enough what time I usually get back," he had said.

At last, however, the snow gave way to sleet, and then to rain. There was one Wednesday when the rain, already falling when Helena arose, continued with increasing intensity, accompanied by numbing gusts of wind as she crossed the factory forecourt. At lunchtime there was no change, and she returned from the town centre soaking wet despite her umbrella. By the end of the afternoon her coat and shoes had still not dried out. She had been working late, completing some correspondence and bringing her filing up to date, and when she finally descended she found that most of the factory workers had already left. The rain still drove against her, and the wind pushed the car door back in her face as she tried to open it.

She turned the ignition key and heard only a hollow click. The pilot light disappeared. She looked at the dashboard in disgust.

"Now, what's the matter with that?" she said aloud, and tried again. This time there was not so much as a click. She sat for a minute or two in silence and then turned the key a third time. Still no response. She felt tired and cross, although she knew perfectly well that this was only a minor irritation, and that she could perfectly well walk home, or catch a bus, if need be; but she could not bring herself to step out again into the rain that was sweeping across the yard.

Through the windscreen she caught sight of an indistinct vehicle turning into the forecourt. The side window enabled her to identify it as it pulled up beside her. It was Jim Sergent's car. He got out and tapped on the window.

"Hello, still here?" he said. "Are you having some difficulty?"

"My wretched car won't start. There doesn't seem to be any life in the battery. I'd be awfully grateful for some help."

"Well," Jim said, "I don't claim to be an expert, but I'll certainly have a look."

The car still declined to respond to the turn of the ignition key. Jim shrugged.

"I would think the leads must have got damp. Not surprising, with all this rain. I could try to push-start it, but you really need a downhill slope for that, and in any case I don't think there's room in the yard to do it. I'll tell you what, you leave it here for now, and I'll get one of the mechanics to have a look at it in the morning. I'll run you home this evening."

"Oh, I wouldn't want to put you to any trouble."

"No trouble at all," said Jim gallantly. "If you don't mind waiting for a couple of minutes. I came back because I meant to take some balance sheets home, and then found I'd forgotten them. Would you like to lock your car up and sit in mine?"

He opened the passenger door. The car was an elderly Hillman showing signs of rust outside and smelling distinctly of dog inside, but Helena was not disposed to complain. She climbed in with pleasure, blessing the forgetfulness that had brought the accounts clerk back.

Jim Sergent returned with a packet inside his coat. Het got in. "Now, where do you need to get to?"

"Donne Close, It's on the south side of the town, not far from the Feathers. If you follow the ring road as far as the third roundabout and then turn left ..."

"Well, that's easy, anyway. I live in Parham St. John. I can drop you off and then carry on past the Feathers until I get back to the Tollersfield road, and go that way round."

Jim set the old Hillman on course. He drove it rather as if it were a tank, not very fast but with the purposeful air of one not to be deterred by either traffic or terrain. Helena wondered momentarily what would happen if they met a bus on the wrong side of the road.

"Sorry about the state of the car," he said abruptly. "Bit doggy, I'm afraid. I do clean up the back from time to time, but it's a bit of a wasted effort this time of year. He brings half the field back with him every time we go for a walk."

"What sort of dog is he?" Helena asked politely.

"Several sorts. Terrier, mostly. Goes off his head if he smells a rat or a rabbit."

Helena had never owned a dog. David, as a young man, had considered having one, but had decided that, with the long hours he had to work and regular periods away from home, it would be impractical. Helena did not envy Jim the prospect of having to turn out that evening to take his dog for a walk.

"Will you have to take him out this evening?"

"Alas, yes. As short a walk as he'll tolerate, which generally means a mile and a half or so. We'll probably finish up drying out at the local. They all know him in there." Jim negotiated the second roundabout with strict observance of the Highway Code as to signals.

"Have you always had a dog?"

"On and off, yes. My family had two or three when I was growing up. We didn't have one recently; my wife didn't want one about the house while she was ill. I got this one after she died. I needed the company, you see."

Helena nodded, offering no comment. Jim had coloured slightly, and neither of them spoke again until she was nearly home.

"Is this the turning?"

"Yes, this is it."

Jim drew up outside the house.

"How would it be if I called for you in the morning, at about a quarter past eight?"

"That would be a great help. But don't bother coming right up here. I can wait on the corner if you like."

"All right, then, I'll look out for you on the corner. But if the weather's still like this I suggest you wait inside and I'll come up and sound my horn when I get here."

"That's very kind of you, Jim. Thank you for the lift. I hope I'll get my own car right tomorrow."

"I've no doubt they'll sort it out," said Jim. "See you in the morning, then."

He drove away with a casual wave of the hand. Helena set about drying her coat and shoes before preparing her meal. The rain, however, had penetrated further, and she had to change out of her office clothes altogether and put on an old jumper and a pair of slacks she used for decorating or cleaning. Her hair needed washing after the rain; *so far as appearance is concerned*, she thought, *I must have matched Jim's car pretty well. Not much to choose between me and the dog for elegance.*

During the evening she listened from time to time to the wind still whining among the bare branches of the trees and shaking the doors and windows with sudden angry gusts. She could picture Jim Sergent, no doubt in heavy coat and boots, leaning forward into the wind, with his glasses misting up, as the dog led him eagerly forward along the lanes. Canine company must be a mixed blessing; even if she had not had the children, she would not have chosen a dog as a companion. Still, if you were brought up with dogs in the family... Did Jim have many friends in the village? He hardly seemed the type to club with the regulars at the local; but then, she reflected, the day of the old-fashioned country pub, with farm hands drinking scrumpy in the snug and a bench outside for the use of the Oldest Inhabitant, was long past, if indeed it had ever existed. Nowadays the village locals were full of accountants and stockbrokers.

Helena brought her mind back to her family. Karen talked more and more about Greg; they seemed well on the way to becoming inseparable. No doubt she would soon be asking whether she could bring him over for the weekend. Chris was beginning to look forward to the summer; he had made friends with two other students who were thinking of taking an old minibus abroad, to camp in it, and had asked him whether he would like to go with them and give them the benefit of his skills as a mechanic. Their proposed destination was Italy. Chris would have liked to take some formal driving lessons; David had taught him the rudiments, but nowhere near enough for him to take the test without further tuition. Time and money being in short supply, he had settled for the moped, economical and easy to park, while he was studying; now he was starting to regret the lack of a car.

No word had come from Gill, although she had apparently taken the trouble to send the landlord a month's rent in advance by post. Evidently she contemplated returning at some stage. Karen had spoken to Gill's mother, whom she found less intimidating than Mr Aubray, and who had manifested no surprise and little concern. She did not altogether regret Gill's absence; it meant that she could invite Greg to the flat without fear of intrusion. The visits from Gill's student friends and other acquaintances had ceased in her absence.

Karen's weekend visits to see her mother were as infrequent as ever. Helena had a vision of a summer with both Karen and Chris away, seeing nothing of them for several weeks, a bleak prospect. Perhaps she should invite her parents, Aunt Marie permitting, and no doubt they would invite her back to stay with them for a while. That would see out a reasonable proportion of the summer. It was a sad contrast with the earlier part of the previous year, when they had been planning the summer holidays with high excitement. The memory brought a stinging moment of grief, something for which she had had no time for several weeks. Hoping to alleviate it, she picked up a library book she had already had for too long, intending to finish it, but the story was not a comforting one, and she laid the book aside after she had read a few pages.

The wind was quietening now, and when Helena drew back the curtains for a moment she could make out a star or two here and there, where the clouds were beginning to break up. She pulled the curtains to again, and went and made a cup of hot chocolate, which she took upstairs to her bedroom, wondering idly what Jim Sergent might be drinking at his local. Then, no less idly, she picked up an ancient shopping-bag which she had found in the study, and recognised as one she had used many years previously, while still at school. She had put it in her room, intending at some time to see what was in it, and now seemed as good a time as any.

She found an old purse containing an eight-sided threepenny bit, some archaic postage stamps, and a door key which she identified as belonging to her family's old house in Newcastle, sold some twenty-five years earlier; a letter to a school friend who had moved away to Wiltshire, which she had omitted to post, notwithstanding the presence of the stamps; a pocket German dictionary; a nail file; a small Bible; two old-fashioned pocket-style tickets from one of the Newcastle public libraries; and embroidered handkerchief, and a comb. *Rather a disappointment*, she thought, *not much there to give me a quiet hour of nostalgia.* She read the letter; it had been written in the middle of a series of examinations. The friend had been apprehensive, presumably as a result of having had to change schools in mid-course, and Helena's letter had been written with the purpose of encouraging her. She remembered then why she had not posted it. Her friend had telephoned — from Wiltshire! (there had been no STD at that time) — to say that the papers had been much less frightening than she had feared, and Helena had judged the letter unnecessary. For a moment she wondered where her friend was now — married, with a family, in all probability; or maybe divorced, or widowed like herself, who could tell? She had not kept up much with school or college friends, finding sufficient companionship in David, and in time, in her family; she had felt that to try to prolong old friendships, once you were married, was somehow artificial and maybe hazardous. Of course she had no way of knowing what had become of this particular friend, or what her married name, if any, might be. *All your life you seem to be creating links with people, only for them to be broken again, by adulthood, removals, change and eventually death.*

I'm getting morbid, she told herself, and put the letter back. She thumbed through the dictionary, recognising odd words here and there, although most had gone from her memory. The she opened the Bible at the place where it was bookmarked by a bus ticket. She had been chosen to read a lesson at the final assembly of the summer term, and being a perfectionist, had been rehearsing it to herself. It was, unimaginatively enough, the Twenty-third Psalm. She closed her eyes and repeated it once again to herself, surprised to find that she was still word-perfect. It was a mechanical exercise to begin with; but suddenly she became more aware of the words, *Though I walk through the valley of the shadow of death... Thou art with me... goodness and mercy shall follow me all the days of my life.*

She stopped, thinking back to her experience in the church and wondering whether the phrases had been inspired by some similar moment in the life of the psalmist. She knew that Psalm 23 was her mother's favourite, as it was for many people, especially when they began to feel old, for the reassurance it seemed to provide; but the notion that it might actually correspond to something one had already experienced was something entirely new. She had meant to speak to the curate, but a certain self-consciousness had deterred her. The Psalm spurred her to a fresh resolve. She would go to another poverty lunch and try to make an appointment.

Helena put the bag back in the study, but left the Bible out and placed it one of the drawers of the bedside chest. She did not feel confident enough to leave it on top; she could imagine David's disapproval. "Religion," he would say, if pressed to give an opinion (for he had always been reluctant to offer one, knowing the risk of giving offence), "to me, is a kind of psychological crutch for people who can't cope with life. If they find it a help, then good luck to them. But I've never felt any need of it, and I've no great respect for them that sell it. The intelligent ones are too half-hearted, and those that really believe never seem to be able to see anyone else's point of view." (In which, of course, he was unconsciously paraphrasing W.B. Yeats). Helena had an idea that this rationalisation had concealed a deep-seated hostility, which, she believed, must be derived from some experience of his, long before they had met. She had accepted and loved David as he was, and had been content to follow his way of life, which, certainly, had been moral enough, without question. Now, when she would have liked to ask him about it, it was too late.

Her mind was troubled when she went to bed, and she did not sleep easily. Against the echo of the words of the Psalm she heard David's voice; against her moment of consolation in the church, she weighed all the years of pleasurable companionship they had enjoyed together. When at last she slept she dreamed of their wedding day, and the Vicar was reading the vows; but suddenly she was alone in the church, and the notes of the organ had become a tangle of cacophonous discords, which eventually resolved themselves into a horrendous twanging of electric guitars, issuing from the radio alarm clock, followed by the voice of an announcer proclaiming, apparently with great satisfaction, that it was precisely six forty-five a.m.

Heavy-eyed, she peered round the edge of the curtain. The rain and wind were gone, and the sky had cleared. With an aching head she washed and dressed, wondering why she had been so disturbed. Coffee and aspirin eased the headache, however, and she was in better spirits when she arrived at the corner of the road to wait for Jim Sergent. For the first time there was a hint in the air that the winter was on its way out. The wind, much moderated, had swung to the south-east, and it was mild enough for her to smell the damp earth. She stood on the corner and looked across the open fields on the other side of the road, where a farmhouse was just visible on the horizon, unsure whether she should look forward to the spring with pleasure or apprehension.

Jim Sergent drew up in the Hillman, got out and opened the door for Helena. As she climbed in, Helena noticed that he had made an effort to render the interior of the car a little more respectable; the rear seats had been brushed and sponged, the ledges dusted and the mats swept, and he seemed to have applied some kind of household polish to the facias.

"Good morning, Helena. I hope you haven't been waiting too long." Very correctly, Jim closed the passenger door behind her. "Don't think I'm fussing,.." he explained, as he engaged the clutch. "The catch on that side is a bit dodgy. I'm always afraid if I have a passenger that they might fall out when we're going round one of these roundabouts."

He was not really at ease with her in the car. Either he was shy by nature, or he had become accustomed to driving alone, except for his dog, Helena supposed. He seemed to be taking refuge in an exaggerated show of courtesy. She had to induce him to talk.

"It was still very wild last night, wasn't it? You must have got awfully wet taking the dog out."

"Oh, a bit. I'm used to it, after all." Jim concentrated on passing a slow-moving lorry.

Helena tried again. "Did you manage to get the figures sorted out?"

"Yes, just about, thanks."

He was not to be drawn into conversation this morning. Did he resent her presence in the car? No, that was too strong, there was certainly no hostility in his manner. He drove as he had the previous evening, tensely, yet very deliberately, unwilling or unable to relax. At work he was much the same, spending most of the day hunched over his papers, discussing the company's receipts and expenses very seriously, and rarely joining in the light-hearted chat that regularly passed between Brian Farrelson and George Bushmell. It seemed to irritate him, although it was rarely prolonged and never malicious. They were contented, easy-going men, astute and careful enough in business, but always able to break out of their routine for a minute or two. To Jim this evidently seemed frivolous and unnecessary; he was capable of concentrating on figures for hours at a time, and apparently regarded it as vital to do so. Helena glanced at him covertly as he negotiated the last roundabout, eyes unwavering behind the dark-rimmed glasses, mouth set above the long chin. David would probably have termed him a miserable so-and-so; was that his real nature, or was it what bereavement had done to him? If so, would it eventually have a similar effect on her? But she remembered, his wife's death had not been the first of Jim Sergent's misfortunes. Brian Farrelson had hinted at some earlier troubles of some sort; and then, the first time she had met him, he had just been injured and had his car damaged in an accident. So far as she could judge, he must detest the idea that people felt sorry for him, preferring to hold the world at arm's length. She could understand that to some extent; she herself had had the benefit of Claire's practical support, and the removal had distanced her from friends and casual acquaintances. She would have hated, when still suffering the first shock of bereavement, to be surrounded by the likes of Susan Cumber, whose simpering voice suddenly sounded clearly in her mind as they arrived at the factory. Jim got out first and opened the door for Helena, again with a politeness that was slightly exaggerated.

"I'll have a word with Ernie," he said. "He usually knows what needs doing when one of the vans is playing up." He strode off in the direction of the maintenance bay.

Ernie appeared in his usual overalls.

"Mr Sergent tells me your motor won't go," he said. "I'll have a look at it for you, if you'll just let me have the keys for a few minutes."

Helena fished the keys out of her handbag. "That's very good of you," she said. "If I can just get it home, my son will probably be able to put it right for me over the weekend."

Ernie took the keys and walked over to the car.

"Don't wait out here, Mrs Halstow," he advised her. "I'll come up and see you when I've found out what's wrong with it."

Half an hour later he came in to the office, keys in hand. "Well," he said, "I've done what I could, Mrs Halstow. I've put the battery on to recharge, and I reckon it'll get you home all right, but it's really just about had it — it looks as if it's been there ever since the car left the factory. All the bad weather this week can't have helped, either. Anyway, I think that's all it needed."

"Well, I'm very grateful to you for your help. I hope I haven't wasted too much of your time."

"You're welcome." Ernie tuned to leave, caught Jim Sergent's eye and winked. Jim seemed embarrassed. "Yes," he added, "thanks, Ernie."

"Can't leave a lady in trouble, can we?" said Ernie, as he disappeared through the door.

Jim coughed. "If it would help," he volunteered, "I'll run you over the town at lunchtime. There's a good motorists' discount store there. We could bring a battery back and put it in your boot to take home with you."

Helena was taken by surprise, not by the suggestion itself, which was modest enough, but by the readiness with which it came. It was as though Jim was anxious to be friendly whenever there was anything to be done, but shrank from becoming involved in conversation. She accepted the offer graciously.

But the purchase of the battery had to be postponed, because one of the machine operators was caught in the eye by a loose belt shortly before noon, and Helena's lunch hour was taken up with first-aid ministrations and the recording of the incident. Brian Farrelson was furious.

"It was only last week we had the service engineers here. It's unbelievable that they missed a fault like that. The lad could have lost the sight of his eye, and we'd have been first in line to be sued. I'll have them straight back here tomorrow."

Fortunately, the eye did not appear to be seriously damaged, although it would be black for a day or two.

"Never mind," said Jim Sergent when Helena finally came upstairs to the office. "You drive your car home and put it in the garage. I'll give you a lift again tomorrow, if you like, and we'll go into town in the middle of the day, as we intended to do today. I'll tell you what, we'll have a snack at the Rose. Make up for missing your lunch today."

This was added with a strange mixture of warmth and reticence. How is it, Helena wondered, that after four months of working at the desk next to mine, he's still struggling to break the ice between us? An odd character.

"Thank you," she replied. "I must say it's been a while since I last had lunch out. It would make a nice change."

***

At lunchtime the following day, therefore, Helena and Jim were seated at a table in the dining area of the Rose, a tiny pub just off the main square, having first stowed the new battery in the boot of Jim's Hillman. He had bought one for himself at the same time. "It hasn't much wanted to start in the mornings," he explained. "I've been charging the old battery up overnight, but it's really time I got rid of it."

"The battery, or the car?" Helena enquired with a smile.

"Both, really, but I'm afraid the car will have to soldier on for a while yet. Anyway, if I had a new car the dog would soon make a mess of it."

The dog again. Jim's conversation seemed to centre on his car and his dog. If their lunch together was not to be unspeakably tedious, now was the time to break new ground. Helena cast about in her mind for a way to lead on to a more profitable topic with reasonable subtlety. Finding none, she simply remained silent for a few moments, and then adopted a direct approach.

"Jim, there's something I've been meaning to ask you, if you wouldn't think it unduly inquisitive. May I?"

Jim looked at her warily.

"I don't mind what you ask," he said slowly, "but I can't guarantee that I can or will give you an answer, of course."

"Well," Helena continued, "as you know, I lost my husband recently. That was probably the main reason why I came to work for Danesburgh Cartons. You're the first person I've met here so far who's been through a similar experience, and I wondered how you've managed to... well, adjust... because, quite frankly, I'm finding it hard."

Jim hesitated, making a point of finishing a mouthful.

"I'm surprised to hear you say that," he replied at length. "Not about finding it hard to adjust, I didn't mean that. You suddenly lose someone you've been closer to than anyone else in the world, for years and years, it's like having your arm cut off. But you've never talked about it before, have you? Not to anyone at work, anyway. You've not known us for long enough. And so far as I can see it isn't affecting your work at all. I can't remember a secretary who could cope with everything the way you seem to, and believe me, I've seen a few come and go."

Helena appreciated the compliment, judging that Jim was not a man to indulge in flattery, and acknowledged it.

"That's a very nice thing to say, and I'm not sure I deserve it. But I do enjoy the work, you know. It was a long time since I'd had a job, and I was very nervous to begin with, but everyone's been so helpful and friendly."

"Yes," said Jim. "They're a good crowd, by and large. I don't think I'd have stayed otherwise."

"Have you been with the company long, then?"

"Fifteen years, coming up. I'd had a business venture that failed, and I was looking for something reasonably secure and not too demanding while I got over that. Danesburgh Cartons were just expanding at that time. They'd moved out of their old building on the other side of the town, and their books had been kept by an old boy who hadn't retired when he should have done. The move got him to go in the end, he didn't want to come over here. The books were in a terrible state. I took them home every night for weeks. My wife got well and truly fed up with it. 'How much longer are you going to stay up with those figures?' she used to say." A note of bitterness entered his voice. "And the figures outlived her," he concluded. "I'm still taking them home at night."

"Figures or no figures," Helena commented, "at least you were at home in the evenings. That's more than my husband used to be, in the early days at least. Off on the road at six o'clock on Monday morning, back at ten on Friday night. Although he did get good holidays to make up for it."

"Your husband was a rep, was he? That's a job I'd have hated. Always trying to make a sale, always trying to get in front of your competitors, make your target or risk losing your job. I can't think of anything worse."

"David loved it," Helena said. "It was his life, every job he took on was a challenge, to see what he could do with the product, how to present it, how to make it attractive. He did it so well that in the end he was getting offers of jobs when he wasn't even looking for them."

"The head-hunters were after him?"

"Yes, that sort of thing. That was one of the reasons why we came here. He didn't want to accept anything unless it was his own choice. He wouldn't ever be pushed into anything."

Suddenly in her mind's eye Helena saw David fighting for life in the ambulance, and screwed up her eyes. It was the slightest of grimaces, but it did not go unnoticed by Jim.

"Something hurt there, didn't it?"

Helena nodded. "Yes. You think about the best things, the most memorable qualities of the person you loved, and then you realise that it ties in with what happened with David when he died, how he wouldn't accept it, he kept trying to tell me it wouldn't happen, he'd be all, right. He put up a terrific fight. By then time the second attack came he had nothing left — no strength."

"I'm sorry." Jim's eyes behind the glasses were showing compassion now. "It must have been very unexpected then? No early warnings?"

"None at all. He'd been a bit tired, because he's been working harder than ever, but then he always had worked hard."

"I do sometimes wonder," Jim said, "if you lose someone like that, which is worse, to have them go completely without warning, and be terribly shocked, or to have to watch them suffer for years and years and have to pretend you think they're going to get better. That was the hardest thing for me. I knew very well what the outcome would be for Brenda, and I'm fairly sure she did too, at least towards the end; but the doctors wouldn't officially let us give up hope, they kept saying the treatment was working, right up to about three months before she died. Then they came clean and said they'd done all they could. There were times when she'd scream at me to tell her the truth. That was another thing, it changed her personality, so that sometimes I hardly recognised her as the woman I'd married. Then there were the times she was in hospital. I'd be over there all the time I wasn't at the office, until they turned me out. I can tell you I didn't take any books home just then." Jim paused, but Helena offered no comment. "Since then," he continued, "I've tried to put the whole business of her illness and death out of my mind, and just remember her as she used to be before she got ill."

"Does it work?" Helena asked quietly.

"No, not really. 'In sickness and in health', the marriage service says. You can't perform a kind of mental divorce if your wife is terminally ill, it's part of your life together, right up to the end. You asked how I had adjusted. The honest answer is that I haven't. I miss Brenda every single day of my life, and it's already been two years." Unexpectedly, he smiled, the same serious smile Helena had seen on her first day at the office. "Now I've bared my soul to you, do you think it'll help?"

"It always helps to talk things over, doesn't it?"

"That depends on the listener. I think I've got to know you well enough to rely on you not to gossip, and I don't usually make a habit of giving away confidences. But I don't think I could say the same about many of the people in the office; or anywhere else, for that matter." He looked at his watch. "Time we were getting back, isn't it?"

"Yes, I suppose it is," Helena agreed. Thank you for the lunch, and thank you for the sympathetic ear. I'll just get my coat."

Their return together did not go unnoticed by the sharp eyes of Marlene Smetters. "'Ello, I wondered 'ow long it would be before them two started gettin' interested in each other."

"Now then, Marlene," said the workmate. "You mustn't start putting two and two together and making half a dozen."

Marlene was unabashed. "Well, stands to reason, dunnit? After all, she's a widow, he's a widower, both serious types — made for each other, I'd say." And she and her friend turned back to their machines.

Helena had no such thoughts in her mind. As she climbed the stairs she was merely concerned that it was Friday, and Chris would be home, and she had done no shopping. It would have to be beef burgers, or something else from the freezer, that evening.

Driving her home after work, Jim Sergent reverted to his uncommunicative mood of the previous evening. It was as though their conversation over lunch had never taken place. He deposited the battery carefully on the garage floor for Helena, and then merely said "Have a good weekend. See you Monday," and drove away with a casual wave of the hand, not even waiting for her thanks.

Chris arrived late, having been held up by a signal failure on the line. He was apparently trying to grow a moustache, in imitation of some film star or other, and a layer of down straggled across his upper lip like dirty cobweb. Karen would have discouraged him with a wry comment, but Karen had not been back to Danesburgh for several weeks, as her social engagements with Greg had multiplied. Every telephone call from her brought news of some party, disco, dance or outing.

"I hope you're paying your share towards all these dances and so on," Helena had said at one point. Karen had laughed. "I would if Greg needed me to, Mum, of course I would," she had said, "but, honestly, Mum, he's well able to afford to treat me."

Meanwhile Chris was steadily progressing towards the annual examinations, due relatively early in the summer term. The Italian trip, furthermore, was as good as fixed, and any spare time he had in London was spent working on the minibus. Ornithology was forgotten for the moment. When he unpacked his bag there were travel brochures and Michelin maps side by side with his text books. He wandered about the house, whistling to himself; he had fitted the new battery to Helena's car before she realised he had gone out to the garage, and it was only when she heard the engine start up that she knew what he was doing. She delighted in his growing self-confidence; it was rather like watching the needle of a barometer rise towards the fair-weather mark. Thank God, both he and Karen seemed to be profiting from their independence, and not abusing it.

She was amused, in the evening, to hear Chris in his room, rehearsing polite enquiries evidently culled from a traveller's Italian phrase book. "*Per favore, signore, dov'e il...*" he stumbled over what followed and began again. "*Ho bisogno di acqua e benzina*," he continued, again finding the pronunciation difficult. Evidently he was intent on earning his trip.

The weekend sped by. Between meals and study sessions Chris helped his mother to turn out the garage and dispose of a good deal of unwanted material at the local recycling centre. He promised to perform a similar operation during the Easter vacation for the study and the loft, in response to Helena's suggestion that a little spring cleaning might not come amiss. This decision had actually been an indirect result of the lifts Jim Sergent had given her during the week; from the initial state of his car, she had begun to speculate as to what his home must be like, with only the dog to keep him company; and this in turn had prompted the thought that, once the evenings were lighter her own house could benefit from a good clear-out and clean-up. Chris had groaned to begin with, "Oh, Mum…" But when it came to it, he rather enjoyed putting his physical strength to good use.

As March gave way to April, Helena busied herself in the evenings with dusters, mops, carpet shampoo and the like. Karen had decided that she would like to bring Greg over at Easter, and while Helena felt no excessive need to impress Karen's suitor, as he now evidently was, she wanted to give a fair account of herself and her home. At the weekends Chris lent a hand with some of the more awkward jobs, and also turned his attention to the garden, tidying up the flower beds and planting what early vegetables he could; but it was still too cold and wet to do much outside.

The soil was mainly composed of heavy clay. "It's a good thing," Chris commented as he removed one heavily caked wellington boot, "you haven't got a garden the size of the one we had in Colmleigh, or it would take me till Easter just to turn it!"

Between Christmas and Easter Helena finally established herself as an indispensable part of Danesburgh Cartons. Josie Barritt, who, since the accident, had regarded her with a blend of slightly exaggerated admiration and affection, reported to her regularly on Wesley's progress at school, occasionally bringing in photographs or pieces of craft work which she placed on Helena's desk with great pride. Helena, in return, became an honorary aunt to Wesley, and from time to time passed Josie a packet of sweets or a child's book for Wesley; on his birthday she bought him a model aeroplane, having ascertained that his interests lay in that direction. She met Josie's parents in the town once or twice on a Saturday, and stopped to talk, surprising Chris, who still thought his mother knew no one in the town apart from the office staff. He noticed the high esteem in which they held Helena.

"They think a lot of you, don't they, Mum?" he commented.

Helena laughed. "It's mutual. They're a lovely family."

Brian and George treated her with cheerful yet respectful familiarity, while recognising that she was not inclined to join in the occasional social events they organised for the benefit of the workforce generally. As an efficient and sympathetic dispenser of first aid and aspirin, and on occasion, advice and assistance to the shop floor workers, she got to know two or three local doctors, social workers and the Citizens' Advice Bureau, in connection with problems in which she had, more or less willingly, involved herself. If there were one or two workers who still shared Marlene Smetters's original assessment of Helena, they had revised their views, or at least modified them to *Takes everything a bit too seriously*, or *Not really the sort you can have a laugh with.*

Jim Sergent, however, remained something of an enigma to her. Despite their lunching together at the Rose a couple more times, she could not decide whether he was a friendly introvert whom life had dealt with harshly, leaving emotional wounds, or simply a prickly individual, ill at ease socially, who recognised the fact. Helena found herself wondering what his wife had been like; whether she had been, or believed herself to be, capable of brightening his view of the world, and possibly also palliating some of the misfortunes that seemed to have quite undeservedly come his way; but then she recalled David's insistence that people made their own luck in this life.

Naturally unaware of these speculations (of which Helena secretly felt a little ashamed), Jim remained courteous but mainly inscrutable. A few clues, however, did come to light. He admitted to an interest in organ music (and a certain disappointment that none of the churches in Danesburgh possessed a halfway decent organ), and in the Iberian peninsula generally. An uncle of his had fought on the Republican side in the Spanish Civil War, and this led him to spend his holidays, as often as he could, searching for some of the people he had heard about. Although not linguistically gifted, Jim had learnt enough Spanish to be able to read some of the works of García Lorca; and Don Quixote was high up in the canon of his literary heroes. The *Knight of the Sorrowful Countenance*, Helena reflected was not a bad way of describing Jim himself, with his rare and serious smile, and she imagined him in the grip of some archaic obsession, riding to rid the world of some imaginary menace, in his Rosinante of a car. Had he once worshipped some Dulcinea? She decided that was taking the fancy too far; he was, after all, a practical, sensible accounts clerk, not some impoverished aristocrat, unhinged by hunger and a surfeit of courtly adventure stories. But the image obstinately persisted, and when now and again she looked up from her work and caught sight of that long bespectacled face, deep in contemplation of the company's finances, she saw for a moment that *Knight of the Sorrowful Countenance*, preparing for battle with some economic giant of his fantasy.

***

Karen arrived with Greg late in the evening on the Thursday before Easter. No old Volkswagen this time; she stepped out of a small Volvo, a sports model, not the current year's, admittedly, but only a couple of years old, still highly polished and free from rust and discoloration. Greg appeared, carrying two cases; not much taller than Karen herself, dark-haired and even-featured, in casual jacket, open-collared shirt and well-pressed trousers, all of which, to Helena's eye, were manifestly expensive. Karen hastened to introduce him.

"Mum, you remember Greg, don't you? You know, from my twenty-first."

Helena did remember Greg; he had stood out among the young men there, as much for his ability to say the right thing as for his undoubted good looks.

"Mrs Halstow. Lovely to see you again. How are you? I do apologise for arriving so late. I hope it hasn't caused you any inconvenience."

"Not at all. Yes, I do remember you, of course. I'm delighted you've come. Do come in."

During the rest of the evening Helena watched keenly for clues as to the way the courtship was developing. It was not easy. Greg, poised and discreet, affected the air of a City businessman. That might be something he used as a shield when meeting strangers socially, or when he felt he was on show. Karen, for her part, was uncharacteristically nervous, saying little of substance and giggling rather too much. Chris, Greg's junior by some five years, withdrew to the fringe of the conversation; Greg's apparent self-assurance evidently made him feel uncomfortable, and Helena felt a shadow of resentment at seeing her son's self-esteem this affected. Not that there was any element of calculation on Greg's part; on the contrary, he made a point of encouraging Chris, emphasising the future role of technology in business, the already expanding use of computers in banking, insurance, property development and the rest. He himself was well advanced in his professional training, and expected to pursue a career which, although he did not mention the fact explicitly, was likely to be highly remunerative.

Helena had to admit to herself that, from a social point of view, Greg would make an admirable fiancé for Karen. He represented a step up the ladder, for, while David had been a highly successful businessman in his way, he had achieved that success without losing sight of his relatively humble origins; Greg, on the other hand, was clearly bred to it. Helena wondered whether Karen could match him; her education was more limited, her social experience sketchy, although the energy which she had inherited from her father, together with a certain measure of ambition which he had never possessed, would go a long way to compensate for any such deficits. As a couple they looked particularly handsome together; but Helena looked in vain for the kind of adoration that had inspired David to write letter after letter to her, brought him back out his way to Newcastle on numerous occasions, and driven him to seek her out that afternoon at Colmleigh railway station, on her return from work. If Greg were capable of such intensity of feeling, he kept the fact well concealed.

Helena rebuked herself. He's only just arrived, she thought, and he's still young, and he's not from a world where a show of passion is an advantage. Give him time to settle. Even so, she could not feel fully at ease all evening.

***

The next morning was bright enough, but the sunshine was neutralised by an easterly wind that bent the new daffodils in the garden until they were almost touching the ground, and sent anyone out walking early hurrying indoors again after the merest turn up the road and back. Remembering Boxing Day, Helena planned to take the family out to the Feathers for a drink before lunch. Greg, the perfect guest, was immaculate when he appeared after a minimum of time spent in the bathroom; Karen achieved the same result using the maximum time available; Helena and Chris fitted in somewhere in between. Everything was going smoothly enough until Helena went to the refrigerator to take out the chicken she was intending to roast while they were out.

"Oh, dear," she said in a dismayed tone.

"What is it, Mum?" Karen enquired from the lounge.

"I don't like the look of this chicken. And it doesn't smell too good, either."

Karen came out and looked.

"My God, Mum, it's off, it's absolutely horrible. You can't cook that."

"I'll have to take it back and get another one," Helena concluded. "I think the supermarket's open today. I'll go into town and sort it out. If I'm not back in half an hour or so you go on to the Feathers, and I'll join you out there once the lunch is in the oven."

She carefully wrapped the offending fowl in its polythene bag, put the whole package in a carrier and took it out to the garage, where she deposited it with distaste in the boot of her car. She apologised hurriedly to Greg, who had come out to ask whether he could help, and drove quickly into town, making straight for the supermarket. At that point she realised that she was not sure she still had the till receipt, but by good fortune the bag in which the chicken now reposed was the same carrier that she had brought it home in, and the receipt was still at the bottom. The exchange was effected without fuss by an apologetic meat manager, who immediately ordered a check on all remaining poultry.

Emerging into the cold again, she discovered that the market square, where she had parked, had subsequently been closed to traffic by a couple of special constables. For a moment she wondered whether there was a bomb scare; then common sense reasserted itself. Danesburgh was a quiet country town with no particular military associations; and in any case, the handful of shoppers in the square were not being moved away. At the further end of the market place she caught sight of a crowd of people advancing slowly towards her. Some sort of demonstration, then, perhaps. She knew that some of the local farmers were unhappy with certain Common Market legislation. But as the crowd came closer she noticed that there were no banners, and no angry chanting. Instead, the leaders carried three great, rough wooden crosses, and the mood of the followers, although serious, did not exclude a murmur of friendly chatter among the various groups that were present, perhaps a hundred or so in all.

Helena's grasp of her wheel tightened with impatience, for she was anxious to get her substitute chicken into the oven. She watched the procession file past, and suddenly realised that she was recognising a few faces. Immediately conspicuous, Josie Barritt, with young Wesley trotting at her side; her parents following, in company with another couple of similar age, Eric and Rhoda Broughmer from next door; they had a younger couple with them, presumably their son and daughter-in-law, who, Helena knew, were staying with them over Easter. One of the cross-bearers, a heavily-built man with thick black eyebrows, whom Helena struggled to identify; then it came to her — Keith Ormondroyd, David's boss, who had come to the funeral. And then another face to whom she could ascribe no name, a young woman in an anorak and dark trousers; it was not until later that Helena realised it was the nurse who had comforted her, the night of David's death.

On an impulse she got out of the car and followed the procession at a little distance to where it regrouped in front of the church. There, a platform had been erected, with microphones, and a couple of clergymen took their places on it. Printed sheets were being distributed, but Helena, reluctant to become involved, kept back and did not take one. She stood and shivered in the cold wind, for, having intended to return quickly, she had not bothered to put on her warm coat. Inwardly she was in the grip of a peculiar kind of argument; one voice — was it David's or someone else's? — telling her that she had no place among these people, and a second voice pointing out that they included several whom she liked and respected, and who showed no signs of eccentricity or over-piety. They were now into some kind of service; most of it was lost to her, the words carried away by the wind. One part, however reached her clearly. It was the account in the Bible of the incident where the disciple Peter, trying to keep warm in the courtyard, is recognised as one of the followers of the Accused, and gives way to panic, swearing brutally at the inquisitive woman who noticed his northern accent. She remembered the story from her Sunday School days, although she had not read it again for many years; then of course, she had shared the general childish condemnation of Peter, but now she found herself appreciating the bewilderment in which he might have found himself, the emotional turmoil into which that night had thrown him. In such circumstances an exhausted man might well say the very opposite of what he truly believed, to avoid having to explain the inexplicable. When you were trying to make sense of a situation in which all you ever hoped for was suddenly destroyed, the last thing you wanted was to be asked embarrassing questions. How much more fortunate she had been herself, in the moment of her desolation, to have an understanding sister who simply put her to bed.

The service drew to its conclusion. Helena was still standing a few yards from her car, lost in thought, when the church clock, striking the hour, brought her back to the present. It was midday, and the family would have been waiting for her for nearly an hour, and the she still had a chicken to roast. She sped back to the car and drove home much faster than she would ever normally have dared.

She arrived at the Feathers half an hour later, extremely embarrassed; but her embarrassment was forgotten when she caught sight of Karen, with Greg's arm round her, their heads close together as if sharing a confidence, while Chris, sitting opposite them, was grinning from ear to ear at something one of them had just said. The awkwardness of the previous evening was manifestly absent.

"Hello, Mum. Where have you been all this time? You've missed at least one glass of sherry."

Greg got up immediately. "What can I get you, Mrs Halstow? Martini, sherry, or would you rather have fruit juice?"

Helena opted for grapefruit juice, and explained why she had had to come in the car.

"I'm awfully sorry. There was a procession going on in town, and I couldn't get out of the square to begin with."

"On Good Friday? What sort of procession?" Karen evidently had some kind of carnival parade in mind.

"It was...people from the churches. They carried three big wooden crosses into the square. And then they had a kind of service in front of the church."

"Good grief," said Karen, "I thought it was only in places like Seville that they did that. Oh, well, you're here now, that's the main thing. I'm glad you've brought the car. I wasn't looking forward to walking back, this wind's freezing."

Chris thought he recalled a similar event in Colmleigh. "Don't you remember Mr Cumber saying he'd seen all these people in the square and wondered what was going on."

Greg said that he had met the Cumbers, whom his father knew, but did not elaborate. The conversation turned to Colmleigh affairs in general. Karen had rarely concerned herself with local news unless it affected her personally, but Greg was well informed and volunteered several pieces of information that interested Helena. There was, for example, a planning application to demolish the former Corn Exchange, a bingo hall for most of Helena's time in Colmleigh, and erect a hypermarket on the site, and the local preservation society were seeking to have it listed. Greg and Karen found this amusing, and Helena had to concede that no one had previously suggested that the old building was of any architectural or historic interest.

"So someone from the Preservation Society came to all the bingo sessions for a week, and all the players were asked to sign a petition. Some of them didn't want to sign, apparently, because they didn't want to let on what they'd been doing with their money. It was mostly married women, of course, and the funny thing was that the ones that were most worried had husbands who'd put more on a couple of horses that they'd spend in a month on bingo. They were scared stiff of being found out."

Helena thought of Marlene Smetters, that assiduous bingo player. She couldn't see Marlene being smitten with fear in such a situation. Still, you never knew what people's home lives were like...

Karen giggled. "You don't bet on horses, do you, Greg?"

"Not likely. I only bet on certainties."

"What would you call a certainty?" Chris challenged him.

Greg responded with a mischievous smile. "Well... For example, you see that old boy by the door, with those other three characters, all talking at the tops of their voices?"

"The one with the handkerchief sticking out of his pocket?"

"That's the one. Well, I would take a bet that any minute now, he's going to get up and say something like 'Well, I'd best be off now, see you later', you know the sort of thing, and walk out."

"How can you know that?" Chris was dubious.

"Did you hear a car hoot outside?"

"Yes. Why?"

"That's the car he came in. I noticed it through the window earlier. You couldn't mistake it, it looks as if it had been patched up with bits from the scrap yard. Someone dropped him off here an hour and a half ago, and now they've come back for him."

The gentleman in question got up, and with a cheery goodbye, shambled out.

"Ah," said Karen. "But that's going by something you know and no one else does. It isn't fair."

"Of course it isn't," Greg agreed. "And you can't do it in racing, or any kind of sport, not without getting involved in something shady, at any rate. But when it comes to finance, well, if you study the markets carefully, there are usually signs that give you a clue as to what's likely to happen. You can get it wrong, of course, and people sometimes do, and then they lose out well and truly. But if you're careful, and don't over-stretch yourself, you can do very well with a little know-how and a lot of patience."

"Provided, of course," Helena added, "that you've got some capital to invest to begin with."

"That helps, of course," Greg admitted with a faintly ironic smile.

It was still chilly when they left the Feathers, as fast-moving grey clouds were beginning to cross the sky.

"Ugh," said Karen. "It looks as if it's going to turn wet again. I'd have liked to show Greg the Manor. Do you think it'll be open today?"

The Manor was an impressive Jacobean house on the western edge of the town. The former home of several Dukes of the county, whose line had finally died out, it was now owned by the National Trust and open to visitors during the summer season. Although not among the foremost of the region's stately homes, it nevertheless housed a number of appealing works of art and some splendid antique furniture and porcelain,. Its official name was Bardstone Hall, but it had been known as 'the Manor' for generations. The original brick building, with its rectangular windows set in stone blocks in the façades, had been extended by the addition of wings in the eighteenth and nineteenth centuries, more or less in the same style, with an odd turret or two, and the result was reasonably harmonious, if a little of the symmetry of the original design had been lost in the process.

"Well, we could go and see after lunch," Helena suggested. "The chicken should be ready soon. Suppose we go back and eat now, and then we'll see what the weather's like."

Although a relatively simple meal, lunch left everyone feeling less inclined to go out to the Manor than to collapse into an armchair and stay there. After half an hour, however, Karen, to Helena's mild surprise, offered to give her mother a rest by washing up, with Greg and Chris assisting by drying and putting away. Karen had never been particularly eager to help with household chores in the past, and Helena wondered whether this was simply a show of willingness aimed primarily at Greg, or whether teenage egotism was beginning to give way to a more mature and less self-centred attitude; a metamorphosis that was capable of producing some startling contradictions while it was in process. Whatever Karen's motivation, Helena took care to manifest a proper gratitude for the favour, which even extended to a cup of coffee afterwards. Chris, while noisily stowing the saucepans, was whistling; not a current pop song, few of which could be whistled, but an unexpectedly recognisable rendering of *Spanish Eyes*, which had been playing over the piped system in the Feathers that morning. It was a good moment, and Helena savoured it.

Another half an hour, and they were out again, in Greg's car this time, turning in at the wide gateway that led from the main road into the drive that formed the approach to the Manor. This was some half a mile long, ending in a gravelled courtyard, which in summer was not available for parking; but visitors so early in the season being few in number, there was no restriction, and Greg was able to pull up almost opposite the main door. Fortunately so, for the clouds had darkened from grey to sooty black, and large drops of rain were spattering the windscreen.

Beside the low wall bounding the courtyard stood a decrepit Hillman, which Karen surveyed with distaste, and which Helena recognised as Jim Sergent's. As they got out, Jim himself came into sight round a corner of the building, with a recalcitrant-looking dog on a lead. The creature was of well above average height, brown and woolly, rather like a smallish Airedale, and visibly extremely muddy. Dogs were not, of course, permitted to enter the house itself, and had to be kept on leads in the formal garden, but at the rear of the house there was a wooded area, stretching away for about half a mile. Once a game reserve, it was now available for general recreation, and popular with children's organisations for picnics and wide games. Evidently Jim had decided that it would be a good place to give his dog an opportunity to roam free for a while.

The animal was clearly not happy at being restrained by the lead once again, and Jim was having to drag it along against its will, with impatient exclamations; but as he caught sight of Helena and greeted her cheerfully, the dog, sensing the change in his tone, bounded forward, almost pulling him off his feet. Two enormous and very dirty paws waved in the region of Helena's waist.

"Get down, will you?" Jim admonished the dog.

"Hello, Jim. I didn't expect to meet you here. And this is the famous dog, is it? I can see he must lead you a bit of a dance."

"Yes, Sit down. *Sit.*"

"What's his name? You've never told me."

"Monty. After Montmorency. You know, the dog in *Three Men in a Boat*. A similar character, though I fancy rather smaller than this one."

Helena gravely introduced her children and Greg.

"We were going to see if the house is open. The season usually begins about Easter, doesn't it? Have you been inside?"

"No. I really came for Monty. He loves those woods. But I wouldn't mind a look round if it is open. I haven't been inside there for a few years now."

Jim steered Monty into the back of his car. "On guard," he instructed the dog, without much conviction. Monty looked sorry for himself, and lay down on the seat with his head on his paws.

"Oh, well," said Jim, "not a lot there worth guarding, anyway."

They trooped into the house, handing the entry fee to an elderly gentleman sitting at a table.

"Thank you very much. I'm glad to see someone coming in. It's been very quiet so far today."

"Early days yet," said Jim. "Wait till the summer."

They toured the house unhurriedly, each finding something to enjoy. Karen admired the fabrics of the short four-poster bed with its velvet canopy, the silver set out on the dinner table. Chris's attention was caught by a superb eighteenth-century German clock. Greg, who occasionally dabbled in antiques, could identify the styles of many of the items of furniture. Helena concentrated on the paintings, mostly portraits of the various Earls and their families, and lingered for a while in the library, examining the former owners' collections. Jim proved knowledgeable on the history of the house, and the region as a whole; he could quote the dates when it served as a rallying point for the King's men during the Civil War, and more prosaically, as a radio station and supplies depot in the Second World War. By astonishing good fortune the house had never been bombed, although it must have been conspicuous from the air; perhaps it had been protected by its proximity to the air force bases.

"I always used think," Jim said, "that it shouldn't be possible to keep places like this in one family. But I've changed my mind about that, because you can often see in the history of a family home a kind of history in miniature of the whole nation. You know, war and peace, poverty and prosperity and the rest of it, side by side."

Greg looked at him with interest. "If you don't mind my saying so, you ought to have been a schoolmaster."

Jim smiled sadly. "I nearly was. It's what I always meant to be. But circumstances didn't permit."

At the door, as they completed the tour, Helena turned to him. "If you're not too busy, would you like to come back and have a cup of tea with us?"

"I say, thank you, that would be a very nice idea. But what about my awful dog?"

"Oh, I'm sure we can accommodate Monty. He'll be no trouble."

"Wait till he's been in your home for a while before you say that," said Jim ominously.

They emerged into a flurry of cold rain that made them gasp and then dash for their cars. Hearing his master approaching, Monty barked and scrabbled at the windows of the Hillman. Jim opened the door to an ecstatic welcome

"Anyone would think I'd been away for a fortnight. Get down, will you," he grumbled.

Jim's Hillman lurched round the corners after the Volvo as it sped back to the house, precipitating the unfortunate dog from one side of the back seat to the other. On arrival, despite Helena's invitation, Jim insisted on leaving Monty in the car.

"For one thing," he explained, "he's used to having the run of my house. I'd rather not risk him doing any damage. And for another, it's one way of making sure I don't outstay my welcome."

Helena made reassuring noises and disappeared into the kitchen, where Karen joined her. Greg politely took up the conversation where they had left off at the Manor.

"You were saying you meant to be a teacher, but something prevented you?"

"Oh, that's ancient history now," Jim replied with some embarrassment.

"It's not that I want to be inquisitive," Greg continued, "but a colleague of mine at work trained as a teacher and then didn't follow it up. He sometimes regrets it now, or says he does. I wondered whether you did."

"Difficult to say. For one thing, I never got as far as training. I was supposed to go to university when I'd done my National Service, but my father had a stroke about that time, and I had to drop the idea and go into the business. He'd got a couple of small stores in North London, nothing very impressive, but quite sound, and he owned them jointly with an old chap who'd started them up in the twenties. He took Dad on when he was demobbed, and when he retired Dad ran the stores on his own for a bit, and then I got roped in. I started off knowing absolutely nothing about business, but Dad had half a dozen permanent staff who knew it all backwards, and I picked it up as I went along."

Helena and Karen had come in with the tea during this latter part of the narrative.

"Do go on," Helena said.

"Well, I found eventually that I needed a business partner. I wanted more time at home and less of a work load. I took on a younger chap I'd known slightly for a couple of years, who said he was looking for a chance to build up a business of his own. Unfortunately for me, it was a bad decision. He seemed keen and well educated, but in fact he was neither. What was worse, he was a gambler. When I first got to know him I thought it was just an occasional punt, he liked to go to the races now and then. I even went with him a couple of times. Then after a bit we seemed to be getting in to trouble with the bank, cheques coming back unpaid, that sort of thing. He always had an answer, but in the end he couldn't cover it up any longer. He'd been drawing money on the store's account, entering it against supplies to be purchased, and betting with it. To be fair, he paid it back, or what he could of it, when he won; but mostly he lost it. Like a fool,

I tried to bail him out, but it wasn't any good, he was really hooked on it. To avoid bankruptcy we sold out to a grocery chain, at a substantial personal loss."

"So what brought you out here?" Greg prompted him. "It must have seemed a bit of a backwater after London."

"Well, I ran into Brian Farrelson, that's our general manager at Danesburgh Cartons, at a pub we stopped at one day. I'd known Brian in my Service days, we'd always got on well, even though we're not much alike, as Helena will tell you. He'd just got started with Danesburgh Cartons — or Phillipson Cartons, as it then was, that was before they moved out. He was looking for an accountant really, but when I told him what I'd been doing he said I'd fit the bill, and frankly, I'd had enough of trying to run my own concern; after my experience, I didn't have much confidence in my own judgment. So I decided to give it a try. I told myself that being in the country would suit my family better, house prices would be lower, and so on. Brenda was a bit doubtful at first, she thought I ought to stay in London because the opportunities were better there. But she got used to it. She never liked it much out in the village, though, she'd much rather have lived in the town. Poor girl, she never saw that wish fulfilled. She never complained, though."

"And your son? He must be grown up. Do you see much of him"

"Not a lot. He took up catering as a career, and now he's under-manager at a restaurant near Northampton — quite a good place, but it means working long hours, and he can't often get away. And then he got married to an Italian girl he'd met at college, and they took her mother to live with them, if you can believe it. I can't stand the woman. Giulietta's all right, that's his wife, but she's under her mother's thumb, and then they're always having her family round for one reason or another. I'm afraid I keep well away."

A reproachful comment rose to Helena's lips, but remained unuttered. She had no doubt that she herself would have endured hours of unengaging company rather than lose contact with her children. She found herself comparing Jim's withdrawn attitude with David's gregariousness. David would have found ways of endearing himself to both the daughter-in-law and her mother. Presumably Jim's son had succeeded in doing so; he must be very different from his father, then.

"Is your son like you?" she enquired, and then felt she should apologise for her inquisitiveness. But Jim was neither offended nor particularly surprised at the question.

"He looks pretty much like me — a bit broader in the shoulders, maybe. In character I suppose he's more like Brenda. He enjoys lots of company, he's good with people. He needs to be, too, in that job. And with that family."

"Yes, I suppose it must take the right sort of person," Helena added vaguely. It sounded as though Jim had been the odd one out in his own home, even before the arrival of the Italian contingent. She really must not pursue that line of thought any further; it would seem as if she had invited Jim to a tea-time interrogation on his background. To curb her curiosity, which she was beginning to find rather alarming, she resorted to offering more tea. This, however, was interpreted by Jim as a polite and oblique indication that the period of his welcome had now run its course.

"No, I really mustn't stay any longer, Mrs Halstow. I've prevailed on your hospitality for too long already. Thank you for the tea, and it's been a pleasure to meet your family."

Greg sprang up to fetch Jim's coat. *Why doesn't Chris think of things like that?* Helena wondered. *Greg must seem more at home here to Jim than my own son does.*

She saw Jim to the door with a friendly "See you Tuesday", and watched him get into the Hillman, where he appeared to be wrestled to the floor by an ecstatic Monty. Finally managing to restore order inside his vehicle, he waved a hand and drove away.

Having closed the door, Helena was making for the kitchen to refill the teapot when Karen's voice reached her clearly from the lounge.

"God, what a wet blanket. I don't envy Mum having to work with him all the time. I hope she doesn't get too friendly with him. He'd be here all the time, looking for a bit of sympathy."

Helena considered this summary judgment with some incredulity. Chris and Greg evidently did not concur.

"I reckon you're a bit hard on him." That was Chris. Greg, having paused to think, then came in more lucidly.

"I suppose he might seem like that to you. But I think he's had a few knocks and they've turned him in on himself. I'm not surprised his business failed, though. He didn't strike me as dynamic enough, he really ought to have been a research man, or an archaeologist or a naturalist, something like that. I doubt whether he'd even have made it as a schoolmaster, he'd have been torn to pieces. He can't even control that dog of his."

"Well, whatever he ought to have been," said Karen firmly, "he's just someone who works at the same place as Mum, so far as I'm concerned, and I don't like to think they see each other outside working hours. He isn't the right sort for Mum, however nice he is."

Helena suddenly realised that this outburst on Karen's part was fuelled less by malice than by a furious compulsion to protect her father's memory. Chris evidently sensed the same thing.

"Hang on, Karen. I don't think there's any question of that. After all, I've been here quite a few weekends since Mum started working, and she's never mentioned him to me before. And so far as I know he hasn't telephoned or anything. You know Mum. She wouldn't take it lightly if she thought he was getting interested in her. She'd worry about it, and go all broody and quiet. She hasn't been like that at all, not that I know of, anyway."

Karen was perceptibly relieved. "Oh, well, perhaps I'm just getting the wrong end of the stick. But you know how I feel about Mum and Dad. And I don't think I'm altogether wrong about Mr Sergent. He sounds as if he hasn't talked to anybody properly for ages, and Mum's awfully good at listening and not saying very much."

Greg's voice, teasing. "I'm not surprised. She must have had plenty of practice with you around." A thump followed, from which Helena deduced that Karen had hit him with a cushion. She clattered the cups and saucers around as she digested what she had heard.

To begin with, the conclusion to which Karen had apparently jumped irritated and embarrassed her. It was as though Karen had brought with her the attitudes and assumptions of her own office colleagues, and applied them to something that really did not go beyond a business association. Compounded with this was a sense of guilt at having eavesdropped, albeit unintentionally, on their conversation; not, she supposed, that they would have been particularly embarrassed themselves to know that she had heard. Gradually, however, she warmed to their esteem, even though Karen's was obviously mingled with a degree of self-interest and no little pride in her father, for whom there could at present be no possible substitute. *If I ever did think of marrying again*, she reflected (and was surprised at catching herself even speculating as to the possibility), *Karen's feelings would have to be treated with the utmost sensitivity.* Then she found herself thinking of Gill, who had been treated with no such delicacy. *Poor Gill; whatever has become of her?* Helena's thoughts took a new turn, but before they could proceed further the door handle turned noisily and Chris appeared.

"Thought I'd see if you needed a hand, Mum. You've been out here for ages."

For the rest of the afternoon, and into the evening, they talked of less profound matters. Chris gave Greg a detailed report on the state of the minibus that was intended to convey him and his friends to Italy in the summer, alarming Helena, who decided that she would have been happier if he had been going in Jim Sergent's car. Chris maintained, however, that the vehicle would be in perfect condition by the end of July.

"We've already started getting the replacement parts. And Phil's got a mate who works in a bodywork repair shop. We'll do all the work, but we'll get it checked professionally before we go. It'll look great, and it'll go like a bomb. You'll see."

"Give me a ring when you come to fix up your insurance," Greg offered. "I've got a contact in a company that specialises in student travel insurance, and I might just be able to get you some discount on the premium."

Chris happily made a note of Greg's office telephone number. Helena noticed that the difference between their ages was far less obvious now than when Greg had first arrived. Even Karen seemed impressed with her brother's enterprising spirit, although she affected an elder sister's air of condescension.

"Watch him, Mum. You'll be finding yourself with an Italian daughter-in-law."

"No way," Chris exclaimed, blushing but not unduly ruffled.

The evening passed comfortably with the aid of an old American comedy film on the television. While Helena was pleased at the way Chris and Greg seemed to have accepted each other, she could have wished for a little more time to observe them together, for Karen and Greg had been invited to a party at the home of one of Greg's numerous family members, situated about half the way back to Colmleigh, and for that reason were not planning to stay the whole weekend, but would stop over at Greg's parents' house until Monday evening. She could not fault Greg's behaviour, and his manners were impeccable; it was simply that she felt she had not had the opportunity to discover much of what lay behind the charming manner. She would almost have liked to confront him somehow with a sudden crisis or provoke a disagreement between him and Karen, but that, of course, was not how one treated a guest.

Saturday was a day of comings and goings, a fragmented day. The weather having improved, Karen decided that she wanted to visit the Danesburgh shops in the morning, and disappeared early, ferried into town by Greg, who returned almost immediately. He and Chris then brought out Helena's car, and chatted equably amid a clatter of tools and revving of the engine. They decided that the wheels needed balancing, and having obtained Helena's consent, Greg drove it to a neighbouring tyre centre; on the way back they put it through a car wash, and then spent some time and energy polishing it. Helena found herself using up much of the morning, which she would have liked to devote to keeping the family together, in cooking, making coffee and doing housework which, she thought rather irritably, could just as well have waited until Karen and Greg had gone. Her irritation evaporated, however, when Karen came in with two large pots of hyacinths.

"You don't seem to have any flowers about the house this year, Mum. When Dad was alive we always did, didn't we?"

Helena embraced her daughter, blinking away an incipient tear.

"They're beautiful, Karen dear. You're right, I really haven't got round to thinking about flowers this spring. To be honest, I don't even know whether there are any bulbs sprouting in the garden. I just haven't looked! Thank you, darling, these are a real tonic."

So after lunch they inspected the gardens, front and back, and indeed there were a dozen daffodils pushing up sturdy green shoots amid a host of less desirable flora in the earliest stages of growth. Parts of the back lawn were waterlogged from the heavy rain of the previous day, and the fences, although not very old, were already showing unmistakeable signs of rot at the bottom; but a concerted effort in a few weeks' time would soon set things to rights. Karen knew little about gardening, and Chris's experience was limited to digging, hoeing and mowing, which he did enthusiastically enough, but without much discrimination. Greg, however, knew someone who had studied horticulture and was hoping eventually to manage, or even own, a garden centre, and promised to pick his brains when they next met.

"Maybe he'd come over for the day?" Chris suggested hopefully.

"I'll ask him," Greg agreed. "Although he's likely to be pretty busy this time of year. Still, there's no harm in asking."

Then Chris suddenly remembered that he needed some stationery for the coming term, and Greg offered to drive him into town; so Helena was left alone with Karen for half an hour.

Karen, as usual, wasted no time in coming to the point.

"Mum, what do you think of Greg? Do you like him?"

"Really, dear, I don't think I know him well enough to say. I can see he's polite, well brought up, considerate, and so on, and he seems to have hit it off with Chris. I'd like a bit more time, though… Are you serious about him, then?"

Karen frowned slightly.

"That's a bit old-fashioned, Mum. I like being with Greg, we have a lot of fun together, but we aren't serious, not like that — at least, I'm not, and I don't think Greg is, either."

"You don't know for certain, then?" Helena asked quietly.

"Well, you can't ever be certain, can you? Not really. And none of my friends want to be serious yet. We just want to enjoy ourselves while we're young."

"That seems natural enough," Helena agreed, although she couldn't help comparing the doubts Karen expressed with the certainty of her own feelings for David at the corresponding stage of their courtship. Yet if Karen were not serious about Greg, why should she have sought Helena's opinion of him? Maybe she was simply being disingenuous, or playing down her feelings as a precaution, in case Greg eventually disappointed her. Karen, she realised, was vulnerable, but also astute enough to realise it. She fervently hoped that Greg was honest; it was the major question she had asked herself, and found herself unable thus far to answer. Not that he had given any cause for suspicion; but she felt he needed to prove himself by something more than good manners and a few offers of assistance, which might or might not be forthcoming.

"Come on, Mum, you're brooding," said Karen. "Come and see what I'm wearing tonight."

So Helena broke away from her reflection to examine the dress, a deep green confection which, without being vulgar, verged on the spectacular.

"This is beautiful, dear," she said, conscious that it was the sort of dress she would never have contemplated wearing herself, even to a party. "Is it the sort of thing the other girls will be wearing?"

"Oh, yes. Well, not exactly the same, but this kind of style. You know Greg's family are well off. His sister gets her clothes made specially by someone up in London. I can't do that, of course, but this is from *Chez Mireille*, you know, the new boutique in Crown Street, oh, no, of course you don't know it, it's only been open a couple of months."

Karen chattered on about Colmleigh, while Helena wondered once again about Greg and his social background, both evidently sources of attraction for her daughter. It was something peculiar to Karen in the family — for all his ambition, David had never been in any way a social climber; he had derived his satisfaction from his work and his achievements, rather than any kind of status. Nor had Helena ever had any social ambition; in her family, pretentiousness had always been put firmly in its place with Presbyterian severity. She felt vaguely uneasy about the kind of life into which Karen seemed to be being drawn; she might hold her own among the students who came to the flat, but Greg's people sounded as if they were a very different matter, older, more sophisticated, and she feared, possibly less scrupulous. She found it difficult to convince herself that Karen would not be somehow at risk.

"Mum, don't look so worried. They're all very nice, normal people." Karen seemed to have read her thoughts.

"Yes. Yes, I'm sure they are… What are you doing for the rest of the weekend?"

"Well, I expect I'll need most of tomorrow to recover from tonight. It'll go on quite late, you see. And then Monday, we're invited to Auntie Claire and Uncle Bernard for the day. You knew that, didn't you?"

Helena had known, and couldn't think why it had slipped her memory. She made a mental note to phone Claire for a chat in the week. Claire was nobody's fool; it would help to know her opinion of Greg.

By the time Karen and Greg climbed into the Volvo, the sky had clouded again, and as they drove away, the first drops of rain spotted the path in the front garden while Helena and Chris were waving goodbye. Helena had made Karen promise to phone her the following afternoon, on pretext of finding out how the party had gone. Greg, courteous as ever, had promised to look after Karen, and had struck exactly the right note when he thanked Helena for her hospitality, complimentary, without being over-effusive. His charm, Helena thought, was truly remarkable; he could become something quite outstanding in whatever he chose to do. It would be as great an asset as David's vitality had been to him. Only, David had had no capacity for dissimulation. *Why don't I trust him?* she asked herself furiously, as the rain began to fall more heavily.

"Come inside, Mum, it's pouring," said Chris.

The house seemed suddenly empty to Helena in the evening. Left alone with her, Chris seemed to revert to his uncommunicative condition, and was inclined to spend the rest of the time stretched half in and half out of an armchair, in front of the television set. Helena watched it too, but distractedly, her mind still full of Karen and Greg, until, by some retrocursive process, they were replaced by the recollection of Jim Sergent and his rarely visited son and daughter-in-law. There was no doubt that Jim's story had left her rather more wary of Greg than she had been at the start of the weekend. It illustrated how adulthood and marriage could draw your children away into an entirely alien world, socially speaking, where you couldn't reach them even if they needed you; but of course, they didn't need you by that time, they loved you, or at least you hoped they still did, but they didn't need you. Almost for the first time, Helena contemplated a home from which both Karen and Chris would be gone, not temporarily for college or a job, but permanently, so that she herself would then always be the visitor. The alien.

Then common sense reasserted itself. It really didn't happen that way; she would make them welcome, they would enjoy coming back to stay with her from time to time, she would get to know their friends, and then, please God, there would be grandchildren, to admire, to spoil a little, to look after when they wanted an evening out. Jim hadn't mentioned whether he had any grandchildren. Strange.

Chris yawned. "Drink, Mum?"

"I'll get it."

Helena made hot chocolate, and then went to bed, leaving Chris watching yet another film, which would continue until well after midnight. She was asleep by the time he reached his room, even though he clattered a little in the kitchen, where he made a point of washing up the mugs.

***

To her surprise, Helena awoke feeling refreshed. A gleam of white on the bedroom door suggested sunshine outside, however vapid; the rain had cleared in the night, although broken clouds still chased one another across the sky on a fresh westerly breeze. Then she heard the bells, and realised which day it was, and she suddenly felt younger, and glad to be waking, and no longer burdened by disappointment at Karen and Greg's departure the previous day. Chris reaped the benefit of her quiet euphoria to the extent of a cup of tea in bed, although it had really been his turn to get up and make it.

"Chris, as it's Easter, I'd rather like to go to church this morning. Would you come with me?"

Chris was surprised, but obliging, as usual.

"Church? Well, OK, why not? If it'll please you, Mum."

So at half past nine they were discreetly seated in a pew half-hidden behind a great grey stone pillar, at the top of which nestled a small loudspeaker. No danger of failing to hear the vicar's sermon, as Chris commented. Although built to accommodate a far greater congregation, the church did not lack for worshippers of all ages, whole families, wide-eyed toddlers cherishing promises of large pieces of Easter egg after the service; elderly ladies in neat felt hats; serious-looking men in suits and ties, farmers in brown and green tweeds; teenagers in jeans, a man in a wheelchair in one of the aisles. The sobriety of the architecture was offset by a wealth of spring flowers, placed with careful artlessness and highlighted by a shaft of sunshine diffused by the great stained-glass window behind the altar.

The choir filed in, singing an anthem that was quite unknown to Helena, who was unfamiliar with church music. As they finished, the vicar stepped from the side to a position in front of the altar rail and declared firmly, "Christ is risen." And the whole congregation, with the exception of Helena and Chris, responded in unison, "He is risen indeed."

Is that usual? I wish I'd been ready for it, Helena thought. Then they were into the first hymn, happily one that both she and Chris remembered from their respective schooldays; and the sense of worship began to come back to her, took hold of her so that she was at ease, conscious of being in the right place, as if God Himself had given her an approving nod. As the service progressed, Chris did his best to follow the responses, thumbing the pages of the Prayer Book in an effort to keep up; but Helena was confident now, and needed no prompting. John Farthing, the curate, read the Gospel lesson; it was, naturally enough, the passage that recounts how a distraught Mary Magdalene was reunited with her Lord, and Helena found herself able to feel something of Mary's delight at the sound of her name affectionately spoken by the hitherto unrecognised Jesus.

Another hymn, and then the vicar began his sermon. And Helena was transfixed as he commenced with the text, *I am the resurrection and the life.*

Immediately the image of the crematorium rose up before her, with the horror of the coffin sliding beyond the curtain. It was so powerful that she turned pale and shuddered. Chris realised what had happened and slipped his arm under hers. She gave a weak smile of gratitude and forced herself to concentrate on the vicar's words; and very slowly the nightmare receded. He spoke of Mary Magdalene, and Helena thought, *yes, Mary loved Jesus and thought she had lost him, but Jesus came back. David won't come back.* And a quiet reply seemed to come from somewhere unidentifiable but close at hand, *Helena. David?* she wondered incredulously, but she knew at once that of course it could not be David. Then perhaps it was a trick of her imagination, an effect of shock. She looked about her; the congregation were following the sermon with varying degrees of attentiveness; a foot or two shifted here and there. Chris was listening too, but she could not make out whether the words were registering with him, or whether he was in a daydream of his own. *I'm being silly*, she thought, *no one here knows my Christian name.*

No one? came again that voiceless reply. *Then why are you here? What are you celebrating?* And the implication struck her just as the vicar was concluding, "We are not paying homage to a martyr. We are not venerating the memory of a great man. We are here to meet someone who is as alive as we are, indeed more so. Christ is risen; he is among us this morning. Thanks be to God."

It was then, as the final; hymn began, that Helena knew without the slightest doubt that she believed, that she had always believed, that she would not again neglect her faith or the responsibilities attached to it. She felt that she needed to know more, to talk, to question, to explore. Who could help? The faces of the people in Friday's procession came to her mind. Rhoda, Josie; she might even approach the vicar himself; or maybe John Farthing, although was he perhaps rather young? The hymn ended, the Benediction followed, and the organ announced the conclusion of the service.

Chris got up and stretched.

"All right, Mum? I thought you were about to pass out in the sermon. Rotten luck the vicar had to pick on that text."

No, Helena thought. *No, it doesn't belong to the funeral any more. Nor do I. I'm free from it.* Aloud, she said, "Yes, dear, it gave me a bit of a turn when I heard it, but I got over it, with your help." *And someone else's*, she added silently to herself.

They shook hands at the door with the vicar, now more clearly identifiable as a tall grey-haired, bespectacled man whose ascetic appearance was softened by a kindly smile. John Farthing, on the other side of the door, recognised Helena.

"Hullo, we've met before, haven't we? I can't quite remember when. Nice to see you again."

"Yes. I came to one of your poverty lunches a few weeks ago. I'm sorry I haven't managed to get to another one. It seems such a good idea."

"Never mind," said the curate, "there's one every week. You're always welcome, any time you can make it. I'm glad you've come this morning, too. Easter is special, isn't it?"

"There is something about it," Helena replied a little guardedly. The church porch didn't seem the best place to discuss matters of consequence, and she was conscious of Chris standing beside her. "This is my son, Chris, by the way, he's staying with me over the weekend. He's at college," she explained.

"Hullo, Chris. You must be coming up to some exams, then?"

" 'Fraid so," Chris replied cheerfully.

"I wish you well. Do you manage to get home most weekends?"

"I have been, but I don't suppose I'll be able to come home so often this term, until the exams are over."

"Well, then, I hope I'll see you again in the summer. And you, Mrs ..?"

"Halstow." *Did I not tell him before, or has he forgotten?*

"...Mrs Halstow, I hope we'll see you again before then, now the winter seems to be over at long last. Let me give you a copy of the parish magazine. That'll tell you what's on this week, and it also lists our various services." He picked up a printed leaflet with a greenish cover and handed it to Helena. "Thank you," she said politely.

"Not at all." The vicar was beckoning to him. "Excuse me."

Helena concluded that she could not talk to John Farthing, not at this stage. He was young and enthusiastic, but it seemed he had yet to learn the skills of listening, of remaining passive until the right moment. *I'll ask Rhoda in for coffee one evening*, she decided.

The rest of the long weekend passed pleasantly and uneventfully. As the weather continued to improve, Helena and Chris donned old trousers and wellington boots and set about tidying the garden a little further, trimming and removing dead growth, pruning undisciplined rose shoots, and turning and weeding out the borders. They bought and planted two or three shrubs, and knocked nails into loose fence palings, dodging indoors whenever a shower threatened. By Monday afternoon both the front and the back garden looked surprisingly respectable.

"If Greg's friend does come over, at least he won't think it's a complete wilderness now," Helena commented as she returned the last of the tools to the garden shed.

Chris left for London after an early tea, promising to work hard (of which Helena had little doubt) and telephone at least once a week. Helena enjoyed the prospect of a short week at the office, and wondered how to spend the following weekend. She had rather built up to the Easter holiday in her mind; now it was over, she had no immediate plans, but a great deal to think about.

***

Karen returned to her flat late the same evening, pleased with the day, and indeed, with the whole weekend. The party had been magnificent, and she was aware that she had attracted considerable admiration, and not a little envy, among her friends. Aunt Claire and Uncle Bernard had made her and Greg very welcome, and Greg had got on very well with them; *is there anyone he doesn't get on well with?* she wondered. He had brought her to the door, and now, after a suitably lingering goodnight, she was composing herself, like her mother, for the week ahead.

She turned the key in the lock and pushed the door open. The light was on in the passage.

I didn't leave that on, did I? she thought, puzzled and a little irritated.

The sound of rock music assailed her ears from the living room, and the unmistakeable aroma of caporal cigarettes hung in the air. As she opened the internal door, she almost fell over a dilapidated hold-all. A familiar, unkempt figure was draped over the sofa with her feet up at one end.

"Hullo, Karen," said Gill.

Karen choked back her instinctive reaction of "Oh, no." She had got used to being the sole occupant of the flat. It had been a convenient retreat for the times when she and Greg had wanted to be alone together. If Gill were back, then presumably, by implication, so were her motley assortment of student friends. The days of peace were gone for good. Then Karen recalled the circumstances in which Gill had left, the state of the flat, the anxiety, and she erupted.

"Gill, for God's sake, where have you been? What the hell happened?"

Gill looked up. Her face was paler than ever, and there were dark patches under her eyes. She looked exhausted, half-starved and deeply worried.

"Karen, please. I'll tell you."

Karen folded her arms and stood like a schoolmistress confronting some wretched first-year junior.

"Well? Come on, then, I'm waiting."

"I've been in Paris."

"*Paris*? My God, Gill, why on earth did you go *there*? And I know international phone calls cost a lot, but they do have a postal service over there, you know."

"But didn't Sarah phone you, then? I told her to make sure you knew."

"No, she did not — whoever Sarah is." Karen relented a little. "Come on, let's have the whole story."

"Well, you remember that weekend you were going to your mother's, and I was going to London, with Francis and Jane."

Karen recalled having heard Gill mention the names once or twice.

"Well," Gill continued, "when I left I was feeling really miserable. You'd gone away, and I'd had a bad mark from the college for one of my essays. And I'd also had a letter from my mother that had upset me — I won't go into that now —, and what with one thing and another, I just wanted to get away for a bit. Then, when I got to London, I met some people I knew a bit. There was Sarah Lottman, she's in rep somewhere, and a man called Derek Hollaton who works for the BBC, and then there was this French air hostess who he'd met and invited to a party once, Joëlle her name is, and we got talking in French. She'd got a flat not far from Orly airport, where she stayed between flights, but she was off to Canada at the end of the following week, and then Martinique, I think it was — anyway, she wasn't going to be there much of the time and she wanted someone to keep an eye on it. She'd just split up with a boyfriend, otherwise he'd have been looking after it for her. Well, Joëlle invited me over. I couldn't believe it, it was too good a chance to miss. And by sheer chance I found I'd already got my passport in my bag. Francis and Jane said, 'Don't bother going back to Colmleigh, you can stay with us until Wednesday'. So on the Monday, I drew some money out, sent Mr Ahmed a cheque for the rent, bought a few clothes and so on, and on Tuesday I met Joëlle and she arranged a cheap flight for me, because she gets a few complimentary tickets for short trips now and then, and we had a meal together. She's very nice, very French, her father's a bank manager in Toulouse and her mother teaches in a primary school there.

"Anyway, on Wednesday, just as we were about to leave, I realised I hadn't phoned you, but I didn't like to ring you at work. I knew Sarah would be at her place, because she was just about to start rehearsals and she was studying her part. I know she's a bit dotty, but I never thought she'd forget to phone you altogether."

"Wait a moment, Gill," said Karen, interrupting her for the first time since the beginning of this narrative, "you say you didn't come back to the flat. Why was it in such a mess when I got home on Sunday night, then? "

Gill looked startled. "Mess? What sort of a mess?"

"Well, it looked as if about twenty people had had a wild party there. Smoke and ash everywhere, empty bottles, sticky door handles. Horrible. I had to open all the windows and leave them like that for hours."

Incomprehension slowly gave way to anger on Gill's face.

"I bet that was Gavin. The *bastard*."

"Who the hell is *Gavin*?"

"He's Hilary's boy friend. Well, one of them. I once lent Hilary a key when she wanted to come here, when we were both going to be away. I bet he found it and made a copy of it. He used to work in the heel bar at Dring and Pusey. He could have easily done it at work."

"You silly fool," said Karen. "Fancy giving someone like Hilary a key. Now we'll have to get Mr Ahmed to change the lock. We'll have to say we lost the key and we're worried someone might have found it and kept it. Anyway, you think this Gavin, or Hilary, might have decided to use the flat for a party?"

"Well, I don't suppose they started out with that idea. I guess they were all at a party somewhere else, and then when that got a bit quiet they thought of coming over to see us…"

"Not the first time that's happened," Karen admitted.

"…and when they found we weren't there…"

"I can just hear Hilary saying, 'Never mind, *I've* got a *key*'. Yes. Well, there's one thing I'll tell you for nothing, it's not going to happen again. I got the shock of my life. And I was scared stiff that someone might have left some pot or something, and I'd get run in for having it in the flat."

"Oh, Karen." Gill looked woebegone. "I'm awfully sorry I've caused you all this trouble."

"You," Karen said sternly, "are a walking disaster area."

Instead of smiling, as Karen had expected, Gill buried her face in her hands. Karen, surprised and already regretting her words, went over to her and put an arm round here.

"It's all right. I'm not half so mad with you now you've given me some idea what happened. Look, I'm starving, and you look as if you could do with something to eat, as well. I'm going to put some soup on, and then we'll go to bed. Episode Two can wait till tomorrow."

***

Both girls overslept the next morning, and Karen hardly had time to speak to Gill before leaving for the office. Greg met her — it had become the usual thing — at lunchtime.

"Greg, Gill's back. She's been in Paris."

"Has she? Lucky Gill."

"Well, I'm not sure she's enjoyed it. She looked awful last night, all pale and hollow-eyed. I'm trying to get the story out of her. Anyway, I'm afraid it means I won't have the flat to myself any more."

"Never mind," said Greg comfortably. "We can always go to my place. Plenty of room there."

"I know that, silly," Karen replied. "But would you mind if I didn't see you tonight? I'm a bit worried about Gill. I've got a feeling she needs somebody about the flat at the moment, and not one of her weird friends. Anyway, I promised to talk to her again this evening."

Greg sighed half-seriously. "So you've decided to be your flatmate's keeper, have you? Think of me when you're having your tête-à-tête. I shall be playing patience in the study, trying to while away the long dark evening."

"Liar," said Karen. "You'll be watching *Dallas* as usual. Tell me what happened tomorrow. I bet I'll miss it."

Her misgivings were justified.. She returned home that afternoon to find Gill distinctly unwell, having presumably made herself one her exotically-spiced concoctions and then been unable to stomach the result. It was a couple of hours before she felt comfortable enough to continue her story.

"Well," she began, "I really felt as if I was escaping from prison. I'd got all sorts of ideas. I'd got a long essay to write for the end of term, a kind of sociological survey, and I thought it would be original to use French subjects instead of English, and then maybe I'd get a better mark. And the I thought if I got half a chance I'd see whether I could trace any of my

French relatives. You know my father used to talk about a cousin he had over there.

"So I met Joëlle at Gatwick and we flew over to Paris, and she took me to the flat when she came off duty. It wasn't bad — quite modern, lounge, kitchen, bedroom and bathroom. It was a bit noisy, because it was right on the main road into Paris. I used to look out and think how romantic, but I suppose it wasn't really all that different from the A3.

"To begin with I hadn't meant to stay for more than a few days, just long enough to get some material together for the essay. Joëlle was going to organise another flight for me to come home when she got back from Martinique.

"I found I could get a bus from near the flat all the way to the Place d'Italie, so I went sightseeing for a couple of days. After that I started getting short of money. Then the heating went wrong at the flat. I thought it might work on a meter, but I never found one, and Joëlle was still away. You remember how cold it was in February, well, it was just as cold in Paris. I'd hardly got any extra clothes. I rang the airline and it turned out Joëlle's shifts had been changed and she'd had to fly out to the Seychelles and wouldn't be back until the beginning of the following week at least.

"By the weekend I was running short of food as well. I'd hardly any money left, and I was stuck there with no way of knowing when Joëlle was coming back or how to keep the place warm. I was afraid a pipe would burst or something and then I'd get the blame. I tried to look for my relatives in the telephone directory, but wherever they are, they're not in Paris."

Gill broke off and shuddered. Evidently her stomach upset had not yet abated.

"Are you all right?" Karen enquired.

"God, I should never have had that chilli. Excuse me, will you?"

It was half an hour before Gill returned, looking paler than ever, if that were possible.

"You poor thing," said Karen sympathetically. "I'll get you a blanket and a glass of water."

"Oh, thanks."

After a further few minutes Gill felt able to resume.

"By the Tuesday I was more or less living on black coffee and Gauloises. Then I went down to the *tabacalerie* for another packet, and I saw a notice saying the owner of the café next door needed some help. His wife had had to go into hospital and he was left short-handed. It was too good a chance to miss. I asked him if he'd take me on, and he hummed and hawed and '*eh ben*'d' about it, saying it was against the employment laws and all that, but in the end he agreed. Six hours a day, twelve till two and seven till eleven, five hundred francs a week and meals provided. I said I'd stay for a month, to give his wife a chance to recuperate, and it was just as well I did, because when Joëlle finally got back it turned out she'd miscalculated, she'd used up all her flight discount and I wouldn't have been able to get home anyway.

"Well, there I was, pouring beer and pastis and handing out French sandwiches, and nearly scalding myself every time I used the espresso machine, but it was great fun really. Joëlle got the heating fixed at the flat, and I was getting free meals. And I was also getting some really stupendous material for my essay. I got the *patron* to tell me about some of his customers when things were quiet. He was a funny old man, he'd argue all evening over nothing sometimes, but he had a soft spot for the British, his father and uncle had both been in the Resistance. I had to hear about Jean Moulin for a whole afternoon.

"The one Sunday he won a bet on the *Tiercé* — that's the races — and it was champagne all round. Everybody came in that day. They brought Madame down on some sort of stretcher and put her on one of the bench-seats so that she could join in the party."

"It all sounds very jolly," said Karen. "I still wish I'd known where you were, though."

"That's not the end of it, though," Gill muttered.

"What do you mean?"

"I... I think I'm pregnant."

Karen stared at her flatmate with something approaching despair.

"*Pregnant*...? Gill, how...?"

"The usual way," said Gill with heavy irony.

"I mean who, then?"

"Well, there were some students who used to come in at lunchtime. They were *surveillants* at the local *lycée*, they had to do that to pay their way through university. You can guess what they were like."

"Yes," said Karen. It was her turn to inflect her voice with irony.

"They used to joke about the *petite Anglaise* at the café. But there was one of them I rather liked. He was called Jean-Philippe, and he was studying archaeology. Well, we got friendly, and when Joëlle was away again I took him back to the flat, because he lived a good way away, and his lodgings were really atrocious. I mean, a room in a real old-fashioned French *pension* with a ghastly stuffy stove in the passage and a really great view of the back of a dry cleaner's in the next street. He didn't tell the others, and I don't believe they ever suspected."

"Gill," Karen breathed, "I never thought even you could be that stupid. Is that what's made you ill today?"

"It might be," Gill admitted.

"If you are... what will you do?"

Gill sighed. "God knows."

"No doubt He does," said Karen. "Have you told anyone else?"

"No, of course not. I mean, I don't even know for certain myself. It's just that I feel so peculiar. Quite apart from this rotten stomach upset. Karen, I'm frightened. And I feel ashamed, but mostly frightened. What have I done?"

Karen was silent for a moment. Then she replied,

"Well, obviously, we'd better not say or do anything until you know for sure, one way or the other. Then — if you're right — you're going to need all the help you can get. No more cooking for you, though. You'll have to put up with plain ordinary decent food — none of this chilli with everything."

A smile flickered across Gill's face for the first time.

"All right, I promise. Thanks, Karen, for not chewing me up over all this. You had a right to. You don't despise me, do you?"

"Course not, you twit," said Karen rather more roughly than she intended. "We're friends, aren't we?" She took both Gill's hands in her own. "And in my family, when we make friends, we stay friends. No matter what."

***

It was not until Thursday morning that Helena was able to catch Rhoda to speak to her. Most of Rhoda's evenings seemed to be booked up for weeks ahead; but when she realised from Helena's face that this was more than a casual invitation to coffee, she contrived to miss a Women's Fellowship committee meeting, not, it must be admitted, without a certain sense of relief. Rhoda did not greatly enjoy committee meetings, and this one had threatened to be particularly tedious. After a few polite preliminaries she asked Helena whether anything was worrying her.

"Well, it's not that, exactly. I mean, I do worry a bit, mostly about the children, but no more than most mothers would... Rhoda, I'm right, aren't I, in thinking that you and Eric are — how can I put it? — The only word I can think of is 'religious'."

Rhoda looked a little startled.

"We're Christians, yes. That may not be exactly what you mean, though."

"I mean you're involved in it, not just pretending, or going to church for — er — social reasons, for example."

"I'll admit to that, yes."

"Well, Chris and I went to church last Sunday. It was the first time in years and years. It was my idea, I suddenly felt I ought to. It was something that's been coming on over the last few months." Helena recounted her experiences, the day of Wesley's accident, the Bible she had found in the study, and finally the Easter morning service.

"And I wanted to talk with someone who was familiar with that sort of thing," she finished. "I couldn't really understand what was happening. I was brought up in a Presbyterian church, but all I can remember now is that there were some terribly long sermons. I was never what you'd call religious, and certainly not since I was married. What do you make of it?"

Rhoda thought for a long few moments

"From what you've told me," she said slowly, "it sounds as if you've had the kind of experience a lot of Christians would give their eye teeth for. I'm amazed that you've managed to be so objective about it; some of the people I know would be on cloud nine. All I can say, and this is only my opinion, of course, is that perhaps God has picked you out for some particular purpose of His own, and He's checking to see whether you're ready for it."

"Ready for it? For what, Rhoda?"

"I can't answer that, Helena. You'll have to ask Him yourself. What I can do, perhaps, is tell you the sort of steps you'll need to take, if you're willing to."

Rhoda outlined, as simply and briefly as she could, the essentials of the Christian faith, while Helena listened intently. When Rhoda paused, she said, "Yes, of course, a lot of that's familiar, but somehow it never seemed relevant before. Thank you for putting it so clearly."

Then she fell silent.

"Is something the matter?" Rhoda asked gently.

"Well... David, my husband, never believed in it. He'd got no time for church, or religion. And yet he was so alive, and so fair, and honourable, and decent... and yes, innocent, in his way. Now he's gone... what's happened to him?"

Rhoda thought again for a moment, and her expression was serious.

"All the evidence suggests that no one who denies God can be united with Him after death, and that seems logical enough. But on the other hand, you can never tell what someone else's relationship with God is at any given moment. And God can do anything, *anything*..."

"Do you really think there's any hope, then?"

"I can't honestly say, Helena. What I do believe is that, if your husband was able and willing to commit himself to Christ, however vaguely (and people do sometimes, you know, when they realise they're close to death), then if you trust Christ as well, you'll see your husband again some day."

"And if not?"

"That's the painful question, and I can only tell you what I believe again. I don't believe the Devil gives prizes for loyalty in this world, so I don't think you'd necessarily be reunited with David even if you chose to refuse God out of loyalty to your husband. And even if you did meet him again..."

"Yes?"

"Well, this is pure speculation, but I'm not even sure that you'd recognise him. You see, I've an idea that just as God can make us perfect in Christ by stripping away all the nasty parts of our human nature, the Devil is only interested in the opposite side. So any natural goodness or niceness we might be fortunate enough to possess would be wasted on him. You might find a very different husband from the man you loved."

Helena's lip trembled and she turned away.

"I'm sorry, Helena. That's a terribly hard thing to say. Please remember it's only my idea, and I may be completely wrong." Rhoda was contrite; but Helena had already recovered herself.

"It's all right, Rhoda. You were right to tell me what you believe, that's what I asked you to do. And it's strange; I loved David dearly, and I don't think I was blind to his faults. But over these months since he died, I seem to have got involved with helping other people and looking after them in a way I never did when he was alive. Of course the children are grown up now… We were happy, but we were altogether bound up in our family life. The whole thing seems different now when I look back. I feel as if I'm finding things out about myself that I never knew before."

"And perhaps one of them," Rhoda suggested, "is that you and God need each other. Well, it's getting late. I'll pop home now and leave you to talk all this over with Him. And I'll do the same. You don't mind if I do that, do you? It's one of the things we do, pray for one another."

"Of course I wouldn't mind. Thank you so much.. You've no idea what a help you've been already."

So the two women went to their respective rooms, and before long each was praying, Rhoda, easily enough, and with some emotion, for she was moved by her neighbour's story; Helena more awkwardly to begin with, hampered by her lack of acquaintance with personal prayer; but as she rediscovered the sense of closeness that had taken hold of her in the church she too felt emboldened, and able to make her act of commitment, not without one final question about David, before, placing the whole thing in God's hands.

"Well, Lord," she finished, "I shall probably spend the rest of my life trying to understand all this, but if You really want me, yes, I'm at Your disposal."

3

SUMMER, 1981

Neither Chris nor Karen returned to Danesburgh for some time.

Karen was trying to keep close to Gill without giving Greg the impression that she was neglecting him. She had kept her word and mentioned Gill only in general terms, although she feared the worst, the more so when she heard her flatmate retching in the bathroom on more than one morning; but she tactfully forbore to disclose that fact to Gill, leaving her to make sure for herself when she was ready.

In Leytonstone, Chris was dutifully spending his days at college and his evenings bent over his books and papers, even though the lengthening hours of daylight tempted him to mount his moped and depart for the countryside or Epping Forest, as he had so often in the early autumn. But he forced himself to remember that it was only until the end of May, there would be plenty of time after then exams; and so he studied on, until the inadequate light from Mrs Byles's sixty-watt bulb made his eyes ache, and he closed them and turned on his radio.

Helena, meanwhile, was profiting from her extra free time, especially at the weekend, to make new acquaintances. Rhoda had a circle of friends who met together in one another's homes on occasional evenings, and she invited Helena to accompany her to the next gathering. They were a very mixed group: a social worker, a buyer from the local department store, a couple of housewives, a canteen assistant from one of the factories. Some of them were even shyer than Helena, but all were friendly. Helena soon realised that, compared with most of them, she was a novice where spiritual matters were concerned, but she used her full ability to listen and absorb what was being said. She was surprised by their fluency when it came to praying; they seemed to treat God as an old, respected but nevertheless familiar friend. Sometimes they were direct to a point that seemed close to irreverence. But if that surprised her, she was even more astonished to find herself joining in with her own contribution, simple though it was, as if she had been going to prayer meetings for years.

Others she met at the church services or the Poverty Lunch, which she took to attending regularly. An utterly new world was opening up to her, one where her reawakened concern for people's needs found its natural place, and where there were sources of patience and love and strength to be drawn on. In those early weeks there were times when she could have sung for joy. Brian Farrelson, at the office, was observant enough to notice.

"Helena, you look as if you've won the pools or something. What have you been up to, over Easter? If you weren't so recently widowed I'd say you were having a romantic fling."

Helena smiled. "It's not that. But I am a lot happier now than I was. Maybe I'll tell you about it one day. Not yet."

She felt unable to discuss her faith with the worldly Brian, and ducked the question.

"Well, don't let it go to your head."

She did, however, tell Josie Barritt, whose reaction was characteristically uninhibited. Josie emitted what could only be described as a whoop of delight.

"Ehhhhh! Praise the Lord. That's the best news I've heard for years. I always thought you must belong to Him, whether you knew it or not. Wait till I tell my mum and dad."

Jim Sergent looked up from his ledgers. "Hello! What's got into you two today? Is it somebody's birthday?"

"In a manner of speaking, Mr Sergent. A *new* birthday," Josie replied with a giggle.

"Oh?" Jim looked puzzled.

Helena, a little embarrassed, tried to explain. "I've become a Christian, a believer. You know, what people sometimes call 'born again'. It was a sort of pun."

"Oh, is that it?" Jim looked gloomy and prepared to revert to his figures.

"You don't approve?"

"I don't either approve or disapprove. If it makes you happy, fine. I'd never begrudge that to anyone. But I'm not a religious person myself, so I can't jump for joy either. Everyone to their own belief, or philosophy, or whatever."

Helena felt a sudden wave of pity. Poor old lonely Jim... 'Lucky Jim', Brian had ironically called him.

"It can make a tremendous difference," she said quietly.

"I don't doubt it. Don't get the wrong idea, I'm not against religion. But after what I've seen of life I can't be anything other than sceptical. Experience shapes the personality."

Helena made a mental note to include Jim in her prayers.

***

Sometime around the second week in May, Karen returned from work to find Gill sitting on the divan, looking despondent.

"I've got the result of my test."

"And... ?"

"Positive."

Karen took a deep breath. She would have to be brutal.

"All right. Now let's start thinking out what to do. Number one, are you going ahead with it, or will you have an abortion?"

Gill stared at her. "My God, Karen... "

"No, it's no good sounding shocked. This is real, Gill, and you can't dream it away. What do you want? Can you cope with a baby?"

"I don't know. I've never tried. There weren't any in my family. I was the only one."

"Then think about it now. It's not just you; you've got to imagine yourself in the baby's place. What sort of life is it going to have?"

"Don't, Karen. I don't like to think about it." Gill was close to tears, but Karen knew she could not afford to spare her.

"Well, you've *got* to think about it. Nobody else can decide. If you decide to have the baby, then there are three choices, one, you bring it up as a one-parent family. Two, you offer it for adoption. Or three — if he's willing and there's a chance it would work — you marry the father.... or find some other man who's willing to take the two of you on. I don't know of any other possibilities. If none of those is going to work, I'd say you'd be better to end the pregnancy."

"No, Karen. The idea makes me feel ill. Besides," Gill found a spark of defiance from somewhere, "Jean-Philippe belongs to a clever family. You never know. This baby might be a *genius*."

If Jean-Philippe's so clever, Karen found herself thinking angrily, *what was he doing getting my flatmate into this sort of trouble?*

Aloud she said, "Well, if that's the way you're thinking, let's go on to the next step. I take it that you and Jean-what's-his-name aren't daft about each other are you? Or you wouldn't have come back, would you?"

"Not really," Gill admitted.

"The why on earth did you let him...?"

Gill contemplated her bare feet gloomily. "I don't really know. I was lonely at night, he couldn't stand the room he was living in... He was a quiet sort of boy, a bit sensitive. The others used to make fun of him. I felt sorry for him, to tell the truth."

There was something revealing about the way Gill said this.

"Gill... you've had an affair before, haven't you? You must have, the way you're talking."

"Yes."

"Here?"

Gill looked away. "Once or twice," she said in a small voice.

Karen said nothing. She needed all her self-control. Fighting back a furious feeling of resentment, she eventually continued,

"Well, never mind that now. If you've had an affair before, why didn't you take more care this time?"

"I left so quickly," said Gill. "I didn't think till I got over there, and then of course I realised I'd left my supply back here. I suppose I thought maybe the cumulative effect would see me through until I got back."

"This is getting worse by the minute." Karen's patience was just about exhausted. "First you use our flat as a love nest, and then you go and get yourself pregnant by some twit of a Frog who all his mates laugh at... have you got any more shock-horror revelations tonight?"

At this Gill broke down into noisy sobs, with heaving shoulders.

"Karen, don't go on at me like that. I know I've been a fool, you don't have to tell me. I deserve it all right."

"Oh, for God's sake," said Karen. "Don't wail like that. I'm only doing this because I'm your friend. It's better that I give you a good telling-off now, before your mother and father start on you."

Gill looked up at her, horrified. "You wouldn't tell them, would you?"

" 'Course not, you twit. You'll have to do that yourself."

"Oh, Karen, I couldn't. They're already fed up with me. It'd be the last straw."

"All the same, you'll have to tell them. And Jean-Philippe as well. It's only fair. To you as much as to him. After all, he's as much to blame as you are."

Gill grimaced. "All right. I'll think about it."

"Don't leave it too long, then. Now, the other thing. I'd like to tell my Mum about all this. You've met her, you know you can rely on her to keep it to herself. How would you feel about that?"

"Oh, all right. Yes. I like your mother, she was so sweet to me at Christmas. You all were. But Karen…"

"What?"

"Don't get her all worried about me, will you? I'd hate that."

***

It was the second prolonged telephone conversation Helena had had that week. The first was with Claire. Helena had been intending to have a talk with her sister, principally about Karen and Greg, but Claire's duties had kept her away from home in the evenings, and the discussion had to be postponed. It was Wednesday before Helena finally caught Claire at home. She wasted no time on preliminaries,

"Claire, you've met Greg now. What do you think?"

"Think? In what sort of way?" Claire deliberately passed the initiative back to Helena. It was an old stratagem of hers. She preferred to hear other people's opinions before offering her own.

"Well, they've been going out together for quite a few weeks now, and they do seem to get on well with each other. Karen says it isn't serious, but I'm not so sure. I think she could very well spring an engagement on me in a while. And I haven't quite got the measure of Greg. I don't really feel as though I know him."

"I know what you mean." Claire's voice was sympathetic. "He was absolutely charming with me; he knew exactly what to say, not a word out of place. The boys were highly impressed with him too. He knew a lot about aircraft and model-making and so on. You couldn't tell what he was thinking, though. I'm not saying he wasn't genuine, it's just that he's obviously well trained in public relations."

"Um... What did Bernard think?"

"I don't really know. He hasn't said much. At a guess I'd say maybe Greg is a bit smooth for his taste. Still, that might suit Karen. She's quite a sophisticated young lady, your daughter — or aspires to be."

"Yes," said Helena thoughtfully. "So what you mean is, you're not sure of Greg?"

"I wouldn't say that, exactly. I don't think he's necessarily untrustworthy, anyway. If he's had any dishonourable intentions, he's had plenty of time to indulge them, down at Colmleigh. But the fact that they've been going out for a couple of months seems to indicate something more than just a passing fancy; and if Karen had thought he wasn't suitable she wouldn't have brought him home to meet you, let alone to me, would she? No, as I say, it's just that you don't get to know him on a short visit. If I knew his family I might be able to give a more reliable opinion, but unfortunately I don't."

Helena sighed. "Oh, well. Thanks anyway, Claire. You've really confirmed my own feelings. Now, the other thing I wanted to tell you..." She went on to give Claire a summary of her recent conversion, as she was now beginning to think of it. Claire listened without a word, but when she replied her delight was audible over the phone.

"Helena, dear, that's absolutely marvellous. I'm completely thrilled." Then, more thoughtfully, and surprising Helena, she went on:

"You know, David was a super person, but when you married him we were afraid we'd lost you, in a way. I'm so glad you've come back."

***

Karen's call came early the following evening. Karen had sent Gill out to the Colmleigh public library, suggesting that she might find the quiet there conducive to the completion of her dissertation, and claiming that she herself wanted to vacuum-clean the whole flat. Gill obliged, perhaps suspecting that Karen was expecting Greg, although both she and Karen knew perfectly well that the library closed at eight. She made her way ungrudgingly to the town centre, dressed in her usual scruffy black jeans, the voluminous jersey having given way to a T-shirt bearing the legend 'University of Oregon' surmounted by a denim jacket, and carrying her file and a couple of paperbacks in a plastic carrier bag.

Karen, meanwhile, wasted no time in briefing her mother on all the troubles that had befallen Gill since her sudden flight in February..

"What do I *do* about her, Mum?" she finished. "I've never known anyone so absolutely chaotic. What do you think?"

Helena's doubts about Greg were shelved for the time being as she found herself involved in this new crisis.

"Oh, the poor child. The poor, silly child. What on earth was she thinking of? She's absolutely determined to go through with it, is she?"

"It seems like it, Mum."

"Well, look, Karen, I know one or two people here now with experience in advising on this sort of situation. And also someone who actually was in a similar kind of situation some years ago. And I think it might do Gill good to be out of your flat again for a bit; too many casual friends in and out, not to mention Greg. It's unsettling for her. And for you."

"You can say that again," said Karen with feeling.

"How do you think Gill would feel about coming here for a while? I can talk things over with her, and I'm sure my friends would too, if she's willing to trust them. Nobody knows her here, and Chris won't be coming home until after the exams, and as you know he's talking about going off to Italy after that. She could finish her study course in peace, and we could try to sort out the future a bit for her and the baby. Not that it would be easy, but we could try."

"Do you mean it, Mum? That would be terrific."

Gill, when the plan was put to her, was initially reluctant.

"I mean, it's awfully sweet of her, but why would your mother want to get involved with my problems?"

"Oh, well, that's Mum, she's like that. Anyway, you're our friend, and as I said before, we stick by our friends, no matter what."

"What about your brother?"

"He's coming up to his exams anyway, so he won't be getting home for a few weeks. Anyway, he wouldn't mind. He's a decent sort, my brother, even if I don't always like to admit it. Nothing worries him."

"And Greg?"

"Greg isn't going to be involved. It's nothing to do with him — not at the moment, anyway. He's going up to Birmingham for some course or other on the weekend, so I'll be free to take you over to Danesburgh. Is it on?"

Gill gave Karen a sweet, serious smile.

"It's on. And thanks. You and your mother are much too good to me, but I promise I'll try to be sensible."

"Yes, please do," said Karen with mock gravity. "For both your sakes."

***

Having issued the invitation, Helena fretted and prayed over it incessantly for the next couple of days. She was sure she had done the right thing, in principle, but all sorts of practical problems now occurred to her — social, medical, even legal; her thoughts reverted to Gill at every quiet moment while she was at work. Not that there were many of those; business was steady enough, but there was a worrying increase in the number of late payments, giving rise to fears of all kinds of disaster, from short-time working to total collapse. About a third of Helena's correspondence now seemed to be with the company's solicitors. Not only that, but one of the drivers had been injured in an accident which, he claimed, had been partially due to the condition of the vehicle he had been driving. This meant further correspondence with the solicitors, and collecting evidence from the maintenance personnel. Helena was almost sure in her own mind that there had been no negligence, and that the driver was pursuing the claim out of malice or cupidity. This belief made her angry, partly with the driver, but more with herself, for she was normally reluctant to impute base motives to anyone. So she was uncharacteristically withdrawn and irritable, by contrast with her euphoria of the previous weeks, and wondered at times whether she had simply been carried away by a tide of sentiment. She admitted as much to Josie at tea-time.

"I'm not surprised," Josie responded. "Everybody's in a state at the moment. You should hear them down on the shop floor, all getting at one another. It gets you down. Somebody said they're thinking of getting rid of the tea trolley and getting a vending machine instead. So I said, 'How would I do as a vending machine, then?'" And she held her arms out stiff with a mug in each hand and made whirring and clicking noises with her tongue. Helena had to smile.

"They'd be very unwise," she said. "You're one of the best incentives to work they've got down there. Anyway, how much working time would they lose, with people going for tea and coffee all the time? Not to mention the quality. I shall tell them it isn't a practical proposition."

Thanks, Mrs Halstow," said Josie. "It's good to know I've got someone on my side. Cheer up. Whatever happens, the Lord doesn't change, and He knows how you feel."

Helena's mood lightened for a moment; but then she began to worry about Josie. If times grew difficult, the management would look to make savings where they could, and to them a tea girl might well seem an unaffordable luxury. What else could Josie do? Another problem, another silent prayer. Then back to Messrs Trubshawe, Earle and Locke. "We look forward to receiving your further instructions as soon as possible." Brian Farrelson's legal dossier grew until the sides split and it had to be taped together.

"All this litigation gives me the pip. Why can't we just get on with what we're here for?" he growled.

Thus, on Friday evening, when Karen was due to arrive with Gill, Helena was close to exhaustion. Her will to carry through her offer to Gill was severely affected by fatigue and uncertainty. How could she help without interfering to an unjustifiable degree? At that point she had no clearer plan than to give Gill a few weeks in a settled home, with regular meals and a sympathetic ear; from there on, she would have to be led by the hand herself.

As always, however, when the girls arrived Helena forgot her weariness and perplexity. For long periods now she was not consciously lonely, but whenever Karen or Chris returned, they seemed to restore to her home a warmth and life that had been lacking during their absence, rather like the power a new battery brings to a dimming torch. Karen and Gill clattered up and down the stairs, in and out of the bedrooms, and once or twice Helena could have imagined herself back in Colmleigh on a spring evening, when the children had friends over with them, and she and David worked together, or talked, or listened to music. *But those days are gone*, she told herself, *you've got to keep looking forward now*. Yet the prospect of company warmed her and eased the strain of the working week.

At some cost to herself (for she would have been pleased to talk late into the evening), Helena insisted on an early night for the girls. Gill was still visibly tired, although not so drawn as Karen had found her back at the flat.

"I've been trying to feed her properly, Mum, but it's a losing battle sometimes. She doesn't seem to have had a square meal for so long that her system won't take it any more. She's been living on snacks and black coffee."

Gill had, however, promised Karen that she would give up smoking. "You don't want this baby to be born with a cigarette in its mouth, do you?" Karen had asked with deliberate crudeness, and Gill had meekly handed over the remaining couple of packs of Gauloises she had brought with her from the duty-free shop at Orly.

Karen too was suffering from a surfeit of late nights and early mornings, and in consequence both girls slept late the next morning and did little all day until the evening. By that time Gill was looking somewhat healthier, and Karen had relaxed and lost most of her asperity. Looking at her daughter, Helena decided that, however boring Karen professed to find it, an occasional day spent doing nothing in particular was distinctly beneficial. She hoped Greg was not setting too fast a pace.

"Now," she said with studied briskness, "let's try to make some plans."

She had reached the conclusion that the whole thing would have to be treated as though it were a business meeting, with an agenda she had prepared in advance. Gill, she recognised, was anything but methodical, and if left to herself was quite likely to do nothing at all, or shoot off in some completely irrelevant direction. Karen's influence on her, though sensible, was limited, as her patience was also likely to be; and she was young herself, with a very active life of her own. It would be unfair to burden her with the responsibility for seeing that Gill behaved in a rational manner. All this had passed through Helena's mind when she had first heard of Gill's predicament; she had prayed over it and seen it as a challenge for her, an opportunity to demonstrate her concern for someone outside her immediate family. Furthermore, she liked the girl, and felt for her; although her own security had never been seriously threatened, she had sufficient imagination to catch glimpses of the heavy seas on which Gill had been adrift for so long, where another parent might have dismissed her as a trollop who deserved whatever befell her.

The first practical steps were simple and obvious enough, doctor, clinic, ante-natal classes, reading, diet and so forth. Next came the question of financial support. It was self-evident that Gill had no clear idea of what she would do when she finished her study course; 'social work, or something like that' was the best she could suggest.

"What sort of qualification does this course give you when you finish?" Helena prompted her.

"Oh some diploma or certificate. But I'm supposed to take an exam as well."

"An exam? When?" Helena was horrified, knowing that Chris was already at the count-down stage.

"Oh, it's in the booklet. I've got it in my bag." Gill disappeared upstairs and returned with a dingy, dog-eared tract which looked at least ten years old.

"Here it is. You can take the exam at any of these centres, Birmingham, Brighton, Cardiff, Exeter..."

"Great," said Karen. "Isn't there somewhere a bit closer to Danesburgh?"

"Just a moment... Peterborough. That isn't too far away, is it?" Gill's grasp of the geography of the United Kingdom was none too firm.

"Far enough. But never mind. When is it?"

"Next month, apparently. It's later than most, thank God."

"Well, then," said Helena. "You'd better get down to work for it. What about books?"

"They're in the car, Mum," Karen said quickly. "I made sure of that. I'm not letting her have a complete holiday here, don't you worry."

The best thing, Helena thought, *is for Gill to sit her examination at Peterborough, if she's well enough, and then later, when and if she gets her diploma, she'll be able to apply for some suitable job as soon as the baby's old enough to be left at a nursery.*

"Meanwhile," she continued, "what other sources of income have you got?"

Gill's parents had both salved their consciences to some degree by giving her a reasonably generous allowance and paying her share of the flat rent.

"If they go on paying it while you're here," said Karen, "that isn't exactly fair on them. And if they stop, it means I've got to pay the whole rent myself, and that isn't exactly fair either. What do we do?"

"They must be told." Helena was emphatic. "I don't mind whether together or separately, or which one first, but they must know. One of the reasons I invited you over here was so that they don't get to hear from someone else first."

Gill's face clouded, assuming the expression of an obstinate small child.

"I can't do that, Mrs Halstow. I've been trying not to think about it for weeks, because I knew I wouldn't have the courage. It's no good."

Karen frowned, but Helena looked mildly at Gill.

"Why not, dear?"

Gill was manifestly close to tears. Helena motioned to Karen. "Could you get us some coffee, dear?"

When Karen had gone out, Helena got up, went over to Gill and put an arm round her.

"It's all right, my dear. If you're not ready, I won't try to force you. It's just that... well, after all, it's their grandchild, isn't it?"

"Grandchild!" Gill muttered. "That wouldn't please my mother. She likes to think she's still my age." She laughed without humour. "Oh, God. Her *grandchild*. Oh, God."

"Now," Helena said reproachfully. "That isn't the best way to think about it, is it? She is your mother." *Honour thy father and thy mother*, she thought. *Even if they behave abominably? Yes, even if they do.*

Gill recovered her composure. "I'm sorry," she explained. "It's just that... well, I learned something I didn't know before, just before I went to France. More than anything else, that was why I went. I'd written to my mother about something, and Dad had been decent and sent me some extra money. I think he'd had a tax rebate or something. I said something quite ordinary, like 'that was kind of him, wasn't it?' and the next thing I knew I got a letter back from her saying he was worse than useless, he'd never suited her, and what was more…" — she gulped hard — "In any case he wasn't my father at all, she'd been six months gone with me when they married, he thought I was his daughter but my mother had already had someone else as well, someone who'd skipped it as soon as he found out I was on the way… So my mother married Dad to give me a surname. And there I'd been all these years thinking he was my father. And to be fair, he always behaved as though he was. I don't know, perhaps my mother never told him; although I think she probably did, that night when I got so drunk, three or four years ago. So you see, things fell apart even more. I just couldn't take it. I had to get away."

Helena took care to conceal her feelings. Her initially angry reaction was tempered by the suspicion that Gill's actions had perhaps been a little more calculated than she was willing to admit.

"Are you sure," she said carefully, that once you arrived in Paris you weren't looking for some way to pay your mother back? It wouldn't be surprising, would it?"

"No!… Well, perhaps, in a way. But most of all I just didn't care what happened then. All I wanted was for someone to need me around for a bit, and Jean-Philippe was there. Poor old JP. His parents would have gone up the wall if they'd known. They thought he was being so good. He showed me one or two of their letters. You'd never think people could be so puritanical."

"We'll come back to Jean-Philippe in a moment. Let's try and sort out the problem about your parents first. At least they ought to know where you are; I mean, supposing they wanted to contact you urgently for any reason."

"They won't." Gill was categorical.

"But you can't be sure of that. Look, why don't you give me their telephone numbers, and I'll ring them and tell them you're with me. Would you be able to speak to them then?"

Gill looked away.

"All right," Helena concluded. "I'll have to do it myself then. I'll do what I can to smooth the way for you later. Now — Jean-Philippe.." Helena gave Gill no time to object. "What do you think his reaction will be?"

"I think he'll be terrified. He'd have no idea how to cope."

He's not the only one, Helena thought, and reproved herself immediately.

"Not now, but later? Is he the sort of boy who'd want to take an interest in his child's upbringing and education — or nationality, even? Would he feel it was his duty to help out financially? Would he come looking for the child? I'm trying to look ahead, to think what might happen, you see."

"Well, he doesn't have any spare money at the moment. And I can't see that he'll ever be wealthy, not as an archaeologist. What do you do with that sort of training, except dig up ruins and give lectures? I think he felt himself it was a bit ridiculous. All his friends were studying engineering or bio-chemistry, that sort of thing, and there he was looking back to ancient history. So no, no money. Anyway, I wouldn't blackmail him or anything like that, he was too nice. I know. I'll write him a letter and send it to him at the café, marked private and personal, or something like that."

As Helena was digesting this the door opened a crack. "Can I come in?" Karen enquired. "The coffee's been made for ages."

After their coffee, Helena sent Gill off to her room to draft her letter to Jean-Philippe.

"How are you getting on, Mum?" Karen stretched her legs out luxuriously on the sofa.

"I hope we're getting somewhere, but she's dreadfully disturbed, you know. Psychologically, I mean."

"Tell me about it," Karen interposed with a smile.

"I just hope she won't take off again on her own. You saw how she reacted when I suggested she ought to tell her parents. I'll have to be careful."

Karen looked more serious.

"Mum, I didn't mean you to get involved like this. All I wanted was some advice. You're doing far more than I intended to ask you. And Gill isn't easy, even though she's sweet in her way. Why are you doing it?"

Helena had expected the question at some point and had even rehearsed her answer, All the same, it did not come fluently.

"Well, dear, I haven't told you before, because I haven't had any time with you to myself. The fact is, I became a Christian a few weeks ago."

"A Christian? I didn't ever think you were Jewish, Mum," Karen said facetiously.

"No, I mean a real one; a committed one, a practising one, if you like. I'm sure God had been saying things to me over the last few months, but it was only at Easter that I really made up my mind. Or gave in, rather. I still don't completely understand it, but it's made all the difference. I feel as if I've got something to give, and the Bible talks about looking after the widows and fatherless. Well, I feel God's looking after me, as a widow, and maybe I can help someone who's fatherless, in a manner of speaking."

"I haven't got a father now either, Mum," Karen reminded her.

"No, dear, but you had him all the years you were growing up, and his influence will always be a part of you. Gill's never had a secure family background."

"Well, Mum, I'm surprised at you, really. If I'd known you'd gone all religious I'd never have told you about Gill. I'd have thought you'd be all stern and moralising."

"Not necessarily," said Helena. "I don't pretend to approve of what Gill's done. But she knows well enough how silly she's been. It's not my place to rub it in. But you never know, I might just be able to repair some of the damage, and I'd find that a worth-while objective."

The expression on Karen's face, during the conversation, had passed from scepticism to curiosity and now verged on awe.

"Mum, you didn't need to get religious. You've always been a saint without trying!"

No, never without trying, Helena thought. *But it's different now, somehow. There's some kind of process going on. Karen's right, it's not exactly that I've changed. I'm the same person as I always was... but I feel as if I'm emerging from something. Maybe that's it.*

***

Gill's letter to Jean-Philippe, when she finally produced it for inspection, was quite remarkable. Helena deciphered it laboriously. She herself could never have written such a letter in English, never mind in French; and no matter how fluent Gill's French might be in conversation, she suspected that a good deal of the text was derived from the pages of some paperback novel from the airport bookshop.

"It's way over the top, Gill," Karen protested, when the translation was complete. "And you're letting him off the hook altogether? Anyone would think he was as innocent as a new-born lamb."

Helena took a less critical line. "If that really expresses the way you feel, then very well. But I wonder whether you ought to be quite so keen to have him come over to see the baby. If he does want to, why not let him take the initiative? Then he'll have to decide whether he's willing to take any share of the responsibility."

Gill considered this.

"All right," she conceded after a moment, "that makes sense. I'll alter what I've said." She held out her hand to take the letter back. "I've thought of something else," she added. "Francis and Jane invited me up for a weekend next month. I'd better tell them I can't go. It's lucky the exam comes about then, it'll look like a good reason. Would you mind if I give them a ring, Mrs Halstow? I'll pay for the call."

"Of course, and there's no need to pay for it."

"Thank you." Gill picked up the receiver and dialled a number, but there was evidently no response.

"They can't be there. Probably at the theatre or somewhere."

"If anyone calls for you at the flat," said Karen, "I'll tell them some story or other to begin with. After that it'll be the summer holidays and most of them won't be around for a while. But I swear if I see Hilary I'll give her the telling-off of a lifetime. If it was her that got into the flat that weekend, that is."

***

Next morning, while Helena went to church, Karen and Gill set out for a stroll across the fields. It was a shimmering late spring morning; the sky was a misty blue-white, the air vibrant with birdsong; the sun had just begun to subdue the emerald brightness which had shone in patches, contrasting with the darker tones of the earth where the seed had yet to sprout, but which persisted in the sprays of buds on the branches of the deciduous trees that marked the limits of the fields and lined the horizon. In little more than a few days, winter had given way to near-summer, with no intermediate stage. The frozen weeks of February were now a scarcely believable memory.

"Damn," said Karen suddenly, interrupting the idyll. "The heel's come off my shoe."

She had not thought to bring any walking shoes, and had come out in an open-toed pair with fairly high heels. One of them had crunched against a large, irregularly shaped flint on the edge of the field, and not surprisingly, had fared the worse in the encounter.

"I'm afraid I shan't be able to walk much further," she apologised. Gill, in her invariable trainers, could have gone on, but she was quite happy to stop. The two girls hauled themselves on to the top of a five-barred gate and took deep breaths.

"That's really done it," Karen said, surveying the wreckage of her shoe. "How far do you think we've come?"

"I don't know, maybe a mile and a half? I'll tell you what, if you can't manage, you put my trainers on and I'll walk back barefoot," Gill suggested.

"Don't be daft, I wouldn't dream of it. Anyway, I'm sure I can walk just as far without my shoes as you can." Karen appreciated the gesture, but she had misgivings about the trainers.

"Well, I'm going to take mine off anyway. It's good for your feet to get some air." Gill tugged off her shoes and rested her feet on one of the lower bars of the gate. She gave a sigh of pleasure and half-closed her eyes.

"Do you know, just this weekend, I've felt for the first time ever that maybe things are going to be all right. Not just the baby, everything. I can't tell you what a difference it makes."

"Well, maybe for the first time in your life somebody's getting you organised properly," Karen suggested.

"Maybe. I know I needed it. Oh, look at that dog. Isn't it lovely?"

A large, woolly, brown dog was making its way along the side of the hedgerow, clearly finding much of interest to investigate on its way. Every few feet, with a snuffle and an energetically wagging tail, it would half-disappear among the hawthorn roots. From a couple of fields away its owner's voice could be heard, indistinctly calling it back.

"I know that dog," said Karen. "It belongs to someone Mum works with. He can't do a thing with it."

"Can't he?" said Gill. What's its name?"

"I can't remember."

Gill slid off the gate and knelt down.

Karen did not particularly approve of Jim Sergent or his dog, and was not anxious to meet them again. But it was too late; Monty had caught scent, sound and sight of the girls and bounded up to them.

"Go away, you horrible beast," Karen began. Gill, however, was enraptured, and transformed. As she spoke to the dog there was suddenly authority in her voice, but also gentleness, and it calmed and sat down in front of her, looking hopefully up at her face. Then it laid its head on her knee and remained still, as though it had just returned home after a long day out.

"Good God," Karen said. "How on earth did you do that?"

"I used to work at a boarding kennels when I was younger," Gill explained. "In the school holidays. I loved it, it was so different from being at home. The owners were really kind to me, but the dogs weren't always good, one or two of them were quite bad-tempered when they first came to the kennels; I picked up some techniques from the people I worked with, and most of all I learned how to win a dog's confidence. It's just a knack, really, once you've sorted out whether there are any physical problems, and what sort of temperament you're dealing with. This dog isn't vicious or even nervous, he's just under-trained. He's a bit like me, he needs organising."

"That's incredible," said Karen, looking at Gill and the dog with new eyes. "Do you know, we met them at the Manor at Easter, that's a big old house that's open to the public, and that dog was all over the place. Mr Sergent came home to tea with us and he had to leave it in the car."

"Is that Mr Sergent?" Gill enquired, nodding towards the lean, untidy and bespectacled figure approaching from about fifty yards away.

"Yes," Karen replied shortly.

"He looks shattered," said Gill, and then, looking at the dog, "What have you done to the poor gentleman, then? You mind you say you're sorry when he catches up with you."

The dog appeared penitent, lowering its head and whimpering slightly.

"No, not to me, you silly dog, to your master," Gill added.

Jim Sergent reached the gate, somewhat out of breath, dressed in clothes nearly as ancient as Gill's, and shod in open-toed sandals.

"Sorry about the dog," he began. "He's very friendly, but I can't always keep up with him." Then he recognised Karen. "Hello! Weather's a bit different from the last time I saw you, isn't it? How are you?"

"Fine, thank you," said Karen politely. "But temporarily held up by a broken heel. Oh, this is my flatmate Gill, from Colmleigh."

Jim shook hands with Gill. "I see you know a bit about dogs. This one's a bit of a scallywag, but quite a good-natured one really."

"I think he's lovely," Gill declared. "Now then... I'm sorry, I don't even know his name."

"Monty."

"Now then, Monty, say you're sorry for running off."

The dog solemnly walked over to Jim and licked his hand.

"I say, how on earth did you get him to do that?" Jim's face was a picture.

"I don't really know, exactly," said Gill. "But I used to work in kennels, and you get used to ordering dogs around. They didn't know you to begin with, of course, so you had to experiment, and after a while you developed a sort of instinct with different dogs. What sort of handling they responded to best. I've had one or two like Monty. They were fine once they'd quietened down a bit."

"Well," said Jim, "I'm very much obliged to you for halting his headlong rush. And (to Karen), you say your shoe's giving you trouble? Perhaps I can return the favour and give you a lift back. My car's over in the lane, by the gateway to the next field but one. It's bit of a walk, but it's not so far as walking all the way home."

Karen hesitated, but Gill decided for her. "That's good of you," she said. "Karen would have found it hard going back across the field, the way we've come. Come on, Karen, don't refuse a good offer."

Karen gave in as graciously as she could, and thus it was that Helena, on her return from church, found the four of them (for there seemed no reason why a reformed Monty should not be admitted), settled in the lounge, with Gill's hand idly scratching the back of the dog's head, which it butted up against her every time she stopped. Karen said little, thinking that she might as well have been back at the flat among the students; but she also had to recognise a note of authority in Jim's conversation that had been totally lacking from that of Gill's associates at Colmleigh, and finished up listening intently in spite of herself.

"You don't mind me asking Mr Sergent in, do you?" she asked Helena. "It seemed only fair, after he'd given us a lift home, when my heel had broken off."

"Not at all," Helena responded vaguely. Her mind was still in church, mulling over John Farthing's sermon. "Have you had some coffee?"

"Yes, of course, Mum."

Jim was naturally invited to stay for lunch, and just as predictably declined politely. As he was about to leave he had an idea.

"I'll make a bargain with you, if you like," he said to Gill. "If you're going to be here for a bit after that exam of yours, how about teaching me how to control this villainous dog of mine, and in return I'll give you a few lessons in basic book-keeping. That's always useful."

Gill had explained her uncertainty about her future career to Jim, although not the real reason for her being there. Frankly, book-keeping did not appeal greatly to her. Still, if it meant the chance of training Monty... and Mr Sergent was not such bad company. She could see no reason not to trust him. If, as seemed inevitable, her condition was becoming visible by that time, she felt he would be neither openly disapproving nor indiscreet.

"Thank you very much," she said gravely. "I think I'd like that. Can Mrs Halstow let you know when the exam's over?"

***

Karen was pleased enough as she returned to the flat that evening. Her mother would keep an eye on Gill, without over-nannying her; and Gill, with the prospect of something to do in the summer, would, with any luck, settle down to study. She herself could resume her courtship without interruption. She had promised to telephone regularly and visit at least once a month.

Helena, by contrast, spent a good hour and a half, that evening after Gill had gone to bed, thinking and praying over her next move. Financially, she could cope. Gill was quite prepared to contribute to Helena's housekeeping costs, and indeed insisted on doing so, as she had at the flat, and although her diet was now rather healthier than it had been, it was still on the frugal side. But Helena felt she could not carry on without the sanction of at least one of Gill's parents, and preferably both. The prospect of approaching them caused her some anxiety coupled with impatience to get it over. She debated whether she should telephone or write, or whether she would need to go over to Colmleigh at some stage. And which parent to contact first? Either would, in all probability, telephone the other immediately. Which way would cause less trouble?

"Well, Lord," she concluded. "Supposing I ask Gill and call whichever parent she suggests, would You be good enough to make sure, if it's the wrong one, that they're not there at the time?" And she had to leave it at that.

Next morning, Gill settled down obediently to her studies, and Helena left for Danesburgh Cartons still trying to make up her mind which of Gill's parents to call first. Gill herself had seemed politely indifferent, as though somehow she was not involved in the matter at all; but at least she no longer actively opposed the idea. Helena tried to imagine herself in Gill's mother's place, but found that well-nigh impossible; then she tried another mental substitution, imagining Karen with an unwanted pregnancy, and found herself immediately apologising inwardly to her daughter; but again she gave up the idea. Karen would have told both her and David, difficult though that might have been; but then, Karen would have taken good care to see that such a situation did not arise. A verse of an old song that a guitar-strumming friend of her student days had sometimes sung came into her mind.

What, O what will mother say,
When I come home in the family way?

And then, sharply appropriate, from what Gill had told her,

*She'll tear her hair and bide her tongue,
For she did the same when she was young.*[2]

It would be the mother, she thought, *who would feel the pain of this re-enactment of one of the less edifying episodes of her own youth. Gill's father might well be exasperated, but from all accounts he sounded the less difficult of the two to approach. Perhaps in the end, however, it would depend on which, if either, had managed to settle down again after the divorce, and neither of them had had a great deal of time to do that.*

Still thinking all this over, Helena climbed the office stairs and prepared for the business of the day. For a while her work was sufficiently absorbing to drive Gill and her situation to the back of her mind; but at the afternoon tea-break she decided to take Josie Barritt into her confidence, without referring to Gill by name, but rather as though she were talking about one of the factory girls, among whom such situations were in any event not entirely unknown.

Josie listened sympathetically. "That's a hard question," she said. "And I don't know the answer, not if it's like you say it is with her parents. When I went wrong my parents didn't stop loving me, or each other. It wasn't easy for them, but they stood by me, praise the Lord, and we all worked it out together. And they're really proud of Wesley now. Do you know, he's already talking about going into the Air Force, like his granddad. And his dad, of course. But that's by the way. This girl's father and mother aren't even together any more, you say? Even then if they don't want to know, there must be something wrong. You don't give up on your own child."

---

[2] *Careless Love* (or *Careless Love Blues*). Traditional. "Although published accounts have cited 1926 as the copyright date,[3] W. C. Handy copyrighted 'Loveless Love' in 1921 under Pace & Handy Music Co." — Wikipedia

"Well, you wouldn't, Josie, and I wouldn't," Helena agreed. "But there's no accounting for what people can and will do. Will you think about it for me, and let me know if you have any ideas?"

"Of course," said Josie happily. "And pray about it, too. The Lord knows the way ahead, even if you and me don't."

***

Returning to the office after lunch one day the same week, Karen happened to meet Susan Cumber in the town centre at Colmleigh. The conversation they had was brief, but Susan felt the urge to ring Helena for a chat that evening, having learned from Karen that her mother would be at work all day.

Having first questioned Helena's wisdom in taking up such a dull occupation, and going into colourful details of her recent easter holiday in the Canaries, Susan was quite easily induced to talk about Gill's parents, whom she and Maurice knew slightly, having various acquaintances in common. Helena prompted her as unobtrusively as possible.

"Well, you know, Dawn — and we always used to say what an inappropriate name she had, because she could never get up in the mornings, at least that's what Carol Swanbourne used to say, you know she was at school with her, at boarding school, I mean — well, Dawn's just divorced and married that photographer, what was his name, Gunton, no, Gunson, that was it. Well, from what I hear, it's not working out too well, but you can't really say, can you, not unless you know them, and I haven't seen them to speak to since it all happened; and Gerald… well, I suppose he ought to have thought he was well rid of her, but they say he moped about it for months, and then this Pauline came along, of course she's a lot younger then Dawn, but by all accounts she practically grabbed him by the collar and marched him to down to the registry office… She must have thought she was on to a good thing, well, that was true in one way, because he was doing very well with that company of his, but really… Well, apparently it's got to the point where whatever she says goes… Maurice told me he's given up holding those late board meetings, everything's got to be done and dusted by half past six, and he's off out somewhere with her… He'll be all right until she decides he's too old for her, I suppose, but you never know, it might go on working... But Dawn, well, I wonder sometimes whether she'll ever find a man that's right for her. Some of us always manage to pick the wrong one, don't we...? No, I don't really mean that, actually I'm quite fond of Maurice. He's improving with age... And of course, you and poor David... There wasn't another couple like you among all the people we knew. But there, I don't want to..."

Helena had heard enough for the moment. She stemmed the flow with difficulty, wondering uncharitably how she and David had managed to remain friends with Maurice and Susan all those years. She and Susan were light years apart in interests and temperament; it must have been David's loyalty to his old Air Force companion. She would have liked to put the receiver down; she had thought she detected a spiteful note in Susan's voice, as though she were giving vent to a long-nursed grudge against anyone whose marriage seemed remotely successful. David would have kept it in check, "Now, then, Susie," he would have said (drawing her fire, for she hated that diminutive of her name). "Let's keep personalities out of the conversation if we can't find something good to say about them." And Susan would have reluctantly complied, recognising his authority.

But in any case, Susan had begun to run out of steam.

"Tell me how your two are getting on. Karen looked so pretty when I saw her... Has she got a steady boyfriend now?"

"Yes, she has," Helena said carefully, "and he seems very nice. Very polite and quite conventional, but with a nice sense of humour." She was surprised to find how much better she liked Greg after listening to Susan. "And Chris is in the middle of his exams at the moment, so I haven't seen him since Easter, but I gather from what he's told me over the phone that he's coping with them all right, and then in the summer he's off to Italy with some friends of his, in a minibus."

"Oh, dear," said Susan. "Doesn't that worry you?"

"Well, I suppose it does a bit, but you can't hold on to them, can you, when they're getting grown up?"

The conversation sputtered on like water from a tap with a defective washer. It had continued for nearly half an hour when Helena finally put the phone down, and she felt mentally exhausted, and in no fit state to make any calls of her own, let alone such important ones as she knew had to be made. But at least a picture of Gill's parents was taking shape in her mind;

the father, genial, shrewd in business but easily led emotionally, besotted with his new wife; and the mother, tense and insecure, uncertain whether her last state might prove worse than her first… small wonder that Gill was so disturbed, and had wanted to escape from her parents' tangled lives. It must have seemed as though the ground, always tending to crumble beneath her feet, had finally split apart, and now there the child was, pregnant and peacefully reading *New Society* in Helena's lounge, with all that buried in the depths of her soul… No, Helena could not take the matter any further that evening. She would make it the principal subject of her prayers, and then the next evening she must act.

***

The next day was Friday, pay day at the factory, which kept Helena and Jim busy in a variety of ways for a great deal of the time, particularly inasmuch as the holiday season was about to begin and there were bonuses to be calculated. The managers were worried, for orders had been declining, and there were always those among the workforce who were less than satisfied with what they earned.

"If this goes on," Brian Farrelson was saying gloomily, "we'll have no option but to cut down somewhere. I hate the idea, but we've got to be realistic."

Jim sighed. "What about that big bill we sent to Evanson's? Any sign of payment yet?"

"Not a thing. It's always the same with that lot — hang on to the cash until the bill's several months old and we're on the point of taking them to court. Then they raise some quibble or other to hold it up a bit longer. I'd blacklist them if I could, but they're out third biggest customer, so where else would we go for that sort of order? And their management doesn't give a tuppenny damn about their workers. I've met one or two of them — real bastards, they are. Professional bastards, I mean, although for all I know they're the same at home. Oh, sorry, Helena, pardon my language. That type always gets my goat."

"Well," said Jim, closing his dossiers, "we're solvent this month, at any rate. It's not every business that can say the same."

Helena returned home that evening feeling as if she were on unsteady ground. The suggestion of financial difficulties at Danesburgh Cartons alarmed her, partly for herself, but more particularly for the wider implications. It would be a serious matter for many of the workers, and for their families; and she knew that Danesburgh Cartons was run as economically as possible, with little room for trimming costs. Other local companies might be even worse affected by the financial climate. Then if the worst happened she could probably have managed without work for a while on her own, but not with Gill to look after. And Chris would be home in a week or two, and would probably be looking for the chance to earn a few pounds before his holiday. Where would he find work? Later in the season there might be some fruit-picking, but at present there was little available. Another thought came to her, she had meant to visit her parents in the summer, but how could she leave Gill for any length of time? By the time she reached her front door, her head was aching.

Gill had prepared the evening meal. Perhaps out of deference to Helena, and also out of regard for her own condition, she had kept to simple ingredients, but there was still a distinctly Continental flavour about the result; her spell of work in the Paris suburban restaurant had evidently left its mark. She was beginning to look much better. The dark patches had disappeared from below her eyes, her hair was clean and combed, and her clothes had been dry cleaned, to their immeasurable benefit. Helena noticed, and it was enough to dispel her anxiety for the time being.

It was also enough to give her the final prompt she needed, when Gill had gone back to her room for a further hour's study, to pick up the telephone receiver and dial the number Gill had given her for her mother.

It was a man's voice that answered. "Colmleigh seven five three double two."

"Good evening," Helena replied politely. "May I speak to Mrs Gunson, please? My name is Helena Halstow."

A barking shout at the other end, in a flat South London accent. "Dawn! There's a Mrs Halstow on the phone for you."

Helena sensed rather than heard the response, "Who?" But Mr Gunson had gone. Helena heard the receive being taken up, then a breathy voice. "Hello?"

Helena began cautiously. "Mrs Gunson? Good evening. I hope I'm not calling at an inconvenient time. I don't think we've met, but my daughter Karen shares a flat with your daughter Gill."

"Oh, yes?" Dawn Gunson's voice betrayed alarm and suspicion, even over the phone. "Is she being a problem, then? It wouldn't surprise me."

Nought out of ten, Helena thought. I've worried her already. I'd better get straight to the point.

"No, it isn't that. I thought I should let you know that she isn't at the flat at the moment, she's staying with me."

"With you?" Alarm turned to incomprehension. "Well, I don't like to seem rude, but would you mind telling me why? What's all this about?"

Here we go.

"Well, for one thing, Karen told me that she wasn't managing to study very well at the flat, because all the students kept coming round there and interrupting her. But there is another reason, and it's a serious one."

Partial enlightenment, followed by resignation.

"Go on, tell me. I can take it."

"She's pregnant, Mrs Gunson."

"Oh, God. Well, I suppose I should have expected it. What does she intend to do about it?"

"She wants to keep the baby."

"Yes," Dawn Gunson said in a distant voice. "Yes, she would."

"When she told Karen about it," Helena continued. "She seemed to be in a desperate state of shock and anxiety. She apparently thought there was no one she could turn to for help, so Karen brought her to me. I'm very happy to do what I can for her, because she's Karen's friend and flatmate, but I'm sure it would be wrong to do anything without letting both you and Gill's father know about it."

"That girl," Dawn Gunson said slowly, "has been nothing but trouble since the day she was born. Somehow or other, whatever I wanted or tried to do, she always managed to put a spoke in the wheel. When she was a baby I wanted to go out to work, but I couldn't get her into a nursery and that kept me at home. Then later on, I had to go out to work to keep her when I could have done without it. She should have done well enough at school to be able to go to university, but she left it too late to start working properly. Now she's twenty. She's grown up, and she still can't sort herself out. She'll get dependent on you if you keep her there, I promise you."

"Not if I can help it," Helena replied. "But you're right that she still needs help, and in particular I think she needs to know whether she can look to you at all for it. I'm not suggesting that it's your duty or anything like that, just asking the question."

"Look, Gill has no financial claims on me, if that's what you mean. Her father pays her share of the rent for the flat and sends her money. That was part of the settlement."

"I see. But I wasn't really thinking about money; more about moral support."

"Moral support?" A short husky laughs. "After what I've been through, I don't think I could offer *moral* support to anyone."

"Well, " said Helena. "I won't go any further. I'm sure you'll need time to think about all this. I know I did. My telephone number is Danesburgh 67035, and I'm usually here in the evenings. If you feel you'd like to talk about Gill again, please feel you can ring me. In the meantime I can assure you that Gill is well and in a much better frame of mind, and I think before long she might very well want to talk to you herself, if you'd give her the chance."

Dawn Gunson's tone suddenly became a little warmer. "Just a moment, Mrs Halstow. I have met you, haven't I? At the school, a few years ago, when the girls were in that play together."

A vague memory stirred in Helena's mind. Gill had had a leading part in the school production of… of… no, she couldn't remember. Karen had been assistant wardrobe mistress, or something of the sort, and Dawn Gunson had come backstage at the end of the final performance, at the same time as Helena, a gaunt, tight-jawed woman with wide brown eyes and vivid red lipstick, ill-concealed freckles and long, straight dark hair under a silk headscarf.

"I believe you're right," she said. "I'm sorry. I'd completely forgotten."

"That's all right. Now I know who you are, I feel better. You must forgive me. It's been a shock, all this, especially when it seemed to be coming from someone I didn't know. It's very good of you to concern yourself with Gill, although I'm quite sure she doesn't deserve it. Let me have a day or two to get over the shock, and then maybe I will talk to you again. It can't have been easy for you either."

Did she mean Gill or David? No, she wouldn't know about David.

"Thank you, Mrs Gunson... ."

"Dawn, why not?"

"...Dawn. I'll look forward to hearing from you again. Oh, just one thing, would you rather speak to Gill's father yourself, or would you rather I did?"

"Well, I don't like to put the responsibility on you, but the fact is that I've hardly had any contact with Gerald since he remarried. Nor wanted to, to be honest. If it's not too much trouble..."

"Not at all," said Helena, concealing a certain weariness. "Thank you again, Dawn, for your time. We'll talk again when you're ready."

"Yes, all right. Goodbye for now."

"Goodbye, Dawn."

Helena felt drained, but not dissatisfied. There was something there to build on. Dawn Gunson had sounded much less of a monster than Gill had seemed to describe. Helena's mind raced on. The first priority now was to speak to Gill's father, before her mother could change her mind about not phoning him.

***

Helena's conversation with Gerald Aubray was much briefer. For a start, the telephone was answered by the new Mrs Aubray, who lost no time in identifying herself.

"Hello. Pauline Aubray speaking. Who's calling, please?"

Helena explained her connection with Gill.

"Well, I don't know if Gerald can come and talk to you at the moment. He's very busy, you know." (*How would I know that?*). "Could he call you back?"

A voice could be heard in the background. "Who is it, Pauline?" Mrs Aubray evidently muffled the mouthpiece with her hand, but her reply was still quite audible. "Some woman who says she's Gill's flatmate's mother. What on earth do you think she wants?"

"I suppose I'd better come." The receiver changed hands. "Good evening. Gerald Aubray here. What can I do for you?" The voice was affable, professional. *Just the way he would speak to a prospective business customer.*

"Good evening, Mr Aubray. As your wife may perhaps have explained, it's about Gill."

"I see. How do you come to know her, if you don't mind my asking?"

Helena went through her recital again. At the end Gerald Aubray's tone remained sympathetic, but dismissive.

"Well, as Gill will no doubt have told you, she has a monthly allowance from me under the terms of the divorce settlement with my first wife. Have you spoken to her, by the way? You have? Well, then, you'll know that she and Gill never really got on. Too much alike perhaps. Poor Gill, silly girl. Well, I'll see what I can do, but please don't let her expect too much. I've taken on a lot of new responsibilities, as she knows. And what about the father? Is he willing to marry her...? Is he fit to marry her? What do you think?"

Odd, Helena thought. *Dawn didn't ask about the father.*

"She's written to him. I don't know. Personally, I doubt it. But I'm fairly sure she's made her mind up, anyway."

"I see. Well, thank you very much for putting me in the picture, and thank you even more for taking her on. She needs a firm hand... something I'm afraid I was never much good at where she was concerned, or Dawn either. Always too busy, I suppose... I'm afraid I can't promise to get in touch very often, but I'll drop her a line. May I have your address...? and telephone number, in case of emergency? Thank you very much, Mrs Halstow. I appreciate what you're doing for my daughter. And... er, I'll do what I can to see that you're not out of pocket by it. Goodbye for now."

When, later on, Gill appeared in an old dressing gown of Karen's, Helena wasted no time.

"I've spoken to both your parents, Gill."

"Oh." Gill looked apprehensive. "How did they seem to you?"

"Well, once the shock had worn off, they were friendly enough. Your mother is phoning me back in a day or two, and your father will be writing. To you, not to me. Next time I hope you'll feel able to talk to them yourself. They were both concerned about you."

"Maybe," Gill said, and the look in her eyes was one Helena had not seen for some time. "But I don't suppose either of them wanted me back on their doorstep, did they?"

To herself, Helena had to admit that Gill was right.

"Never mind," she said. "It's early days yet. At least they both seemed ready to listen, and maybe they'll come half way to you if you'll do the same for them. After all, they're both in new situations. Adults have to adjust too."

"Mrs Halstow… you've adjusted, haven't you? I mean to being here, on your own, in a new place. Karen says you've got over… everything, incredibly well. Why can't my parents?"

The question took Helena by surprise. It was, true, she realised, that now, after only eight or nine months, she now went hours or even days without consciously thinking of David. What, she wondered, would he have made of what she was doing now? He had little time for people who allowed their lives to get into a mess. "Sink or swim," he would say. "They'll never learn to cope if there's always someone there to hold their hand." That was one reason why she had managed so well on her own. He would have expected no less of her. But he would not have contemplated sheltering a troubled girl like Gill; he would have said it was the parents' responsibility, and there was an end of it.

"I'm sorry, Mrs Halstow. I shouldn't have asked."

Gill had taken Helena's silence as an indication of grief.

"No, my dear, it isn't that. I was thinking. There are all sorts of reasons. For one thing, my husband placed great value on self-reliance. For another, I had the benefit of a very close and loving family, and plenty of good advice. Then I was fortunate enough to find a job that kept me occupied and involved with people all day, and I've made some good friends here. But I think most of all it's because I've found a faith."

Gill nodded. "I know. Karen told me about that. It's a funny thing, we used to talk about religion sometimes, you know how students do, and she was always dead against it. But she respects your faith, and I believe she's starting to think maybe there's something in it after all."

"Karen's like her father. He had no time for it," said Helena. "It's sad now for me to think that, but it's true. He was never interested. It makes it rather difficult for me to think about him. On the one hand I loved him dearly, but on the other hand, well, you know the saying, 'There but for the grace of God go I'... I can't quite reconcile the two ideas."

Gill thought for a moment or two.

"I wish I'd had the grace of God," she murmured.

***

After a little more time to reflect, Helena found herself feeling rather less sympathetic towards Gill's parents. A letter duly arrived from Gill's father, addressed to Gill, as promised; she forbore to show it to Helena, but merely commented that it was 'the sort of letter he usually wrote'. There was also a cheque for a hundred pounds, which Gill cashed, and handed the proceeds to Helena 'for safe keeping'. Helena wondered what Mr Aubray had told his new wife, if anything.

Some days passed, however, before Gill's mother phoned back. She asked to speak to Gill, who agreed, albeit somewhat reluctantly. After a quarter of an hour Helena noticed that Gill was becoming distressed. Thinking that some bitterness might have found its way into the conversation, Helena gestured to Gill, enquiring whether she should take over. Gill passed her the receiver, but instead of rushing away upstairs, she stood quietly by, and Helena realised that Dawn Gunson was in tears at the other end of the line.

"Do please excuse me, Mrs Halstow. I don't usually get all weepy on the phone. It's just that... well, Gill's so different now from what I expected her to be. If only she'd had someone like you for a mother... I just felt I'd let her down. I can't pretend I wasn't furious at first when you told me what she'd done, but when I'd had a chance to think about it I realised, how on earth could I blame her, really...? What do you think I ought to do?"

Helena glanced at Gill.

"You could probably do with some time to talk — face to face, I mean. Supposing you came over here after Gill's taken her exams. Could you get away, do you think?"

Gill was nodding.

"Yes, I'm sure I could."

"Well, the exams are a fortnight from now. Which day would suit you best?"

A pause. "Mid-week, I think," Dawn Gunson said. "We're very busy at the weekends. Do you work?"

"I do," Helena replied. "But I am due to take some holiday. How would Wednesday the seventeenth do?"

"Wednesday the seventeenth?" Another pause, presumably while Dawn consulted her diary. "Yes, that day seems to be clear. Now, where exactly are you, and how do I get there?"

Well. Helena thought, this is encouraging. We seem to be working our way towards a reconciliation. Thank God...

No word came from Jean-Philippe, however, and Gill did not mention his name again. Helena wondered once or twice whether she had ever posted her letter to him, but thought it better not to pursue the matter.

***

With Gill's examinations due the following week, Chris arrived home tired but triumphant, having, he felt, done himself justice. Despite the strain of the last few weeks, and what Helena always suspected to be a totally inadequate diet while he was away, he seemed to have grown up further since Easter; the months of independence had given him a self-confidence he had totally lacked a year earlier. He greeted Gill cheerfully, as though it were perfectly normal to find her there; and flushed with anger when he heard that Jean-Philippe remained uncommunicative.

"Rotten Frog. If I had the chance I'd go over there and punch him on the nose."

Helena gave him a reproving look, but thought, *that's exactly what David would have said. Maybe there's a bit of him in Chris after all.* And Chris's next piece of news seemed to confirm it.

"Mum, I hope you don't mind, but I'm only home for the weekend."

Helena's face fell. If Chris was growing more like David he would be better company than ever; and she had missed her son.

"Oh, dear. I was looking forward to having you home until your holiday."

"Well, you see, Mum, I wanted to earn some money first. I know you'd have tried to help, but it wouldn't have been fair. And I've got fixed up with a job."

"Oh... What sort of job?"

"Removals. One of my mates has a friend whose uncle runs a small removal business with another guy. My mate always helps out in the summer, but they needed an extra pair of hands this year. And he's hired an extra van for a couple of weeks. I can't do it for the whole holiday, of course, but I've promised to help out for a month."

"Where is it?"

"Not far from the college. I can get there easily from Mrs Byles's, and she's agreed to let me keep the room on for the summer, and then again next year. I don't know for certain yet that I'll want it again in the autumn, but I haven't told her that yet. I thought I'd better not let it go until I've got somewhere better."

"Oh, well," Helena said resignedly. "I can see your mind's made up. What about weekends?"

"Time and a half on Saturdays, double on Sundays, if the work's available, but the regular chap will probably want to do those. I'll have to let you know each week whether I'm coming home or not."

"All right, dear. I'll just have to make the most of having you while you're here. Supper will be ready in ten minutes."

"Aha." Chris gave that familiar grin. "Is it one of Gill's specials?"

"No," said Helena. "It's one of mine."

***

Chris, therefore, returned to Leytonstone, ready for a month's heavy work before the long-awaited holiday. Almost immediately, it was time to organise Gill's two days in Peterborough. She intended to use some of her father's money to book a room in a small hotel, to avoid the need to travel there and back on both examination days. Although she looked healthier than Helena had ever seen her, travelling was beginning to cause her a little discomfort.

Yet, as always, she needed strict supervision; she would certainly have left without her admission card, and probably also without her sketch plan showing the location of the examination hall, had Helena not been there to make a final check. Helena put her on an afternoon train, having extracted a promise from her to telephone that evening to confirm that she had arrived safely at the hotel, and that she knew where to go in the morning — and at what time she had to be there.

Once she had heard from Gill, Helena decided to pray for a while and then to put the girl and her examinations out of her mind. She felt tired. The office was still under strain, as the recession took a firm hold of local industry. Jobs were seriously threatened now; at one point Helena was asked whether she would be prepared to move her typewriter down to the reception desk and replace the lumpish Diane, who had given in her notice.

"Just until things take a turn for the better," Brian Farrelson explained. "Then we'll take on a new receptionist. You won't have a lot to do while things are so slow, anyway."

In the event, however, the transfer did not materialise. A shop-floor accident made it clear that, while Helena might combine the functions of secretary, receptionist and telephonist, if her first-aid skills were needed elsewhere it would inevitably mean that the reception desk would have to remain unattended for an unforeseeable period, which, as Brian had to acknowledge, was unacceptable. He therefore compromised and engaged a school-leaver, whom Helena soon found herself deputed to train. As it happened, Sharon, the trainee, was the daughter of a church acquaintance of Helena's, which gave her the opportunity to get to know the family better; so the change had its compensations.

The truculent Marlene Smetters, became one of the first real casualties of the slump. Never the most enthusiastic of employees, she had recently received two or three warnings about her late times of arrival in the mornings, for which she habitually produced a variety of ingenious excuses. On learning that, owing to falling demand, she and a handful of other workers from various parts of the factory were to be laid off, she stormed up to the office, demanding a direct talk with the management. Brian Farrelson consented, with some misgivings, and was met by a verbal onslaught that might have made his old sergeant-major flinch.

"You've 'ad it in for me ever since I 'urt my leg that time and 'ad to stay orf work with it... I knew very well I'd be the first ter get the sack as soon as you could find some excuse... Look at all them young girls down there, think of nothing else but boyfriends an' spendin' money and makin' themselves up ter look like tarts... don't know the meaning of an honest day's work, some of 'em... What am I goin' to do now, that's what I'd like ter know? All these years I've 'ad to work ter make ends meet… You've chucked me on the scrap-heap, yer know that, don't yer? I shan't get another job at my age, and me with me 'usband at 'ome with chronic bronchitis… it's not right. I oughter sue this company for unfair dismissal."

"Listen, Mrs Smetters," said Brian patiently when at last she paused for breath. "You're not being dismissed at all, you're being made redundant, along with a few others. I'm sorry it's come to this, and I hate having to do it, but the fact is the work just isn't there at the moment. There'll be some severance pay for all of you, anyway, and a decent reference if you do find something else; and if things pick up again in a few months' time we may be able to think about taking people on again. If that happens, of course, we'll let you know. This is happening all over the country, it's not just you."

The promise of a redundancy payment mollified Marlene Smetters to some extent, and she went downstairs again, still muttering to herself. Brian Farrelson whistled, then, rather unexpectedly, grinned.

"Thank God there's only one Marlene Smetters in our place. In London the works used to be full of old battle-axes like her. Scared the living daylights out of everybody."

"Will she get another job, do you think?" Helena asked.

"Oh, she'll get by. She's already working in the evenings. Straight down to the Fox and Hounds from here, pulling pints till closing time. No wonder she's been getting in late in the mornings."

"I feel sorry," said Helena, "for anyone who has to work that number of hours a day. Is her husband really sick, then?"

"Not too sick to walk down to the betting shop every day, from what I hear." Brian grinned again. "You mustn't get too sentimental over people, like that, you know. They'll take you for a ride if they get half a chance."

"All the same, if he really is ill…"

"He's suffering from the same thing he's had for years. It's called 'lazy-itis'. Believe you me, some of our people are in a far worse state of health than old Fred Smetters. Look at poor old Laszlo, for example."

Helena had to acknowledge the point. Laszlo was a middle-aged Hungarian, a refugee after the 1956 uprising, who looked after the men's overall store. He suffered badly from arthritis, and there were days when he had great difficulty in carrying out his duties; yet he was well known to be unfailingly polite and conscientious. All the same, she felt a kind of obscure sympathy with Marlene Smetters, and would have liked to be able to do something to ensure that her source of income was not abruptly cut off. Brian Farrelson, in the meantime, affected an air of ruthless efficiency which she knew perfectly well was feigned.

"We've got to think of the business as a whole, you see, cut out the dead wood, so to speak. We've always found it necessary from time to time. I remember once in London…" but the telephone rang before he was able to share the memory.

Helena went home at the end of the day feeling thoroughly depressed.

The next day seemed even worse, if that were possible. For one thing, there was already a persistent drizzle when she awoke, as though it were late autumn; the town seemed as grey as the sky above it, and the mood at the factory seemed to match it. No one was inclined to make any attempt to raise the work-rate; on the shop floor the workers gathered in knots of two or three, unwilling to settle to their activities; while, in the office, Brian Farrelson's expression alternated between immense concentration and an uncharacteristic scowl, and Jim Sergent stubbed the cap of his ball-point pen viciously against the top of his desk. Even Josie Barritt was subdued; there was more talk of a vending machine being installed.

Just before midday, Brian received a telephone message. When he put the receiver down his face was grim.

"That's it. That's all we needed."

"What's happened?"

"It's Evanson's. They've called the receivers in. You know what that means, don't you?"

Helena knew. David had had one or two brushes with companies on the brink of insolvency. He had a developed a knack of divining where trouble was likely to arise, and had made a point of keeping clear, no matter how tempting the prospect.

Brian answered his own question. "It means we really are in dead trouble. Properly. It means it will take months to get our money, or even part of it, if they're able to pay their unsecured creditors anything at all. I'd better talk to our bank about it. Look, I'll dictate a letter to the receivers, when we know who they are, and you make photocopies of the outstanding invoices. If we don't waste any time putting in our claim, at least it'll show we mean business."

Half an hour later, Jim Sergent got up and came over to Helena.

"I think I need to get out of here for an hour or so. How about some lunch over at the Rose?"

"That," said Helena, "would certainly brighten up my day. Thank you for suggesting it. I'll be ready in five minutes."

They splashed their way across the sodden gardens under Jim's ancient umbrella, the moist air heightening the scent of the roses above the smell of the wet shrubs. In the town centre it was a grim mid-week market day, with the stall-holders half-heartedly vying with one another to attract the handful of shoppers in the square. Not unexpectedly, the Rose was crowded, but after a few moments a pair of middle-aged, heavily swathed ladies left, and Helena and Jim gratefully took possession of a table by the wall.

"Well," said Jim. "How do you see all this?"

"I'm sorry, all what?" Helena realised that, although polite as ever, Jim had said practically nothing all the way from the factory gate. Evidently he had been preoccupied, and the question had issued from his thoughts.

"Danesburgh Cartons. Evanson's. Redundancies. Cash-flow problems. Brian off to see the bank manager. And so on."

"Not very encouraging," Helena admitted. "Do we owe much to the bank ourselves?"

"Fortunately, no. Not compared with people like Evanson's. That's why they fall so hard when things go wrong. No, thank God, our advisers have been sensible and the bank has always been pretty reasonable. All the same…"

The waitress came to take the order, and Jim had to break off for a moment.

"You were saying," Helena prompted when she had gone.

"All the same, I don't very much like the look of things. We're too dependent on people like Evanson's, and if they go they tend to drag smaller companies like us down with them."

"Do you think we're really in serious trouble, as Brian says?"

"I think Brian sometimes reacts too quickly, and he may be exaggerating a bit. We'll probably survive this particular crisis. But in the longer term, I think we'll need to take a careful look at our market and see if we can pick up a few more contracts with companies in expanding industries, where they exist. And exporters, too. Some of our customers are already reducing their orders because they can't sell their own products. We need to be dealing with those who can. The trouble is that such a lot of local industry is stagnant at present, and we haven't got the resources to send scouts out all over the Midlands and East Anglia looking for new customers. And of course, it's a vicious circle; if we can't sell we can't take on new staff."

Two bowls of soup arrived. Mushroom. "I was hoping for oxtail," said Jim. "Ah, well."

"What do you think will happen, then?"

"I'm afraid that lack of foresight may eventually close us," he went on. "Brian's a very good day-to-day manager, but he's not expected to concern himself with long-term strategy. That's for the board, and I'm afraid they're not very imaginative. Too old and set in their ways. A bit like me, I suppose," he concluded with that familiar sad smile.

"It sounds," Helena commented, "as if you mean to go down with Danesburgh Cartons, if and when it folds, like the captain of a sinking ship. Is that it?"

"If and when," Jim said thoughtfully. "I don't know. I'm not really sure what I'd do. What about you?"

"Well, if there's one thing I've learned in the last year or so, it's not to look ahead further than the end of next week. It's as if the entire world had altered. And I don't suppose I'm that much younger than you, for goodness' sake. So why on earth should you think you're set in your ways? This time next year I might be — we might all be — in a completely different situation."

Jim looked at her, still, gloomy. "Well, I suppose you might be right. Though I can't see it myself at the moment. But then, maybe it's just the weather getting on top of me. It's enough to depress anyone, isn't it? There's no excuse for it this time of year, none at all."

"I don't know," Helena replied. "I felt a bit down this morning, but then I thought of young Gill taking her exam today. I remembered my own university exams, and how I hated having to sit and write when the sun was blazing down outside and I might have been swimming, or walking out in the country, or something. It's far better if the weather's dull and wet, you're much less likely to get distracted. I suppose the same applies to work as well. Let's get the foul weather over in the week, and maybe the sun'll come out and shine for us at the weekend."

Jim smiled with sudden warmth. "Well, well. Who knows? Perhaps it will… If it does," he went on after a moment's pause, "would you consider coming out to my humble abode? I owe you at least a cup of tea. And I have promised Gill the chance to show me how to control that horrible hound of mine."

Helena reflected. "That's kind of you, Jim. I think I'll have to see what my family are up to first. If Chris isn't working he may well decide to descend on me on Friday night, and I've told him he needn't let me know beforehand if it's a last-minute arrangement. I love having him home, of course, but he's trying to raise some money for his holiday, so if there's a job on he's almost certain to stay in London. Karen would phone first if she were thinking of coming over, but she has a very full programme in Colmleigh, so I doubt if we'll see her for a few weeks yet. So I should be able to tell you by Friday evening. Would you like to ring me about, say, half past eight?"

"Half past eight," said Jim. "So shall it be. Well, I suppose we should be getting back." He endeavoured to catch the waitress's eye for the bill. "Now, where did I leave my umbrella?"

Helena stayed late at the office that evening, tidying up a few bits of work which, for one reason or another, had been left on one side earlier in the week. By the time she finished, only she and Brian Farrelson were still there.

"Brian," she said. "Are things really bad?"

Although he looked weary, Brian was beginning to regain some of his usual nonchalance.

"Probably not quite as bad as I thought they were this morning. Sorry if I gave you a fright. I'm afraid people like Evanson's have a bad effect on me. They can't manage their own finances, and then when they run into trouble they take perfectly sound businesses with them. It seems so unfair."

"Jim isn't very optimistic about the company's future."

"Well." The old grin was back. "Jim's never very optimistic about anything, is he?"

***

From the factory Helena drove straight to the station. Gill had intended to catch a train soon after five, which would have left her just enough time to collect her things from the hotel and settle her bill. Helena, however, was none too confident of Gill's ability to read a railway timetable correctly, and was anxious in case she might have boarded the wrong train and found herself bound for King's Cross or Doncaster. When the train arrived and a handful of passengers straggled past her, handing an assortment of tickets to the collector as they passed, there was no sign of Gill, and Helena thought for a moment that her worst fears had been realised; but after a couple of minutes her familiar, untidy figure came into view, hair falling over her eyes and trainers soaked by the day's rain, moving slowly. Her pregnancy was now beginning to show, more so, Helena thought, than when she had seen her off only a couple of days earlier.

"Hello, my dear, welcome back. How has it been?"

"Ghastly," said Gill. "Ugh... I hate exams. You've no idea how good it is to see a friendly face after those horrible invigilators. They seem to sit there and glare at you, trying to put you off."

"Oh, I'm sure they're very nice people really. They're only making sure the rules are strictly observed. You didn't let them put you off too much, though, did you?"

"Well... I managed to finish all the questions, anyway. Thanks to you and Karen keeping me at it for the last few weeks. There were some people who didn't even try, and just walked out. So I suppose I can't have done all that badly."

"I'm sure you haven't," said Helena. "Let's get you home now and you can relax. Have you had a proper meal today?"

"Yes... er, sort of. At the college canteen. It was open for us. I had an egg salad."

"Better than nothing. Still, I expect you can do with something hot this evening, especially after all this rotten weather. You look as if you're soaked through. I'll give you a chance to dry out and get you a meal, and then you can tell me all about it."

Gill smiled gratefully and clambered into the car. Helena stowed her bag on the back seat, not bothering to open the boot, and drove carefully home, with Gill sprawled beside her, about as graceful, Helena couldn't help thinking, as a hurriedly packed rucksack, yet oddly appealing, especially in her absolute lack of guile. *What a contrast to my own daughter.* Even so, Karen still carried traces of the child she had been, and no doubt would do so for years to come. *Maturity*, Helena reflected, *is the grand illusion of youth, the more so because it seems to profit so many people to foster it.* Meanwhile, Gill yawned and stretched as unselfconsciously as a cat as they reached the house.

"Oof! Sorry to be so rude… I'm tired out. I stayed up late, reading through my notes."

"That's always a temptation, isn't it?" Helena replied, pulling up on the drive. "I hope it was worth the lost sleep for you."

"I don't really know that it was," Gill admitted. "Still, it was the last thing in my mind before I went to sleep, and something must have stuck there."

"Maybe you dreamed the answers to the questions, then?" Helena suggested, and at once regretted her facetiousness. But Gill took the question quite seriously.

"No. I dreamed I was on top of a cliff, looking out to sea. The sea was absolutely calm and still, and then all of a sudden the cliff-top started breaking up, and I was trying to jump from one bit of it to another, until in the end I was left on one little patch of ground and I couldn't see any of the others. I lay down to get a firm hold on it, and then I woke up clutching my pillow… Do you think it meant something?"

"I am no interpreter of dreams," Helena said. "I usually put them down to eating the wrong thing late at night. Anyway, it didn't put you off the exam, did it?"

"Oh, no. The rain nearly did, though. I didn't much want to go out. It was a real effort."

"At least you weren't tempted to miss the exam and go off somewhere else."

"No. I suppose it was as entertaining as anything else I could have done today, all things considered," Gill said as she disappeared up the stairs.

Later, after supper, Gill produced the exam papers for Helena to inspect. The questions seemed very technical to Helena, except for one or two which she supposed, perhaps naïvely, that she might have made a reasonable job of answering. She wondered how they might relate to the sort of situations in which she had been involved since her arrival in Danesburgh. However, difficult examinations might be, people were infinitely harder to manage; things rarely remained constant for long. It was a question of trying to ride the waves. Helena had serious doubts as to whether Gill would ever be capable of riding them.

"How soon will you know the results?" she enquired, bringing herself back to more immediate matters.

"I'm not sure. Sometime in August, I think… Would you excuse me now, Mrs Halstow? I'm practically falling asleep."

"Of course, dear, see you in the morning."

Brian Farrelson proved to be right. The collapse of Evanson's did not, after all, cause Danesburgh Cartons to founder, and indeed, by way of encouragement, one or two long outstanding payments arrived from other customers after several reminders. Nevertheless, the episode had its effect on the whole factory, and the consequent uncertainty about the future of the Evanson's contract was a continuing strain on the management. There were rumours that a large and successful company might buy Evanson's and maintain its production lines, endeavouring to make it profitable again by improving its efficiency; but even if that were true, they might well prefer to use their existing suppliers. Brian instructed Jim to calculate the figures without assuming that any part of the sums due under the Evanson's contract would be recovered, and ordered a review of the financial situations of all their other customers. That information was not always easy to obtain, especially in the case of some of the smaller firms. No new orders were to be accepted without a good reference, which did not always go down well with potential buyers; one customer asked whether he was expected to bring his bank manager with him. Yet the company worked on without any further serious problems for the time being.

Chris informed Helena that he would be assisting with a removal to Cheshire, which would require his services for the whole weekend, and that she should not expect to see him until at least the following Friday. He sounded as enthusiastic as usual, but Helena wanted to satisfy herself that he was getting enough to eat.

"What? You're joking, Mum. Removal men work on their stomachs, you know. I'm making up a list of the best lorry drivers' cafés within fifty miles of London. My mate knows them all. He's fantastic."

"What about the evenings?"

"Well, sometimes Mrs Byles fries something up for me. And I've usually got enough money left over for a hamburger or something if she doesn't. Honestly, Mum, there's no need to worry. I'm not starving to death over here, believe me."

Helena told herself that she had to believe him; but she made him promise to come home at least once before he set off for Italy, so that she could see for herself.

Karen also telephoned ostensibly, to enquire, in daughterly fashion, after her mother's health and welfare, and how Gill had coped with her examinations; but there was a partially suppressed excitement in her voice, from which Helena sensed that there was something else.

"Mum, is Chris going to be at home with you this weekend?"

Helena was puzzled. Karen was normally unconcerned with her brother's activities.

"No, not this weekend. He's helping with a long-distance removal. Maybe the following one."

Karen actually sounded disappointed. "Don't you know when he'll definitely be coming, then, Mum?"

"Not for certain. But I've told him to be sure to come and see me before he goes off on holiday, abroad."

"Well, can you let me know when he's going to be over there with you?" There was more than a little eagerness, bordering on anxiety, in Karen's voice.

"Yes, of course, dear. But why?"

"Can't tell you now. Take care, Mum. 'Bye for now."

What's got into Karen? Helena wondered *Oh, well, it sounds as if she's all right, anyway.* And she returned to her current tasks, picking up an old pair of heavy woollen socks belonging to Gill, which had apparently been purchased years earlier from an army surplus store, and which Helena had rashly volunteered to mend.

When Jim Sergent rang on Friday evening to renew his invitation, Helena had half-forgotten it and was rather expecting to hear Karen's voice, although there was really no reason for Karen to ring again so soon.

"Oh, Jim. Hello… No, they won't be coming home this weekend, either of them."

"Would you like to come over tomorrow afternoon, then, say about half past two, and stay until the evening? If the weather's good and Gill's up to it, we could go for a stroll in the forest."

"Well," Helena said cautiously, "she's not as keen on long walks as she was a couple of months ago, but I should think she could manage a mile or two, especially if it's with Monty."

"Hmm. If it's wet, I suppose we could always drive somewhere instead… See you tomorrow, then."

"Yes. Thank you, Jim. See you tomorrow."

Gill looked up from a volume of French poetry she had brought with her.

"Mr Sergent? He's remembered, then? Oh, lovely."

"He suggests that we might take Monty for a walk in the forest, tomorrow afternoon. Could you manage that?"

"Try and stop me," said Gill.

***

Helena was not acquainted with the village of Parham St. John, and had formed her own idea of what it would be like by reference to certain villages in the Colmleigh area, consisting of timbered cottages clustered round a well-kept green, sometimes with a duck pond in the middle, and boasting a tea room and perhaps an antiques shop; the kind of village populated as much by artists, stockbrokers and retired army officers as by agricultural workers; a Home Counties St. Mary Mead, in fact. In this she was entirely mistaken. Parham St. John was totally unprepossessing. A decayed wooden signpost by the roadside announced your arrival at the parish boundary, but it was another half a mile before the first houses came into view, squat red-brick buildings roofed with grey slates and displaying identical Edwardian sash windows, their tops slightly arched; small rear gardens could be glimpsed, mostly set to vegetables, with a chicken-house here and there; by one gate there was a notice advertising home-produced honey. At the village centre there was a T-junction, with a public house, apparently of some antiquity, presumably Jim's local, on one corner, and a post office and general store on the other; at the further end of the settlement stood a ramshackle corrugated iron garage and workshop, where motor repairs were evidently carried out. The steeple of a church could be made out on a promontory a hundred yards away on one side; on the other, out unhedged acres of green cereals stretched all the way to the horizon, where a dimly visible dark stripe suggested the presence of conifers, the edge, Helena supposed, of the forest Jim had mentioned.

"This," Gill declared, "is what the French call *un trou minable*. What a place to live."

Having established, with some relief, that Jim's house did not front on to the main road, Helena reversed into the garage yard and returned to the junction, where she took the side road. Here, as the ground rose, the houses gave way almost immediately to the stone wall surrounding St. John's church, from which the village no doubt derived its name. Behind the church lay the usual scattering of tombstones, many now overgrown and no longer standing fully upright, and backing on to the churchyard, a rather larger house, presumably the vicarage at one time. The walls were rendered white, and a dark line a few inches above ground level suggested that a damp course had been inserted at a relatively recent date. To one side there was prefabricated concrete garage, from which the nose of Jim's Hillman protruded. Having identified the vehicle, Helena drew up on the muddy grass verge in front of the house itself.

The front garden was small, and walled like the churchyard. Although Jim had clearly made some attempt to keep it tidy, the grass patch was interspersed with dandelions, thistles, plantains and other less recognisable weeds. The flower beds held half a dozen spindly rose bushes and a single camellia. The front gate creaked noisily as Helena opened it, and could not be latched on closing. The house itself looked as it had been due for redecoration a couple of years earlier, but the windows were clean, and the brass door knocker recently polished.

Helena knocked. From within there came the sound of furious barking, followed by the thump of a heavy body hurled with considerable force against the inside of the door. The barking continued, nearer at hand. Beyond it, and almost drowned by it, came Jim's voice. "Monty! Come in here, now." There followed a scuffling noise, as Monty was presumably dragged away from the door by his master, and an inner door slammed shut on him. The front door then opened, and Jim stood there in the same open-necked shirt and corduroy trousers he had worn when Gill had first met him.

"Glad you could come. Sorry about the dog; he always seems to get to the door before I can. Do come in," he said eventually. "Don't worry. I've shut him up now until you're ready for him."

He showed Helena and Gill into what must once have been the vicar's parlour, a rectangular room with a high ceiling adorned with Edwardian mouldings, a tiled open fireplace, and in the alcoves on either side of it, bookshelves encased in glass or covered by faded chintz curtains. A somewhat ring-marked walnut gate-leg table stood by the window, with a high-backed chair on either side. A round-faced wooden clock ticked busily on the mantelpiece, and beside it there smiled, from an old-fashioned frame consisting of two small sheets of glass wedged into a dark wooden frame, the photograph of a fair-haired woman. It was, Helena thought, an attractive smile. Jim saw her looking at it.

"That's Brenda," he explained. "As I like to remember her, before she was ill. I must have taken that photograph, what? Ten years ago now. It's been my favourite ever since."

"Have you any more?" Helena asked politely.

"I've got a couple of albums in the study. Getting a bit dusty, I'm afraid. I don't often get them out. But you won't want to see those, I'm sure. Nothing more tedious than people who want to show you their family albums."

"Not at all," Helena assured him. "It always interests me to see a few photographs. I think it helps you to understand people better if you can see a few glimpses of their background."

"Really? Oh, well, perhaps later on. Suppose we go for a stroll now, and then we'll come back and have some tea in a couple of hours?

Otherwise, I'm afraid Monty will inflict some damage on the furniture. He hates being shut in there."

He collected an uncompromising-looking lead and went to the kitchen. Gill gave Helena an impatient look.

"It really isn't necessary, you know, shutting him in like that. It'll only wind him up."

Certainly the few minutes' confinement had done nothing to reduce the dog's excitement. He appeared first from the kitchen, nearly pulling Jim over, and made straight for the door. But Gill called his name once, and recognising her voice after a moment's puzzlement, quietened and sat longingly on the doormat, tail wagging hopefully.

"I say. How on earth do you do it?" Jim exclaimed, not for the first time.

"It's not all that difficult. I'll show you."

Jim led the way out to the road. For about half a mile they walked between the wheat fields; Then they reached the edge of a forest, fenced off with posts and wire. A stile offered access, and Jim courteously, assisted Helena, who really needed no help, and Gill, who scrambled over it rather more awkwardly.

"Now," said Jim. "If I were to let him go here, in the usual way you wouldn't see him again for half an hour. What should I do?"

"Well," Gill replied, "is he likely to do any damage?"

"Damage?"

"I mean, is there any game in here, for example?"

"Shouldn't think so. I've never heard anyone shooting around here, and so far as I know the land belongs to the National Trust, anyway. That means lots of people tramping all over it, especially at weekends. Not good for game birds."

"What about people, or other dogs?"

"No. he makes a lot of noise, but I don't think he'd ever go for anyone, and he's never been inclined to fight. He'll just galumph about in the undergrowth and try to catch any squirrels he sees."

"I should let him go, then," Gill concluded. "And let him work off some of his energy. When he's calmed down a bit I'll see what I can do."

They followed the forest path in a broad circle, stopping here and there in an open space, and allowing Gill to take occasional rests, seating herself on a stump or a fallen tree trunk. For the first few minutes Monty kept racing past them in one direction or another; then he disappeared from view for a longer spell, although he could frequently be heard nearby, crashing about amid the ferns. Gill plied Jim with questions about the dog's age, his parentage and habits. Helena was astonished that the girl who had so recently seemed adrift and bewildered could now be so methodical and purposeful. Karen would hardly have recognised her. Could she possibly adapt that sort of expertise to working with people? But people were so much more complicated and demanding than dogs. Helena thought again of the questions in Gill's examination paper; they seemed to have little to do with techniques for dealing with behaviour problems, techniques such as Gill was now demonstrating in subduing Monty. *I'll talk it over with her later*, Helena decided. *It's a sure thing she's never thought in a sensible way about her future; she's spent too much time dreaming, and those student friends of hers haven't helped... Nor have her parents*, which reminded her that Dawn Gunson would be coming to see her daughter shortly, and some preparation must be made for that.

The dog had by now tired sufficiently to be content to trot by Gill's side, and when they reached a clearing she began to outline the way Jim should start training him. From her jeans pocket she produced a small bag of chocolate drops, which were now rather sticky.

"Does he like these?"

"Does he not! If I get these at home for him he goes mad until I give them to him. I've known him to pull the drawer out of the table trying to get at them."

"Well, do you think we might start by getting him to sit? If you'd keep those chocolate drops hidden for the moment. Downwind of him, or he'll smell them straightaway."

The first lesson in the training of Monty was not an immediate success. The dog appeared to be oblivious of what was required of him; either that, or he made up his mind not to cooperate with the peculiar whims, quite out of character, now being indulged by his master. The process was not assisted by the fact that he became aware of the chocolate drops rather earlier than Gill had intended, and much time was wasted in pushing his nose away from Jim's or Gill's pockets. For Helena it was an amusing half hour, but she closely observed Gill's way with the dog, and her patience in endeavouring to impart some of it to Jim, who showed not the slightest embarrassment or irritation at having to learn from so young an instructress. *He is nice,* Helena thought, *but no man ought to be quite so self-deprecating. Although maybe, if he learns to be a real master to the dog, it'll help him to start believing in himself again.*

At length, Jim found he was able to persuade Monty to sit without the stimulus of a sharp tap towards his rear end.

"Now you have to tell him know how well he's done," Gill explained. "And repeat that every time he obeys your command."

"What happens when I run out of chocolate drops?" Jim enquired dubiously.

"Well, by that time I hope you'll have impressed your authority on him, at least about sitting."

Monty wolfed the last of the chocolate drops and departed in earnest pursuit of a rabbit that was ill advised enough to cross their path, about twenty yards ahead.

***

Back at the old vicarage, Jim produced a tea of sorts, evidently prepared beforehand, and consisting mostly of slices of cold chicken and ham, lettuce, tomatoes and wholemeal bread, the last item having been baked by a neighbour's wife who had been friendly with Brenda and seen it as her duty to provide occasional help of that kind. It was something between a solitary man's meal and a guest's; Jim had clearly enlarged, rather than elaborated on his usual sort of afternoon tea, so that there was plenty of food but no sense of occasion. "I hope this is acceptable," he remarked.

"It's delightful," Helena assured him, and Gill nodded enthusiastically. "Have you ever tried..." she began, but caught Helena's eye and left the question unfinished.

"Do go on," said Jim. "Although, I'm afraid I'm not very adventurous where food's concerned. I've tried Italian food once or twice when I've been to visit my son, but I can't say I get on very well with it."

Helena's reply was slipped in smoothly enough to forestall the recital of some recipe by Gill. "Have you heard from your son lately?"

"I have, as a matter of fact. He's doing very well, and thinking of setting up a restaurant of his own. At the moment, he's going into the financial implications. He's quite excited about it. I just hope it won't be a big mistake for him," Jim finished with a shrug of his shoulders.

"Mistake? Well, why should it be?"

"Because," Jim explained, "I think people often try that sort of thing without doing enough market research. I've known restaurants to close down within a year, simply because the owners hadn't considered carefully enough where to site it, who their customers would be, what they might like and what they could afford. Still, he's got his head screwed on — and so has that wife of his, I'll say that for her. And they'll both work themselves into the ground if they have to, so there's a reasonable chance they'll make a go of it."

"Do they have any particular location in mind?"

"Not at present. But they're looking in the trade journals to see what's available. I'll no doubt hear when they come to a decision. If they do."

After tea, Monty was admitted to the room again, and immediately draped himself over Gill's knees and the chintz-covered arms of the chair she sat in.

"Oh, dear," said Jim. "Is that all right?"

"It's all right," said Gill. "Unless my legs go to sleep, then I'd have to move him. But he'll get down if I tell him to. Won't you, Monty?" The dog gave her an adoring look.

Jim went and found the photograph albums, and he and Helena leaned over the table to look at them.

"Our wedding."

The photographs were very conventional, as Helena would have expected, a greyish urban church with a high porch, set back only a few yards from the street. Jim and Brenda in formal pose, with parents and relatives. Various groups. Only one bridesmaid.

"That's Brenda's younger sister. Teaches children with educational problems in London. She writes now and again."

Jim went through the photographs as though they represented another world. Helena suddenly remembered the night after David's funeral, when, in quest of emotional release, she had forced herself to study her own wedding photographs.

"Is this painful for you?" she asked quietly.

"No, not really. Not any more. I've come to terms with it all. Brenda's dead, Stuart's grown up and moved away…"

"But you've stayed here in the village. Isn't it lonely for you?"

"Well… I've got Monty. And if I'm honest, I like the quiet here."

More photographs. Brenda as a young mother, with the baby Stuart in her arms. Holiday snaps, taken in Cornwall, by the look of them. Brenda again, in costume for some dramatic production, or maybe an opera.

"She always loved that sort of thing."

How could Brenda have endured a move from a London suburb to this backwater? What could she have found to do all day? And with Jim bringing his work home in the evenings…

"She must have found this a tremendous change."

"Yes, she did," Jim responded gloomily. "When we moved out from London we were really in dire straits. We could only afford to live out in the village. We always intended to move into Danesburgh when things got better, but somehow… it never happened. Still, it doesn't matter much now."

Gill broke a slightly uneasy silence. "Er… would you like me to wash up for you, Mr Sergent? I promise I won't break anything."

"I wouldn't dream of it," Jim replied. "I don't expect guests to do that sort of chore for me, and especially not after you've already expended a lot of patience and energy training my dog. I'll do it later on. There's not a lot of it. But thank you very much for the offer, all the same."

"Couldn't we both lend a hand?" Helena volunteered. "It'd be done in no time."

Jim gave in, a little grudgingly. "Well… I'm afraid you won't find my kitchen up to your standards."

The kitchen, indeed, could have changed little over the last thirty years, save perhaps for the installation of a fluorescent tube. The walls were covered up to half height in heavy black and white tiles, above which they were painted pale blue, flaking in places and much faded. The floor was quarry-tiled, with an elderly blue plastic mat placed approximately in the middle. The sink was of ancient vitreous chinaware with equally ancient brass taps, and the cooker must have been one of the earliest post-war models. A drying-line frame was suspended by hooks from the ceiling, and in one corner there was an old heating stove, its chimney disappearing through the yellowing plasterboard above. A door at the far end proved to lead to a food cupboard, aerated simply by a grille in a window above the top shelf. Helena looked down, half expecting to find a meat safe, but the floor space was in fact occupied by a small refrigerator connected to a power socket of relatively recent installation.

Helena and Gill looked at each other, sharing one unspoken thought, *Poor Brenda*. Jim seemed to be the least unfeeling of men, yet this house appeared to verge on cruelty.

Jim caught their glance. "Not much of a kitchen, is it? Thirty or forty years out of date. Mind you, it's all in working order; better than some of these modern gadgets, I sometimes think. But there's no doubt that it's hard work."

"Couldn't you get it refitted?" Gill ventured.

"I suppose I could, but it hardly seems worth it. After all, I don't exactly live in the kitchen. And in an odd sort of way it's one of the attractions of the place that it hasn't been modernised. I get home in the evenings and it's as if nothing's changed since I was a young man, full of hopes and aspirations. Silly, but there it is, I like trying to live in the past."

He might as well be seventy-five instead of fifty-five, Helena thought, and decided that something really must be done about Jim. She looked about her as they returned to the sitting room. The carved hat rack in the hall, the plaster ceiling mouldings, the ancient sideboard and fender; all authentic relics of the early post-war years, or possibly earlier still. She could dimly remember the homes of one or two of her primary-school friends, which had resembled Jim's, in the condition it must have been in at that time. There was, she realised, no television set, only an old-fashioned radiogram.

"What do you find to do in the evenings?" she enquired brightly as they sat down again.

"Well, I'm usually out with Monty for at least an hour. Then on the way back I have a quick one at the Plough, next door, and that doesn't leave a lot of the evening."

"But when your wife was alive?"

"Oh, we used to read a lot, listen to the radio, records and so on. And Brenda used to make things. She was clever with her hands, which I never was, unfortunately. Look. This is one of her little ornaments."

It was a minute donkey, improbably but exquisitely fashioned from what looked like some old scraps of grey flannel stitched over a fragile wire frame, is head bowed as though consenting to some burden to be placed on its back, and its tail lightly curving to ward off a molesting fly.

"That's incredible," Gill exclaimed, delicately examining the donkey. "You could make a fortune out of this kind of thing, these days. Didn't she ever really use her skills?"

"Not really. She made some of Stuart's toys, of course, when he was little. And she used to sell a few bits and pieces at the Women's Institute stall, at the market in Danesburgh, sometimes. But it was for her own pleasure mostly. She used to start out with the idea of using up old bits of material to save throwing them away, and she came up with all sorts of things. Doll's-house furniture, for example. She ought to have had a daughter; Stuart never had much use for it, except one or two things that went with his model railway."

Helena was silent again. Imagine Jim married to this talented craftswoman. How silent their evenings must have been, yet filled with intense mental activity. And what of the son, growing up in this odd, old-fashioned home? Had he been attracted by the noisy life of an Italian family, in contrast to the stillness of the old vicarage?

A despondent howl from the next room interrupted her thoughts.

"I'll let him out, now there's no food about," said Jim. He got up, opened the door and went out. A further door was heard to open. Monty emerged with a decidedly guilty air.

"He's been up to something, by the look of it," Jim said, returning. "I'll inspect the damage in a minute."

Gill gently discouraged the dog from clambering on to her knees, and he settled down with some disappointment at her feet, rolling his eyes upwards in reproach.

Jim proposed playing a few records, and disappeared to the study to find them. He came back with an expression of dismay on his face.

"Does either of you know how to re-cover a leather armchair?"

Helena, taken aback, looked at him. "No, why, Jim?"

"Just come and see."

The study was much as it must have been during the last vicar's tenure. The only window being less than a yard wide, the room was dark, cold even in May, and lined on all four sides with shelves and cabinets, where the vicar must have kept his commentaries and theological treatises, and perhaps other volumes too, for country vicars traditionally had hobbies and learned pursuits of one kind or another. Jim had used the shelves to his full advantage; they proclaimed the man who, deprived by fate of the higher education he would dearly have loved, resolves to make up for it in a lifetime of private reading. Every kind of subject was represented, English and European history, politics, economics, astronomy, zoology, ecology, music, art and literary criticism; Rabelais (in translation), Chaucer, a full set of Shakespeare's works, Milton, Dr Johnson, volumes of Dickens, Trollope, Shaw; the entire 1955 edition of the Encyclopaedia Britannica; an enormous pile of venerable copies of the National Geographic Magazine; weeklies and quarterlies, catalogues and reviews, more or less ordered, but bearing the marks of repeated removals and replacements. Under the window stood a heavy oak bureau with a hard wooden chair, probably left by the vicar himself, and in the darkest corner there was a dark brown leather armchair of the kind often associated with gentlemen's clubs. It was this latter piece of furniture that had evidently been the object of Monty's attentions during tea. Not only were the legs indented with repeated gnawing, but the seat was now sprouting kapok, through which protruded the top ring of a rusty spring.

"Oh, dear," said Helena in dismay. "Is that your favourite chair?" She could almost see the vicar, deep in preparation of next Sunday's sermon, hunched over the desk with his authorised version and his notebook, imagining him as an elderly bachelor, left on his own in the evenings when his housekeeper went home, or, if resident, retired to her quarters.

"I do use it quite a bit, when I don't want to bother with a fire in the sitting-room."

How like Jim, Helena thought, to shut himself up in this tiny dark cubby-hole, when after all he's got a fair-sized house to live in; here, he can see himself as the teacher, or maybe the don, that he ought to have been.

Jim himself was rummaging in one of the cabinets, drawing out two or three long-playing records. Helena recalled that he liked organ music and rather expected Bach, but only one of the records proved to be by an organist, and the music itself was by a Portuguese composer whose name Helena was not quite able to establish. The other two were Schubert and *H.M.S. Pinafore*; the latter, however, Jim thrusted back, presumably deciding to seek something more modern for Gill's benefit, and finally producing a selection entitled *Blues from Chicago to Kansas City*. Helena fervently hoped the Schubert would come first. She would have preferred Gilbert and Sullivan to this latest offering, and suspected that Gill would have agreed with her.

As it turned out, however, the music simply served as a background to their conversation, and Helena would have been hard put to remember the order in which it was played. Gill, no musician, nevertheless listened intently for short periods, as if trying to discern some coded message in the harmonies, and then relapsed into a dreamy state, scarcely speaking, fondling the dog's ears. Jim became more animated once his domestic surroundings were forgotten; he described one or two village characters, whom he knew quite well from the Plough, and proceeded to others he had heard tales of, eccentrics, poachers, brewers of improbable-sounding liquors, mole-catchers and ferret-fanciers of the past; all recounted with a dry humour to indicate that none of the stories were to be taken too seriously, amusement taking precedence over veracity. Helena remembered what David had said about such characters, and wondered what Gill might be making of all these improbabilities and inconsistencies.

They got on to politics. Gill wished vaguely that she had Hilary with her, but felt that even Hilary would have met her match here. Jim described himself as left of centre, although somewhat disillusioned, and Helena found herself putting up a defence of the rugged individualism on which she had often heard David hold forth; but she found herself emotionally at odds with her theme, and unable to sustain it. She had to admit to herself that she had never been as tough-minded as David; what in his time had seemed to her to be common sense and enlightened self-interest now had a suspicion of ruthless egoism about it. *Yet,* she thought, *those were some of things I loved him for; they were part of his zest for life, and they helped to hold us together as a family, for he saw us as a part of himself. Now look at us, Karen in Colmleigh, Chris in London, or maybe away somewhere on a removal, and me in Danesburgh with a girl who's no relation of ours at all living with me.* It was as though that unifying force had vanished. But then, she no longer depended on that unifying force, a greater power had taken over, or perhaps it had always been there, but had only now become perceptible.

Gill rocked back and forth to the last of the blues tunes. Jim had stopped talking, realising that Helena was lost in her own thoughts. As she appeared to surface again, he said.

"You've come a long way, haven't you?"

"I suppose I have. But what about you, Jim? Two years on, and you're still living out here, as if nothing had changed. Oughtn't you perhaps to be considering whether it's the right thing to do? I'm sorry, that probably sounds impatient and interfering, but I'd hate to think you were wasting your life here."

"Maybe so. Or maybe I needed someone to tell me so. But let's see how things go with Danesburgh Cartons. I might be forced to rethink the future if things go seriously wrong here."

It was time to leave. Monty was incarcerated in the study once again as Jim bade his guests good night. It was arranged that he would collect Gill on Thursday evenings, so that she could spend an hour helping with Monty's training; a further hour was allocated for accounts. Helena suspected that the tutorial might encompass a wider range of subjects, but that would be of little consequence, and might even be good for both of them. Helena would collect Gill again at the end of the session, probably staying a few minutes for tea or coffee.

They stepped out into the still summer evening. The sky was clear and still light in the west, and the moon, nearing its full, hung like a lamp over the poplars on the distant ridge, but the edge of the forest was lost in the twilight. Helena reflected that the afternoon and evening, although long, had been worthwhile. Not until the evening had the three of them come to be completely at ease with one another, but now, without a doubt, they were friends.

"I hate being alone," Gill said on the way back. "I don't think I could live out here, all on my own, like Mr Sergent. You can feel the loneliness as soon as you go in. Even with Monty there." She shivered a little. "It's not just him living alone that makes it feel like that, though. I mean, you've been living alone for most of the time this year, but your house feels warm and friendly. Mr Sergent doesn't; it was cold, even on a warm evening like this."

"Men don't really know how to make a proper home. They put up with all sorts of discomforts from sheer indifference, a lot of the time. Look at Chris in those awful lodgings."

"But at least he knows it's only temporary."

They thought of the equable Chris for a moment, and then of Jim again. Had he, as a young man, been as cheerfully determined to make the best of what he had, what he was? Probably not. Jim's loneliness was an inward thing, not merely a product of his bereavement. It would take a great deal to change him.

"Well, it'll be good for Mr Sergent to have your company once a week. See if you can make that dog a fitter companion for him."

"Monty," said Gill seriously, "isn't really the kind of dog he needs — at least, I don't think so. But I'll do my best with him."

***

It was in the same week that Gill's mother came over. Helena had originally intended to take a day's holiday, but had second thoughts and merely indicated to Brian Farrelson that, subject to his approval, she would be late in that morning. Her instinct was justified, for Dawn Gunson arrived in good time for one whose enthusiasm for early rising was reputedly doubtful. Either she had changed, or the occasion had seemed of sufficient importance to get her out of bed at such an unaccustomed hour.

She drove up in an emerald Fiat, and presented herself much as Helena remembered her, thin and nervous, brown eyes set wide apart, face slightly mottled, skin taut over her jaw; she wore a plain white T-shirt, blue jeans that looked new and a red cardigan tied round her waist, even though the day promised to be a hot one. She wanted to smoke as soon as she sat down in the lounge, and Helena had to root out the only ash-tray that had been kept after the move, for neither Karen nor Chris smoked, she herself never had, and David had given up years earlier. Helena hoped Gill would not be tempted to start again, but to Helena's intense relief, she merely declined with a polite smile the cigarette her mother offered her.

After about an hour, Dawn Gunson suggested that she should take Gill out for most of the day, for lunch and some shopping, and by implication, some time to talk more intimately. This was what Helena had foreseen, and she agreed willingly; Gill also consented without demur. Once left alone, Helena made herself a couple of sandwiches, for she intended to work through her lunch hour to make up for her late start, and then spent a few moments praying in her bedroom. She would have liked to go into the church, but it was not on her route to work, and she felt it would be wrong to delay her arrival any further.

Brian Farrelson made no comment when she walked into the office, but Jim Sergent, to whom she had mentioned the visit, looked up raised his eyebrows in greeting.

"Did Gill's mother come? You were expecting her, weren't you?"

"Yes. They've gone out together for the day."

"That sounds encouraging. I hope it works out for Gill."

"Thanks, Jim."

Helena absorbed herself in the business. There were more outstanding bills, but at the same time more orders were coming in, which raised the spirits in the office; then, however, the air-conditioning system in the main building failed, one of the shop-floor girls fainted, fortunately not at her machine, and Helena was called down to attend to her. The engineers had to be called in, and work inevitably came to a standstill. One of the drivers was sent out to a cash-and-carry store nearby, one of Danesburgh Cartons' regular customers, and returned with a supply of soft drinks, which were hurriedly refrigerated and distributed.

Helena hoped Dawn Gunson had found somewhere cool to take Gill. Few of the Danesburgh shops were as well-ventilated as the more modern ones in Colmleigh. In the office Helena felt considerably less comfortable than she contrived to appear, and she did not like to contemplate how the temperature must be rising in the factory. She suggested that the workers be allowed to go home, but Brian Farrelson would not hear of it.

"Not unless they come and demand it. But they're all working to earn extra holiday pay at the moment, anyway, which we can hardly afford as it is, let alone if production has to stop for half a day."

The men outside, the drivers and loaders, were scarcely more comfortable. George Bushell breathed heavily and perspired freely as he moved between the office, the bays and the service area. There were irritable remarks on all sides; yet work went on, until at last, at about twenty to five, the air-conditioning came on again, to ironic cheers of relief.

Helena was thankful, when she left, that she had parked on the shaded side of the building, but even so, the car felt like an oven after only a few minutes in the sun. She wound down the window, but to little effect. By the time she got home there was a patch of moisture in the small of her back, and the back of her blouse had half-stuck to the vinyl seat. Indoors, the front half of the lounge was in direct sunlight and unbearable, but the rear half was mercifully shady. Helena drew the curtains, and aware that Gill and her mother were unlikely to be far behind her, prepared long cold drinks and then hurriedly washed and changed into a cotton dress. She had guessed right, for from the bedroom window she saw the green Fiat arrive as she put her comb down.

She opened the front door. Gill came in slowly, pallid and damp-haired. Dawn Gunson followed, sporting an enormous pair of sun-glasses that all but obliterated the top half of her face. At first, Helena feared that the reunion had not been a success, but Gill's smile seemed contented enough.

"Would you mind if I went up for a shower and changed? I'm a bit sticky."

"Of course. You must be absolutely roasted. Perhaps you'd like to freshen up as well, Dawn? It's been so hot all day."

"Oh, that would be lovely. But I'll let Gill go first."

Gill trudged heavily up the stairs, while Helena directed Dawn Gunson to the cooler end of the lounge.

"Please tell me," Dawn began, once seated, "how you've made such a change to Gill in such a short time. She's really been quite happy with me all day, not that I deserve it."

Helena deflected the question. "What did you find to do here?"

"Well, it was beginning to get too warm this morning, so we finished our shopping as early as we could. Then we went out to that pub, you know, the one Gill said you went to at Christmas, they do light snacks there and that was all we felt like; and after that we drove over to the reservoir and sat under the trees and talked for quite a while, nearly a couple of hours I think it must have been. I think we both needed that. I have to hold myself responsible to some extent for the situation Gill's got herself into. I said something unforgivable to her in a letter — I won't go into details — God knows what made me do it, there wasn't a scrap of truth in it. I suppose I was still trying to get at her father through her. If I'd been in her place I don't think I'd have wanted anything more to do with the person who wrote it, even if it was my own mother... especially if it was my own mother."

"I hope you don't mind my asking, but did you discuss it with her this afternoon?"

"Yes. I had to. It was the really big thing between us."

"How did she take it?"

"Like a lamb. She said yes, that really hurt, and she nearly went mad with the pain of it; but since then she's begun to understand the pressure I was under, and things were different now. As I said, she's altogether different herself. Before, I couldn't get through to her, every time I tried she'd go off into some dream world of her own. I suppose it was the only way she had of protecting herself against... well, the sheer nastiness of it all, when we were breaking up. Now, she seems rational."

Helena nodded. "Pregnancy does rather call for a down-to-earth attitude. I think my daughter may have had a hand in making her see that, and getting over the first shock of it. Karen has a rather short way with dreaminess, as Gill will tell you."

"Then I'm grateful to Karen, too. But it really is your influence mostly, isn't it? You seem so settled and sensible and caring, and your home is so peaceful. Gill tells me it's less than a year since you lost your husband? I can't believe how you've managed to adapt so well, and in a new place. and as for taking Gill in... well, I haven't got the words to say what it means to me. Only, thank God you were there when I ought to have been."

"Actually," Helena assured her, "she's been rather good company. And she's made friends with one of my colleagues at work, or at least with his dog. She's helping him to train it properly."

"She always did love dogs. When I was with Gerald, neither of us would have one. She was so unlike either of us... and God knows we were ill enough matched as a couple. What we must have done to her, between us."

Steps were heard descending the stairs, and Gill reappeared, suitably freshened up, and for the occasion, wearing a maternity smock which totally engulfed her small body, so that she looked for all the world like a baby herself.

"Would you like a wash now?" Helena asked politely. "The bathroom is just to the right at the top of the stairs."

Dawn Gunson made her way upstairs in her turn. Helena smiled at Gill. "Has it been all right?"

"Mother's been fine," said Gill. "Really concerned about me. I found I could talk to her almost the way I talk to you. I never could before. You know, as if we were friends, rather than mother and daughter. I think she liked that. And I don't think she's had an easy time since she remarried, but I didn't want to talk about that too much. The only thing is, she was always different when I got her on her own. As if she was afraid to be herself when Father was there. He seems very smooth and easy-going on the surface, but I think she was a bit afraid of him really. He could be quite cruel in some ways, even though he never lost his temper."

"Do you think you can stay friends now?"

"I hope so. I'm ready to try if Mother is."

Helena prepared a simple meal while Gill and her mother sat and talked again. To her, their reconciliation seemed a minor miracle, and certainly an answer to prayer, although she had no clear idea of the likely sequel. In that respect, she had taken Rhoda Broughmer's advice to heart. "Don't expect to see the future mapped out for you," Rhoda had said. "It does happen occasionally, but most of the time you need to concentrate on getting round the next corner." Dawn Gunson's visit had been the 'next corner', but the rest remained unknown. Even when the heat of the day had abated a little, and Dawn was about to leave, things were no clearer. Dawn embraced Gill affectionately enough, planning to invite her back 'when everything settled down at home'. When that might be expected to be was a matter for speculation. Any hope Helena might have entertained at the back of her mind that Gill might return home there and then were swiftly dismissed.

"We've agreed to phone each other once a week," Gill informed her. "If you don't mind, that is, of course. Mother will try to arrange it so that she calls about the same day and time every week, but if she forgets would it be all right if I phoned her?"

"Of course, my dear."

She would not be able to go away during the summer, then. That was something of a blow, for she had counted on seeing her own parents. That would be the next corner. In the meantime, Gill was still wondering at the apparent change in her mother's attitude.

"She still wants to be noticed, but I get the feeling it's a sort of habit she can't break now, not a real need. I mean, look at those sunglasses, and the colour of her car. But when we were out together she really tried to look after me. She kept asking if I felt all right, whether the heat was worrying me, and so on."

"You and your mother," said Helena, "must have made a fine mixed-up pair. But I'm delighted that you've started to find each other again. Try not to let it slip. She might be glad you're there, some day."

***

The following evening, as though by arrangement, Chris and Karen phoned Helena in quick succession. Chris had just completed a longish return trip, which had involved some particularly heavy lifting and the dismantling and reassembly of a grand piano, and had decided it was time for a weekend at home. Helena felt a thrill of pleasure and relief. She had missed her son more acutely than she would have liked to admit.

She had hardly put the receiver down when Karen was on the line.

"Mum, if it's all right with you, I'd like to come over on Saturday. With Greg."

"Of course, dear. I'd love to see you both. Are you intending to stay, though? Gill's still here, of course, and Chris is coming home."

"Oh, that's all right. Greg will sleep on the sofa, or in the study. It wouldn't be the first time he's ever had to rough it."

That's no way to talk about my home, young lady, Helena thought. But she knew Karen didn't mean it like that.

"Well… fine, then. It will be lovely to have you all together. I'll make sure there's plenty of food in the house."

"Don't do anything special, please, Mum," Karen's tone was strangely urgent. "I mean, we don't want to make a lot of work for you."

"Very well, dear."

"Lovely. See you Saturday, then."

It was Gill's evening at Parham St. John again. Helena drove out in the late twilight, the headlights picking our small animals scuttling across the road and into the hedgerow. The prosaic brick cottages of the village stood out darkly against the watered-ink of the sky; the calm of the evening only partially muted an inner excitement that made her grip the steering wheel unusually hard. *Too much coffee this evening*, she thought, mistaking the cause.

Monty had made gratifying progress and would now remain seated, albeit quivering, until permitted to advance, and on Jim's command, too, as well as Gill's.

"Astonishing, isn't it?" Jim said. "You really have someone with a rare talent here. She's been wasted on the social services."

"And how about the book-keeping lesson?"

"Well," Gill admitted, "we never really got on to book-keeping this evening. We started talking about the sociological aspects of life in a small community, and somehow the time just ran away... Perhaps next week?"

Helena smiled. "Perhaps." As they drove away, Gill suddenly said.

"What with you and Mr Sergent, I think I've learned more in the last couple of months than I ever did from my correspondence course. You won't both leave me on my own when this baby arrives, will you? I don't think I could bear that."

"Well, speaking for myself, I'll certainly be there if you need me," Helena promised. "And I don't think Mr Sergent's the sort of person to give up on you or anyone else. And I dare say you're as good for him as he is for you, not to mention the dog. There's no one in the office who could talk philosophy with him, even if we had the time. Which we don't, of course." She looked sharply at Gill for a second. "Are you worrying, then? About the baby, I mean."

"I can't help wondering what it will be like to be a mother. It's an awful responsibility, isn't it?"

Especially on your own, Helena thought. *Yes; it would be criminal to leave you without any support.* Aloud she said, "Yes, it is. But on the other hand, it's amazing how you rise to it."

"Several times a night, I gather, to begin with." Gill made a half-hearted joke of it.

"Well, that at least is being realistic," Helena approved.

***

Chris arrived by coach from London, having taken a half-day off. Helena gave him what was, for her, an enormous hug; it seemed to her to have been far too long since the last time he had been home. Once again, she had the impression that he had grown bigger and stronger. The rigours of shifting heavy items of furniture no doubted accounted for that in some measure, but the moustache that had been a shadow last time was now clearly defined and gave him a somewhat raffish appearance, as if he might be planning to sell you a second-hand car and elope with your daughter. Helena preferred not to mention the moustache, rather hoping that he would shave it off. She wondered what Karen would say about it.

"Have you been finding it awfully heavy work?" she asked instead, as they drove back from the bus station.

"Just to begin with. But you soon learn how to lift things and manoeuvre them. You'd be amazed, Mum, we've had to take things to pieces and put them together again, and hoist furniture through upstairs windows. It's a real art."

"No disasters, I hope?"

"Only one. My mate put his foot in a box of crockery. Luckily it was only everyday stuff, nothing valuable. They claimed it on the insurance. No problem."

"And have you had many long trips?"

"One to Cheshire, and one to the Isle of Wight. Oh, and one to Oxford, but we came back the same day on that one, of course. Otherwise mostly around London, Essex and North Kent. A lot of short moves, some almost in the same street, we could do two in a day if we started early."

Helena listened as Chris described what he had been doing for the past few weeks. *He really is enjoying it*, she thought.

"We've had one or two funny things happen, too," he concluded as they neared the house. "But I'll save those for when we're all together. How's old Gill, by the way? Did she pass her exams?"

"She doesn't know yet," said Helena. "She thinks the results will be out in about six weeks' time. She's well, but a bit sensitive, and a bit apprehensive about the baby, I'm afraid. She really has been trying to sort herself out, though, so you won't tease her, will you, Chris?"

"The idea never occurred to me," Chris replied with mock piety. Helena was confident, however, that he would be considerate to Gill; he had never been inclined to use others as a target for his wit. They went in, and Chris, after greeting Gill affably, took his bags, which seemed unusually numerous and heavy for a weekend visit, into the study, where he proceeded to assemble an old camp bed, with much clanking of steel tubes, and laid a sleeping-bag on top of it.

"Bought it the other week," he explained. "Just in case I ever had to sleep in the van. And I'll be taking it to Italy, of course."

"You can have your own room tonight, at least," said Helena. "Karen and Greg aren't coming till tomorrow. It's funny how you all decided to come the same weekend. Not that I mind, of course."

"Yes, isn't it?" Chris agreed, poker-faced.

And of course, the following morning everything became clear. If Helena had not totally forgotten her own birthday, she had at least pushed it so far to the back of her mind that she would have been hard put to identify the date; and the events of the previous week had consigned it to oblivion. Unknown to Helena, Gill, at Karen's instigation, had collected up the few cards and letters that had arrived prematurely, and kept them in a drawer in her bedroom, so that, on being woken (with tea and biscuits and a bouquet of roses), she had at first no idea of the occasion.

David had always made a big thing of it. Even when she had, in her own judgment, reached the age when birthdays became more of an embarrassment than a delight, it had always been marked with a flourish of some kind: theatre, concerts, a weekend away once or twice, when Claire had been available to look after the children. The previous year, they had been in the middle of preparing for the move to Danesburgh; even so, David had taken time off to drive them down to the coast, where they had lunched at a five-star hotel and spent a carefree afternoon strolling on the cliffs. He had seemed so well then, so full of vigour and enthusiasm; they might both have been twenty years younger. Helena caught her breath at a particularly vivid memory of David walking by her side in sports shirt and sandals, laughing at something or other. She had said at the time, she remembered.

"Are you sure we're doing the right thing?" And he, putting his arm round her shoulders, had replied.

"Of course, I'm sure. This is marvellous, it's a new beginning. The biggest challenge I've taken on yet." Death had been the first and only challenge he had not been able to meet, and the new beginning had been Helena's inheritance.

The sharp pang of grief eased to a milder melancholy which Helena addressed herself to subduing as she opened her cards, which Gill had brought up to her with her tea. All the family seemed to have remembered, including David's parents (an unusual thing), and the cards chosen by Chris and Karen (the latter also signed by Greg), were especially ornate. Among the remainder was one from Jim Sergent, which surprised her; *Gill must have told him*, she concluded, not quite knowing whether to be touched or put out. "A Happy Birthday to an extraordinary lady," Jim had inscribed on the inner pages. "With best wishes from Jim and Monty." No, she could not be put out; the simple greeting dispelled the last of her sadness, replacing it with a gentle pleasure at the compliment.

Chris and Gill were waiting to add their good wishes. Gill insisted on kissing Helena on both cheeks, French fashion; this called for a delicate manoeuvre, which she executed with a determined effort. Chris, less decorous, simply enveloped his mother in a bear-hug.

"Do you know," he said. "I believe you really had forgotten it. We can't have that. No birthday in our family ever went by without a party. Today the rest of us take over, and you just relax and enjoy it."

And Helena was not permitted the merest hand's turn all day long, despite her ritual protests. Karen and Greg arrived loaded with baskets, bouquets and bottles, including champagne. Gill produced from her room an elaborate simnel cake, baked one afternoon during the week and subsequently concealed under the cover of an old sewing machine Karen had occasionally used in Colmleigh, which now reposed at the back of the wardrobe. Lunch had been booked well in advance at the Swan, Danesburgh's only Michelin-starred hotel; dinner was to be Karen and Gill's responsibility. On her return from lunch, Helena found a clutch of parcels waiting for her on the dining-room table, jewellery, and perfume, and delicate ornaments, and a little leather-bound edition of the Book of

Common Prayer, which she was astonished to find was from Karen. Karen, of all people.

"I don't know much about that sort of thing," her daughter explained. "But this seemed to suit you, as you are now, you know? You didn't already have one, did you?"

No, Helena assured her, she didn't. It was the day's second special moment.

The third came right at the end. Dinner, Helena had to concede, for she still affected to doubt her family's ability to boil an egg, had been magnificent. The blue summer evening was calm, the air scented. Chris had been recounting some of his removal anecdotes as they sat on folding chairs in the garden, enjoying the start of nightfall, and had then gone inside with Greg to discuss some aspect of the holiday. Gill was making coffee. Karen moved closer to Helena.

"Mum."

"Yes, dear?"

"Have you enjoyed the day? Really?"

"My darling, it's been glorious. I can't remember a happier birthday, even when... even when your father was alive."

"I wish he'd been here, though," Karen said softly. "Especially..." She broke off.

Helena suddenly knew what was coming.

"Yes, dear?" she said again.

"Especially... as we're sort of nearly engaged, Greg and me."

"Sort of nearly?" Helena enquired with a smile. "That sounds a bit vague. And it's not the impression I got when you were talking about him a few weeks ago," wondering for a moment whether her daughter was influenced by a certain imminent and much publicised royal wedding.

Karen looked thoughtful. "Things have changed since then. It was when Greg went away on that course, you know, when Gill first came to you here. I found I missed him more than you miss somebody you're just friends with. When he got back he said he'd been feeling the same. And well, we both got round to thinking there's more to life than just having good times. I know Greg well enough now, he wouldn't take me for a ride. He really meant it."

"And you?"

"Yes, I'm serious, too."

Helena looked again at Karen's face. Yes, Karen was serious. Nothing to do with the royal wedding. How her two children had grown up in less than a year.

"But I wouldn't say yes if you didn't think it was all right," Karen added, immediately reversing Helena's thoughts with her sudden simplicity.

Greg and Karen, engaged, a wedding on the horizon. Helena's thoughts began to race. She wanted to go to her room and talk this out with God; she was terrified of committing herself prematurely.

"Well, dear, you've taken me a little bit by surprise. I'd like to think about it. Not that I don't think Greg's a splendid young man. In fact, I'm not sure that I didn't think he was a little bit too perfect to be real when he first came here. If you did get engaged, how long would you want to wait to get married?"

"Oh, I think it would have to be quite a while. At least a year. We're not rushing into it. Greg's not qualified until the end of this year, so he wants to make sure he gets the job he's after first."

"I see. Have you told Chris? Or Gill?"

"No, of course not. Although, I think Gill may have guessed. But I'll have to be careful when I tell her. She probably thinks she's blown her chances of finding anyone decent sky high by now. I'd hate to make it seem as if I was rubbing it in."

Helena nodded. "Yes, I think you may be right. But treat her gently, and I think she'll be delighted for you; or at least she'll keep it to herself if it does grieve her at all. But I don't think there's any jealousy in her. Anyhow, you're not saying anything tonight, are you?"

"No, I'm not, Mum. But could you tell me tomorrow if possible because Greg wants to propose to me the proper way, you know?"

"Really? How old-fashioned." Helena smiled again. "But how very courteous. I promise I'll tell you tomorrow, then."

They all talked late into the night, in the manner of long-separated families, until Gill fell asleep in her chair and had to be gently woken and sent up to bed. Chris departed to the study, and Karen and Greg were left together on the settee. Helena studied them, half listening to what they were saying, half absorbed in her own thoughts. She knew that, even if she had wished to, she could not forbid their engagement, and on the face of it there was no possible reason to do so. So far as she could discern, Greg had no undesirable characteristics, and Karen would be twenty-three by the time the wedding took place; older than Helena herself had been when she had married David, and certainly older than one or two of her school friends who were already married. No reason at all; and yet there was tugging at her heart a longing, not expressed in rational thought, that Karen might go further along the road to casting off her prejudices against churches and religion, indeed that she might fully embrace the faith which Helena herself had recently discovered, and marry a believer, set up a Christian home… It was a dream, of course, and she recognised it as such, but while that dream glimmered in her mind, it would be difficult for her to bless her daughter's engagement without reservation.

Karen caught her eye. "Don't look so solemn and serious, Mum. It's still your birthday for another twenty minutes yet!"

Helena smiled again then. "And what a birthday it's been. Let's make some hot chocolate. I want to make the most of those last twenty minutes."

But when midnight had passed and they had all finally retired to their various beds, Helena stayed awake, enquiring urgently of her Lord as to what *He* thought of it all, and what attitude she should take. And at last, the Lord seemed to intimate that she should concern herself with what could be done immediately, and leave the unattainable to *Him*. Upon which, barely an hour before dawn, she fell asleep; and it was fully half past eight before she stirred again, and nine by the time she was properly awake. A grinning Chris stood by her bed.

"No church this morning, Mum?"

Helena looked up at him, still dazed.

"Oh, no, dear. I don't think so. I haven't got you all here for very long, so let's all be together while we can. I can always go to Evensong."

A clatter of crockery came from below.

"Who's that in the kitchen?"

"That's Gill. She told me she'd woken up early and hadn't been able to go back to sleep, so she decided to go down and make herself useful. Breakfast in ten minutes!"

***

Everyone seemed determined to extend Helena's birthday by a day. After breakfast Gill went straight back to the kitchen to start preparing the next meal. Greg got out the lawn-mower, and Chris backed the car out on to the driveway to check it. Karen made a pretence of helping Gill, but at the first opportunity she left her friend and sought out her mother.

"Mum, have you thought? What about it?"

Helena felt the familiar urge to curb her daughter's impatience.

"I have thought, dear, of course I have. But the real question's whether *you've* thought about it enough. You've got to weigh it up carefully; there aren't many decisions you'll have to make that are bigger, if any at all. And once you're engaged, there's always pressure on you to go through with it, even if you're not feeling so sure then. And the longer the engagement, the more it grows. It's certainly not a decision to be taken lightly. Answer me two questions. Do you really want to be married in the next couple of years? And do you want to be married to Greg, as a commitment for life?"

Karen's face was positively grave. "I have thought a lot, and that's very much what I've been asking myself. Yes, I do want to be married. You know how I've always loved you telling us about yourself and Dad. Remember that night, after the funeral? And the weekend? There was something beautiful about it, even at a time like that. We were like kids listening to fairy tales. You were always so happy together, weren't you? Although I think you're happy now, in a different sort of way. And yes, I do love Greg. I think he's marvellous. I don't suppose I deserve him, but I do believe he loves me as well, all the time we seem to get closer. You know what I mean?"

Helena knew; it had happened to her with David. No marriage could have been happier; yet Karen was right, she had discovered a different kind of happiness even in her widowhood. It would have been a gross injustice to David to call it 'joy'; there had been joy in abundance between them; yet it was something more than solace. The sense of loss when she thought of him was never less than acute, but the compensation had been extraordinary and beyond price. *But please God*, she thought, *don't let Karen have to go through the same experience if she's ever to find a real faith.*

She had yet two further questions.

"What about Greg's family? Can you get along with them? And if it's not too inquisitive to ask, do they value marriage?"

"They're great, Mum. His parents are really sweet. And so far as I know, no one in his family is divorced yet!"

"I'm glad to hear it," said Helena. "Well, you seem to know what you want, all right. You always have, haven't you? Still, there's nothing wrong in that. I'm sure your father would have liked Greg if he'd had the chance to get to know him properly, and I think perhaps I've been a little over-cautious. But then, that's like me, as you well know. So yes, you have my blessing, the two of you, and I shall be looking forward to knowing the date."

"Oh, Mum." Karen embraced her. "I'll get Greg to come in as soon as he's finished."

Greg was not quite so debonair when he came in to ask for Karen's hand. He suddenly seemed younger, more like Chris as the latter had been a year or so earlier. *That's all to the good,* Helena thought. It would have been distinctly bad form if he had approached the matter as though it were a business deal, or, worse, if he had been flippant. Nevertheless, she decided not to make it too easy for him.

"Can I ask you a question, Mrs Halstow?"

Good gracious, Helena thought. *This is a bit direct.*

"Did you really not know we were organising a birthday party for you?"

False start. That was not the question she had expected.

"Well, no, I didn't. Not until yesterday morning, and then of course I dawned on me. It was a lovely surprise."

"Well," Greg went on. "That's marvellous because that was what we all hoped and intended for. But Karen and I had something else in mind as well... We've always got on well together, you know that, but over the last few months it's sort of got a bit deeper. We both felt we wanted it to be more than just a — a boy friend - girl friend relationship. And this weekend seemed the ideal to celebrate it. So, er..."

Helena considered this disappointing. Not so direct after all. Now you're going all round the subject. Come to the point.

"Greg," she said. "You understand that if my husband had still been alive it would have been him you'd have had to ask. So I'm going to ask you the kind of questions he would have asked. Number one, do you love Karen?"

Greg surprisingly blushed deeply.

"Yes," he said. "I do. Very much."

"And do you believe in marriage?"

"Yes, of course."

"I'm not sure," said Helena in a slightly reproving tone, "that there's any *of course* about it these days. I mean, as something that's intended to last. Something that's worth working at, and something that gets better and better as time goes on."

Greg looked her in the eye. "I do believe in marriage, and I certainly wouldn't go into it casually. No, it's the real thing or nothing as far as I'm concerned. I'm not saying either of us is perfect but we're not just playing about. We both want to be married to each other, and and I know it's something a lot of people shy away from. And quite honestly, if we'd just wanted to live together, we could have been doing that already. We've had the opportunity in Colmleigh, with Gill being over here. With you. But we haven't, because we don't believe that's right, and we know you don't. And for that matter, neither do my parents."

"Have you actually asked Karen?"

"Not before I spoke to you," said Greg earnestly.

"Well, Greg," said Helena. "You can take it that I approve. I'm delighted for both of you; I don't think Karen could have found anyone better. Now go and ask her, and don't leave it any longer."

Greg beamed. "I will. Thank you, Mrs Halstow." He disappeared to where Karen was waiting in the garden. Helena could see them for a moment, and then they moved out of sight. She went in search of Chris and Gill.

Chris was stretched out under the car, apparently securing the exhaust, and emerged as he heard Helena approaching.

"It's mostly OK, Mum," he pronounced. "But it needs a proper service. You'd better get it down to the garage this week if you can."

"All right. I'm sure Jim will give me a lift to work while it's in for service. But come inside for a minute now."

Chris, black-handed, stood on the doorstep for a moment while Helena looked for Gill, who was not immediately to be found, but eventually appeared from upstairs, perhaps a little red about the eyes, but fully in possession of herself.

Karen and Greg made their triumphal entry through the French windows, for all the world as though they were actors playing in a drawing-room comedy.

"Well," said Helena, trying not to sound arch. "Have you got something to tell us?"

For answer Karen held up her hand, unmistakably adorned with a diamond ring.

"Yes, Mum. We have. We're engaged."

A moment, a fraction of a moment. Then Gill hugged Karen as best she could, and Chris shook hands warmly with Greg, while Helena watched and smiled, thinking of her own engagement and then suddenly imagining David in the midst of them now, chuckling with pleasure. The vision caused a tear to sting her eyelids momentarily; but then the champagne was brought out again. A fresh celebration began, and if either Helena or Gill felt any slight impairment of their delight, both of them succeeded in concealing it.

"Oh, Lord," said Chris. "I suppose I'll have to give you away. Good grief."

That brought relieved giggles from Karen and Gill.

"I suppose so," said Karen. "And make a speech at the wedding."

"Well," Chris conceded. "If you don't mind me reading it off a sheet of paper. I'll get someone to write it for me."

"You'll do no such thing," said Helena firmly. "You're quite intelligent enough to make up your own speech. You've got plenty of time to do it, anyway."

"Gill," said Karen. "I'd rather like you to be my bridesmaid."

"If I can find a baby-sitter," said Gill, her smile a little wan.

"Don't be daft," said Karen warmly. "We'll hire a nanny if we have to. But I don't suppose for a moment it'll come to that. There's bound to be someone who'll look after the baby for you. They'll be queuing up to do it, you'll see. Leave it to us."

"Then yes, of course I will, if you really want me to."

"I take it the wedding will be in Colmleigh," said Helena. "Do you mean to be married in church?"

"Oh, yes." Karen was unequivocal. Greg nodded. "It seems the right thing. And I don't like register office weddings. I've been to one or two. The whole thing's over in a matter of minutes, and then the next couple are there in the waiting room. It seems so flat, somehow. No, we'll be married .. in *style*."

Style was not exactly what Helena had in mind. Still…

"Well, I should hope so," she said. "I wouldn't have expected less. Not from my daughter. Now, then how far had your plans progressed?"

"Quite honestly," Greg confessed, "no further than today. I'm hoping to qualify at the end of this year, so we thought it should probably be some time next year. That might give us time to save up a deposit on a flat. Or if things go really well, we might even manage a small house."

"I think I might be able to get a mortgage, you see," Karen added. "I've been saving with the Bucklersbury for quite a few years now."

"If we both work hard and save hard," Greg continued, "we ought to be well set up by then."

"No holiday this summer, then," said Chris.

"Well, not in July or August," Greg agreed. "But we might get away for a few days in September, when the high season's over. We haven't really thought about it yet."

September, Helena thought. *Again. Already.*

"You've got a lot of details to think out, haven't you?" she said. "But I'm sure you'll enjoy that. Now, I'm not going to try to organise anything for you, but you know that if there's any help or advice I can give you, you've only to ask."

"Oh, Mum," said Karen happily. "I'm sure I'll need *heaps*."

They went on planning, speculating, discussing, until Gill had to dash to the kitchen to save their lunch, which was in danger of incineration. Helena and Karen went to help, in hilarious mood, while Chris looked on in mock condescension.

"If that's what champagne does, I think I'll stick to Coke," he remarked to Greg.

But the meal was rescued, and after that the day, it seemed, was as good as gone, with Karen, Greg and Chris packing their respective cases and leaving all together by half past five after a hasty cup of tea, and a welter of promises to phone.

Helena went off to Evensong, not certain whether to feel elated or apprehensive. She was still not entirely sure she had been right to approve the engagement whole-heartedly, and wanted the guidance she felt she had already received to be ratified. And Gill, who had looked a trifle lost when the others had left, was causing her some concern again; she felt that the girl was not finding enough to do now that the examinations were over, and her future plans were far from clear. Helena had taken her in on the assumption that it would be a relatively short-term arrangement, but she saw no immediate prospect of Gill's returning to either of her parents, nor to the flat, which was patently unsuitable for a mother with a small child, being on the second floor of her building and far from sound-proof. Nor could Helena divine how Gill might earn her living. She might, therefore, have been forgiven for being a little distracted during the service, paying less attention than usual to the sermon, but remaining on her knees in earnest and silent prayer after the final blessing.

She returned to find Gill still rather subdued.

"Mrs Halstow, you've been awfully good, to me, and I don't know how to thank you, but I don't think I ought to stay here much longer. You've got your family to think of, and now the wedding and everything. I've been thinking while you've been out at church, perhaps I ought to go to London. After all, they're much more used to unmarried mothers there, and there'd be more opportunities for me to get a job, and more nursery facilities and all that sort of thing. I'll see if Jane can help. She usually knows about things like that."

Helena was unable to reply immediately, wondering whether this was an answer to prayer or a test of her commitment.

"My dear," she said eventually. "You've been most welcome. I haven't thanked you yet for your part in my birthday surprise, or all your help today. And you mustn't think you have to go now or at any time, not until you're ready and you're sure it's right, not for me but for the baby and yourself. I can see that there might be some advantages to being in London, but I can see some dangers too. If you'll allow me to be honest with you, I'm not sure whether you'd cope, either with that or with the kind of job you've got in mind. I mean, you're not exactly one of nature's dreadnoughts, are you? And I'd worry in case you found yourself being exploited in one way or another. As I say, if you're sure it's right I wouldn't want to stand in your way. But I really don't think you ought to go off to London — or anywhere else, for that matter — without knowing exactly what you were going to. That would be rather a backward step, wouldn't it?"

Look what happened when you went to Paris, was Helena's unspoken thought.

Gill had listened to all this in her usual dreamy, docile way. "Yes. Yes, I do see what you mean."

"Well, look," Helena resumed. "Let's wait at least until you have your exam result. That may give you some idea of what you can do. And in the meantime, I'd miss you, and so would Mr Sergent and Monty. Suppose we carry on as before for a little while, anyway. But you might like to start researching careers a bit more carefully. You've got time — you won't be able to start work until the baby's old enough to leave at a nursery, and in any case there aren't so many jobs available at the moment, not with the recession. There are agencies that might help you to find the right sort of thing. Don't assume that social work is your only option."

"I'm not very good at managing on my own," Gill agreed, as though she had only just taken in what Helena had been saying earlier. "Sometimes I wish I were more like Karen. She always seems to know what she's doing, and how to go about it."

Karen, Helena admitted to herself, was highly capable. On the other hand — and this was harder to admit — some of her apparently most generous actions could be traced to a seed of self-interest. That, of course, she would not mention to Gill. It would undoubtedly have been an easy solution to let Gill go to London; but it would have conflicted with her sense of responsibility; a kind of moral estoppel dictated that she must complete what she had begun.

"Yes, Karen has the ability to organise her life. But you've got talents too, and there are things you'd be able to take on that Karen would never consider. I'm sure your instinct will tell you what sort of things you might try, if you'll let it."

"I know. I'm probably more worried about the baby than I am about the job. How will I ever cope on my own?"

Helena pretended to make light of the question.

"Oh, you'll find there's no shortage of people willing to advise you on how to look after a baby. Some are better qualified than others, of course.

Some will lose interest as soon as the child grows out of the pram stage. There are others who say they love families and produce the most awful children you could imagine. So I'd say go by the children, because if they're the sort of children you'd want your own children to grow up like, then you'll probably do well to take advice from their parents. That may seem obvious, but when you're in a situation where you don't know quite what to do it's easy to fall into the trap of listening to the first person who seems willing to help."

Gill digested this in silence.

"How do you feel about babies generally?" Helena added.

"I don't really know. I've never had much to do with them. Apart from occasionally sitting for someone, you know, but then I only had to look in every so often to make sure the baby was all right, because it was already asleep. I must have been lucky, because I never had any problems. But I haven't got any relatives with young children, and Francis and Jane have always said they don't want any. So I don't really know," Gill ended, realising she had repeated herself and looking a little sheepish.

"At least they haven't put you off altogether?"

"Oh, no."

"Well, I suppose that's the main thing. Most of us have had to pick it up as we went along. At least you don't have to learn it all at once, as if you had to take an exam in it."

Gill shook her head.

"I sometimes wonder whether it is the right thing, I'm doing, though. If I'd had an abortion I'd have been back at the flat by now, maybe in a job, instead of being a worry to you. and I might even…" She broke off.

Helena guessed what she had been about to say.

"Well, I suppose you just might. But from what Karen's told me I'm not sure you're mixing with the kind of people who take relationships seriously. And anyway, you made the decision on the best of moral grounds, so if it was right then it must be right now. I don't think you'll regret it in the end. In the meantime I'm very happy for you to stay here as long as you want to, provided that it doesn't cause any difficulties between you and either of your parents."

Gill was not entirely reassured. "I know, and I do believe you. It's just that, well, I think seeing your family here this weekend made me sort of feel I was intruding. I've no right to expect you to look after me like this."

"Gill," Helena said. "Since I moved home, I've seen my family disintegrate, in a manner of speaking. Both my children are away most of the time now. That was always going to happen sooner or later, but I'd counted on having my husband with me for many years. Now that he's gone, I could have been dreadfully lonely. The fact that I'm not as lonely as I might have is due to a number of factors. but one of them has certainly been having you here with me. So rights don't come into it. You're doing something for me as well. It's mutual."

"You're not just saying that?" Gill insisted.

"No. I wouldn't say it if I didn't mean it."

Gill exhaled a sigh. "That's marvellous. But please don't ever let me become a nuisance, will you? I couldn't bear that."

"Don't worry," said Helena. "You won't, I promise you."

As it happened, a couple of days after that conversation, Gill greeted Helena on her return from work with the news that her mother had telephoned that afternoon with an invitation for Gill to go and stay with her for a fortnight, while her husband was away on some film shoot or other. The invitation was for the third week in August; Chris would still be away.

"How do you feel about it?" Helena asked.

"I ought to go, didn't I? I mean, we've been trying to patch things up. And it would be easier with just Mother and myself there. Yes, I'll go."

Unexpectedly, Dawn Gunson telephoned again the same evening. *It's almost*, Helena thought, *as if I were her mother. Dawn more or less asked me whether I would let her own daughter go and stay with her. Strange woman; no wonder Gill's so unsure.*

Once the arrangements were confirmed, Helena began thinking about a trip to Scotland, to see her own parents. She wondered whether she could face the prospect of driving such a distance alone; on the other hand, she found herself suddenly longing to see them, and to be in the north again after so long. Late that night, she wrote them a long letter encompassing the weekend party, Karen's engagement, Gill, and her proposed visit; and her heart grew lighter with every paragraph.

Shopping in the supermarket later that week, Helena encountered a figure whom she at first failed to recognise; but the voice, when she heard it directed at the checkout girl, was unmistakeable.

"I'll 'ave it in a paper bag, dear, them plastic ones are no good, they don't last no time."

White waves had replaced the tight blackberry curls, but the voice was unchanged. It was Marlene Smetters, expensively dressed and manicured and clearly prosperous.

"Hello, Mrs Smetters. I'm sorry I didn't recognise you. How are you these days?"

"Oh, 'ello, dear. Long time, ennit? I'm fine. 'Ow about you? Still over at Danesburgh Cartons, are you? My Gawd, what a place. Best thing that ever 'appened to me, I reckon, when I got the push from there."

"You certainly look as if you're managing all right," Helena agreed. "I'm glad it's worked out well for you."

"No thanks to them over there, though," said Marlene emphatically.

"Oh?"

"Nah. That redundancy pay they give me didn't 'ardly last a week."

"Then?"

"'Ad a big win on the 'orses, didn't we?" said Marlene complacently. "Accumulator bet, it was. My 'Arry couldn't believe it when they all came up. Never known nuffink like it. Gawd, we had a time that night. Biggest party ever. We was doing 'Knees up, Mother Brown' till two in the morning."

"And nobody minded?"

"Nah. They was all in there wiv us!" Marlene concluded triumphantly.

"So now you're a lady of leisure?"

"That's abaht it."

"Well, then, congratulations. I'm very pleased to hear it. Make the most of it!"

Marlene looked at her.

"You're a real lady, ain't you? Not a bit jealous. I've 'ad some aggro since I got rich, you'd be surprised the people what didn't like it one bit. Not you, though." She moved a little closer to Helena. "I'm sorry I called you those names, up there in the office. You're all right, you are."

Helena was touched by the unexpected apology, so long after the trivial offence.

"Please don't give it a thought, Mrs Smetters. You were worried about money then and I was an extra complication for you. We're all liable to get irritable in circumstances like those."

"I'm glad there's no 'ard feelings. See you abaht, then."

"Yes, I expect so," said Helena, conscious that if she had been less financially secure she might have been tempted to indulge in a little rancour herself. She paid for her own groceries and carried them out to the car.

Marlene had been right about Danesburgh Cartons, however; the place was changing, and she would have found it increasingly uncomfortable. While the company continued to stay afloat by dint of diligent pursuit of payments due and the acquisition of two or three reliable customers, the need for economy grew ever more pressing in the directors' eyes; thus it was that, despite Brian Farrelson's valiant defence of the remaining personnel, several jobs had to be terminated and some others reduced to part-time working. This round of cuts brought the long-threatened installation of a drinks-vending machine. It was a blow to Josie Barritt, who, however, accepted it with equanimity, at least outwardly; but it brought angry reactions from some of the workers, who saw it as an initial step in the introduction of automation generally, and feared for their own jobs, and furthermore were not greatly pleased at having to drink their coffee from waxed cardboard cartons. Brian Farrelson found himself caught between two opposing forces, and grew markedly tetchy in the office as a result.

Helena similarly felt a division of sympathies. She was desperately sorry for Josie, who, whatever she said openly, would be concerned at losing her job, poorly paid though it undoubtedly was. Yet, at the same time, she could not be unaware of the financial situation in which the company found itself, and began to perceive the gathering clouds of which Jim Sergent had spoken a month or so earlier. Recognising the difficult situation in which Brian had been placed, she did her best to lighten his burden by working cheerfully, asking as few questions as possible, and dealing with routine work on her own initiative wherever she could.

Jim, curiously, seemed somewhat less melancholy than he had been in recent weeks, and seemed to be concentrating less hard on his work. Once or twice, Helena noticed him gazing vaguely out of the window that overlooked the loading-bay, watching the loaders and drivers at work, or looking at the patch of green garden area that was just visible between the two warehouses on the opposite side of the road. He made no mistakes, and kept his work up to date, but his absent-minded manner, more pronounced than ever, irritated Brian, who consequently snapped at him two or three times in the course of the week. Jim accepted this apologetically, but remained distracted.

The summer had suddenly become heavy with apprehension. Chris came home for the last week before his holiday, and half-deliberately filled Helena with alarm by listing in detail the equipment he was gathering together to enable him to make temporary repairs to the minibus, should any prove necessary. The vehicle sounded to Helena as if it would be hard put to reach the other side of London, let alone Italy. She was only partially reassured when he produced the insurance certificate, and she recognised the name of the company.

"If it does break down and you can't repair it, you will be able to get home, won't you?" she pleaded.

"Don't worry, Mum," Chris replied with his usual easy smile. "We're ready for anything. I mean, *anything*."

So he went off on the Sunday evening with a misshapen old grey rucksack on his back, having given her a colossal hug and promised to send her a postcard at least once a week, and she wondered for two or three hours why she wanted to cry, and then decided that it would be a better idea to pray. And God was good, for she got her postcards.

***

A week later, Helena was packing her own luggage. Although it meant more driving, she had agreed to deliver Gill to her mother's home in Colmleigh, and then planned to stay overnight with Karen at the flat, to catch up with recent news. It was hard to believe that she had not been back to Colmleigh since the family, except Karen, had left a year earlier, and she wondered whether it would be like, a homecoming, or whether the whole place would suddenly have become foreign and unwelcoming. Gill, for her part, was nervous, uncertain whether a longer reunion with her mother would be tolerable for either of them, and once or twice Helena caught her looking longingly at the cigarettes on display at the local newsagent's shop. She knew that Dawn Gunson was a heavy smoker, and hoped that Gill would not find the temptation irresistible. In the end she gave Gill a spare key, together with strict instructions to return to Danesburgh if she felt under serious strain at any time, and let her know immediately by telephone if it happened.

But when they finally arrived at the Gunsons' extraordinary split-level villa on the outskirts of Colmleigh, with its surrounding plateau of lawn interspersed with clumps of rhododendrons, Gill's mother quickly made it clear that Gill was welcome, at least initially; and Gill was entranced by the pair of King Charles spaniels that came out to greet her with snuffling enthusiasm. A splendid lunch was served by an assiduous Mediterranean maid. This was clearly not the home of a mere provincial purveyor of wedding photographs. The rooms were decorated expensively, although not to Helena's taste, with pedestals and Art Nouveau mirrors and ceramic tiles.

"God," Gill murmured when her mother was out of the room for a moment, "imagine Father in the middle of all this. He'd be in a daze." But the house fascinated her, and as Helena left she was contentedly thumbing through an album of French poster reproductions, having, to Helena's great satisfaction, politely refused her mother's first offer of a cigarette with her coffee.

Karen, as usual, was full of news and tales about parties and concerts and discos, and when Helena went to hang her coat in the wardrobe in the spare bedroom she could hardly find room for it. *She must be keeping the Colmleigh boutiques in business single-handed.*

"I am saving, Mum, really I am," Karen protested, reading Helena's thoughts. "It's just that I can't resist a bargain."

Helena smiled at her. "Colmleigh must be a good place for bargains, then."

"Well... it's not like London, of course. But it's not bad."

They sat and talked for an hour and then strolled about the town centre, where the Saturday crowds were just beginning to thin out and disperse to the car parks, or queue for buses to take them home. At one point, Helena tried to imagine that she and Karen had been shopping while David and Chris had been gardening, or out playing golf, and that soon they would all be sitting together at the table, teasing one another over the salad. It was no good, though; Colmleigh now was just another town, to be visited for her daughter's sake. She was surprised at the lack of affection she felt for the place where they had lived happily for so many years; was she no longer the same person, then?

"Just the same as ever, you see," Karen remarked brightly, oblivious of her mother's mood.

There was a Greek restaurant in a narrow thoroughfare running parallel to the High Street, in what was known as the 'old' part of the town, and Karen and Greg invited Helena to dine with them there. It was one of their favourite places, and Greg, characteristically, was on very friendly terms with the owner, who promised them a special menu, and special it certainly turned out to be, with a range of wines and liqueurs Helena had never previously encountered. Much as she enjoyed it, however, she was conscious of a longing now to be rid of Colmleigh, and impatience for the morning, to be on the road north, to see her parents again after such a long absence, and — perhaps unknowingly — to be away alone, and sit and think and read and pray, and have time to come to terms with herself; a new self, as it seemed to her. Then came an immense weariness, compounded by the restaurant lighting, the smoke and music and voices and wine. Karen chattered incessantly through the meal, and afterwards danced with Greg and urged him to dance with Helena, but to Greg's credit, he sensed that Helena was not so disposed.

"I think your mother needs to rest," he said. "Let's go now. She's got a long journey ahead of her tomorrow."

This time last year I'd have danced, Helena thought.

Karen swallowed her disappointment and accepted an early Saturday night with as good a grace as she could, and Greg left them at the flat, reminding Karen of a lunch date with friends the following day.

***

Helena woke up feeling altogether different. Colmleigh town centre was, if anything, even quieter than Danesburgh early on a Sunday morning, and only one or two inveterate dog-walkers were about when she looked out at the street at half past eight. A hazy sun hinted at a warm day to come, and Helena was pleased at the prospect of travelling north. She had elected to cover the better part of the journey on Sunday morning to avoid the heaviest traffic, and had booked an overnight stop at a motel near Kendal, leaving, she calculated, half a day to complete the journey on Monday. Having quickly washed and neatly made her bed, she packed her overnight items back in her case. Karen appeared in the doorway, yawning.

"Mum how can you be up like this on a Sunday morning? It's so early."

"I remember," Helena mused, "a little girl who once got up at half past five on a Sunday to watch the sun rise. I wonder what happened to her."

Karen giggled. "Oh, God, yes, I remember. But I was too late, and anyway it was raining buckets. You wouldn't get me up for the dawn now, not unless I'd been up all night anyway."

"Well, it's the only holiday I'm having this year," said Helena. "And I intend to make the most of it. Where's the nearest garage for petrol?"

"On the London road, about half a mile out of town."

Karen prepared a light breakfast while Helena completed her packing, and then, as they were about to sit down, she opened a cupboard and drew out a carrier bag with half a dozen packages in it.

"I was hoping to take Greg up to meet Grandma and Granddad," she explained. "But I don't think we'll have a chance now this summer, so will you take these things up for me, Mum, please? And tell them I haven't forgotten them."

Dear Karen. "Of course I will, dear. I'm sure they'll be delighted. I wish you could get to see them, though; but still, if Aunt Marie permits, perhaps they'll come down later in the year, and then you could come over. They're bound to want to meet Greg."

"Of course, they will be. And we ought to go and see Nan and Gramps too." They had always distinguished the respective pairs of grandparents thus. "I doubt whether they'd come up again if they could help it. I'm afraid the funeral put them off Danesburgh forever."

"That would be kind," Helena acknowledged. "It might cheer them up a bit."

"I don't know that anything would," Karen said gloomily. "Still, we'd better go anyway. At least it isn't too far, we can get there and back the same day."

Helena gave her a reproachful look.

"Well, Mum, be honest, they are a couple of old miseries, aren't they?"

"Never mind. Just think *noblesse oblige* for a day."

"I'll talk to Greg about it, then."

At half past nine Helena gave her daughter a parting embrace, and having checked her route round the outskirts of London for the eighth time, set the car in motion for the longest journey she had yet undertaken alone, reminding herself that she had all that day and half the next if she needed it. The first part, despite some road works and one-way systems, was not too difficult; the route was familiar from previous trips. When she found herself on the motorway, however, she was nervous to begin with. It seemed so endless, and all the traffic seemed to be moving so fast; sports cars shot across her bows from access roads, and enormous coaches overtook her at what seemed like suicidal speeds, creating side winds that took her by surprise, so that it felt to her as if the car was in danger of swerving off course. After a while, however, she became used to it, and found that without conscious intention she too was driving faster. She eased the pressure of her foot on the accelerator pedal a little, out of respect for her car's elderly engine, and as London fell further behind the traffic thinned out, and she settled down to the tedium of the long journey. Rather before she expected it, she was on the verge of the industrial Midlands with their innumerable chimneys and power stations and brick housing estates. Pleased with her progress, she stopped briefly for coffee somewhere south of Birmingham, and then continued steadily, through the Black Country and out into the countryside of Staffordshire. About an hour later she was in the Potteries. At Newcastle-under-Lyme she turned off for lunch, taking in the hills and hollows covered with Victorian artisan dwellings, with glimpses of green where fields were visible between the rises, and where the former slag heaps had been grassed over. The conurbation had the air of a leathery old workman in retirement, contemplating a well-kept square of garden, the coal and clay long since washed from his hands but still deeply worn into the creases and wrinkles.

Helena would have liked to explore, but that would have meant increasing the burden of driving, and her eyes had begun to ache a little. She contented herself with a light meal, not wishing to make herself drowsy, and contrived to make it last until the restaurant was on the verge of closing for the afternoon; she was pleased to have been allocated a corner table, concealed from the main dining area, for she had once or twice felt nudged by concern that she might have to fend off over-solicitous strangers who noticed that she was alone. As it happened, however, the only people who spoke to her were a retired couple on their way home to Rhyl from a holiday on the south coast. They reminded her slightly of her own parents, which reassured her. They wished one another a safe journey and went on their way, and soon afterwards Helena was back in the car.

The afternoon proved more tiring. As green pasture changed once again to industrial landscape, and then back to fields, Helena found that her pleasure in the journey was being diluted by fatigue. Near St. Helens an accident had thrombosed the road, and although the police cars and ambulance had long since departed, the area resembled a broken ant-hill where the crushed bodies of some of the insects causes consternation among the rest. Helena caught a glimpse of a car overturned on its roof, a spectre which cast over the rest of the day a shadow that was not to lift until at last, that evening, after the simplest supper the motel could provide, she locked the door of her room and turned to her Bible. Having missed church in order to travel, she felt an unexpected sense of loss, as though she had had to cancel an appointment with a friend at the last minute; but now it was more as if the friend had telephoned to say, "That's all right, I don't mind a bit."

By good fortune Helena's neighbours at the motel, if indeed there were any, appeared to share her desire for a quiet night, for there was no sound from the rooms on either side. At length, she turned the light out and slept. Tomorrow she would be in Scotland.

***

She started out early, rather expecting a Monday morning of the kind she had been familiar with at Colmleigh, where by eight o'clock the London road was packed tight with sales representatives' cars, heating engineers' vans and lorries of various sizes; but the road to the Border proved surprisingly quiet and clear, and the fifty-odd miles to Carlisle were no more than a prelude to the main part of the day's journey. By the time she reached the end of the motorway, she was ready to relax and acquaint herself with a part of Scotland she scarcely knew, for, although her mother came from Ayrshire, her father was a Lothian man, and she had happy memories of Edinburgh, and her grandfather showing her the Castle and the Royal Mile. She drove on at a more leisurely speed, stopping briefly at Annan and Dumfries, and enjoying the forests of Galloway and the glimpses of the lochs. And at last she sighted the neat-tiled roof of her parents' bungalow, tucked into a fold of the hills and facing south for the sun; and as she knew she should have expected, they were watching for her at the window, and the front door was open before she had the handbrake on.

Although she didn't quite know how, Helena had somehow been afraid that they would have aged out of all recognition, but on the contrary, they were in joyous good health, and only a little tired by the demands of Aunt Marie. But they had missed her; they had talked and worried about her for months, and wanted to know everything at the same time, so that she could hardly begin to explain one thing, or describe another, without being interrupted and led off in a different direction, by her mother at least, although she knew her father was no less eager to hear everything she had to say. It was lovable and a little exasperating, and Helena promised, over her second cup of coffee, to give them as full an account as she could of the months that had passed since the funeral.

The exercise proved fruitful, for, in reviewing the year's events so as to make them intelligible to her parents, she was able to place them in perspective for herself. Frank and Elspeth McCallogh listened intently then, confident that nothing important would be left out, until, late in the afternoon, Helena recounted her goodbye to Karen of the previous day. Only then did her mother respond.

"Well, my dear, it certainly sounds as if you need a holiday. Who'd have thought you'd find so much to do? But no doubt, it's all been for the best."

And they were determined to give her a holiday. The only thing they requested, which Helena would have been glad to do in any event, was that she should see Aunt Marie a couple of times during her stay. She took her share of household chores, although there were few of those, and treated her parents to a shopping expedition to Glasgow, with lunch included. But for much of the time she was free to explore and enjoy, sometimes with them but often alone. She travelled widely in the car, covering miles of hills and forest and coastline; but her favourite place, to which she returned at some time almost every day, was a simple wooden bench on the hillside above the village, set by the side of an old shepherds' track, and little used, for the pathway was steep. The seat commanded a broad view of grassy slopes surmounted by rocks, with patches of heather and gorse scattered here and there, and a single point where the line of the cliffs dropped to reveal a semi-circle of blue-grey sea. She took to making her way up to the bench during the evenings, after high tea, once the washing-up was done and her parents had settled to reading or some other peaceable activity, having talked together for a while first.

The same question seemed to arise nightly. Put in its simplest form, it was 'what next?'. In a way she had not experienced back in Danesburgh, Helena became conscious of the uncertainties of her situation. From this distance, nothing seemed altogether secure for her; not her job, for the company's future was quite likely to be threatened further; nor her family, for both her children were moving away from her into a different world as they reached adulthood; nor Gill, almost a surrogate daughter now, but who could say what she would be like, or what decision she might take, after a week in her mother's company? Then there was the wedding, and in her present frame of mind even that seemed a precarious prospect, so far had her parents' long-harboured anxiety taken root in her own mind. She tried to look further still ahead; they were fit and active now, but sooner or later they would need her or Claire to be closer at hand, and it was unlikely that they could be persuaded to move south again. She tried to contemplate coming to live in Scotland permanently, but it was no use. That would put as much distance between her and her own children as she had had to travel to visit her parents, and besides that, Gill's immediate needs were still uppermost in her mind. She began to think back again, looking for signs of God's providence now, and soon realised that they were not hard to find.

Quite apart from her own rekindled faith, she suddenly saw a path laid out for her, not starting but ending at that hillside bench. It began even before that moment of need that had driven her into the church in Danesburgh, the day of Gill's disappearance and Wesley's accident. She might not have had Rhoda Broughmer as a neighbour; she might not have been offered the job at Danesburgh Cartons; Karen might never have thought of bringing Gill home with her at Christmas. As it was. all those events had helped her over the worst of the early days after her bereavement, without quite knowing how. It had been a year when she had been caught up by a great and loving Person whom she had been slow to recognise; a year of grace. Whatever might follow, nothing would alter that.

And she would walk slowly back down the hill and rejoin her parents, who marvelled privately at her serenity, and just as quietly thanked God for it.

Only Aunt Marie troubled her. The old lady, whose mind had clouded now, failed to recognise Helena at all the first time, then confused her with Claire; but on the second visit, just as they were about to leave, she suddenly took Helena's hand and said, with all the licensed tactlessness of the very old and infirm, "You're too young to stay a widow, my girl. You find yourself another husband as soon as you can. That's my advice."

Helena smiled, trying to conceal her embarrassment, and nodded ambivalently; but Aunt Marie insisted. "Don't you be ashamed, now. There's nothing wrong with getting married again, provided you find the right man. Just leave it another year, and then you'll have done your duty." Then she lay back as though the effort had exhausted her, and dozed off; and Helena felt irritated with the old lady, and cross with herself, and then suddenly sad, for she guessed that when she left for home at the end of the week she would not be going to see Aunt Marie again. If she was right, it would mean that the burden on her parents would be lifted; they themselves had not so many years ahead of them that she could afford to neglect them, certainly not many when they would be able to travel to see her. And again she felt guilty, and gently took the old lady's hand. "I have thought about it, Aunt Marie. And if the time comes when it's the right thing to do, of course I'll do it."

Aunt Marie opened her eyes for an instant, and her face assumed a satisfied expression before they closed again.

It was the only occasion on which Helena's visit coincided with one of Aunt Marie's lucid moments, which, according to Mr and Mrs McCallogh, were becoming rarer all the time. "If you'd been able to come in the spring she'd have known you straightaway," her mother said, not reproachfully but with regret. Helena did her best to comfort herself with the idea that somewhere within that rapidly dimming consciousness was a glimmer of appreciation that she had come; had Aunt Marie not acknowledged it, albeit in a different context, when she had said, "You've done your duty now?" Perhaps that was stretching things a little; but it did go some way to allaying the uncomfortable feeling, long muted but now sharp and painful, that in assuming one responsibility she had severely neglected another. It was something she prayed over on several evenings, particularly while alone on the hillside bench, without any clearer answer than a reminder that God arranges *His* people's circumstances as *He* will, and reserves the right not to explain.

***

When the time came to leave, Helena knew her parents were profoundly sad. It had been much too short a visit. They had known, of course, that their daughter could not stay with them for long this time; but farewells come no easier with age, and there was no possibility of arranging a reunion yet. All too soon, the travelling season would be over for the year. Yes, they would keep in touch by telephone, but they needed to see her, to know for certain that she was all right, not grieving, or lonely, or overwrought. She promised to try by some means or other to persuade Claire to come up before the winter; that would not be easy, for Claire found it difficult enough to keep a day free, and often complained that she had not enough time for her own family. Still, it was her duty as much as Helena's, so she might be shamed into it. *What a way to look at seeing your parents — it ought to be a pleasure.* But that, of course, only made her think of Gill again.

There was a distinct smell of autumn in the air as she stowed her luggage in the boot of the car. The previous evening had been cool and misty, and she had put on the Shetland jumper she had been intending to pack. Summer was already coming to an end, and she wondered again how she would feel as she approached the season of her last days with David. Those days had been so busy with the move, with settling Karen into the flat she was already looking forward to leaving again, with Chris's study course and lodgings, with David's enthusiasm for his new job; and again she thought, *what now?* That time seemed to return with the autumn smell, perhaps earlier in Scotland than it would have at home, and yet it was far distant, the property of a different age. The life to which she was returning in Danesburgh was infinitely more challenging and beset by uncertainties than she could have envisaged a year earlier. So, the evening before, she had sat on her bed and prayed for strength and discernment; and now promising to return, she embraced her parents warmly but without lingering, and set an easterly course away from the bungalow, waving as she reached the bend in the road, and began to concentrate her mind on Danesburgh again.

Chris should be waiting for her at home; she knew he had been planning to return in the week, and had left a spare key with Rhoda next door so that he could get in. He would have brought some food in, even though it was only likely to be sausages and pies, that sort of thing; and would have done his best to have some support ready. He would be full of stories about Italy, and she would listen and smile, and be reminded of David; he would ask after his grandparents, and might even write to them. Without a doubt, he was her principal consolation for losing David. It would be good to have him home for a few days before he returned to London.

What Gill would do, she could not be sure. She had refrained, as a matter of policy, from trying to contact either Gill or Dawn while she had been away, apart from sending them a postcard for the sake of courtesy; thus she did not know what to expect, or what kind of influence Dawn and her friends might have had on the girl. She could not even be certain that Gill would want to return to Danesburgh. Seen through the prism of a restored relationship with her mother, Colmleigh might represent a more attractive option. It was unlikely that her pregnancy would raise many eyebrows where she was now, although she might come to embarrass her mother by reason of her reduced mobility. *I shall be glad to hear that she's all right*, she thought, simply enough, *and after all it's only been a couple of weeks*. Then she began to consider the situation at the office, wondering whether there had been any good news to encourage Brian Farrelson, or whether, on the contrary, things had grown worse in her absence. Were they so dependent on customers like Evanson's that they might go under? She had a sudden odd vision of the entire workforce standing and helplessly watching the entire factory building collapse around them, leaving them untouched, like so many Buster Keatons; then a quirk of imagination caused her to substitute the comic actor's face for Brian's, and then for Jim's. At that point she found herself obliged to overtake a tractor, and forced herself to concentrate on driving.

Realising that she would not have to circumnavigate London this time, she had started out early with the intention of completing the whole journey in a day. Unlike her parents, Chris would not be anxious if she were late home, and she was prepared to take her time, leaving the motorways and crossing the moors into north Yorkshire, and so on to the historic Great North Road, where the place-names, as she read them off the signposts, spoke of stagecoaches and highwaymen. She lunched in York and wandered about the old city for an hour, after which the time and the miles fled away, and almost before she realised it, she was within forty miles of home.

By then, easy and agreeable though the drive had been, her head was beginning to ache, and she was glad as she neared Danesburgh that the journey was coming to an end. Nevertheless, the hours at the wheel had left her a little disorientated; the outskirts of the town, even the close and the house itself, were temporarily unreal to her, she was back too soon to accept them. She left her case in the boot and went straight inside to put on the kettle for a cup of tea and the immersion heater for a bath, with her mind still obstinately registering Ayrshire and York and the road south.

Of Chris there was no sign, but when Helena opened his bedroom door she saw that he had left a bag under the table and a couple of guide books on the bed. Thankful for this evidence of his safe return, she made and drank her tea, and then ran the bath and got in. It was something she had denied herself at her parents' home, for, whether or not they needed to be, they had always been sparing with the heating, and she had not wished to interfere with their ways. This bath, therefore, was doubly welcome, and she allowed herself a few extra minutes to enjoy it. Just as she was deciding that she really must let the water run out, she heard a rumble and a squeal of brakes at the front of the house, a door slamming, and Chris's voice. "Great! Mum's home already."

Helena climbed out of the bath with a certain air of resignation, and hastened along the landing to her bedroom, clasping the bathrobe tightly round her. She really was not prepared, either mentally or physically, for any company other than her own son. She dressed hastily and glanced out of the window, to behold a minibus of well advanced years, painted in what looked like household gloss of an improbably brilliant sky blue, the side windows plastered with so many stickers and badges so that the view from within must have been reduced to practically nil. A roof-rack was loaded with an assortment of bags, rucksacks and sports and camping gear, precariously secured with rope, and the whole vehicle had sunk so far on its suspension that a cat would have had difficulty in wriggling underneath it. Helena gaped at this apparition; and then illumination, and amazement, and alarm, and relief, and anger, followed one another as she almost cried out loud. *They've been to Italy and back in that thing...? And now he's brought them all back here. It's too much. Really.*

Waves of laughter floated up from below. Helena finished combing her hair, and with a final adjustment to her collar, marched downstairs as if to defend her house against an invading army; but she entered the lounge and Chris stood there, sunburnt as she had rarely seen him, with his arm round the shoulders of a fair-haired, athletic-looking girl in shorts and T-shirt; next to her, an immensely tall, thin, bespectacled youth appeared to be about to demonstrate some sort of trick with a bottle-opener; a smaller, darker lad was seated on the sofa, but immediately got up as he saw her come in. Then suddenly two more girls appeared from the kitchen, one plump and fuzzy-haired, with great startled-looking brown eyes, and the other slight and dark like the smallest of the boys.

There was an embarrassed silence for a moment, and then Chris, realising that everyone was looking at him, said with a studied artlessness worthy of his sister, "Mum, you don't mind, do you? We wanted to have a party tonight, for the end of the holiday, and for you coming home as well."

Helena's resentment evaporated.

"There's nothing I'd enjoy more," she said, gallantly and untruthfully.

Introductions swiftly followed. the fair-haired girl was Julie, the small dark one Louise, and the plump, fuzzy one, improbably, Mercedes. The lads were Phil (the tall one), and Gareth (the small one), and Gareth and Louise were brother and sister. They were all thoroughly polite and well-mannered, even if they did tend to dissolve into helpless laughter at what seemed to Helena to be the slightest of witticisms; *but that*, she thought, *might just be the effect of exhaustion. I'm sure they're all in need of a good night's sleep after touring in that vehicle outside.* To their credit, they did not over-indulge in the wine they had evidently brought home with them, nor did the girls seek to take any liberties with her kitchen. Nor, again, did they expect her to entertain them. They all wanted to relate some anecdote or other, in which Chris figured prominently, and his face went a shade redder under the tan. After a couple of hours Helena felt as if she had known them for years; and it looked as if Chris had found in Julie enough cause to abandon ornithology altogether, and if he was not careful, the study of electronics as well. She would have to talk to him about that.

It was, inevitably, a noisy gathering, and just as inevitably, it was suddenly one o'clock in the morning, far too late for them all to be thinking of going home, and Helena found herself organising spare beds and mattresses, cushions and whatever else could be found to put two of the girls in Karen's room, the third in the room usually occupied by Gill, and the two boys in the study; and they all spilled out of the house to look for things in the minibus, or on its roof, with half-suppressed giggles and groans as they bumped into one another in the dark, while Helena looked anxiously for signs of waking neighbours. The nearest of those, however, must have been either away or oblivious, for not a single light went on.

At last, they were all installed more or less comfortably. Helena reflected, as she climbed wearily into her bed, on the disparity between the evening for which she had been preparing herself on the drive home, and the one she had just spent. *O Lord,* she prayed, *it'll be one mad scramble in the morning, and I doubt very much whether I'll make it to church. You won't mind, even if it's the second time in two weeks?* And before she fell asleep the Lord replied quite clearly, *no, Helena, that's quite all right, you weren't to know what was waiting for you here this evening.*

And yet, in the morning, to her great surprise, they were all up early, and she found herself in the minibus with them, on her way to a Non-Conformist chapel, where neither she nor Chris, let alone any of the others, knew anyone, but where they nevertheless joined with gusto in Charles

Wesley's hymns, clapped in time to the choruses and even produced Bibles to follow the points the pastor was making in what to Helena was an inordinately long sermon. Chris seemed a little baffled by it all, and looked at his mother apologetically once or twice, as if to say, "I'm not used to this kind of thing either."

After the service they sat in the minibus and finished their supplies of sausage rolls and cheese and fruit, before returning to the house to collect their bags and rucksacks once again, and with enthusiastic thanks to Helena, departed; and the sound of their singing could still be heard as the minibus rounded the corner.

"Your friends are certainly full of life," Helena commented as she and Chris walked back up the drive. "Now tell me how all that came about."

Chris grinned sheepishly. "Well, originally we didn't intend to get back till today. But last week the minibus began to play up a bit — for the first time, I should say — and I wasn't sure we could get the spares we needed. So we decided to head for home, only slowly, to give ourselves plenty of time in case the bus broke down. But we were lucky, it did hold out, and we got to Calais a couple of days early. Then we had another bit of luck, because someone who was meant to be on the ferry with a camper-van or something got held up, and there was a spare place. So we thought, why not go now and wind up with a party when we get home? And well, our house was the biggest, and I really meant the party to finish in time for everyone to go home last night, before you got home yourself. We'd have cleared everything up, of course."

"Of course," Helena acknowledged with only the faintest hint of sarcasm. "And how did your original three turn into six?"

"Well, I told you, didn't I, that Gareth's sister was thinking of coming with us. And then Merce and Julie were Louise's friends, and they offered to help with the food in exchange for us taking them on the trip with us. Originally the fourth guy would have been Mac, but he had to drop out. Actually, it worked out very well. I was quite surprised, really."

Helena, however, was not surprised. Even after such a short acquaintance she could tell that Chris had fallen in with a group of youngsters who shared his absolute lack of egoism and his willingness to make the best of a little lack of creature comforts here and there. They made a good team, less worldly than Karen's circle of friends, less bohemian than Gill's. Chris had been fortunate.

"And Julie… is this just a holiday friendship, or do you think you'll be seeing more of her?" she enquired.

"Oh, Julie's off to teacher training college in a few weeks' time. But I dare say we'll all get together now and then. We've had too good a time to let it all drop just like that." And Chris launched into another string of tales of their exploits in Italy, culminating in the occasion when Phil, having yet again mislaid his glasses, had spent several minutes trying to walk from the boys' tent to the minibus, colliding with three trees on the way.

"We thought he'd found his way in the end, and then he got tangled up in someone's washing. They'd got a big blue towel out in the line, and it was pretty much the same shade as the minibus. And there he was with all these wet clothes wrapped round his head, mumbling *'scusami, scusami'*."

"Poor lad," said Helena sympathetically. "He didn't try to drive without them, though, did he?"

"No chance. I lost count of the number of times we were late starting out because he couldn't find them. In the end we made him tie the ends together with a long piece of string and hang them round his neck… Boy, I'm tired, Mum. I bet you are too, aren't you? That was a long drive you did yesterday."

"It was, for me. Though it wouldn't seem much compared with the distance you must have covered. Well, let's see about some lunch, and then maybe we can put our feet up for an hour or two."

But Helena was due back at Danesburgh Cartons the following day, and her Sunday afternoon rest had to be sacrificed to the business of unpacking and sorting clothes. She would have enjoyed the familiar calmness of Evensong, but guessing that Chris would not appreciate another dose of church the same day, she decided to stay at home with him. Almost for the first time, she had the opportunity to tell him about her parents, her concern about their remoteness from Danesburgh, and the advancing senility of Aunt Marie.

Chris listened then in his turn. "Poor old, Auntie. Can't be much fun for them, though. And not much of a holiday for you, Mum."

"Oh, I didn't do too badly. I had a few trips out while I was there. And it was good to be in Scotland, even for a short while."

Chris pretended to wince. "You won't go and retire up there, will you?"

"Retire?" Helena was startled. It was an idea that had never previously occurred to her. She had always assumed that David would retire eventually, but she herself? "I've never thought of retiring. After all, I haven't been back at work for a year yet. I doubt whether I'd qualify for a pension."

"Well," said Chris, "it's a long way ahead, I suppose."

Fifteen years. Yes, to Chris, at twenty, a long way ahead.

***

In the evening Helena made some telephone calls: firstly to her parents, to confirm her safe arrival the previous evening; then Karen, who was about to go out to some concert or other, and sounded her usual exuberant self; and thirdly to Dawn Gunson, to find out whether Gill had enjoyed her stay, and whether or not she was ready to return. The background noise at the other end of the line suggested that there was a party in full swing. It was not easy to make out to whom she was speaking, but eventually Helena realised that Dawn had put Gill herself on.

"Yes. Yes, thank you, Mrs Halstow. I've been quite all right. Really quite well."

"Do you think your mother would rather keep you there, then, or is she happy for you to come back to me? At least until the baby's born?"

"We've been talking about that. She thinks it would be better for me to stick with the same doctor and so on, if possible. So, if it's all right with you?"

"Yes, of course. When will you come?"

"Well, there might be a job going over here later. I've got to see somebody on… is it Tuesday or Wednesday? I can't remember now, but I've got it written down somewhere… Anyway, it's this week."

"That sounds interesting. Look, if your mother's agreeable, suppose I come over next weekend, and then I could drop Chris off on the way. He'll be starting the new term the following week."

***

Monday began badly. Helena overslept, for no immediately apparent reason, and had to rush out to work with no more breakfast inside her than a cup of coffee. Chris, exasperatingly, had not stirred. Autumn was perceptibly close again, the morning grey and misty; the sort of morning that Helena rather liked in the usual way, adding as it did a touch of mystery to the most ordinary of surroundings; but this morning she only registered that the traffic was slower than usual. The lights were on at Danesburgh Cartons when she arrived, giving the buildings a wintry look, despite the plentiful and still green leaves on the surrounding trees, and suddenly, illogically, she felt lonely and dejected. It was something she had experienced before at the same time of year, but it had nothing to do with the approach of autumn; rather, it was a reaction to her holiday. Idleness had never suited her; the summer tended to create a kind of void that needed to be filled with concern and activity. She recognised the feeling and walked into the office with a purposeful step that was intended to dispel it.

Brian Farrelson looked up as usual.

"Hello, there. Had a good holiday? Been north of the Border, haven't you? What was the weather like up there?"

"Good morning, Brian. It was fine, thank you. I've had a good rest, and done my duty by my parents, and the weather wasn't bad at all. How have things been here?"

Brian pretended to grimace, and then chuckled. "I reckon we'll survive for a bit longer yet."

Helena set to, sorting and filing, and gradually her mood lightened as the rhythm of her work took hold of her. She realised that, for all her love for her parents, and for all the welcome they had given her, she had not been altogether comfortable with them; they inhabited a different sort of world from hers now, gentle and restricted, confined to their corner of Ayrshire, a world in which they would remain by their own choice even when they no longer had Aunt Marie to care for. They would have liked to keep her there, if they had been able; but, for better or worse, she belonged in Danesburgh now, and would not have been happy to stay long there.

She had almost regained her usual briskness, and was ready to persuade herself that everything was back to normal and nothing much had happened while she had been away, nor was likely to happen in the immediate future, when Jim Sergent came over to her.

"Good holiday, Helena?"

"Yes, thanks, Jim. Very good. But I'm glad to be back."

She had missed Jim more than she had realised, perhaps more than she had expected.

"Good. Have you got a few minutes for a chat at lunchtime, or do you have a lot of shopping to do?"

Helena smiled. "I expect I can find a few minutes. Shall we walk over to the gardens, perhaps?"

"Good idea."

The gardens were still displaying an abundance of roses, but dry petals were gathering at the sides of the footpath. They walked on the wet grass, stirring up craneflies which fluttered dizzily in front of them to settle again few yards ahead. Brown conkers and their spiky green cases were strewn about under the horse chestnut trees. Helena and Jim sat down on an ornate wooden seat with their backs to the uneven stone wall. For a moment neither of them said anything. Then Jim spoke abruptly.

"You know I'm leaving Danesburgh Cartons?"

Helena was startled. "No, Jim. You've never said anything to me about it."

"Sorry. I suppose I haven't. But I've been thinking about it for quite a while, and in the end I had to make up my mind. I remembered something you said to me quite a while ago. 'This time next year', you said, 'you might be in a completely different situation'. And then at my home, the first time you and Gill came out there, you said you'd hate to think I was wasting my life out there. I think you've been trying to nudge me into some kind of action for a long time."

"I have?" Helena was surprised to find that she had placed her hand on Jim's, or, to be more accurate, on the back of his wrist. "I didn't realise I'd said anything that would stick in your mind like that… What do you intend to do, then?"

Jim seemed to brace himself to explain.

"Did I ever mention that my son was looking for a place of his own to run?"

"I believe you did, yes."

"Well, he's found what he wants. Or, rather, I found it for him. You know the old roadhouse on the Cambridge road? Well, George Bushmell knows the present owner quite well, and says he wants to give it up. He's getting on a bit now, the owner. My son reckons it's the kind of place he could turn into a gold mine. There's a lot of potential with the amount of traffic that passes the door these days, and he's had a fair amount of experience. He'd turn the place into a high-class restaurant, but with a special menu for children, you know the sort of thing, to suit regular travellers and people going on holiday as well. And then, if it does well, he'd have room to use it for wedding receptions and that sort of thing, and even add some chalets, if he can get planning permission. It's quite a big site."

Helena nodded. "Where do you come into this?"

"Well, first of all, I'd be keeping the books, of course. Secondly, he hasn't got the capital to finance the site purchase and start up his own business as well, not to mention all the refurbishment the place needs. So the idea is that I'll sell the old vicarage and move in over the shop, so to speak, and sink the proceeds as a share in the business. It ought to work."

"But I thought," Helena objected, "that you didn't get on with your daughter-in-law, or her mother, or someone."

"Oh, that. No, I can't pretend that Mamma is one of my favourite people. But maybe I haven't tried very hard to like her. In any event, though, to do her justice, however, much she gabbles on sometimes, she does know how to cook. And that's something we'll need, of course."

"She's coming too, then? You've got it all planned? It sounds like a bit of a risk. Suppose it doesn't pay?"

"In that case," said Jim. "I shall have to think again. I don't suppose I'd be out of a job for long; every business need someone who can balance a couple of rows of figures. I'd find something else, I'm sure."

"But you'd have given up your home."

"Home?" said Jim. "It hasn't really been that since Brenda died. That would be the least of my worries."

Helena said nothing in reply to this. Jim coughed, the artificial cough of someone unsure of what to say next.

"I was going to say," he began. "I mean, to ask you, rather… I suppose you wouldn't be, well, interested in coming in on it? Not financially, of course, I don't mean that. But you know, to do something like what you did at Danesburgh Cartons. Correspondence, bookings, supervision, that sort of thing."

The question, when it eventually emerged, took Helena aback.

"Jim, I've no experience of any kind of commercial catering, except a few weeks as a waitress in a store restaurant, up in Newcastle. I really can't see that I'd be any use to you."

"I know. But what office experience did you have before you came to Danesburgh Cartons? You made yourself indispensable quickly enough at the factory. I've watched you cope with all sorts of things — and all sorts of people. I'm sure anything you set your mind to you'd do well. And if I'm going to be surrounded by excitable Italian women, I could do with a calm, sensible Scottish lady nearby to keep me sane. Obviously, I don't expect you to say yes or no now, but will you think about it? There's no enormous rush, of course. I'm not selling up tomorrow. There's a lot of bargaining and planning to do first."

Helena smiled. "You've said some very kind things there, Jim, and I don't know that I really deserve them, but you've taken me rather by surprise, and I don't quite know what to say. At the moment, my feeling is that I've been through quite enough changes in my life for one year. But if there's one thing I've learnt, it's that you have to be ready for anything. I'll think about it seriously, I promise you." Then a thought struck her. "May I make a suggestion?"

"By all means."

"If your restaurant does get off the ground, would you consider taking Josie on? She'd do a marvellous job there, and she'd be glad to get back to work, especially for someone she knows. It's been hard for her since they made her redundant."

"Josie. Do you know, I never thought of her. It's certainly an idea. We'd have to sort out some transport arrangements for her, I suppose… But I'll bear that in mind." Jim paused. "I think perhaps we'd better get back now. I don't need to say this is all in the strictest confidence, do I? I know you won't spread it around."

"Not a word shall pass my lips," said Helena with mock indignation.

***

The week seems to have passed almost before it's begun, Helena thought, *because Chris is going at the end of it.* Despite herself, she could not suppress a twinge of maternal possessiveness; he was so obviously looking forward to resuming his student life. He even spoke with indulgence, if not with affection, of Mrs Byles.

"Will you be able to get home at the weekends this term?" Helena asked as casually as she could.

"Sure. But not every week, Mum. I've already said I'd go down to Cardiff with Gareth and Lou one weekend, and then Julie wants us to go and see her at college when she's settled in, you know… And Phil and I are going to give the bus a good going over. It needs it after all the miles we did in it."

Helena knew it was no good. It was perfectly natural for Chris to prefer company of his own age now; it was a point he had taken long enough to reach, and it was not as if he never gave her a thought. As if reading her mind, he said with the usual grin, "But don't worry, Mum, I won't forget that you like to see me regularly. I'll be popping over from time to time. And you'll have Gill here for a bit longer, anyway, won't you? Give her my regards. I'm sorry I'm missing her this time."

On the Saturday, therefore, Helena made the awkward journey from Danesburgh to Colmleigh again, pausing at Leytonstone to leave Chris to the rudimentary welcome of Mrs Byles. She had not arranged to see Karen on this occasion, judging the time too short, and drove straight to the Gunsons' house, arriving just after two. She had had no lunch and felt hungry; she told herself that she ought to have left home earlier, but then comforted herself with the thought that they could stop for tea somewhere on the way back. That would break the journey for them.

Dawn Gunson opened the door to her, as flamboyant as ever in slacks, silk blouse and kerchief, her hair now gathered in a chignon.

"My dear, Helena, how lovely to see you. Have you had a good holiday? Can I get you a drink, now?"

"Thank you, Dawn, but I'd rather not at the moment. Yes, I have enjoyed my holiday, thank you. How are you, and how is Gill?"

The usual courtesies having been observed, they went through into the lounge, where Gill was sitting on the sofa with her feet on a low stool. She looked well, but rather more tired, Helena thought, than when she had left her, and there was a suspicion of yellow about her fingernails. She got up a little unsteadily to greet Helena.

"Hello, Mrs Halstow." Her voice was husky. "I'm just about ready, but would you like a cup of coffee or something first? Have you had anything to eat?"

Helena was suddenly impatient to get Gill back to her own home. The Gunson house had something about it that tautened her nerves; whether in the colour scheme, the way the furniture was arranged, the pictures on the wall, or whether there was simply something about the ambiance, independent of all those things, she could not have said. She accepted the cup of tea, trying not to appear reluctant. Strange how the place was affecting her more than it had on her first visit; perhaps it was something to do with the fact that she had then been about to go away on holiday, and had needed the change.

Gill made tea for her mother and Helena, bringing it in on a brass trolley with a patterned glass tray top. It was China tea, green and delicate; evidently Gill's exotic tastes were inherited, or learnt, from her mother. Dawn Gunson lit a cigarette, and looked at Gill, who glanced at Helena and then gave the slightest shake of her head. It was an odd little pantomime, which left Helena feeling excluded by their air of connivance, their mute exchange. She was not sure whether to feel pleased that some sort of bond had evidently been forged between them, or suspicious, on the other hand, that Dawn Gunson's influence on Gill might not have been for the best.

In the end, it was half past three by the time Gill's luggage was in the car. Gill had apparently acquired a quantity of new clothing for herself and the baby; it would be interesting to see whose choice it had been. There was also a bag of books, mostly paperbacks with titles printed in large letters on brightly coloured covers, no doubt pressed on Gill by her mother in the belief that she would need them to help her through the coming hours of enforced inactivity. Apparently Dawn shared and approved Gill's predilection for the *grande passion*. *I'll get her on to* Anna Karenina, Helena thought, *that should keep her going for quite a while, and perhaps after that she won't find so much to interest her in these.*

They drove sedately back through Saturday afternoon in London, and stopped on the other side at Monken Hadley for tea and Danish pastries. Until then Helena had been forced to give all her attention to the traffic, for she hated the congested London streets and the impudent manoeuvres of London drivers. Gill seemed reluctant to talk, although she showed no sign of discontent. When they were on the open road northward, Helena relaxed and smiled at her.

"You're very quiet."

"I'm sorry," Gill replied. "I've been trying to sort out my feelings about… well, about 'home', if you can call it that."

"Can't you?"

"Not really. The trouble — or one of them — with Mother is that she doesn't know how to make a home, a home. It wouldn't come right with Father, and I'm not sure whether it's coming right now."

"Oh, dear, I'm sorry to hear that."

"I don't mean that she doesn't get on well with Leo. I think they suit each other rather well, from what I can make out. No, the real thing is that she wants to treat the house as a kind of permanent exhibition. She's always changing things round, having rooms redecorated, and so on. And there are people coming in and out, people they know professionally, and she wants to impress them all. Not so much her friends, at least not while I was there, there were only one or two who came more than once. But Mother was always like that. It was one of the things she and Father never understood about each other; he wanted to keep his social life out of the house, at the golf club and so on, places like that, and didn't want hordes of visitors at home."

"Did that disturb you?"

"It did a bit. I didn't think it would, not when I remembered all the people that used to come up to the flat, but I must have changed since then. I got a bit on edge with it."

"So you won't find it too boring back in Danesburgh?"

Gill gave Helena that familiar slow, sweet smile.

"It's never been boring, Mrs Halstow. And I'm looking forward to training Monty again. I hope he hasn't forgotten how to behave while I've been away."

Helena thought of Jim, someone else who hadn't been able to make a house into a home. She could not, of course, disclose his plans to Gill; but as he had said, it would not all happen tomorrow, and if he did move it would not be too far. Anyway, once the baby was born dogs would certainly be of secondary interest only to Gill for some considerable time.

"It's only been a fortnight, hasn't it? And I'm sure Mr Sergent wouldn't have forgotten to practise with him," Helena reasoned. Then she remembered something else. "Oh, by the way, Chris sent you his regards. He's just gone back to London for the new term."

"Oh, thanks. Did he have a good time in Italy?"

"A high old time, by the sound of it. So good that I don't think we'll be seeing so much of him at the weekends this term. He's found himself a rather nice girlfriend. He says it isn't serious, but I'm not so sure."

"An Italian girl?" Gill enquired.

"Oh, no. Very English, by the look of her. A student teacher, just starting at college."

Gill smiled again, with a glimmer of brightness in her eyes. "He deserves somebody nice. But you'll miss him, won't you? I know how much you looked forward to seeing him last term."

"Yes," Helena agreed. "But it wouldn't be fair to ask him to miss out on seeing his friends, especially girl friends." She paused for a moment. "He used to be so shy. I want him to have the chance to make up for lost time."

"I don't think he's wasted his time," Gill said gravely. "I think I've wasted a lot more time than he has. I'd give anything for the chance to start again from the time I left school."

"Then you wouldn't be here to keep me company while Chris is away," Helena pointed out. "Often things that seem bad at the time turn out afterwards to have had a purpose — or at least to have some kind of compensation. I've often felt over the last year as if I was being carried along by the things that happened to me, and it's a comfort to think they're all part of a plan that's designed to work out well in the end."

"I don't know," said Gill. "I mean, I actually tried to make something happen, didn't I, and God knows I succeeded. And now I wish I hadn't. I shall have this baby, and I'm sure I shall love it and care for it, but there'll always be a part of me that wants to believe that it isn't the best thing, or at least not as good as being free."

Helena looked at her, wondering whom she had talked to at her mother's home. This was not the Gill she had left there; she clearly had some work ahead of her, and some prayer, if the girl's peace of mind were to be restored.

But when the journey was over and the bags unpacked, and Gill was once again curled up in her favourite chair sipping chocolate, she was already a good deal more cheerful.

"It's good to be back here, Mrs Halstow. Mother was kind to me in her way, and so were her friends, but they somehow seemed to be more concerned with my rights than my feelings. You know, maternity benefit, jobs with creche facilities and so on. I do know a certain amount about that sort of thing anyway. But none of them would have thought of doing what you've done for me. I wish I could do something for you in return, but I can't, can I?"

"You don't have to, my dear," Helena said gently. "Perhaps the day will come when you have the opportunity to do something for me, or maybe for someone else — it doesn't matter; and maybe that baby of yours will do something wonderful one day. That's the great thing about being a Christian, there's no balance sheet. You accept God's love, and the love of other people, and you give it out again where and when you can, and where and when it's needed. I think that's what's called 'grace'."

"Grace," Gill mused. "Maybe, if it's a girl, that's what I'll call her. As a reminder."

"It's a wee bit old-fashioned." Helena adopted a Scottish idiom in an attempt to conceal that she was moved by this declaration. "But none the worse for that. Now, what about that job you were telling me about over the phone?"

"Well, I'm not sure about it. It's in London. It's nothing very exciting — only an office job, looking up records and that sort of thing; but I suppose it would do to begin with, for a few years until the baby reaches school age. And there's a bed-sit available that's being used by the girl who's leaving the job, next Easter. I needn't start till then."

Helena started. Easter was, by anyone's calculations, a long way off. The she scolded herself; it would leave time, much-needed time, for the rebuilding of Gill's relationship with her mother, time to get used to being a mother herself. And there might be a better job available before then anyway, if she did prove ready for it.

"A bed-sit doesn't sound very practical," she said. "And in London… we talked about that before. Do you think you can cope with it?"

"I've got to do something," Gill said morosely.

"Well, why not keep that option as a last resort and then start looking seriously in the new year, if you like. You never know. Something much better may come along."

"I'd like to think so," Gill admitted. "But I don't like to impose on you any longer than I need to. And Father will be thinking I ought to be supporting myself and the baby. I know him. He can't stand idlers, and he can't believe that anyone can ever be out of work unless that's what they want. He's always worked hard, and he can't understand anyone who doesn't. Some of Mother's friends used to drive him mad. He hated them because they'd be round there talking while he was out at work. If they came in the evening he wouldn't stay in the house with them."

"Have you been in touch with your father lately?" Helena asked, seizing the opportunity.

"Well… no, I'm afraid not. He doesn't know I've been at Mother's, and I didn't see any point in telling him. He'd only think I'd gone even further downhill."

Helena sighed.

"Well, let's prove him wrong, then. I know. Why don't you send him a print of one of those photographs we took at Karen's engagement? I doubt whether he'd know you, you look so well."

Gill shrank back into the armchair. "Oh, no, please, Mrs Halstow. Not yet."

Helena gave up the idea. She must not become obsessed with the business of reconciliation. *Leave it to the Lord…* Gill had clearly become moodier and more introspective through being with her mother, and needed help again. Two steps forward, one step back… better than nothing, of course, but still frustrating. Perhaps an hour or two with Monty would make a difference.

"All right, my dear. Not if you don't feel ready for it."

Gill relaxed perceptibly.

"It's not that I want to keep up the bad feeling, honestly. But I'm only just finding my way with Mother again. I don't want to spoil it."

"Do you feel at ease with her now?"

"More than I did. But it isn't — easy. She's always dashing about, doing things at the last minute, changing her plans... It's not peaceful like it is here. I get the feeling she'll never settle down and be happy."

The words confirmed Helena's own impression. It had been a house where such activity concealed a certain lack of purpose, an enervating void.

"Well," she said calmly. "You can get back to our quiet routine for a while. You can tell me what you've been doing a bit at a time. What have you been buying over in Colmleigh, for a start?"

4

AUTUMN, 1981

The autumn days began to close in on Danesburgh, with their still, grey mornings and early twilights. After a few days Gill lost most of her fretfulness, but still seemed listless and passive. Helena tried to encourage her to go for walks, and they went to see Jim and Monty to continue the dog's training, but the shortening daylight hours meant that the sessions had to be transferred to Sunday afternoons, and the weather was not always suitable. Gill spent a good deal of time immersed in books, sitting on the sofa with her legs tucked under her, and responding slowly to Helena's attempts to make conversation, though not impolitely. It was as if she had entered a chrysalid stage, storing up her energy for the unknown state of motherhood to come. Even the long awaited exam result note, which confirmed that she had been awarded a pass and would receive her certificate in due course, failed to raise her from her torpor for more than an hour or two. She did not attempt to telephone her mother.

Jim, whose intellectual gestation curiously seemed to be keeping pace with Gill's physical pregnancy, said little about his plans, and Helena knew better than to ask about them. She found herself wondering what Danesburgh Cartons would be like without the 'Knight of the Sorrowful Countenance'; she would have admitted to being mildly and discreetly fond of him, but she knew she would not leave her present job for the proposed restaurant. She wanted to be a friend, but that would have brought her too close to being one of the family, and her natural caution warned her that things might not go as Jim was hoping, or that indeed the whole thing might come to nought. She regarded it as a compliment that he had asked her the question, and years later came to wonder whether it had been intended as a prelude to a proposal of quite a different nature. She wondered what she would say when Jim was ready to talk about it again, hoping that he would understand, but she did not mean to go into the reasons for her decision, and knew he would not press her for them.

She saw little of Karen and Chris, and that was as she had expected. They did get together at a weekend or two, and then they were merry and affectionate, but she knew their hearts were elsewhere now. Chris still brought his books home, but fewer of them, and spent much less time studying in his room, for which Helena was grateful, but hoped he was not slacking; he assured her, however, that he was putting in plenty of hours' work at college, and at Mrs Byles's, and anyway he was finding the course much less difficult to follow this year, which she supposed might well be the case.

Karen and Greg gave the impression of being completely in control of everything they were doing. All that remained was for Greg's professional qualifications to be confirmed; it seemed certain that he would then step into a rewarding position with some leading company or firm, proceeding steadily towards high responsibility. There remained in Helena's innermost psyche a remote tremor of concern that something might go wrong; not so much a genuine fear as a sense of reluctance to allow another disaster to take her by surprise as David's death had done. Thus far did her faith fail her; but she never disclosed the fact to anyone but her Lord.

October, inevitably, set her memory racing. She wanted to commemorate the date of David's death with some act of remembrance, but shrank from the idea of driving up to the crematorium. Without consciously intending to, she had avoided the place altogether since the funeral, preferring to find a route that spared her the need to pass the gate. But she decided that for his sake she must go once a year at least; his love deserved that much. So she steeled herself and arranged a morning away from work. She thought of taking white chrysanthemums, but having bought them, she changed her mind and put them in a vase in a prominent position in the lounge, to Gill's evident approval, for she came and tucked her arm under Helena's in mute understanding. One bloom, however, Helena did keep to take with her.

She was just getting into her car when Eric and Rhoda Broughmer came out from next door. Rhoda was carrying a small case with her. She recalled then that her neighbour had been waiting for some time to go into hospital for a minor operation of some kind. Perhaps the time had arrived. Helena got out again.

"Hello, Rhoda, dear. Hello, Eric. Is this the day, then?"

"Yes, this is it." Rhoda smiled. "After all this time, they want me at last."

"I'll be remembering you. And if there's anything I can do for Eric while you're in or I'm sure Gill would be delighted to cook a meal or two."

"Thanks, Helena." Eric was as shy as ever. "I think I can manage all right, but if I do find I need any help, I'll know where to come."

They left in different directions, and before long Helena was at those iron gates. She looked round about her as she approached the crematorium, lawns and laurels, holly with green berries beginning to appear. She had hardly noticed her surroundings the previous year. Standing at the place where David's ashes had been scattered, she felt the whole of the past year dissolve, and found herself back in that bewildering, echoing blackness, feeling for Chris's hand to hold.

But only for a moment. She drew a deep breath and spoke silently, David, I did love you dearly, and that hasn't changed, but I belong to God now, and unless *He* has something in mind that I don't know about, I doubt whether we shall meet again in heaven.

The thought brought tears to her eyes, and even as she blinked and turned away, she thought of Karen and Chris. They were David's true memorial; something of the best of him resided in each of them, more recognisably as they reached maturity.

She had work to do. Gill's pregnancy was advancing. Chris would soon be looking for a job, not to mention a car. Karen and Greg would be compiling their guest list. Danesburgh Cartons needed her, first of all, that afternoon.

And tomorrow?

Tomorrow she would have to nip out at lunchtime and buy some more flowers. Some brighter ones, this time.

For Rhoda.